A Soul's Warfare:

Book 1: The Hot Marble

by Rosemary B. Althoff

ISBN: 978-1-956654-44-8

CHAPTER 1

THE SKEPTIC

It was one o'clock in the morning, deadly quiet, and Lewis Brahmindura was wrestling with God. Equations of gravitational resonance physics went round and round in his head, along with the writings of his favorite atheist role models. He sighed, turned on the lamp, and went over to his desk to gather his thoughts in his journal.

At that moment, a nudge inside made him look up. His eyes roamed to his bookcase. They focused on the black book his religious parents had given him six years ago: A Bible. It seemed to be calling him. Lewis got up and reached for it, and when he opened the Bible at random, it came to the book of Ezekiel.

As he read, images formed in his mind: Cherubim covered with eyes, beryl wheels turning, heaven like a crystal expanse over them. And above all that, the text described a sapphire throne with a glorious man seated on it. The prophet's vision was all very strange. Who was that glorious man?

Lewis muttered. "What does that man have to do with anything in my life? It's weird!"

He pushed the Bible back into the shelf. Then he wrote:

> *How can anyone know if God is real? Jesus, Allah, Krishna, Amaterasu, Buddha .... Sorry, folks, but*

heavenly thrones and cherubim and wheels covered with eyes are not real. Spirits and ghosts and demons are not real. God is not real, either. These are all myths, stories people use to explain what they don't understand or to comfort themselves. Science is real. When we understand the universe, we will know god.

His mind could not quit roiling around with the God-questions, so he diverted his thoughts to his job.

It's been amazing to work with Dr. Zhartha on our project. The data suggests that we're close to a major breakthrough! Using the power from even a tiny black hole and gravitational resonance, people could walk through walls, and materials could be moved across far points nearly instantly!

My experience with that physics is what commended me to the Shields. They've offered me a position with a huge increase of salary. The Shields is a large, growing weapons manufacturing company. They said that I would be protecting my country. Should I take the job?

For some reason he felt uneasy. Images of bombs and attack rifles swarmed in his head. *Suppose they used the weapons for the wrong purpose?*

Lewis closed the journal with a *snap!* and went to bed. However, his sleep was shallow: He felt that he was travelling through the stars, and the universe's expanse was infinite. There was no God in it, just space and time. He whirled in a vortex of gravity, on and on and on, until he felt sick.

CHAPTER 2
THE MARBLE IS FOUND

Patrick Brahmindura nudged open the back door to the deck with a plump hand and sat down outside on the back steps. The Alabama summer day had been a scorcher, but a tiny breeze cooled him a little where it lifted the sweat from his T-shirt. It was a hand-me-down from his older brother Lewis, more than twelve years old, with several large holes in the armpits, but it was precious in his mind. Yes, the T-shirt was getting a bit too tight for a ten-year-old, especially around the stomach, but he felt good when he wore it.

The back door eased open, and Patrick turned around. The kitchen light haloed a pair of expensive sandals, long skinny, hairy legs, khaki shorts, a loose white polo shirt with a coffee stain on it, and his brother's smiling face topped with wavy dark brown hair.

"Hi, Lewis," Patrick asked, "any success fixing the Home Systems Controller? The air con's dead, the dishwasher won't work, and there's no Internet. I'm roasting!"

Lewis grinned, holding up a black computer case. "Air con, appliances, phones, and the computer network are back! There was a glitch in the software, and I corrected it. The system can talk to itself again."

"Hey, thanks, bro'! Wow! Hey, can you stay a while and

play some video games with me?"

"Sorry, Sport—I've got to convert myself from helpful older brother to research physicist when I get home and get some work done."

Despite the "no" answer, Lewis's brown eyes sparkled with affection. Patrick felt warm inside, a good sensation very unlike the day's thermal agony.

"See you tomorrow, bro', at breakfast with the fam'." Lewis said. He playfully reached down and mussed up Patrick's thick brown hair.

"Stop that!" Irritated, Patrick thought, *Even if my brother is a genius physicist, he should leave my hair alone!*

Lewis slipped into his used silver biodiesel Mercedes. He beeped good-bye as he backed down the driveway, and Patrick waved until the car was out of sight.

Sweat still coated his skin in a jacket of heat. His T-shirt clung tightly, damp down the back and under the armpits. He thought, *I guess I'll go in now. I can pound on the piano, play some games, or watch a movie.*

Instead, he sat there, looking out into the evening sky. A few early stars crept out overhead like intense tiny laser dots. Near the dark blue horizon, he saw bright Venus. It was a very, very pretty sky. As the last light faded, Patrick looked up and down the street, watching the lightning bugs turn themselves on and off. They looked like stars floating over the grass. He began to whistle softly, as Lewis often did.

Then a dazzle of white light arched from sky to Earth, and Patrick blinked, his whistle turning into a hiss. "That was no lightning bug," he said. Excitement pumped in his chest, *Wow, that could be from some aliens. They might want to capture me and take me to their planet!* Leaping to his feet with a big grin almost splitting his face, he called to the world, "Adventure, here I come!"

*　*　*

Something clattered; the screen door thumped and banged into his back. "Ouch!" Patrick yelled. "What did you have to do that for?"

His little sister Gracie came out to join him on the concrete porch. "I heard something about an *adventure!* Where is it? Can I come, too?"

Patrick considered. He was jealous of Gracie. Although she was only eight years old, she was already tall. He often envied her fair skin, hazel eyes, and auburn hair that she'd got from Mom. Plus, she was athletic and popular at school.

Patrick, however, often felt ashamed because he was plump, short, dark like Dad, and awkward. One of the kids at school had even teased him with the "N" word. Tonight, though, his spirit surged. *I'm important! The aliens came for* me!

Gracie bugged him again. "I wanna go with you!"

"Go away, Gracie. I mean, *Greasy!*"

But his sister wouldn't let up. "I wanna go!"

They argued for a while, and finally Patrick gave in. "All right, all right." He nodded toward the place where he'd seen the dazzling flash come down from the sky. "I saw a meteorite or something weird like that, over there." He pointed toward a vacant lot down the street.

"Let's go look!" Gracie jumped down the steps, while Patrick had to scramble to keep up with her.

"Maybe it's a meteorite," he puffed. "But they usually burn up before they reach the ground …"

"Wouldn't it be great if we found one? I could use it for show-and-tell in my science class."

"If I find it first, it's mine!" Patrick claimed. A short distance down the curving suburban street, he and Gracie came to high grass in a field that had not yet been converted into houses. Patrick scanned back and forth. Away from the pinkish glow of the streetlight, the area was quite dark. Somehow, he felt queasy about going there.

He wiped his sweaty face, while Gracie chattered, "Hey, Pat—

"Don't call me 'Pat!' My name is *Patrick!*"

Gracie went on, "If it's a meteorite, what will it look like?"

"It'll probably look like a rock, dummy."

"Then how will we know it's a meteorite?" Gracie asked.

"We'll know when we find it." *But I don't want it to be just a rock. I want it to be from the aliens, 'specially for me!*

"Hey, look!" She swished through the tall grasses into the dark.

Meantime, standing on the curb and peering into the gloom, Patrick grumbled, "She always beats me to the good stuff!" Yet, he didn't want to go any further. Spooky dark had always bothered him, and he sensed that this dark was … "*malevolent,*" the big word came to mind. It really irritated him that he was scared, and Gracie wasn't.

Soon he heard her shout, "I got it! I got it!" Then she shrieked.

"What's the matter?" he yelled, alarm bursting in his chest. He tore through the grass toward Gracie's voice.

However, before Patrick reached her, a palpable boundary oozed against his skin. It felt just like sticking his hand in cold black goo at the Halloween haunted house. "Yuck!" His hair crawled on his neck. This presence wasn't an animal or a human, and he was sure it had no body. Yet it had a "feel," the way he felt that bully in his class who told the world that Patrick was "fat" and "stupid" and "a loser."

It whispered in his mind, *"Come on, come on. Join me and I will make you a hero!"*

Patrick stopped. *Yes, I do want to be a hero!* Did the thing have that power?

But he remembered the bully, and his mind changed. This wasn't fun! This wasn't what he'd imagined the adventure to be!

The presence taunted him, *Are you scared, little boy?*

You're evil! You won't make me a hero! Patrick crouched in the grass, feeling like a little bunny trapped in front of a big snake. The center of the dark thing was right ahead.

Gracie shouted. "Ow, ow, ouch!"

Patrick's heart pounded until he thought it would burst. Inside he yelped, *I'm stuck! Gracie is in trouble, and I can't get to her! Help, help!* Still afraid, he tried to push through the horrible, invisible wall.

Fat boy! the evil presence mocked him. *You are a pig, and you are slow!*

The space between him and Gracie seemed thick, almost impossible to move through. He couldn't even see her!

"Hurry up!" he heard her cry. "This darn meteorite burned my hand. Patrick, hurry up!"

Thrusting fear aside, Patrick broke through the nasty presence and headed toward Gracie's voice.

"Are … you … okay?" Patrick called. He was panting.

Gracie cried, "I'm so scared that I'm about to pee in my pants! And I feel something nasty out here; I think that awful meteorite is haunted!!"

"I'm coming!" When he reached Gracie, he hugged her. His little sister was shivering.

"I'm really, really scared," she whispered.

Patrick realized, *I'm hugging a girl!* Quickly, he let go. "What did you find?"

"I don't know. It looks like a marble. And it's super-hot! I touched it and I'm going to have blisters!" Gracie's voice trembled.

When he looked at the object, Patrick's fear shrank into a mere bother. *This is really Adventure!* "Give it to me," he ordered. "I'll make a pot-holder out of grass so I can hold it." Patrick snatched a wad of grass and cradled the object in it. The marble in his hand glowed with a warm amber color like honey in sunlight. "Wow," he breathed.

"This marble is evil!" Gracie cried. "It's haunted! Throw it away!"

"No, Gracie, I'm keeping it. Come on; let's get out of here!" Patrick grabbed the wad of grass with the marble in it and began to run.

"Wait for me! I'm scared!" Gracie cried behind him.

But Patrick headed toward the streetlight. At first, he felt like he was running through a thick oil spill that smelled bad, coated his skin, and made him so sick that he could hardly move. However, he kept going, leaving Gracie wailing, "Don't leave me here!"

CHAPTER 3
GRACIE AND STARS

L ewis is really, really late for breakfast," Gracie complained. She heard her stomach growl loudly, sounding like something in a zoo.

Since Mom and Dad had breakfast on hold until Lewis could come, Gracie ran to her hideout in the woodsy back yard to sit under the special tree where she'd stashed a notebook and a pen, wrapped in plastic. *Maybe I have time to start another story,* she thought. *In this one, aliens from outer space try to take over the world.*

However, the idea darkened her insides because that reminded her about the *thing* in the field. She knew that it hated her; it wanted to kill her, or, worse, turn her into slime. Despite the August heat, she shivered. No, aliens weren't fun right now. Carefully, she put the notebook and pen away and ran back to the house.

No car. *Lewis isn't here yet.* To fill the time, Gracie walked to Mom's rose garden. When she bent down close, she saw that drops of moisture like diamonds still clung to the leaves. She felt the soft tangerine-colored petals of an exquisite tea rose and leaned over to smell its perfume.

She looked up. The sky was clear and blue, heavenly blue.

As Gracie stretched upward on her toes, arms up, head back, she imagined herself soaring upward. As she got closer to heaven, all the stars blazed big and bright. Now she pictured angels in shining robes and dazzling wings, shouting, and singing. Then, at last, she saw Jesus sitting on a rainbow. His beautiful face lit with joy when he saw her, and he held out his hand.

At that moment, she heard the loud rumble of Lewis's car pulling up onto the driveway, and Gracie's thoughts swept back to the Earth. "Lewis is here!"

Sprinting out of the garden, Gracie flung herself on him and hugged him. Like a gentleman, Lewis opened the screen door for her. "After you, my dear," he said in a princely tone. She gathered her skirts, and floated inside, her head high.

Dad and Mom and Patrick were already seated at the sunny breakfast nook. "Good for you, Gracie," Dad said. "You found your brother and brought him in. Okay, family, time to say the blessing." He bowed his head. The rest of the family got quiet while he prayed. But Lewis did not bow his head or fold his hands.

Gracie took a small bite of her pecan roll, then looked again at Lewis. When he doctored his coffee, he absent-mindedly spooned sugar into it over and over. *Yuck!*

Gracie rearranged the strawberries and blueberries in her fruit salad, and Patrick was chewing his third pecan roll, when Dad asked Lewis about his work. Immediately, the conversation got boring.

"We're analyzing particle tracks and gravitational resonance," Lewis said. "If our project is successful, we could benefit the whole world."

Gracie tuned out as Lewis went on, "Recently, we used a focused ultrasound beam tuned to the molecular resonance of a plasma solution of radioactive thorium to compress nuclei whose electrons have been burned off at a very high temperature."

Gracie couldn't understand a thing. But Lewis kept going, "And then we compressed it very, very fast to simulate the conditions of an imploding star." The word *star* caught Gracie's attention. She loved stars. But imploding didn't sound good.

"The results are promising. If we succeed in doing that properly, everything we throw at it will go into the core of compressed nuclei, but nothing will come out. Then we should see a mass wave with gravitational resonance approaching infinity. The event horizon of that singularity produces energy, not the singularity itself."

Gracie sighed. *Why can't Lewis talk like normal people?*

"Hey, Lewis," Patrick broke in. His round face looked blank. "What's a singularity?"

"A black hole," Lewis explained.

"A black hole?" repeated Gracie. A black hole sounded scary. She remembered the dark thing in the field and shivered.

He answered, "A black hole is the ultimate squished matter. Light can go in, but it can't get out—that's why we call it 'black'—and it's a 'hole' because it's a discontinuum of space/time. When a big star burns out of fuel, that's what happens. The weight of its own gravity compresses it into a black hole."

Her happy mood evaporated. Gracie felt stricken. Her stomach knotted and she put her fork down on her plate. "A star can burn out? Why would *anybody* want to make a burned-out star?"

"To make energy," Lewis said. "Lots of energy."

Dad continued the conversation. "The news said that some people are opposed to your energy project. They say that making a black hole could suck the whole Earth down it."

Gracie stiffened all over, and her stomach felt filled with ice. If even stars could die, if the whole Earth could be sucked into a black hole like water going down a drain, then the universe was a very, very scary place. She looked at Lewis. There was a new sparkle in those big, brown eyes. Apparently, he thought that making a dead star that could gobble up the Earth was a good thing.

"A singularity the size of a pinhead wouldn't do that. It would just sink down to the Earth's center of gravity and stay there. Any reduction in the Earth's mass would take millennia. And its event horizon will produce energy. That's what we're trying to do, to tap into the event horizon's energy. With that much energy, we can do remarkable things!"

Dad went on, "Isn't that big new corporation, the Shields, doing something similar? Except, I heard that they are into weapons research."

Lewis said slowly, "Sort of. They approached me recently. They even offered me a big salary if I'd come work for them."

"What do you want to do?" Dad asked. "Do you want to take them up on the offer?"

Gulping coffee, Lewis spilled some on his shirt and then replied, "I don't know. It sounded exciting, and I'd continue the energy research, just in a new angle. But the Shields specialize in *weapons*. That bothers me. I won't commit without knowing more about them ..."

When they had all finished breakfast, Patrick punched Lewis's arm. "Come on up to my room, bro'. I've got something to show you."

"I'm coming, too!" Gracie insisted.

The three of them went upstairs.

In Patrick's bedroom, Lewis looked around at socks and action figures and Legos strewn on the floor. "You're as messy as I was when I was ten!"

Gracie sniffed. "Patrick, your room stinks!"

Letting his sister's comments slide off, Patrick got the marble out of a little jewelry box and dropped it into Lewis's upturned palm. "I think it's an alien object," Patrick said solemnly. "From outer space."

Gracie frowned but didn't say anything ... yet.

Lewis held up the marble and looked at it in the light. His eyebrows drew up. Gracie saw that he was skeptical. "I doubt it,

Patrick. This is probably a meteorite. Some tektites are round and amber like this. Tektites are glass balls associated with meteorite craters. It's true, this one is symmetrical and smooth, but that's not so uncommon."

Patrick protested, "I did see a flash! And the marble was hot when we found it. Wasn't it, Gracie?"

"Yeah, ..." she began, "But I didn't wanna bring it home! It scares me!"

Patrick flashed Gracie an intense, warning look that told her to shut up.

Gracie knew her brother didn't want to look like a sissy, but *she* was the one who had blisters on her hands, not him. And *she* was the one who got left behind in that field. She looked Patrick in the eyes. "That ghost was real! I didn't make it up!"

"Oh, it wasn't so bad," Patrick said.

"You liar!" Gracie insisted. "It was horrible!"

Patrick shrugged, which punctured Gracie's full anger sack, and she hissed through her teeth, "You know, bro', that there was an awful *thing* out in that field when we found the hot marble!"

Patrick ignored her. Instead, he turned to Lewis. "I want you to do research on the marble! Maybe ..." His voice dropped to a whisper, "Maybe it has powers. "You know, *alien* powers!"

"Humph," Lewis snorted.

Patrick wouldn't let up. "Please, please, please!" he begged.

Gracie stomped on one of Patrick's grubby bare toes. "I swear, there was a ghost where we found the marble." She remembered with a shiver the hate she'd felt. "We oughtta throw it back where it came from!"

As usual, nobody listened to her. Lewis was already taking the marble. He gave Patrick a small smile. "Okay, okay. I'll take this and run some tests on it when I can. Don't look for an immediate result, however."

Gracie felt like having a temper tantrum, but it was no good. Patrick was going to get his way, and Lewis was going to "run some tests" on that stupid marble. She wouldn't be surprised if the ghost came back!

CHAPTER 4
THE ATTACK

Late that night, Lewis awoke. *What's that noise?* Rain hissed and pounded; lightning flashed through his bedroom window. He lay still and listened. Usually, he liked storms, but tonight he felt tense as the violent weather carried on. Besides the noise of the storm, he heard another noise just outside his bedroom door. It was small, a mere shuffle, but it was creepy. *I'm just hearing things,* he thought and closed his eyes.

The noise came again. This time it made no pretense to be subtle. Jumping out of bed, an electric panic spreading through his veins, Lewis looked for a weapon. *I'll grab the chair.* He lifted it, ready to break it over somebody's head, and took one step toward the door. Before he could take another step: *Bang!* The bedroom door smashed open against the wall. Lightning flared; Lewis saw a huge figure advancing.

The courage of adrenaline shot through him. Lewis jumped forward with the chair. Raising the chair above his head, he brought it down hard. *Crash!*

No success—the attacker knocked it away with a sweep of his arm. A big fist slammed into Lewis's stomach. His breath rushed out; he doubled over; nausea paralyzed him. Next, the attacker kicked him in the groin. Screaming, Lewis tried a clumsy kick of his own, aiming at the attacker's own groin, but strong hands caught his foot and twisted. He fell hard. While he lay stunned on the floor, the attacker began kicking his sides and ribs. Lewis feared that his ribs were cracking and that his kidneys would start bleeding. "Help me! Help me!' he shouted, curling up into a ball. He rolled from side to side, but the kicks kept coming, each one a violent agony. Suddenly, the attacker bent down and clamped a hot hand around his throat. Hysterical, Lewis flailed his arms and legs; he kicked back against the attacker's shins; he tried to twist out of the hold, but he could not escape.

The fingers around his throat squeezed harder, and then harder. Lewis had never imagined he'd be choked to death, and not being able to breathe *hurt!*

Close to his ear, the dark figure whispered, "Are you wondering why I came? This is why: I'm from the Shields. We want what you've been working on. Work for us, or what's happening to you could happen to someone in your family. Imagine your little brother and sister. Yes, we know their names: Patrick and Gracie." The hold on his throat eased. "If you call the police, you'll regret it." Hissing, the attacker continued, "You'll hear from us in a few days. It'll be a call from an unknown number. Answer all your calls; I repeat, all of them. One of them will be ours." The intruder let go and kicked Lewis in the back. "Keep your ears open, Wonder-Boy. We need you. We intend to connect to another world. You know how to do it."

When he could think again, Lewis became aware that he was gulping like an asthmatic covered with cat hair, and his pajamas were soaked with cold sweat. At first, he was afraid to move. Then, dragging himself to his feet, he turned on the light and scoped the bedroom. His desk chair was broken and … there were blood stains on the rug. Gingerly, Lewis tiptoed out of the bedroom and stepped into the living room. No intruder was there. Crowding the wall, hoping that the invader wasn't waiting for him, Lewis rounded the breakfast bar into the kitchen. Nothing had been disturbed. He sagged against the wall. All clear; the attacker had left.

His eyes caught the stuffed brown teddy bear that Gracie had given him on his birthday. It sat on his kitchen counter beside the breadbox, and he had felt warm inside every time he saw it. He didn't feel warm tonight. "Would that guy do it, Bobbie? Would he really hurt Gracie and Patrick?" His usual baritone voice sounded hoarse in his ears.

Sure, he would, stupid, Bobbie seemed to reply. *Look at yourself in the mirror.*

Lewis straightened up and stumbled to the mirror that hung in the bathroom. Surprisingly, his face looked normal except for a small bruise on his cheek. However, his throat was encircled with violent red marks. "Wow." His knees buckled; he grabbed the sink to keep from falling; he was violently sick into the toilet. Slowly, he made himself look in the mirror again. *It happened; it really happened!* Terror swelled inside him so that he thought he would burst. *They could hurt Patrick and Gracie, or the rest of my family! But I don't want to work for them! What can I do?* Walking like a zombie across the living room, he opened his patio door. For several minutes, he stood outside in the heavy rain, letting it soak his wavy hair into a dripping mess, letting it wash away the sweat and the stink of fear.

CHAPTER 5
A HELPING FRIEND

At 3:00 a.m., Fred Jontz stood in the kitchen, trying to vaporize a big droning fly with his homemade laser. The laser worked fine, but his aim wasn't very good. He might be a stellar engineer, but he wasn't a sharpshooter.

His phone jazzed, and he took the call. "Fred, thank God, you're there!" Lewis' voice sounded trembly, like a saxophone with a bad reed. Fred wondered if he had a cold. Lewis went on, "I could really use your company right now. Will you come up to my apartment? I know I'm calling late …"

"Sure, Lewis," Fred answered, "I'll be right up."

He felt a spreading pleasant warmth in his belly at the thought that he could do something for Lewis, instead of the other way around. Not only did Lewis and he work at the same place on the same project, but they lived in the same apartment complex. Ever since they'd met at the conference at CERN two years ago, they had been close friends.

Meanwhile, the fly continued to drone, and Fred wiped at a smoking spot on the kitchen wall with a damp paper towel. "Next time," he promised the fly balefully, and went out toward the elevator.

Soon he was knocking at Lewis's door. "Hey, it's me, Fred!" he called, but not too loudly, lest he disturb the neighbors.

The door opened quickly. "Come in," Lewis croaked. "I need your help with a really big problem."

His tall, skinny body looked as tense as his voice sounded. In fact, tension filled the whole apartment, and to soften it Fred joked, "What's up? Do you have one of your brilliant ideas for us to work on?"

As soon as he spoke, Fred experienced a flash of hot jealousy behind the breastbone. *Why does Lewis have all the great ideas? Is he the genius and me the dummy sidekick?*

Immediately he felt ashamed. *What's wrong with you! Why are you jealous of your best friend?* He knew that low self-esteem often slimed his thoughts, even with Lewis, but he couldn't always stop it.

Lewis did not answer right away. Not only had he sounded strange, but he also looked strange. There was an ugly swimming-pool green scarf around his neck, his usually glossy and wavy dark hair stuck out in every direction, and the clueless big, brown eyes that so many women swooned over—which had been another trigger for Fred's jealousy, ever since he had seen gorgeous Maria and sexy Mikiko preen themselves every time Lewis walked by them at work—those eyes were sunken with fatigue and circled with shadows.

"Uh," Lewis finally said, "can I bring you something to drink? A cola or a beer?"

"A diet cola, please."

Lewis stumbled to the kitchen and came back with a cola over ice. When he handed it to Fred, a little sloshed out. Fred saw that his hand was shaking. "Sit down, Lewis," he said, very concerned now. "Tell me what's going on."

"Tonight, I had a home invasion." Lewis's tone was matter of fact, as if he'd taken a walk in the park.

"*What?*"

"Yes. The man beat me up and told me they would hurt my family if I didn't work for 'them.'" He pulled on the scarf, and

Fred caught a glimpse of livid marks.

"Oh, my God! Lewis, the guy strangled you!"

"Yeah." Lewis swallowed. He described the attack briefly, then went on, "I do know who 'they' are."

"*Who?*" A chill went up Fred's back. "Some terrorists? Our energy project could be a powerful in the wrong hands."

"Listen to this: Some recruiters from the Shields company approached me several weeks ago about working for them. They said they want me because I'm familiar with the energy project and they offered a large salary. I wasn't sure if I wanted the job."

"Are you sure it's the Shields?"

Lewis at last showed some emotion when his eyes flashed and narrowed. "Yes! I did my research: The Shields have invested in corporations that make weapons and conduct chemical research. I'm sure they're up to something. The man who attacked me said something about 'they need me to connect with other worlds.' And here we are, learning to walk from point A to point B right through mass using gravitational resonance.

Fred couldn't quit staring at Lewis's throat. "Shouldn't you go to the police, my friend?"

"No!" Lewis's hand touched his scarf. Fred heard a tremble in his voice when he whispered, "The man said they would hurt my family if I went to the police."

Fred found his own voice dropping when he said, "What are we going to do, Lewis?"

"I don't know. I'm in a double bind! I'm caught between betraying my company, maybe even my country, or hurting my loved ones." Lewis put his face on his hands. The emotion finally broke out of him, and Fred held him while he sobbed.

CHAPTER 6

THE MARBLE STORES "MUSIC"

Once he calmed down, Lewis told Fred, "There's no way I'm going to get back to sleep tonight. And I don't want to be alone."

"Sure! I'll do anything I can do to help. I'm staying with you the rest of tonight, Lewis. Should I take you to the ER for your throat?"

"No!"

Fred sighed. Lewis needed help, but he had to wait until his friend was ready. Meanwhile, as they sat on the sofa, drinks untouched, there was no sound except for the steady patter of rain against the patio door. Eventually, Lewis straightened up.

"Here's something we can do. It will take my mind off … well, off what happened. Lewis took a long breath. "Patrick asked me to analyze his 'hot marble.' It's late, and there will be nobody using the lab. Plus, we've both got security clearance."

Lewis handed Fred a battered little jewelry box.

Fred opened the lid and picked off the cotton wad. Inside lay a round glass object. "Looks like a marble," Fred remarked. He picked up the marble in his large fingers, noted that it was exceptionally smooth and looked man-made. "It's pretty. Nice amber color." He handed it back to Lewis. "So what?"

They were silent again. Outside, Fred heard the steady rain, and inside he felt his stomach roiling and his pulse skipping like a squirrel. "Maybe you're right. Maybe analysis of that thing can take your mind off the ugly threats. Then he asked, "What is it with that marble? It seems like such a trivial side-track." He handed the marble back to Lewis.

"It is. That's just the point."

As Fred and Lewis got up, Lewis groaned. He moved like an arthritic old man. "All right, let's go to the lab," Fred directed. "We can play with the marble until everybody comes into work." He ordered firmly when Lewis fumbled for his car keys, "I'm driving. You're in no shape to drive."

Lewis did not argue.

*　*　*

At the Bergman Research Complex, they showed their IDs to the all-night guard, were admitted to the building, and after optic scanning rode the elevator down to the lab. Lewis talked. "Here's the story about the marble. Patrick and Gracie found it yesterday evening, and they thought it was something special. I figure it's just a tektite, but we might as well, I mean, take my mind off things ..." His voice trailed off. Then he continued, "Anyway, Patrick begged me to analyze it, and I said I'd do it."

*　*　*

Fred analyzed the marble with instruments that produced ultrasound, and Lewis examined the crystal using light. They used atomic force microscopy to map its shape and structure. Just before the morning crew came in, they put up everything and went to breakfast.

*　*　*

Seated in a booth, Fred and Lewis talked. The restaurant was dimmer than Fred remembered, but bright enough, and the smell of warm food helped dispel the sick fear in his stomach. He grabbed the syrup for his pancakes and said, "All, right: We analyzed the marble, and now we know that it's more than just a marble."

"Somebody made the thing, plus it apparently has some advanced function," Lewis agreed.

Fred drew out the small notepad from his nerd pocket, along with his mechanical pencil. "Yep. This is what we found in our analysis." At length, in order and in detail, Fred summarized the tests they had run on the marble: "We did some x-ray diffraction spectroscopy, proton nuclear magnetic resonance spectrography …"

"The object is a spin glass," Lewis added. For the moment he seemed to have put aside his danger, and his voice sounded excited. "The glass appears to have been grown in monomolecular layers. Each layer—only a molecule thick—has its own resonance pattern. The resonance patterns don't look random because I calculated predictable algorithmic patterns in, between, and among layers—"

Fred felt another flash of jealousy. *What kind of brain can calculate atomic patterns so easily?* However, suppressing the jealousy, he thought, *I have my own insights.* "Yeah, the resonance patterns are like spreading activation in the nervous system. In fact, there are even resonance relationships in the nuclear sub-structures that contribute to its overall 'music.'" Fred felt himself smile inside. "It's a neural network, firing signal patterns like the brain."

"You're right on target," Lewis agreed. "The marble is a very advanced unit for information storage; as you say, it's a neural network. I'm not sure yet what the patterns mean and what information is stored in it; however, that little marble is capable of storing an absolutely incredible amount of information, in petabytes, not gigabytes." The excitement in his voice dwindled. "Fred, I'm in a real pickle. A scalding hot pickle!" Lewis stared at his plate and sighed. "And so is my family."

Fred thought about that and looked at Lewis's face. His friend still wore that awful green scarf. His face looked gray, a sick man's face. "Lewis," he urged, "I'm taking you to the ER."

Lewis shook his head. "No."

"All right then. If you're not willing to go to ER, or the police, or maybe even Homeland Security, you should go to *someone!* Somebody besides you and me definitely needs to know what's going on." Fred started on his bacon, gobbling it down in a few bites. *I always eat too much when I'm upset.*

Lewis shook his head again. "No." He nibbled at a slice of toast, ate one mushroom from his omelet, and put down his fork. When he spoke again, his voice sounded desperate. "I can't endanger my family!" He looked at Fred. "Or you."

"Then, let's tell Dr. Zhartha. He's discreet, and he knows the people who can help you. Fred downed another big bite and continued, "Look, Lewis, you're going to show up to work with bruises on your neck. People will know something bad happened."

"No, they won't! I'll take a week off work. I should look fairly normal by then."

"Lewis, you can trust Dr. Zhartha."

Lewis sipped some coffee. "He's on vacation. I don't want to disturb him when he's with his family."

"You are so stubborn!" Fred exclaimed. Call him!" He had a powerful urge to shake Lewis for trying to manage these terrible events on his own.

Lewis looked down and frowned. "All right, all right. I can tell him about the hot marble. That's as much as I can promise. I'll beg Dr. Zhartha to meet with me as soon as he can."

Fred snapped, "Don't say, 'as soon as he can.' Lewis, getting help *now* is extremely urgent and important when you and your family are threatened by those creeps!"

Lewis's brows drew together, "Don't you think I know that? But I repeat, as you just said, my family is in *danger!*" His voice broke. "If … if it gets back to those people that I told you what they want me to do …"

Fred glared at him.

"They might hurt you, too, Fred."

"I'm your friend. And I'm big and mean and I can protect you."

Lewis sighed and slumped. "Okay, okay, I'll text Dr. Zhartha right now to schedule a private meeting. But I know it might be a week before I can see him, because …"

"Aw, too bad. Text him anyway!" Fred emphasized.

"Okay, okay." Lewis tapped out a message on his phone. Before he put it down, he had a reply:

"I can see you Saturday at 3 p.m. at the office."

Fred saw a shadow cross his friend's face. Lewis exclaimed, "Heck, Fred, Mom and Dad are going out of town next weekend! I'm supposed to watch Patrick and Gracie, and I've promised that I would take them out for a picnic on Saturday afternoon!"

"You think you have to entertain Patrick and Gracie with all this going on? No. You've got to cancel the picnic. Suppose the Nasties get to you before that?"

Lewis thought. Fred heard him breathe deeply. His eyes brightened a little, and he straightened. "I have an idea. Fred. But I'm counting on your help."

"Sure. What's your idea?"

"On Saturday, when I see Dr. Zhartha, you and I can take Patrick and Gracie to the park. They'll have their picnic, then we'll take them to your place. You show them a movie and make your famous spaghetti supper. Meanwhile, I'll go to Dr. Zhartha at 3:00 p.m., and –

"And you *will* tell him what happened tonight. And take that darn marble with you!"

CHAPTER 7
SHIELDS AND THE MARBLE

Saturday morning was too cool for August. It felt like fall. Also, it was cloudy with a few spits of rain. But Gracie was looking forward to the picnic so much that she didn't mind at all.

"We'll have the picnic," Lewis told them. "We can climb the hills and work off some energy. After that, Fred and you can take in a movie at his apartment. I have some business to take care of, but I'll be back to join you for Fred's famous spaghetti."

Gracie jumped up and down. "That sounds *great!*" She was ready. Her body was full of physical energy. She had dressed for action, wearing her toughest pair of jeans, a plaid shirt in soft browns, and the best pair of walking shoes that she owned, the brown leather lace-ups. Also, she had remembered to bring a good raincoat.

"What about the rain?" Patrick complained. Gracie sighed. Patrick was being obnoxious today.

"I don't care if it rains! I want to go outside!" Gracie insisted.

"It's just drizzling, and we *will* have a picnic," said Lewis. "There is a very nice pavilion at the park." He and Fred opened a kitchen cabinet and pulled out a cooler and some paper products.

While Lewis and Fred carried the picnic supplies out to the car, Gracie saw Patrick grab something that had been lying on the counter by Lewis's car keys. "What's that, Patrick?" she asked.

His face looked as innocent as an angel's. "Just some snack crackers to feed the squirrels. Maybe I can get one to eat out of my hand."

"You're gonna eat them all yourself!" she accused. "You eat all the time!"

"Yeah, I'm a growing boy."

"You're only growing sideways!"

"And you're going to be a red-headed bean-pole," Patrick shot back.

Lewis called, "Kids, we've got to go!"

*   *   *

The four of them piled into Lewis's car and they drove off. As they traveled, the sun peeked out between the clouds. Gracie's spirits rose with excitement. *We're going to have fun!*

When they turned into the park entrance, the grass and trees looked green and fresh, dazzling with droplets of water in the sunlight. Rich foliage hung over the road, and swells of earth rose, covered with tall poplars, maples, and pines, and crowned with tall old oaks.

They got out of the car. Gracie raced Patrick to the large picnic pavilion. "I'm hungry, let's eat!" Patrick exclaimed, when Lewis joined them in the pavilion.

"You could eat the crackers in your pocket," Gracie pointed out.

Patrick's eyes shifted to one side. "I guess I'm not that hungry. I'll wait."

Gracie wanted to tease her brother about his appetite, but she chose to drop the subject. Lewis told them, "I brought everything we need for hot dogs and Some-Mores," and her mouth watered.

For almost an hour, Gracie and Patrick dabbled in the stream and ran up and down the hills. They walked like tightrope artists on the pavilion's benches while Fred and Lewis made lunch. After a while, Lewis called, "Food's ready!"

"Oh, boy!" Patrick exclaimed, leaping off a bench with a mighty thump. He looked dirty and happy. "We get to eat!" He reached for a hot dog with a grimy hand.

"Some people are coming," Fred noticed. "Wow! Look at that!"

Gracie took a small bite of her hot dog and watched as eight SUVs and a humongous tractor-trailer pulled up into the parking lot. Two people got out from each SUV and two from the semi. All the men – there were no women – were all big and tough looking. They made Gracie very uneasy.

"Oh, great," Patrick muttered to her, "Those are people from the Shields. I know that because I heard that many of 'em wear some kind of identification ring."

Gracie noticed large gold rings with black stones on their left hands. *This group doesn't look nice at all.*

The newcomers didn't look pleased when they saw her group in the pavilion. One of the men came up to them. His eyes brushed over Fred, Patrick, and her as if they were nothing, but when they came to rest on Lewis, they narrowed. "Hello, Mr. Bramendra," he drawled. "What a jaw-cracker of a name you have! And, what a surprise, seeing you here."

"My last name is 'Brah-min-du-ra," Lewis answered. "It means, 'Justice of God.'"

Immediately Gracie did not like the man. He had a thick neck and a heavy, pocked face, which she could have ignored, except his pleasant greeting sounded fake.

Lewis asked, "Do I know you? Aren't you with the Shields?"

"Well, our company did offer you a very lucrative job." He did not offer his own name. "So, I've heard your name. You're currently working with Dr. Zhartha on the energy project." His voice sounded oily. He added, "Just go on with your picnic."

Lewis did not reply. In fact, Gracie noticed, a muscle in his jaw kept twitching and he wouldn't look at anyone.

Gracie and he and the others ate as the Shields crowded onto benches in the pavilion. The men sat without talking, hardly moving. Gracie felt a crackling tension in the air. Now her hot dog tasted dry, and the bottled water flat. She could hardly choke down the food. Even the warm, melted marshmallows and chocolate on graham crackers that Lewis made lost their flavor.

"Time to leave," Fred murmured to Lewis when everyone was done.

"Yes."

They began to pack up. *They've ruined our picnic!"* Gracie thought, with a hot prickle in her chest and her teeth clamped shut. She had never felt so angry.

As they were leaving the pavilion, Lewis put his hand into his pocket. His face paled. "Where is it?" he exclaimed. Fishing in his other pocket, he cried, his voice frantic. "I was sure I brought it with me! Oh, my God, where is it?"

"Hey, Lewis," Fred said, "it probably just fell out of your pocket in the car. I'm sure it's there."

Meanwhile, Gracie saw Patrick rifle into the picnic basket. "Stop that, Patrick, she scolded, "Let's go!"

However, he grabbed the marshmallow bag, popped one in his mouth, and then noticed that his shoe was untied. When he bent over to take care of it, a little box fell out of his pocket. The lid came off, the *marble* dropped out, and it rolled to the feet of the heavy-faced leader. To Gracie's amazement, it began to glow warm and bright in the gloomy pavilion.

"Excuse me, I lost my marble," Patrick joked. He blushed, and he couldn't look at Lewis. "Excuse me, excuse me." He reached down to retrieve it. "Ouch! It's hot!"

"Patrick," Gracie began to scold, "You sneaky –

The Shields' leader grabbed Patrick's wrist. "What do you have here, boy?" His voice sounded sweet, but the smile on his broad, pocked face showed too many teeth.

"N—nothing!" Patrick answered, trying to shake off the man's grip.

Lewis glared at the leader. "Let go of my brother," he ordered, his lips curling back from his teeth, the light of battle in his eyes, and his fists clenching. When the man did not let go, Lewis whipped out his phone and began to call 9-1-1.

Several of the Shields jumped up. They grabbed Lewis' arms and snatched the phone from his hand. One of them crunched it underfoot and threw it into the bushes. The leader's eyes gleamed with the marble's reflection. "You!" the man exclaimed to Lewis. "This is the *noretha!* How did you get it? Tell me!" He twisted Patrick's wrist.

"Ow!" Patrick yelled. He dropped the marble and the leader seized it.

At that instant, a swish of tires on wet asphalt broke into the tension. One blue SUV drove into the park, its window open and its driver gaping. Lewis shook off the hands that had held him back. "We're going," he stated. "And I'll take that!" In one smooth motion, he grabbed the marble from the leader's grasp. Now his jaw was set. Showing no fear, he circled his arms around Gracie and Patrick, guiding them outside the pavilion, keeping his body as a bulwark between them and the Shields, while Fred carried the picnic basket.

As they left, a tether of tension stretched between them and the men in the pavilion. Gracie felt like it pulled tighter and tighter. Her heart fluttered as if a bird were trapped inside her rib cage. *Once we get in the car, we'll be safe,* she thought.

Not far away, the blue SUV cruised in a large circle, its driver and passenger looking at everybody. Gracie could hardly breathe. *Maybe the Shields won't chase us now.* However, the vehicle drove away.

Gracie and the others approached Lewis's car. But when Gracie glanced back, a feeling like a hurtling down elevator swooped in her stomach. Several of the men reached into their raincoat pockets. *Do they have guns?* She felt a scream building up.

"Lewis," called Fred from behind, "Hurry up and start the car! I'll guard the kids!"

With a nod, Lewis sprinted the few remaining yards, getting out his keys while he ran. "Go, Lewis," Patrick cheered. "Go, go, go!" Lewis reached the car. He started to open the door.

Fred shepherded her and Patrick as they raced. They had about ten more steps to go, but the Shields, chasing them, coming fast, were only a dozen yards away. The men's hands came out of their pockets. *They do have guns!*

To Gracie's horror, Lewis dropped his keys. When he fumbled to pick them up, Patrick ran into him so hard that they crashed into the car door, which slammed shut again.

Lewis yelled a bad word. He tried to open the door, but it wouldn't open, and he shouted, "Patrick! Doggone your hide!" He finally jerked the car door open again, but Patrick, Fred, and Gracie had jammed together so that they couldn't get inside.

Gracie had just raised her foot to enter the car when everything seemed to move away. The car, the trees, the parking lot, even the Shields faded out. She saw her brothers and Fred through a dimming fog, and then the world blinked out like a television set turned off.

I can't move! Help! Help! She felt, brushing against her skin, a soft, thick, velvet curtain. Or could it be a thick cobweb? Or a monster's mouth? Panic rose in her, a searing light brighter than any flashbulb engulfed her, and she screamed.

CHAPTER 8
THE MASTER OF REST

Meanwhile, on the world called "Horizon," *Lanthra,* in the middle of the night, High Magus Daniel heard soft scratching at his front door. Jumping out of bed and grabbing his sword, he felt his heart lurch in his chest. *Is Lord Charon trying to assassinate me again?* However, when Daniel opened the door, he saw only one of his night guards, Officer Jamie. He took a deep breath and lowered the sword.

Officer Jamie announced, "Your Excellency, your protégé, the young magus Mark Gregory, sends a message. He says you must come to the University laboratory as soon as possible. It is extremely urgent." Officer Jamie, Daniel's secretary's son and his night guard, was not smart, but he was as sturdy as a draught horse. His eyes gleamed in the lamplight. "Your Excellency! Please hurry!"

"Were there any more details in the message?"

"Someone has broken through from …" he bent down and whispered, "*that* planet."

* * *

Daniel and Officer Jamie headed for the College of the Magi. The flagstone path became a broad brick walkway that wound under stately trees, lit at intervals by lamps on wrought iron posts. While the two men half-walked, half-jogged, Daniel imagined the worst: *Lord Charon has succeeded in using the noretha and connecting the worlds. He will bring the Shields from Earth with their weapons.* His heartbeat hammered, so he practiced a calming exercise. First, he inhaled slowly and deeply. Holding his breath, he let his fears slip out of his chest and down his arms onto the upturned palms of his hands. When his heap of burdens had become so huge that he could no longer support it, he exhaled and let it drop.

"There," he said aloud. "Master of Rest, I give you my dear daughters Deirdre and Myra, my position as High Magus, my country Bardia, my province Rockeerie, my people, and my own life."

The reply from his Master took his breath away. *Lord Tahei Charon is too strong for you. You* will *be overrun, Daniel. However, continue to rest, even while you struggle.*

*   *   *

Not far from the College, Daniel sensed danger. *What now?* His hand went to the hilt of his sword.

The avenue curved through a pleasant copse of tall trees. Daniel had always enjoyed this part of the walk, with fresh-scented pine branches and a bridge arching over a pebbly stream. However, it was there that he felt the presence of the demon.

He stopped and put hand out to slow Jamie. "Wait," he said.

Officer Jamie stopped beside him on the bridge. Daniel could hear the big man's breath. His own breath burned in his throat. *There it is.* He sensed the demon about three feet above them.

Jamie started humming nervously. Daniel noticed that the man was shivering. *It's not that cold. He feels the hate, too.* Daniel gritted his teeth hard. The winter night was supposed to be beautiful, mysterious, filled with spirit—not like this! Now the air felt contaminated, infiltrated with spiritual sewage water.

Like a cockroach looking for a crack to hide in, the invisible being stroked their souls. Daniel groaned. *How many of these pests have gotten loose into my world through that that connection to Earth?*

He knew, from his magus training, that the parasite was probing for weakness such as a core of resentment or shame or fear. Once it found an entry, it could slip inside. And feed. And stir up more resentment and fear, a feast to which it could invite its friends. He shuddered. *How dare you! How dare you, Tahei Charon, to invite such filth into our world!*

There was plenty of resentment and fear in his soul to attract spiritual vermin, but he trusted the Master's protection. *Bizeor,* Earth's demons, were nothing, powerless unless one made them so. However, Jamie did not know that. His fear would give it power.

You cannot touch us, he told it. Anger sizzled through him. *We belong to the Master.*

The demon laughed at him. *You are a poor guardian. I cannot touch you, but I can seize him. I will fill this stupid boy full of maggots!*

A hard, hot knot of rage formed in Daniel's belly. Breathing deeply, he struggled not to take the demon's bait. *You have no power over us. We belong to the Master.*

The bridge creaked as Jamie shifted. "What are we waiting for, Your Excellency?" the guard asked. His voice wavered.

"Nothing, Jamie," Daniel answered. "Let's go on."

Jamie raised his sword. "There's something here! Get behind me, Your Excellency!"

The demon sneered, *See his fear? I am already biting him.*

I am nothing, but the Master calls me his servant, Daniel replied. Leaning into his authority, he snapped, "Get out of here! Go back to your hellhole. Now!"

An unexpected breeze rattled the pine boughs above. A big pinecone bounced off his head, and then Daniel felt the demon fade from local space and time, just as a spark fades on a spent sulfur match.

"Gone!" he said. His hand relaxed and fell away from his

sword. "Let's go on now, Officer Jamie."

Cold air burned Daniel's throat as he came to the building that housed the ancient laboratory. Passing through the gatehouse, they stopped at the entrance. *Passing to Earth is as easy as passing through this door,* he thought, *if you have the right technology. No wonder the ancients shrugged aside the One Law and visited the forbidden planet.* How often he had longed to go there! But that was strictly against the Law. Not only that, but his portal at the College of the Magi was deliberately disabled. He and other magi in Bardia could only observe.

"I'll be all right now, Office Jamie. Go back to your post."

Daniel softly spoke a word of command. Immediately, the ornately embossed metal door vanished. A mound of dry leaves at the doorsill swirled as his cloak passed over them. Then, to any onlooker's eye, he also disappeared.

Reappearing in a high-ceilinged stone tunnel hundreds of feet below, he stood in front of another door, smoky glass, beveled around the edges, but without handle or knob. A simple thought from him would open the door as it had the first.

He hesitated. *Tonight marks the end of the old world. Beginning now, Lord Charon will begin to destroy the separation between the people of the universe. Earth's curse will multiply in all the worlds!*

Daniel pleaded into the silence, "Life is too heavy for me. How can I bear this pain?"

It is too heavy for you, and you cannot bear it. That is why you need Me.

Daniel sighed a great sigh. "If you are so powerful, how could you let my wife die?"

The Master's voice came to Daniel, heard heart to heart, *You ought to remember—Death cannot stop me. Not yours. Not mine. Not Ielen's.*

He felt a great calm. Every cell in his body realigned to a healthy position, and he knew that the Master loved him. It was time to go into the laboratory and see what his magi could show him.

CHAPTER 9
DIFFICULT ARRIVAL – SOMEWHERE

Swoosh! The velvet surface of who-knows-what brushed Gracie's skin, but next she hit a firm surface that smelled like leaves and moss. "What happened?" she shouted. Her right side felt bruised but not broken. Her loudest voice sounded small because she was surrounded by a big noise, like water pouring from a giant spigot in a tremendous space.

Her chest still heaving, Gracie rubbed her eyes. Beside her, Lewis wiped his forehead with his sleeve. "Where's Patrick?" she asked, gasping.

Patrick lay on a ledge several yards away. He rocked back and forth, grimacing and holding his ankle.

"Patrick!" Lewis cried. "What's wrong!"

"My ankle," Patrick answered through gritted teeth. "It's like I went through a curtain, but when I got to the other side, someone pushed me, really, really hard, and I fell."

Lewis rushed to him and bent down.

Patrick's voice cracked as he asked, "Where's the car? Why are we here?"

"Here? Where's here?" Fred asked.

Gracie turned around to look out over the cliff. When she saw how deep the gorge was below, how high the rocks above, her breath caught in her throat. A chill prickled her spine.

Fred huddled his hands inside his pockets. To Gracie he looked terrified. "It's really cold out here! If we don't get back home soon, we could die of exposure!"

"Take the marble for me, Fred," Lewis ordered. His voice was calm. "You have a pocket with a zipper. Remember what we thought it might be? Don't lose it!"

Fred received the marble and dropped it into his zippered pocket.

"What do we do now?" Gracie asked.

"We have to climb out of here," Lewis told her.

Gracie and the others stood on a ledge halfway down a great gorge. Below boiled a wild river, and above loomed cliffs topped with winter-bare trees. The gray sky was a narrow bright ribbon above the two walls of the gorge. Gracie swallowed. She looked down at the rushing water, up at the high walls of the gorge, and her hands suddenly became slippery with sweat. The water below boiled and churned; the yawning space seemed to pull her forward. Her stomach did a vigorous somersault.

Setting her jaw firmly, Gracie flexed her arms and stretched her legs to prepare to climb. *If Lewis is willing to climb this cliff, then I guess I can, too.* Gracie suddenly felt peaceful, as if her fear had shrunk to the size of a small biscuit.

First, Lewis pulled off his jacket. Next, he took off his shirt, and T-shirt and tore the T-shirt into strips. Shivering violently even after he put his clothes back on, Lewis wrapped Patrick's ankle, using the cloth strips like an Ace bandage.

"Patrick, you'll have to put weight on the ankle while you climb," he said. "Also, I want you to go first so I can steady you. Are you willing to try?"

Patrick nodded, his eyes wide.

"This will brace it a little."

"It feels better now," Patrick said.

"Good job, Sport," Lewis ruffled Patrick's hair. This time Patrick did not complain.

They all looked at one another in silence for a second. Then Gracie said, "I'm ready."

*　　*　　*

Fred clenched his teeth. "Okay, I'm ready, too. Let's do it." After Patrick began, Lewis followed, calling out each handhold and foothold. Gracie came next, and last Fred.

While he saw Gracie scramble up the cliff, spry as a little green lizard, Fred's knees trembled violently. His hands were so sweaty that he could hardly grip the rock.

Suddenly, he felt a cold, oily presence near his ear. A sly thought flitted through his mind, *This fiasco is all Lewis's fault. How could somebody as smart as Lewis have made such stupid choices? He should have never let the kids and you handle that blasted marble. He was just trying to show off, wasn't he?*

"Get away!" Fred yelled at the thought.

Startled, Gracie handhold slipped, and she almost fell.

"S . . . Sorry, Gracie," Fred apologized. "I didn't mean to scare you."

Fred felt unclean. *Why did I think like that?* he wondered. *I just ripped my friend to shreds! What came over me?* He shook the water droplets from his soggy hair and continued to climb up the gorge. He tried to reassure himself, *I don't really feel that way.* But when he pictured Lewis, there was a knot of anger in his gut.

*　　*　　*

"Yo, Patrick, we're playing follow the leader and you're It," Lewis joked lightly as he talked his brother around a bulge in the cliff. So far, he felt very calm, or maybe too shocked to allow any fear. As he climbed behind his brother, he gave Patrick a hand, a gentle push, tug, or lift, and kept up a smooth routine.

"Good ..." he called down, "we're almost to the top of the gorge. As Lewis strained to steady Patrick up a few more feet, his thought was, *I'm going to be late to see Dr. Zhartha this afternoon!* He laughed to himself. He was not going to make that appointment. At least the Shields were not going to be able to hurt him or his family. *Maybe being teleported wasn't a bad thing.*

A compartment of his mind that was not focused on climbing assessed what had happened. Unbidden, a mean little voice whispered, *You were stubborn, Lewis, as usual. That's why you're stuck in a gorge. God is teaching you a lesson and keeping you from getting too proud. After all, you say you are an atheist. He is probably watching, having a great guffaw.*

Lewis clenched his jaw. Sheer persistence would get them all up this cliff, even if God was laughing at him. His arms and legs trembled with fatigue, but he kept moving, inch by stubborn inch.

At last, the top! Lewis pushed Patrick over roots and soil to the top of the gorge. While his brother crawled away from the edge and sat on a patch of green moss to rest, Lewis remained on the edge of the cliff, waiting to help Gracie and Fred up the last few feet.

His body was so hot from climbing that he no longer felt the cold. However, in a few minutes, he knew his sweaty clothes would cool off and he would be in serious trouble. For now, he could appreciate a little of the beauty of the place. *Is this what going to heaven like? You pass through the valley of death, and come up into paradise?*

Firmly he reminded himself, *Don't get religiously sentimental. There is no heaven.* Meanwhile, roaring tons of water, rugged cliffs, huge and ancient trees, and delicate lichens and moss had replaced his familiar suburban environment. Even the austerity of winter could not mask the grace of nature in this place. The air smelled fresher and cleaner than he had ever experienced.

*   *   *

Gracie and Fred were almost to the top of the gorge. Lewis stayed where he was to help them up the last few feet. Once Gracie stood on the top, catching her breath, she looked around. The trees were bare; there was a penetrating wind, a cold, icy wind under a low gray sky. And soon, she felt like she was in a refrigerator. *It's winter here!*

"Where in the world are we?" Gracie and Patrick asked at the same time.

"We're here, wherever here is," Fred joked, sweat dripping down his forehead and soaking his shirt in a dark "V" over his chest. He pulled his jacket tightly around himself.

They stood close together in a cluster and surveyed the wilderness. Patrick had found a stick and was leaning on it.

Fred exclaimed, "We're in Daniel Boone country!"

They stood on a ridge. Wind that sounded like someone blowing into a microphone beat against their ears. Before them, a forested slope dropped steeply, covered with trees behind trees behind trees. Behind them, stark choirs of trees rose in ever-taller ranks toward endless mountain ridges. There were no houses or cars or roads in sight.

Gracie and the others looked at Lewis, who let out a long sigh. "All right," he said. "Follow me. We're going downhill."

*   *   *

After about an hour, although they shivered from the wind, they stopped to rest. "Look!" Gracie shouted. Horses and riders approached; they reminded her of a troop of Mounties. They wore wide-brimmed hats, brown uniforms with heavy cloaks, and sparkling silver insignia on their shoulders. Gracie sighed with relief. Not only had somebody found them, but they all looked friendly. She and the others waved and called, and the troop rode up to them.

One of the riders, a man with crinkly brown hair and a full beard, addressed them. "I am Captain Gregory. I'm here to meet you." The captain smiled, "It looks like you are glad to see us, too."

CHAPTER 10

YOU'RE ON LANTHRA

Why are you here? How did you know to meet us in this wilderness?" Lewis cried.

Gracie wondered why that was important. After all, they were rescued!

"I am the commander of the Bardian Army in the province of Rockeerie. At the order of His Excellency, High Magus Daniel, we were sent to locate you and bring you to our home." Captain Gregory's face grew serious. "Others would like to locate and take you, too. However, I fear that would not be a pleasant experience."

He turned to his troop. "Wrap them in blankets, cloaks, any warm clothes you can, and let us depart!"

Captain Gregory and the Bardians helped them mount horses, which Gracie did not mind at all. She loved, absolutely loved horses. However, they rode on, and then they rode on some more. By the time afternoon approached evening, she was thinking, *I'm so tired. If only we could ride in cars or trucks!*

Just when she thought she couldn't go any further, they stopped at a high plateau. There was a wonderful view of a valley, and at another time, Gracie would have been delighted. However, now she was so tired she wanted to fall off the horse and lie on the ground. "Let me help you," her trooper said. She went limp and let him ease her down.

Captain Gregory called, "We'll camp here."

While the Bardians prepared their campsite, Lewis, Patrick, Fred, and she, all huddling in blankets or cloaks, sat on the ground. Lewis folded his arms around Gracie to keep her warm. Her body ached and her mind ached. *Mom and Dad will be worried sick, and there's nothing I can do about it.* The thought hurt her stomach.

The sun, setting over her right shoulder, reflected burgundy from a deep river far below. On both sides of the river, the treetops glowed with bars of orange light. It was beautiful, but her stomach flapped inside like an empty bag, and she asked Lewis, "When will we get to eat?"

"Soon," he told her, giving her a gentle hug, "soon."

By now, all the soldiers had set up small, primitive shelters and had gathered for supper. Soon, unheated food and drink passed from hand to hand. Gracie ate crunchy multigrain bread, chewy smoked turkey, and sweet dried apples, washed down with cold water. No one started a fire, and she wondered why.

Although it was getting hard to see in the evening dusk, Gracie noticed one of the troopers approaching. He looked about Lewis's age. In clear English, he stated, "I'm Lieutenant Rel." Feeling sleepy, she leaned against Lewis and drowsed while they talked.

*   *   *

"This is my first question, Lieutenant Rel," Lewis said. "Where are we?"

"Yep," added Fred. "Give us a little geography lesson."

The lieutenant began, "You are from Earth, the planet of the treasure. However, now you are on Lanthra, which means 'horizon.'"

"We're on Lanthra," Lewis echoed. He added, feeling irritated, "And I have no idea why you call Earth the planet of the treasure; it begs the question, so tell me what that means."

Lieutenant Rel sighed. "I don't have time to explain that

now. Soon we will have to be silent."

Lewis slumped. He felt exhausted. The chilly air froze his back even while Gracie on his lap kept him warm; he ached all over; and his butt felt permanently smashed from riding the dratted horse.

Fred held Patrick. "You must have some nifty short-cut between points A and B in the universe. This is stuff right out of science fiction."

Rel sounded happy when he said, "Ah … I watched science fiction movies when I studied Earth culture at the College of the Magi. Godzilla, Martians, Vulcans … sometimes my friends and I stayed up all night in the College laboratory, laughing our heads off!"

Lewis almost fell off his rock. He had to shift quickly to keep Gracie in his arms. "*What* did you say?" he exclaimed. "*How* could you see our sci-fi movies from another planet?"

Captain Gregory snapped, "Quiet! We're not out of hostile territory yet."

When his ears registered the word, "hostile," Lewis felt sick "I can't believe this. We're on another planet, in the winter, in hostile territory … What is going on?" Gracie, fast asleep, was hot and heavy in his arms, and he wasn't sure he could hold her up much longer. That word, "hostile," frightened him, especially for the kids. "What does all this have to do with us?"

The trooper explained, "I am sure that the enemy Nark's Wolf Riders and Lord Charon's Horned Edge magi will want to question you *because you are from Earth*. And they are not gentle."

CHAPTER 11
FORDING THE WINERUSH

It was too cold to sleep well, but Lewis managed to nod off. A short time later, he felt a light touch on his shoulder and awoke. "Time to go," Lieutenant Rel whispered.

While the Bardians got the horses ready, Rel said, "We shall exchange clothes. We want to make sure you are not captured."

A chill ran up Lewis's spine. "What about Patrick and Gracie?"

"The children, Captain Gregory thinks, will be safe as they are."

"And, what about *you*, should you be captured?"

"We are soldiers, trained in war. Better us than you."

Lewis was silent. He shivered while he peeled off his clothes. Rel handed him a uniform, riding boots, and a cloak that fit reasonably well, and he struggled to put them on in the dark.

Fred sounded loud as he joked. "My guess is that we've got parts in a Civil War reenactment. I hope they give me a sword!" He laughed, and Lewis winced.

"Shhh," Rel hushed him.

Lewis felt a tap on his wrist. "Take off your watch," Rel said softly.

"Even my watch? It's a gold Rolex! My Dad gave this to me when I graduated from college!" he whispered with a jab of anger.

"Yes! It gleams in the moonlight. Trust me. I will return it later."

After the exchange of clothing, Captain Gregory approached Lewis and Fred. He spoke in a low voice, "We have to ford the Winerush River, the border between Bardia and Torpatath, which is called Tor. I believe there will be enemies waiting to ambush us at the ford. I'll do my best to get us all safely across the river."

After adjusting saddles and gear, the troop mounted; even Lewis awkwardly hauled himself upright onto his horse's back. One of the Bardians made a little chuckling sound, and the horses willingly walked forward. Following the others, his horse descended a steep slope, rocking from side to side. Lewis hung onto the reins and the beast's mane with a desperate grip. *I hate horses!* he thought.

Eventually, he could hear the faint rushing of the river, and in the moonlight shone silver ripples of its water. Two moons were visible above the mountain slopes. *Okay, we're on Lanthra.*

Soon, Lewis heard a crunching noise. They had reached a gravely spit by the riverbed. He gripped saddle, mane, anything, as his horse slid on its haunches down the steep, muddy bank into the river. But, thrown off balance, Lewis jerked forward, rebounded back, overcompensated, and toppled off the animal into the water.

The cold water shocked him; he could hardly breathe. When he found strength, he yelled, "Help!"

At that moment, other yells pierced the air. "Fred! Patrick! Gracie!" he called frantically. *God, I cannot bear it if one of them gets killed!* An arrow whistled past his ear.

Somebody pulled Lewis up by the arm. Shouting at him in an incomprehensible language, the person grasped both his wrists and tugged him further into the river.

Oh no, he screamed inside, *I'm being captured!*

His captor hissed at him, "Get back on the horse!"

He knew that voice. A gold glint on the man's arm was his

own Rolex watch. "Rel!" he gasped. He dazedly waded through icy water to his beast.

An arrow whizzed past, very close—he felt a whiff of air on his cheek and saw several moonlit streaks cut into the shallows. Helping him mount the horse, Lieutenant Rel urged, "Go, Lewis! Hurry!"

As his horse swam, Lewis heard such screaming all around him that the hair rose on his neck. Arrows glinted past like dim sparks.

Behind him, he heard a triumphant, "Try a taste of wet boot in your kisser!"

He glanced back. A man had grabbed Fred's leg and was trying to pitch him off his horse. With a mighty kick, Fred knocked away the would-be attacker. Lewis heard a loud grunt and a splash as he hit the water. Swimming hard in the current, Fred's horse passed his and reached the far shore.

With great heaves of its strong legs in the river, Lewis's horse swam until it reached the other side of the river and followed Fred's up the steep bank. Once all of Captain Gregory's troop reached the Bardian side of the Winerush, the ambush was over. Lewis searched frantically until, in the faint glimmer of the moons, he made out double shapes on two horses. *At least Patrick and Gracie are alive.*

Fred's voice came as his horse drew up alongside, "Are you okay?"

"Yeah, sure," Lewis answered, trying to sound confident, but he felt embarrassed because his voice shook.

Meanwhile, Captain Gregory called, "Follow me to Nutman!" The Bardian survivors galloped down a rough trail toward safety.

CHAPTER 12
THE CITY OF NUTMAN

Hours later, Lewis ached as his body jarred up and down because of the wretched beast's slow trot, but his eyes and ears and nose observed the world. He smelled rich forest mould and the fresh air of early morning. In the brush downhill to the left, a quail called, *Bob, bob, white!* Another echoed further downhill, more faintly, *Bob, bob, white!*

Under the trees, at first, he could see only a dark predawn gloom. The moons had set. However, in a few minutes, sunrise—his first on this planet—began with a glow of optic purple. Gliding quickly through the trees, the early sunlight mutated into glowing peach. Lewis lifted his head and wished that the warmth would penetrate his wet clothes. From peach to bright pink, the colors evolved slowly to full morning light.

The path turned another corner. Immediately, the mammoth trees gave way to a view of a valley, and Lewis saw a walled city below, nestled into the side of a small hill. *That must be Nutman, the capital of this province,* he realized, remembering Lieutenant Rel's geography lesson. *That's where we're going.*

Turning, he looked back for Patrick and Gracie and Fred. Their heads were bowed down over their horse's necks, but Gracie looked up, caught Lewis's eyes, and waved. Lewis counted the Bardian riders. *Five missing,* he thought, *including Rel.* He felt his weary head droop.

At last, they arrived at the city. The troop crossed a bridge over a burbling creek, and they stopped at an iron gate. Captain Gregory called, "Old John, open the gate! Hurry!"

An elderly man with a head full of white hair, a grizzled beard, and tufty eyebrows sauntered out of the gatehouse. "Good morning, Captain Gregory." He bowed and let them through.

Weary though he was, Lewis noticed Old John staring at them, especially at him. This wasn't just a curious stare; it was so intense that Lewis felt uncomfortable, as if he had been jabbed.

After the troop entered the gate into the city, Captain Gregory brought his horse close to Lewis. His face was drawn and tired, but his eyes seemed kind. "I want to tell you what I have in mind for you and the little ones, so that you don't worry," he said. "I plan to take the children to my own home. My wife Sadie will see that they have whatever they need. You and your friend will go with my men to the barracks and rest. This afternoon, you will all go to the High Magus, and he will get you more permanent housing and food."

Too tired to speak, Lewis nodded. Captain Gregory and the two soldiers sharing horses with Patrick and Gracie rode to the right. Lewis and Fred filed obediently into line and rode with the rest of the troop to the left.

For the rest of the ride, Lewis saw through a gray haze. They finally came to a courtyard. Lewis groggily ticked off what he still had to do: *Get off the horse. Don't fall. Let them take the beast away, thank you. Goodbye, beast, and good riddance! Follow Fred. Go through that doorway. Down the stairs. Down the hall. Into the room. Oh good! A bed!*

*   *   *

He awoke with a start. Someone was shaking his arm.

"Wake up, Lewis." It was Fred. "We're supposed to go see the His Excellency, Daniel, the High Magus of Lanthra. And we've got to get ready *now!*"

CHAPTER 13
DEIRDRE

Fred, Lewis, and the children approached Nutman's massive provincial capitol building, which was surrounded by a high stone wall. There, they stopped at a guardhouse, where a black-robed young man looked at them with great interest. "I bet that's a magus," Fred whispered to Lewis, who nodded. Captain Gregory said a few words to the magus, and the young man rang a bellpull. A deep chiming like a London clock came from the other side.

At that moment, Fred's nose began to run. He wiped it on his sleeve. Immediately, he thought, *You slob; have some manners! You're going to a formal interview with the High Magus of this whole world!"*

Nearly sick with embarrassment, Fred stepped away from his group to hide and wipe his dripping nose on his sleeve. But his foot tapped a loose brick, and he toppled over, banging his face on the pavement. When Lewis helped him up, Fred berated himself. *Why is the fool always me? Why can't Lewis be the one with the runny nose and the tripping feet?* He touched his face, and his fingers came back with blood.

Meanwhile, the magus at the gatehouse chanted, *"Golanoya!"* The entrance to the capitol building's grounds not only opened; it vanished, shocking Fred to the core.

"Wow!" Patrick and Gracie cried.

"This is one example of the old technology," explained the magus. "It is based on manipulation of sound, which is allowed on Lanthra."

"Huh?" Fred said, but suddenly he felt a fount of liquid running inside his nostrils. "*Yuck!* he cried. Before he could wipe his nose on his sleeve again, the young magus handed him a handkerchief.

Meanwhile, Captain Gregory gestured to two more people approaching, a tall man about his age and a young woman. "Meet my son, Mark, who is a magus in the College who works with High Magus Daniel. Also, meet Deirdre, His Excellency's older daughter."

Fred felt his heartbeat skip as the two people came forward. He glanced at Mark, who wore a gray robe with white lining at the sleeves. However, his eyes fixed on Deirdre, and immediately, he felt his face get hot.

The first thing he noticed was her luscious body. She was not as tall as he preferred, but she had all the right curves in the right places. She wore a marvelous Kelly-green riding skirt, matching vest and cape, and brown leather knee-length riding boots. Her golden wavy hair hung down to her waist. Because of her straight-backed, quick authoritative manner, Fred thought she might be in her mid-twenties, but when she got closer, he saw that she was only about eighteen years old. *Wow, I like them young.* Fred felt the palms of his hands sweat.

Magus Mark Gregory greeted them, and then the lovely girl said, "Welcome to Lanthra, our world, and to Bardia, my country." Fred wondered, *Are she and Mark an item? I hope not. I hope she's available.*

Fred loved her accent. It had a delightful lilt. Plus, when she took his hand with a soft but firm touch, his body quivered. "My name is Frederick Jontz," he said gallantly. "But my friends call me 'Fred.'"

"Fred," she said, with a bright smile. Her voice was wonderful, like an expensive guitar with elegant timbre.

He bowed to her low, despite his injured nose. When he straightened, he looked into her eyes. He smoothed his hair and flexed his muscles. But … her lovely violet eyes were on Lewis. She gave *Lewis* her brilliant smile. With a courtly gesture, Lewis took Deirdre's hand and touched it to his forehead.

Fred's stomach twisted. He ground his teeth. *You stay out of it, Louie. I want this woman. She's mine.*

*   *   *

The company passed through the gate. Deirdre and Mark led them to the entrance of a tall, cream and rose stone building at the crown of the city's hill. It had a shining gold dome, and a green flag with a white oak tree flapped from the peak. Deirdre pointed upward. "This is the Forschwynn building, named after the family that saved Bardia from Lord Amen Charon's conquest. That time is called the Great Rebellion."

Fred's party started up the marble steps. Lewis shepherded Patrick, who limped badly. Gracie came close and clung to Fred's arm. He liked that. Gracie always soothed his soul. He could feel her pulse beating fast, like a little bird. "Nothing to worry about, sweetie," he reassured her. He patted her hand, and felt her heartbeat slow a little.

People ascended and descended the steps, just as they might in a government building back home. Most were dark-skinned like Lewis and Patrick; some had blond or auburn-hair like Gracie and himself … and Deirdre. The Bardians conversed in a language that sounded to Fred a little like Gaelic, with rolling, lilting inflections. At the top of the steps, at a great door bound with brass, Deirdre stepped aside. Two guards opened it for them to enter.

When Fred passed through the door, he hoped that Deirdre's eyes would brush over his big chest and strong arms with approval. However, his stomach lurched when he looked back and saw Deirdre's face. Her eyes were on Lewis again. She studied

Lewis as if he were a masterful work of art. Fred hoped she would notice his friend's skinny body and tired slump, but instead he knew that Deirdre had focused on Lewis's big brown eyes, dark, wavy hair, and serious, intelligent face. She looked at him much, much longer than she had looked at Fred. His insides twanged like a steel string snapping off a guitar. When she smiled a brilliant sunglow smile at Lewis and her eyes darkened with desire, Fred felt sharp claws dig deep into his back.

She wants Lewis! He inwardly seethed. His hand swept his stinging shoulder but felt nothing except his cape. Yet the pricks were still there. *I hate you, Lewis,* he thought.

You're a fat slob, Fredrick Jontz, a wicked little voice said in his head. *Why should any woman like you, stupid big blond jerk with a flabby belly and a runny nose, much less a beautiful daughter of the High Magus! You always were second best to Lewis. All right, maybe if he were out of the way, she'd like you. But you haven't got a chance with him around.*

For a moment, Fred considered knocking Lewis "accidentally" over, hoping he'd smash his face. *But no, she'll probably fuss over him even more if he gets hurt. Women do that.*

They crossed a marble vestibule. Their steps rang on the stone and their voices echoed. Hating Lewis with all his might, Fred again felt the sharp pricks on his shoulder, painful as mean cat's claws.

Deirdre led them to a smaller chamber where warm afternoon sunlight flowed in through stained-glass windows. She said, "This is my father's office. Please call him 'Your Excellency.' And this is his secretary, James."

A thin man with dark brown hair and a well-trimmed moustache arose from his desk. "Welcome."

Deirdre began the introductions. As she spoke, her eyes smiled into Lewis's, and Fred's stomach began tying itself into angry knots. "Meet Lewis Brahmindura. Also, meet Lewis's brother, Patrick, and his sister, Gracie, and ..." she seemed to search her memory, "Dick Jontz."

She smiled at him again, but his insides had gone rancid.

"Fred," he muttered. "My friends call me Fred."

"I'm sorry," she apologized. "Fred Jontz."

"Wait here," James said. "His Excellency will see you shortly."

Deidre bade them goodbye.

CHAPTER 14

THE TREASURE AND THE CURSE

Gracie liked the High Magus Daniel. The man was short, but he was so graceful that he must have studied ballroom dancing. Clear afternoon sunlight haloed his curly blond hair. His entire office was light, warm, and elegant—just like him. White and gold, with odd nooks and corners, it reminded Gracie of a perfect quartz crystal. She drew in an awed breath at the view through its clear windows.

"Please sit down," Daniel said. He indicated a comfortable-looking couch and chair arrangement near the bay window, and they took seats while James bowed and left the office.

Gracie sat next to His Excellency's chair, which made her feel special. However, across from her, Patrick's face was gloomy, even scared. Fred seemed upset, even angry, and when she looked at Lewis sitting beside her, she saw that his face was dark and troubled. Her own tummy began to squirm, but she told it, *Quit! Even if I do miss Mom and Dad.* But her tummy kept twisting.

Smiling, the High Magus began the introductions. "I am Daniel, High Magus of Lanthra, which means 'Horizon,' just as your planet is called 'Earth.' My various titles include High Magus of the Order of the Magi in Lanthra, the Viceroy of the

Rockeerie Province in Bardia, and visiting Professor of Earth Studies at the Bardian university in our capitol city, Kingsport."

All the man's titles flew over her head. Gracie decided immediately to think of him as Daniel. *But I had better call him "Your Excellency!"*

Lewis asked, "I wondered … Why can you speak English? Aren't we on another world?"

"There is only one language on Lanthra," Daniel explained. "We never built a Tower." He smiled, and Gracie wondered what he meant. He went on, "However, anyone who has studied at the one of our Lanthran universities can speak several Earth languages, especially, here in Bardia, English."

Silence fell with a thud onto the gorgeous carpet. Daniel leaned forward in his armchair and put his hands on his knees. His voice went into teaching mode. Even as excited and nervous as she was, Gracie paid careful attention, even more than she listened to her teachers at school. *I'm on another world,* she thought, which made her feel dizzy.

Daniel said, "Lanthra was completely unspoiled for centuries. All our people were careful with the environment, with creatures, and with each other. Plus, Lanthra's magi, scientists and philosophers developed technology that could observe and communicate with far places on this planet, other worlds, moons, and more. You were brought here by such technology."

Fred growled, "If you have such fantastic technology, then why do you send troops on horses who fight with swords and bows and arrows? Where are your cars, trucks, and trains?"

"Since the Great Rebellion, we do not use electronic technology. Also, Lanthra had no great Flood, so there is little petroleum."

"Then how did we get here?" asked Fred. "Surely there's electronic technology somewhere on this planet!"

"Some is used, restricted to our colleges. But otherwise, we use sound and various resonances."

"Why us?" Lewis blurted. "Why are *we* here!"

Gracie reached for Lewis's hand and clung to it tightly. It felt cold. He was upset; she was upset; they were all upset. His hand began to clench Gracie's until it hurt. But she held on. *He needs a comfort dog, that is, a comfort girl, and maybe my hand can help.*

"I believe that your passing through the Horned Edge's nexus was a *mistake*. My enemy's scientist, in a fit of spite, threw the *noretha* to Earth. Patrick and Gracie, you found it first. Now our enemies can use you to work for them – and so can we, but I believe that both chance and spiritual design brought you all here. Radyah has a purpose for you."

Daniel's office was silent for a while. Gracie watched her brothers and Fred and the High Magus.

"Who are your enemies? What is the conflict about?" Lewis asked. "Tell me again, because I don't understand."

Daniel answered, "My principal enemy is Lord Charon, ruler of Tiorpatath, which you might call To. He and his barons made an alliance – we call it a *plot* – with people on your planet who call themselves 'the Shields.' That is a weapons manufacturing company."

"Yes," murmured Lewis. "I know."

"Lord Charon intends to exchange our ancient and powerful communication technology for Earth's warfare technology and the alliance will conquer both planets."

"Shields!" interrupted Fred. "Wow! No wonder those men in the park were so mean!"

Lewis shut his eyes and took a deep breath. He said, "The Shields blackmailed me. One of them beat me and threatened to hurt G … er, my family if I didn't work for them." His eyes opened, looked at Gracie, and a tear rolled down his cheek.

Gracie felt sick to her stomach. *They hurt Lewis! They could have really hurt us when we were in that park!*

"So, here we are in the middle of a plot to conquer two worlds." Fred said heavily. "How do you know that we have better motives than Lord Charon and the Shields?"

Daniel nodded. "That was a concern. However, my magi have observed you since you found the noretha, which you call the marble." He smiled slightly. "You do not fit the profile of *Saoma*-worshipping people.

"Huh?" Fred asked.

"Saoma is a demon. It and its servants, the *bizeor,* want to eat souls. Saoma-worshipping people are cruel. They even practice human sacrifice."

Gracie couldn't help it; she burst out, "Ew!"

Patrick leaned forward. "'Bezubs,'— that's what the word *bizeor* sounds like – demons."

Daniel's eyes flashed. "Yes, they are our enemies. More than five hundred years ago, the magi called the Horned Edge, chose to serve Saoma. They nearly captured our whole world. And so began a horrible war that we call 'The Great Rebellion.' I will not describe it! Finally, the magi of my order defeated the Horned Edge, with Radyah's help and the courage of the Bard."

"Who was the Bard?" Patrick asked. He looked excited and leaned forward.

"The Bard was a person from the family called the Forschwynns. He roamed the countryside and played the lute so skillfully that he changed people's lives. The music freed them from emotional and literal slavery. Strengthened, we won the war and this country Bardia was established."

"Wow," Patrick breathed. "I want to be like the Bard."

Gracie thought, *He always did want to be a hero!*

Fred interjected, "What does Earth have to do with Saoma and demons and the Horned Edge magi and the Shields?"

Daniel answered, "On Earth—this is the part nobody wants to hear—there's a curse. In a metaphor, I'll call it a disease. Imagine a vile beetle that feeds on blood. When it bites a person, it injects a deadly virus. That person rots, all the way down to the roots! Some people on your own planet serve Saoma; some serve

Radyah, but all have been infected.”

Silence fell over the group. Disgust, disbelief, and doubt showed on their faces.

“Here is the good news,” Daniel said. There is no world like yours. Let me emphasize this: Earth is unique in the universe!”

“What do you mean?” asked Lewis.

Daniel’s expression brightened. “From Earth came the universe’s greatest treasure. Your treasure is eternal life!”

Gracie tried to take it all in. *This sounds kinda like Sunday School,* she decided.

“Is that like magic?” Patrick burst out. Gracie nearly grinned. Her silly brother’s mind had grabbed his favorite subject. “Or ninja power?”

Daniel smiled at Patrick and leaned forward. “Yes and no. This power is not ‘magic’ in the way that you usually understand it. However, when people hear in one of Earth’s liturgies: ‘… with angels and archangels and all the company of heaven,’ you are hearing a little part of it.”

Gracie thought, *I know what angels are. I have a Guardian Angel.* She was sure she could feel her angel sometimes. Plus, Mom had given her a little angel pin to wear on her shoulder. When her hand went up to her shoulder, though, she didn’t feel it. *I left my angel pin at home. Will I ever see it again – and Mom and Dad?* She felt like someone was ripping her heart out.

“Christianity,” Lewis commented. He folded his arms over his chest. “God and Satan; angels and demons.”

Daniel nodded. “Lewis, you are exactly right. I am talking about Jesus, whom we call *Radyah.*

Gracie saw Lewis’s muscles tense. She thought, *Lewis doesn’t believe in Jesus. That’s why he wouldn’t say the table blessing with us.*

“So, your world has adopted Christianity from Earth. Why? Don’t you have your own religions?” Lewis asked. His arms were crossed; his ankles were crossed.

"No, we do not have our 'own' religions. With technology we watched all the religions. The Lanthran magi believed the promises of the Jewish prophets. Our magi saw Radyah being born that night when the angels sang to the shepherds! Later, your own magi brought him gifts."

Patrick's eyes brightened. "Magi!" he echoed softly. "They're real!"

Even though her hands trembled, and she had to clasp them together, Gracie smiled to herself. She could picture baby Jesus, angels, shepherds, wise men: They were her close friends.

"Our magi saw the miracles, heard his sermons, and, with terrible fear …" Daniel took a deep breath, "we watched him die by the Roman torture called crucifixion. But when we saw him rise from the dead, we began to understand … and now many people in Lanthra worship him in the *tharadyah,* our chapels."

They go to church! Gracie thought, her eyes widening.

"John Lennon would be rolling in his grave," Fred joked, but Gracie didn't know what he meant.

Daniel leaned forward and let another silence fill his beautiful office. Then he said,

"Because of the concern of bizeor infection, our ability to travel through to Earth has been disabled. You were brought here by Lord Charon's system, but from here you cannot leave!"

Lewis went stiff as if he had been petrified. Patrick's mouth dropped open. Across from them, Fred's face had turned red, and Gracie felt bile rise from her stomach. *I can't go back home!* her thoughts wailed. *I'm so scared! I want to see Mom and Dad!*

It was a total interruption for their frail composure when Mr. James came into Daniel's office carrying a large, covered silver tea tray. "Coffee? Cider? Scones, anyone?" he asked.

"Ermm," Fred growled aggressively, but accepted a scone, "

Gracie could not eat. Fear was growing, tingling down in her tummy. She wanted with all her heart to go home. She pleaded, "Isn't there *any* way we could get back to Earth? I want to go home!" Her whole body shook, and she could hear her voice small and trembly.

"Not from here. And even if we could renew that technology, the answer is No. The Lanthran magi have one law: We can observe Earth, but we cannot go there."

"Then, what will we do? How will we tell our family where we are?" Lewis broke in.

Gracie saw that Daniel's eyes shone with compassion, but she could not feel a thing. She had become completely hollow inside, empty and numb. Daniel looked at them each in turn. A corner of her mind registered that the afternoon sun gleamed golden through the window and a sweet bell rang down in the city somewhere; however, none of her senses had the power to reach her heart.

"I will do everything I can to help you," Daniel said. "I will give you, Lewis and Fred, a place to live and work at the College of the Magi. I will give you, Patrick and Gracie, a home with the Gregory family and a Bardian school to attend. You will all have anything that you need."

Lewis squeezed Gracie's hand. Fred hugged Patrick's shoulders. Gracie felt a hot tear roll down her cheek. She sensed that all their emotions hung delicately balanced like a house made of cards, and, at any moment, a card could slip. Soon they would *all* end up bawling.

CHAPTER 15
DANIEL'S PLANS

A week later, Daniel sat in the locating chamber beside Mark. The monitor showed Lord Charon's secret chamber in Tor under his palace's white marble dome. From there Lord Charon and the Horned Edge magi had watched the Earth and communicated with the Shields. At this moment, Daniel saw Charon's assistants, two magi named Millie and Rick that he remembered from their days at his College in Nutman.

*   *   *

Lord Charon's two scientists bustled about in the cave chamber. Millie was tall, blond, square as a cow, and perpetually frowning. Rick was shorter, dark skinned, and his broad face seemed nearly expressionless. They wore the black and silver robes of the Torish magi and gold rings on their left middle fingers.

"Hurry up, Rick," Millie snarled. "Hand me my tool." She rattled one of the chains that dangled bizarrely from the amethyst-encrusted wall. "Do you want to become like one of the Blue People? A sacrifice to the *bizeor* because you are so useless?"

Rick replied meekly, but with a touch of sarcasm in his bland voice, "Here's the tool that you want, dear. It's much smaller than mine."

*   *   *

Daniel grimaced. "They were nice, once."

Mark said, briefly, "That is not a nice place."

Daniel remembered magus Remi's temper tantrum, his screaming fight with Lord Charon, and his throwing the noretha into the nexus. "They have become vessels of Saoma. How many others will be corrupted by demons before this is over?"

"Too many," Mark said, and Daniel shivered. "What about our visitors from Earth?" asked Mark. "Will they become slaves of Saoma, too?"

Turning away from the scene in Tor, Daniel told Mark, "I do not know. Young Patrick is still a puppy, eager for adventure. His sister Gracie is full of faith. I'm sure that she is in no danger. Fred, however, is full of jealousy and low self-esteem. The bizeor may already have their claws into him."

"And Lewis?" Mark asked.

"Lewis is a key figure in this story. All of them are important, of course. However, in Lewis I sense something extra. For one thing, his creative work amazes me. He reminds me of the ancient magi – which may work both ways: for the light or for the darkness. I sense that he has a soul-dragon, a secret desire that he keeps trying to suppress. That could be a great gift, or it could be his undoing."

"What do you mean?" his protégé asked.

"A dragon does not always stand for an evil snake; it can be a neutral metaphor for the soul. And the soul is the part of us that yearns to become real—forever."

The young magus looked at Daniel and grinned. "I'm familiar with soul dragons! Mine wants to be the next High Magus."

Daniel chortled. "My dragon jumps with joy at the thought! You step in my place, and then I can retire. Mine wants to raise goats on Deirdre's estate in Smythe."

Mark snorted, but exclaimed, "High Lord, look at the monitor!"

Daniel came back to the present. "Yes, *fean,* what is it?"

Pointing to the monitor, Mark said, "Here comes Lord Charon."

*　　*　　*

Inside the cave chamber, Lord Tahei Charon snapped at Millie and Rick, "Ye canna' repair the thoyo-on? What more do you need?"

Millie replied, curtseying low, her robe sweeping the polished stone floor, "We need time, my lord." Her voice was obsequious, like dripping motor oil. "Because your former head magus Remi threw away the noretha, the thoyo-on was badly stressed. We maintained the nexus for so long that the system burned out. My staff have repaired a few malfunctions in the sonic system, but we can't find the real problem. We cannot connect with Earth, or to anywhere!"

Lord Charon's eyes narrowed. Tall, elegant, and graceful, he wore a sable black robe with gold lining, inverting the colors of the High Magus. The ruler of Tor swept aside his silky black hair with one hand, and then slapped the obsidian table monitor, making the others jump. Even Millie cringed to half her size. Rick nearly faded into the wall.

*　　*　　*

Daniel and Mark leaned forward. "This is it," Mark whispered.

*　　*　　*

Charon commanded as the large gold Horned Edge ring on his left hand flashed, "I must have a full connection to Earth before the Council of the Magi!"

"We'll do what we can," Rick mumbled. "But if we don't have the parts …"

"Then you will have to get them before the Council of the Magi," Lord Charon interrupted, enunciating every word, "when we invade Nutman and take the High Magus prisoner."

*　　*　　*

Both Daniel and Mark jumped. Daniel felt he might faint. Immediately he made himself take a deep, deep breath, letting it out very slowly. *You told me this would come, Master, but I am so afraid!* Yet, they continued to watch their monitor.

* * *

Lord Charon told his scientists, "Remi's dead. However, another expert may be familiar with the mechanics of a *thoyo-on*, a system that opens our way to Earth. Most of the parts of my system and the Bardian system are completely interchangeable, as you know. This expert will steal the parts from the College of the Magi in Rockeerie."

Both Millie and Rick winced at the words "another expert." Millie rolled her eyes, trying to recover from the hint that she and Rick were disposable.

Rick squeaked, "And who is your expert?"

Lord Charon smiled at them, but the edges of his brilliant white teeth showed. He replied with cool amusement, "My own protégé, Barth Layhew." His eyes looked far away for a moment. "We'll steal what we need very soon. After that, we'll invade Daniel's province and take him and other hostages to keep Bardia from counter-attacking us. Meanwhile, continue to repair our system with all the resources that you do have."

Millie dipped in a heavy curtsey. Rick ducked his head with a resentful look.

Charon, flanked with two gray-and-silver uniformed bodyguards, spun gracefully around, and ascended the spiral staircase to the upper halls.

Millie turned to her husband, snarling. "You're such a smarmy wimp! Couldn't you have stated the problem in the positive? Charon will feed us to the rats if you keep that up!"

* * *

Daniel felt nauseated. "We've heard enough for now," he told Mark.

His assistant whispered, his face white, "So … they're

planning to invade us and seize the College."

Daniel nodded. "We have to move the whole College, including the locating system. And then we will evacuate the province as completely as possible." Meanwhile, he thought, *Dear Mighty Father, you've told me what will happen to me: I will be captured and taken to Tor. I ask you to let me stand firm in the Council when Tahei Charon seeks to change all our principles.*

*   *   *

Striding fast through the university park, followed discretely by some military magi, Daniel mused, his stomach going sour. Given what he had overhead today, what should he do?

Don't evacuate too suddenly, he reminded himself. *Charon mustn't know that we know his plans.*

Horrible images of berserk Torish soldiers burning, killing, and raping his people threatened panic in his mind. Daniel pushed the fear away.

As he and the bodyguards arrived at the residential area and passed through the gate, he muttered to himself, "Some of our families, especially ones with children, can go west to Smythe. I'm sure the Thamaon will be amenable."

Daniel began the next set of plans. "Hmm … what about the others? I know that Smythe would not shelter thousands of our people."

As he walked down the lane past rows of mansions, he noted that purple, yellow, and white crocus were popping up in the gardens. The little flowers cheered him. "All right," he murmured aloud to himself, "Here's a way to clear the city. The 500th anniversary of the Bard's victory that stopped the Great Rebellion of Saoma's magi will come next month. How convenient! How apt! Sir Edwin can arrange a huge celebration in his Forschwynn Province. It is well defended and the original home of the Bard— what could be more natural? Our people can congregate there."

Daniel's murmurs turned to thoughts. *Very well … to get started, I'll ask Sir Edwin Forschwynn to host our city. I will also ask him to lend us his son, young Sir Thomas, as soon as possible. The young man is a masterful musician, a descendant of the Bard himself. He can draw great crowds and stir up their hearts to go to the celebration! That should work to distract Charon ... yes ... Just as the Bard did in the old days, he'll lead our people out of harm's way!*

"But what about the people from Earth?" he asked aloud, but not so loud that his guard could hear him.

Let's see ... Patrick and Gracie can go with Deirdre and Myra to Smythe, to Deirdre's estate there. But what about Lewis and Fred? Charon might come after them, even into Smythe, because they are familiar with Earth's technology.

Keeping his voice soft, Daniel complained, "Master, why would you bring a physicist and an engineer to our world? They could develop weapons, or they could even become channels for the bizeor!"

The Master replied in his thoughts, *I have a plan for them as I have for you.*

"What about the children and my people?"

They will be safe.

"But … will the College of the Magi be enslaved by Lord Charon?" Daniel imagined the College absorbed into the Horned Edge system and their vicious god Saoma. His skin crawled.

No. However, you will be taken to Moorway to facilitate the Horned Edge agenda.

Daniel couldn't breathe. Sweat broke out on his forehead. He began thinking extremely fast.

The Master warned—and for a moment, he reminded Daniel very much of his dear Ielen *You are working very, very hard. Stop it! You can't make everything happen the way you want it to go.*

"Why not?" Daniel growled. "Why do you have to act like Ielen? She was always telling me that!"

However, just as he reached his mansion, he felt a friendly little tickle in his mind. *Think about what you just said. What a silly question!* He imagined that a warm, soft hand slapped his butt, just like Ielen used to do in their intimate moments.

CHAPTER 16
PATRICK AND GRACIE'S NEW "NORMAL"

Patrick and Gracie left school in the late afternoon and walked uphill on a cobblestone street to their new home with the Gregory family. The rich blue sky looked lofty, and the light deepened as it would close to evening in Earth time. On the horizon, the sun began to set with brilliant orange, yellow, pink, and even purple glows. He could see two moons, but he'd learned that Lanthra had six moons, and usually only two could be seen at one time. A three-moon night was exceptional, an occasion to be celebrated.

Patrick felt that school was awesome. It was much harder than his school back in Huntsville, but that made it fun. Plus, the emotional climate around him felt wholesome; he was making friends! He congratulated himself because his Lanthran language was getting to be smooth fast. His feet danced a bit. *Friends!* he thought. *Finally, I have friends! They don't make fun of me here.*

At that moment, Patrick did something that surprised him, something that he'd never have expected: He confided in his sister.

"I like it here," he said. "Even though I miss Mom and Dad, and I know they must be worried sick about us, I really like this place."

Gracie did not reply. She was silent for so long that Patrick felt uncomfortable. "How are you?" he asked.

Gracie blurted, "Patrick, I miss Mom and Dad, so much!"

Now Patrick wished he hadn't brought up the topic.

Tears flowed down Gracie's cheeks. "The Gregorys are kind," she said, wiping her eyes, "But my sad feeling goes on and on. It feels like a big dough-ball in my stomach." Her voice broke. She quit walking. Her face reddened, and she hid it in her hands as she sobbed.

Patrick reached out and held Gracie to his shoulder until she calmed. "Can we go now?" he said. "It's getting dark." They walked downhill toward their new home. Patrick babbled, "These streets are so narrow that there might be enough room for a pair of motorcycles to run side by side—but there aren't any motorcycles. Look! A donkey-cart just passed us. It looks like it's carrying a big load of dirty laundry!"

Gracie broke in, "Patrick, don't you feel sad like I do?"

"Well … sure!" *Well, that's not exactly true. I don't feel much of anything. Maybe I'm just brave,* he thought. Patrick added, "Usually, I try not to think too much about home … uh, Earth home." He wondered why he wasn't upset like Gracie. Wouldn't it be normal to be homesick? A memory came to him of visiting the dentist. Before having a cavity filled, he'd had a shot of Novocain. Well, he felt like that right now.

CHAPTER 17
FRED AND THE MARBLE

Late out of bed and walking quickly to work at the College of the Magi with Lewis, Fred fumbled with cold fingers to fasten his shirt.

Lewis commented unnecessarily, "We're running late."

"Yeah, yeah, yeah, I know. I had trouble getting up because my friends Dale and Sia and I stayed out late at the Red Oak. But the music was fantastic! You should hear the new fellow who plays there … Sir Thomas Forschwynn. Dale called him the Bard of Bardia! I can't wait to get you to the Red Oak Tavern with me!"

"Well, I don't know," Lewis hedged. "I'll probably have supper with the kids at the Gregory's house …"

"Come on, Lewis," Fred urged. "You spend all your time with them when you're not at work or sleeping. You've got to make some friends. In fact, Sadie has invited Sia and Dale for dinner tonight. You'll meet them, have time with the kids, *and* hear the bard play."

"Okay," Lewis agreed.

What Fred didn't mention to Lewis was that, besides his new friends Dale and Sia, he had also met a really interesting fellow, Barth Layhew. The man's blue eyes hid his thoughts, so he would be a good poker-player, but he was also intelligent, well educated, and told great jokes. And what he said gave Fred a new perspective on the Bardia-Tor conflict. *He presented a very compelling argument for the Torish side. I'm still considering whether I might just believe him.*

Meanwhile, inside the College's walls, the *click, click, click* of the booted feet of students and professors in black robes with capes sounded like an entire percussion section. At the entrance of the laboratory building, he and Lewis stopped at their favorite kiosk of hot breakfast foods. A team of the physically fluent Blue People stood around a portable food wagon and handed out baked goods, fruit, and drinks in return for shining ducat-like coins called *ion*—the Bardian equivalent of a silver dollar.

Fred and Lewis ordered hot meat pies. Fred commented to Lewis, "Never thought I'd be spending an *eon* on breakfast!"

Lewis nodded, not getting the joke.

A Blue Lady wrapped Fred's pie in a napkin and handed it to him. The fur on her hand felt soft as a kitten's paw. She bobbed her breasts and stuck out her phenomenally long red tongue in greeting.

Fred signed a perfect "thank you" in the Blue People gesture language, grabbed the hot pie and a cup of "brew" in a blue ceramic cup, and led Lewis toward the College's laboratory. Their footsteps echoed in the marble vestibule while Fred sipped his brew as fast as he could without burning his mouth. He commented, "This stuff smells all right, but I can't really call it 'coffee.' To me it tastes more like hot burned rubber."

Lewis smiled a little.

Fred downed his last swig of the syrupy brew.

Soon they reached the Lanthran "instant elevator" to the deep-underground laboratory where the Bardian locating system operated. "Ready?" Lewis asked, throwing back his cloak, which had a smear of meat pie on it and a wet splot of brew. Fred saw that he hadn't noticed. Typical Lewis.

"Sure, let's go, Fred replied. "We get to practice the cute trick that transports us from here through a couple of hundred meters of bedrock to the laboratory." He estimated that the interior transportation saved him and Lewis a thousand steps of winding staircase—times two. Except … there was no winding staircase.

Fred and Lewis entered a little room. It looked cheerful enough, well-lit with blond maple paneling, a parquet floor, and an ornate hammered ceiling. It smelled funny, however, like ozone.

Lewis put his hand on a gold plate that adorned the wall and disappeared. Then Fred did the same. Nothing spectacular happened, except that he felt his stomach swoop like a kid's on a swing.

He now stood in an anteroom with a high, arched roof, looking at a handsome door, dark as smoke, but without handle or knob. "Wow! What a way to travel!" Fred's eyes lit brightly. "Think of the cartage possibilities on Earth: no more subways and buses and trains. Transportation would be so much easier!" He went on, his brain whirling with the possibilities, "Imagine the money we could make if we could export this technology to Earth!"

"Absolutely not! Hush!" Lewis put a finger to his lips. "Remember Fred, Earth is anathema to these people. Now, okay, let's get into the lab." He spoke, the door vanished, and he passed through.

Stepping behind Lewis into the locating chamber, Fred noticed that they had arrived before their new boss, Dr. Zadok. "We're on time after all," he noted with satisfaction. He joked to Lewis, "Now we get to wait until 'Dr. Strangelove' makes his entrance."

Lewis winced.

Fred had decided on Day One that he could not stand Dr. Zadok. The man talked in a loud staccato, walked with a military swing of his heavy shoes, and maintained a formal body space at all times. His bristly moustache, beaky nose, and penetrating dark eyes reminded Fred of bird … a big turkey vulture.

Lewis yawned. "That so-called coffee didn't do anything for me. I'm sleepy again." Sitting on a sofa and closing his eyes, he folded his arms and crossed his legs.

Fred jittered, looking around at the locating chamber. The décor was more Lewis-style than Fred-style. The furniture was covered with plush apricot, the walls with silver silk, the dark gray marble parquet floor shone with glints of mica, and the obsidian black locating table reflected the elegant room like a full-length mirror. Not only was it too elegant, but it was too quiet.

I'd rather have a wood floor with sawdust on it, a bar, a jukebox, and cowboys. Oh yeah, and lots of women.

The silence bothered him. He paced around. How long were they going to be stuck here? What was he going to do here? He was an electrical engineer, specialized in the arcane mechanics of subatomic electromagnetic research—all of which were banned in Lanthra. *Except in special spots like this—where I have to work with Dr. Zadok.*

Fred imagined making toys such as his homemade laser flyswatter. Here in Bardia, the technology police would come and get him. Speaking of technology police ... his new buddy Barth had told him stories: A whole town wiped out by Daniel's military magi just because they were using electricity to heat water; a family butchered because they invented an electric winch to stack hay bales. *Apparently, Daniel the High Magus is not as nice a person as he pretends to be—the little prick!*

While he waited, Fred jittered a piece of string in his pocket. After a while, he tapped his feet. *Hurry up, Dr. Zadok! I'm getting bored!*

On the couch, Lewis snored.

Fred stood in front of the upright obsidian table, sucked in his belly, and looked at his reflection on its polished surface. *I look pretty good!* Tall, broad-shouldered, strong. Blond hair, blue eyes, wide sunny smile. Nice clothes, too—he really liked the cloak, boots, and other clothes they had given him. He was really looking forward to seeing Deirdre tonight at the Gregory's.

Fred stepped closer to the obsidian table. *Zadok calls this system a thoyo-on, but I call it the Toy.* His hands itched to feel the controls. He longed to hear the hum as the locating system sympathetically harmonized a path through the universe, plucking one of the cosmic strings the way the bard plucked the strings of his lute.

Why not? Lewis is taking a nap, Dr. Zadok is late, and I need something to do.

He found the indentation on the control panel. *It won't hurt to peek.* He brushed it with his index finger.

Immediately the table showed a soft, swirling random mass of color. "Cosmic noise," Fred grunted. "Gotta tune to the right station."

The "tuners" were the marbles, like the hot marble. *Ho, ho!*

Crossing through a door on the side of the laboratory, Fred found the glass cabinet, like a museum case, where the little round amber marbles were stored. He knew that each one held the gravitational signatures of coordinates between two or more moving positions in space, like fancy algorithms that could follow endless strings of changes. He found the one that was labeled, *Pigolanor* meaning, "Don't Go There"—the Lanthran designation for Earth. This was the hot marble, the one Patrick and Gracie had found, winking at him like an amber eye.

Hey, since I can connect to Earth, maybe I can find a way to get Lewis and the kids back home. It's worth a try, anyhow.

A teeny voice in his mind whispered, *And, then you would have Deirdre all to yourself.* He caught himself rubbing his hands together. Immediately he felt guilty, like the evil villain. *Stop it, Fred!* Checking that he was still alone, except for Lewis snoozing on the couch, he slipped the little piggy out.

The hot marble fit nicely into the slot in the table controls.

Ah, the lovely hum, the bursts of color showing exotic stars and galaxies as the system sorted out the gravitational signatures to find the one that led to Earth.

There it is, my—home planet in its blue and white glory—gorgeous! He felt a thrill that raised every hair on his body.

Let's see ... this control, here, just a tiny bump a few centimeters away from the marble slot—this one controls the zoom tuning. Fred brushed it and saw the image on the table look closer or further away as he manipulated his finger against the bump. *This is wonderful! I can even see back and forth in time! (At least, up to a relative point, where the "present" is at the located position.)*

At first, his movements were wild. Finally, he got better, and zoomed downward toward the Earth's surface. *Where do I want to look? Back home? Nah – try the White House!*

He found the White House. With some wobbles, he got a view of the Oval Office and to his delight, the President was there, talking to the Chief of Staff. He heard the Chief say, tantalizingly, "Reliable sources say that a private company has acquired weapons of mass destruction ..." However, the picture wavered and soon he couldn't see or hear anything.

Rattled, Fred paused. He thought, *Now I understand our situation better. Lord Charon plucked a cosmic string to Earth, apparently telling those Shields at the park, "Red Rover, Red Rover, let weapons and weirdos come over." Lewis and Patrick and Gracie and I ran over instead. Not knowing what we were doing, we ran right out of our own world and into this one. Stupid of us, getting caught here like sparrows flying into a gymnasium. But at least we prevented the weapons transfer.*

What he'd heard finally sunk in. *Weapons? Weapons! Even nuclear bombs?*

CHAPTER 18

DR. ZADOK

At that moment, the door vanished and Dr. Zadok entered the locating chamber. Fred snatched the marble out of the control panel. The monitor blackened. Hoping his new boss hadn't seen anything, Fred spun around, standing at attention.

The old scientist looked rumpled and tired, his wiry hair sticking up in a cowlick where he had forgotten to comb a spot. He didn't seem to notice that Fred had been playing with the locating table.

"Good morning," Fred greeted him cheerily. It felt great to be the only wide-awake person in the room.

Lewis's eyes popped open, and he sprang up from the couch. "Good morning, Dr. Strange—I mean, Dr. Zadok." Fred was amused to see a bright pink hue to Lewis's perennially tan skin.

The old scientist said dully, "Soon we will have to dismantle our locating system."

"What?" Lewis squeaked.

Fred felt his mouth contracting into a frown. "More of the ban on technology stuff?"

"No," Dr. Zadok shook his head. He straightened with visible effort to his usual stiff posture and looked at them eye-to-eye for the first time. "Daniel, the *Radhegoya*—the High Magus—has a plan because of a possible invasion." The skin tightened around his eyes. "If we do nothing, the Torish might capture this locating system and take it to their own laboratory. Then, they could connect with the forbidden planet! Therefore, we plan to relocate vital parts of our thoyo-on as soon as possible. Naturally, you understand that this information must remain private."

"What does that mean for Fred and me?" Lewis asked.

Dr. Zadok turned his head slightly and scrutinized them with his glittering black eyes, looking, Fred thought, like an old buzzard. "For a few more weeks, while we back up the system – we use the thoyo-on as is. After that, we start the disassembly."

Fred groaned, "From scientific research to manual labor."

Dr. Zadok ignored him. "Learn! Learn everything you can about the system! You, my experts from Earth, will have to work with our magi to assemble it again later. Beginning today, you will back up all the information, including the schematics for building the system and its computer and all the instructions for using it. Yes, back them up, and back them up again!"

"Oh great," Fred muttered. "Sounds fascinating. I thought I'd start to learn the fun part, but now it's over."

"After collecting and organizing data from our entire system's plan," Dr. Zadok continued, "we will fully remove the locating system from the College of the Magi here in Nutman. Everything must be done very carefully so that we can build the system again when we return."

"Return from where?" Lewis asked.

"That is yet to be decided," Dr. Zadok said stiffly.

Lewis stepped back, his eyes wide. "Will my brother and sister be with me?"

"I am not the one to make that decision." Dr. Zadok's beady eyes were hooded.

Lewis balled up his fists. "What expertise do Fred and I have that makes you want to take us away without my brother and sister?"

Zadok's bushy eyebrows drew together. "This system has not been disassembled since the Great Rebellion! And some of it is based on electricity—illegal since that time. My scientists are the best, but they are not as fluent … they have less experience with the old technology than you do."

Dr. Zadok paused. then continued, "As for what you will do when you are away, you will teach the magi at the College-in-exile as much as you can about the Earth technology. Those are my orders from the High Magus."

"So, we'll teach them our electronic magic?" Fred joked.

Dr. Zakok speared his with a glance.

Fred gnashed his teeth so hard that he bit the inside of his lip, but he tried to keep his features from showing his irritation. The old goat reminded him of a particularly nasty teacher he'd had in the eighth grade. Mr. X—Fred couldn't remember his name. The teacher had decided from the first day that Fred was stupid and a troublemaker and had badgered him the rest of the year.

Dr. Zadok's nostrils flared, "Mr. Jontz, His Excellency will have you trained as magi, and then you will learn the 'magic' in our science. The magi call it, 'the Magic of Release.'"

Fred wrinkled his nose. "Release? From what?" The expression reminded him of a picture he'd seen of lost souls in purgatory. One scared human was millimeters from the stinging point of a devil's tail. *If that's magic, I don't want it.*

CHAPTER 19
LEWIS FINDS LOVE

Where is Fred?" asked Sadie Gregory during supper. Her radiant tropical beauty dimmed as she frowned with concern.

"Oh," said the Gregory brothers at the same time. Allen cleared his throat, while Mark went on, "Fred's coming, along with his new friends."

"Who are those?" asked Patrick, his voice muffled because he was stuffing food into his mouth.

"Dale, Sia, and some guy named Barth," Lewis answered.

"Pass the bread, Professor Brahmindura," Mark said.

Lewis barely heard him. *I will have to leave Patrick and Gracie after we dismantle the locating system!* Forgetting to pass the basket, he pulled out a bun. He dimly heard Allen snort, but he didn't pay attention. He tore his bun into perfectly uniform small pieces and created a geometrical pattern on his plate.

A light whoosh of refreshing cool air brushed against his cheek as another guest breezed into the Gregory's house. "Hello," came Deirdre's voice. "Sorry I'm late; may I join you?"

From the table came a chorus of "We're so glad to see you!" Sadie jumped up to set a new place at the table … right beside Lewis. He looked up, and Deirdre smiled. Her intense, intelligent blue eyes sparkled, and her wonderful skin glowed.

Lewis's hands quit their mathematical constructions and his thoughts quickly tore away from his worries to Deirdre. She was wearing his favorite color—blue—and smelled fresh and spring-y from her walk to the Gregory's house. Lewis saw that her thick golden hair had been pinned up, showing her soft neck.

After getting settled, Deirdre began to serve herself from the bowls on the table. "Pass the salt, please," she said to Lewis.

Immediately, he reached out but knocked over the saltshaker. He recovered it and gave it to her. Her hand brushed his. She met his eyes, and Lewis was surprised to see that she seemed more interested in him than in the salt.

Having Deirdre next to him was like touching soft golden velvet after being wrapped in a black gunnysack. Lewis ate, finally tasting the food, sipped his wine, and listened to Deirdre's warm, firm voice as she described her day. "I've been packing for Myra and Patrick and Gracie to come with me to Smythe when we evacuate." While she talked, Lewis noticed the captain and Sadie looking into each other's eyes and the way that they often touched each other. *I'd like that in a relationship like that with Deirdre,* he thought wistfully.

Deirdre touched his hand, and he jumped. "Tell me …" she began, but at that moment, the front door banged open, letting in a great gush of chilly air.

"Yo, Lewis!" Fred shouted. "Yo, Patrick and Gracie! How are y'all?" He bowed to Sadie and Captain Gregory and waved at Allen, Mark, and Deirdre. His eyes lingered on Deirdre. "Is it too late for us to come to dinner?"

The captain smiled and said, "Not at all. Come on! Get your plates from the cupboard. You know where they are."

Fred—and three other men—entered Sadie's cozy kitchen, filling up the room.

"Please excuse the imposition," apologized Fred to Sadie. "Since I bragged about your excellent cooking, my friends, Dale, Sia, and Barth wanted to meet you all … especially you, Lewis."

Fred smiled. "So, I invited them to come along; I hope that's all right."

It took a few minutes for the visitors to settle down. Elbows knocked, legs stretched, apologies and courtesies were said, and soon there were ten people squashed around the table.

Patrick glowed. "This is fun, Fred! It's like trying to fit everybody into a little car!"

Deirdre smiled at Fred. "Glad you could get here! I don't see you often enough!"

Fred blushed to the tops of his ears; Lewis wondered why. "Oh, wow," Fred exclaimed and sniffed. "You've done it again, Sadie. A feast!"

As if the guests could not see for themselves, Patrick recited the menu, savoring each item: "Large yellow potatoes, boiled and fluffy, served with fresh butter; meatloaf—except it's not animal meat, because Sadie's a vegetarian—fresh spring peas from Sadie's garden; soft bread rolls with strawberry preserves, sharp yellow cheese; red wine; and stewed apricots with spices from Eleaemana. By the way, that's where Sadie's from."

"Yes," Sadie nodded.

Dale spoke for the first time, "Thank you for receiving us." He accepted a large helping of meatloaf, took a huge spoonful of potatoes and put three buns on his plate, at which Patrick glowered. The man's pert, humorous face reminded Lewis of a leprechaun. Dale had tweaky eyebrows, a mop of curly dark hair with some gray in it, and he grinned with an air of bonhomie. Lewis thought he could like him, except that he was greedy.

Next, Sia spoke, "I'm honored to be present in the Gregory home." He bowed his rather triangular face to Captain Gregory, who inclined his head slightly in acknowledgement.

Captain Gregory answered—and Lewis was surprised to hear that his voice was rather cool, "And I'm glad to see you again." There was a slight emphasis on the word *again* which Lewis did not understand.

He looked at Sia more carefully. The man was stylish with shoulder length hair. Fluffy white lace at cuffs and collar adorned his shirt. To Lewis, he brought up images of a cavalier—he might have been brandishing pistols and a sword—but there was something tricky about him, because the calculating, shifting expression of Sia's eyes did not match his carefree gestures.

The third newcomer at the table, Barth, leaned his chair against the wall to make room for his long legs, which meant that he crowded Lewis, who also had long legs. Barth was a big man with intelligent blue eyes. Although he resembled Fred because of his blond hair and size, he was more massive. Lewis did not like Barth's over-full lips. They were just too red. *Does he use lipstick?*

Barth reached for a bowl of the potatoes—his forearms were as big as large hams. He smiled at Lewis, his face cherubic. "Glad to meet you. I hear that you're already the College genius." His baritone English was crisply enunciated.

"Uh … er," Lewis stammered, not knowing what to say.

For a second, Barth's eyes seemed to emit strange static. "You probably know a lot about the locating system by now."

"Not really," Lewis said. He thought, *Have I missed something?* Barth came across as the jovial, bluff fellow, a big drinker and hearty talker. However, for some reason, Lewis felt the willies up his spine. Unwilling to show his immediate dislike, he arranged his remaining peas into a matrix and drew a function with butter and Sadie's special vegetarian meatloaf.

Barth, Sia, and Dale began to monopolize the conversation, addressing mostly Fred and leaving out the others. In a moment, however, Lewis became aware of a light touch on his arm on the non-Barth side: Deirdre. She leaned close to him. "What is the matter?" she asked. "You look troubled."

Not wanting to tell her (yet) how much he liked her, and avoiding his distaste for Fred's new friends, he chose a "safe" topic; he told her about his day at work. "It's not a secret—we have to move the lab because Lord Charon wants to invade and seize it."

Deirdre's eyes narrowed. She murmured, "The bizeor hate us; the demons are so cruel." Next, in the same low voice, she said, "Thank you, Radyah, for keeping Lewis, Patrick, and Gracie safe! And Fred—do not forget him."

Lewis didn't know how to reply. *She believes in a God and a devil. I know evil is real, but are there spiritual entities at war? Should I tell her that I am not a religious person?*

His face must have shown his skepticism, because Deirdre took his hand. "You don't believe there is God. However, don't be afraid. It is all right to fight with him."

"What?" Lewis exclaimed.

Her eyes met his, radiant with affection. Covering his left hand gently but firmly with her right one, Deirdre added, "Your soul is at war; I sense it."

The others at table were wrapping up their meal with the cheese and apricots, but Lewis could hardly eat. *Religion. If this radiant person believes in God, I feel warmer toward that concept. But ...* He stood his ground to maintain his honesty, "I'm an agnostic. Why should my soul be at war if spiritual beings don't exist?" A part of his mind noted, *Now I am a step up from an atheist. When did that happen?*

Deirdre smiled as if she could read his thoughts. "There is an Earth poet named Francis Thompson who wrote a poem titled, 'The Hound of Heaven.' The Hound is pursuing you, Lewis."

His stomach, his chest vibrated with conflict. His mind buzzed. However, he resolved, *I don't think God exists!* At the same time, he felt an intense desire welling up inside that was not only romance but deeper. He felt a radiance coming from her, a calm power: Suddenly, he realized that he felt closer to Deirdre— even though he hardly knew her—more than he ever had with anyone. His soul yearned to live with her, be like her, and (he thought with a little guilt) have her.

Even after dinner was finished and everyone got up from the

table, Lewis couldn't quit looking at her. *Deirdre is so beautiful!* A few honey-blond curls, long and slightly wavy, escaped from her pinned-up hair, and he wanted to finger them. He could imagine touching her … actually, she had been touching him! *On purpose! Wow!*

Unfortunately, Barth had noticed. He kicked Lewis's foot, and he muttered into Lewis's ear with meatloaf breath, "She's sweet on you, Louie."

CHAPTER 20
THE BARD OF BARDIA

Lewis walked quickly uphill to the University's residential section to meet Deirdre. Overcoming his shyness, Lewis had asked Deirdre to come with him on a date, and she had said *yes!*

Instead of the green and red unmatched outfit he'd put on, Sadie had made him wear a flowing dark gray cloak over a fine cotton shirt and formal trousers and boots. Sadie had told him that he looked great, and he stood up straight. Yet despite the beautiful evening, his mind roiled. *I want our relationship to go further, but what should I do about the God-thing? Deirdre believes in God. I don't believe in God.*

As he walked toward the mansion where Deirdre and her family lived, he saw many carts and wagons rolling out of the city gate. People were headed for the 500th anniversary of Bardia's founding. *There will be a huge gathering at the Forschwynn province,* Lewis thought. *Too bad I am going to Kingsport to be their Earth-familiar scientist I'm going to miss my sister and brother, the Gregorys, and Deirdre so much!*

Meanwhile, the whole city knew that the Bard of Bardia, Sir Thomas Forschwynn, was playing at the Red Oak Tavern for a few more days. Many people had put off their trip to hear him.

*   *   *

Armed and vigilant security guards admitted Lewis through the gate to the lane toward the Deirdre's father's mansion. Warm yellow lights showed in the windows and a tang of wood smoke made him feel at home. His heard warmed; his soul quieted.

When Lewis knocked on the door at Deirdre's house, Daniel himself opened it. "Hello?" His Excellency Daniel looked sleepy and cozy in bedroom slippers even though the evening had just begun.

Deirdre's little sister Myra peeked at Lewis from behind her father She waved and giggled. "Deirdre! He's here!"

"Good evening, Your Excellency," Lewis began, bowing. "I'm—"

"I know, Lewis. You're escorting Deirdre to the Red Oak Tavern to hear Sir Forschwynn's concert. Good idea—he's amazing. You'll have a wonderful time."

When Deirdre appeared, Lewis's heart melted. *She looks amazing!* Tonight, Deirdre wore a meadow-gold dress, and her blond hair was twisted back into a chignon. He took her hand, and they left together. From the High Magus' mansion and the flagstone lane, Deirdre and he walked together while the escort followed discretely behind.

Lewis kept sneaking looks at Deirdre. "It was warm today," he said inanely to make conversation. "But the weather is supposed to change later tonight. Patrick—my favorite weather prophet—predicted that it's going to storm." He looked appreciatively at her bare shoulders. "Are you going to be warm enough?" he asked.

"I'm ready," Deirdre said, laughing. She opened her small purse and pulled out an embroidered shawl, supple and thin as smoke. "The Blue People wove this special material. It's beautiful and warmer than it looks."

The gatekeeper let them outside the university wall, into the old section of Nutman. At that point, Deirdre dismissed the guards. "We call this area Forion," Deirdre told him, as they continued down a lamp-lit brick-paved street, along with other couples and groups of talking, animated people.

"Let's see … that means, "to go into a big place," Lewis said, refining his Lanthran.

"It can mean that," Deirdre nodded, then she grinned. "It can also mean, "Make a lot of money.""

"So, this is the trendy end of town." Lewis eyed the slate-roofed houses and shops. The buildings in Forion were taller and narrower than elsewhere in Nutman; the steep, brick-paved streets were like canyons, exciting ones that he'd want to explore. Overhead, a strip of starry sky showed the clear dark blue of evening and two moons. As they walked, Lewis began to relax, and the two of them talked about anything and everything. Their eyes met. Smiling up at him, Deirdre wrapped her soft, strong fingers around his. Lewis imagined what it would feel like to kiss her. *She is so beautiful.* What he liked best, however, was the self-assured, tensile strength that he felt in her personality. He sensed that she didn't need him, she just liked him, and that aroused him more than anything else about her.

"There's the sign for the Red Oak Tavern," Deirdre pointed down the street.

"I haven't been there yet," Lewis said.

"I have. You'll like it."

He let Deirdre guide him, hand in hand, across the street and up to the tall building with a red awning and a big lantern over the front door. The lantern light ebbed and flowed on the street in a rhythmic pattern because the wind was picking up, swinging the lantern back and forth.

"Listen," Deirdre said. He put his arm around her, and they paused for a moment in front of the tavern.

An eerie sighing reached their ears. It rustled in tree branches overhead. "The dragons are singing."

"You're joking?"

"No. They are real dragons – beautiful, extremely dangerous, but not evil."

Lewis thought with a jolt of his inner dragon, the one he repressed. Despite himself, it spoke, *Time travel. You want to discover a way for time travel.*

Isn't that just my pride? Am I just trying to be rich and famous? he answered.

Yes, but I put that desire in you. Trust me.

Who are you? Lewis inwardly asked the dragon. However, the mental conversation faded, and he turned his attention to Deirdre.

They lingered outside the tavern, looking up into the sky. Stars twinkled behind the fine array of waving oak branches. "It's so beautiful. The sky is clear, the stars and moons are bright," Lewis said.

"The cold white one is *Noditlabath*, and the blue, orange, and green one is *Sewega*," Deirdre told him. "The colors on Sewega are where they took out copper. People used to mine the moons, before the Great Rebellion, but the magi ordered our pass-through technology to be shut down."

She put on her shawl and leaned against his shoulder. Lewis savored her warmth. He felt that, if they stood outside together any longer in the warm, windy twilight, he would bend down and kiss her. To his own surprise, he did bend down, and Deirdre lifted her face toward him. He felt her soft rose-petal lips and a little poke of a playful tongue. At that second, another couple going into the tavern saw them and tittered. Lewis hurried pulled apart.

"Let's go in," he said, sure that he was blushing.

He pulled the heavy oak door open, letting out a puff of warm, smoky tavern air and the sounds of soft music. A server approached and gestured toward the far wall. "Standing room only, so pay up, and I'll bring your drinks to you back there."

Lewis presented his writ, and they found a place against the wall. After a while, Deirdre and he received large ceramic mugs of frothy ale.

"Oh, good," Deirdre said. "Tom Forschwynn hasn't started playing yet."

Lewis sipped his ale. It was good, cool and smooth. He liked the froth. "Do you know him?"

"Yes," she nodded. "He has been a guest at our house a number of times when he is in this city. Tom plays concerts all over the northeastern continent. His music gives me a sense of mystery. Sometimes it sounds happy, sometimes it sounds sad, but always … it takes my soul to deep places. People say that his lute is magic. I asked Dad once, and he told me that the lute is magic only when the Bard of Bardia plays it, because the Bard's music comes from the desire of his heart—from Radyah."

"The singing Lord." At once Lewis felt the dragon stir in the deep place of his soul, saying, *I'm the desire of your heart. I also serve the singing Lord.*

What *singing Lord? What do physics and time travel have to do with God?*

His dragon stretched and challenged him: *Do you want to find out?*

Deirdre looked at him, and he came back to the moment. "Just distracted," he said. Changing the subject, he added, "Have you been here before?"

She nodded. "I've come with Mark and Allen a number of times." Seeing the look on his face, she laughed and touched his cheek. "When I mentioned Allen …"

"I know. I got jealous." He changed the risky subject. "Maybe Fred is here."

Looking for Fred, Lewis scanned the crowd. Round tables that normally sat six to eight people now sat twelve or more. Men and women talked merrily, drinking beer or ale in big mugs. The roasted nuts and warm bread sticks on the tables smelled wonderful. Pleasant music already filled the common room.

"Look! To the very front!" Deirdre touched his arm.

"What?"

The man on the stage was Fred. Lewis watched with mixed joy and amusement as his friend, dressed in a catchy blue outfit with high brown boots, strummed a slow rock rhythm on a mandolin, making easy listening music. Unself-conscious, for once, Fred gazed dreamily into space, fingers sliding expertly over the strings.

"I didn't know that Fred played the mandolin," Lewis said. "Wonder of wonders … what other secrets has my friend hidden from me?" Lewis and Deirdre waved at him from the back of the room, hoping to catch his attention.

They succeeded. Fred's eyes snapped toward Lewis and then to Deirdre, where they lingered. He nodded, especially at Deirdre and then broke into a love song.

> *You are the light of my eyes,*
> *You are the wine on my lips,*
> *You are the song of my soul; let me into your heart.*

The tune flowed like smooth, clear water. Fred sang in a beautiful tenor, pouring out emotion. *Is he singing to Deirdre?* Lewis felt uneasy. A little prick of jealousy stuck him in the chest, but he pulled it away. *If he loves her, what could I do? Just accept his feelings. After all, Deirdre is the one who will make the choice between us.*

As if she knew what he was thinking—and she probably did—Deirdre squeezed his hand. Lewis's heart sped up, dancing in his chest. *It seems she has chosen* me.

His heart nearly burst with surprise and love.

When Fred finished, he stood and bowed. A rain of applause followed him as he descended the steps that led off the stage. Fred neatly waved the Blue People's version of "thank you," and Lewis heard a few people laugh.

"Ho, Lewis! Deirdre!" Fred greeted them, wading through the crowd.

Lewis grinned. "Fred, I didn't know you could sing so well! You've been hiding that talent from me! And how did you get to be part of the warm-up performance?"

"I asked. I tried out, and the Red Oak people said yes."

"I enjoyed hearing you very much," Deirdre gave Fred a hug, standing tiptoe to reach him. "Thank you for singing that love song. What style of music is that?"

"Um, Country-Western, I guess," he said, returning the embrace.

The embrace lasted a little too long. Lewis gritted his teeth and stiffened, but he told himself, *Deirdre is the one to choose.*

"Yeah, that's my style," Fred answered, his arm possessively around Deirdre.

"Hey, come on, Deirdre. Look about five tables behind the guy with the huge beard—there's where my friends are sitting. We can get seats for you and Lewis—we'll fit you in despite the dirty looks from other people standing up."

Still holding Deirdre, Fred edged around tight-packed chairs and people's protruding legs to a table, while Lewis followed. Fred began the introductions. "Deirdre, Lewis: Remember my friends who came to dinner: Dale, Sia, and Barth?"

"Yes. Thanks for letting us sit with you," Lewis said.

Quickly, Fred pulled out a chair for Deirdre and sat down beside her.

Feeling outmaneuvered, Lewis took the seat between Dale and Barth. "Glad to see you again," he said with a forced but friendly smile.

Dale scanned Lewis up and down. "People keep saying that you're a 'whiz kid,' Dr. Zadok's favorite scientist. Not many people are as brilliant as you, they say." He grabbed a handful of nuts and tipped back his chair, munching.

Lewis mentally put caution tape on Dale's comments. "Um, thanks," he said.

Ignoring Lewis and looking at Deirdre, Sia said, "How are you, my lady? How's life in Smythe these days?" From his chair he managed an elegant flourish.

"Quiet and pleasant," she replied. Her manner changed a little, and Lewis felt that she had become a lioness, alert, keeping her claws sheathed. "We're plowing while the weather is good."

Sia's lazy eyes caressed her breasts, and he gave a half-smile as if thinking, *I'd like to plow with you.* Lewis's blood heated fifteen degrees Centigrade. He imagined smashing Sia's face into a pulp but forced himself to stay polite. He glared at Fred. *You've picked a sorry lot of friends!*

"Hey, Louie ..."

Turning toward Barth, Lewis forced his face to stay pleasant. Barth stretched those red, full lips in a smile, and, in the big man's intelligent eyes, Lewis glimpsed a dangerous, angry power, like a high-voltage spark.

However, Barth's face looked extremely impressed with Lewis, "When I was still a student in the College, majoring in Earth studies, I worked with Dr. Zadok for a while. He fired me, like he does most of his interns. You must be really special to stay on his good side."

Lewis began to retort, but at that moment a waiter breezed by, edging through the packed crowd as easily as a wraith, carrying a tray with another round of ale for them all. Lewis wanted to deflect all the praise. However, while he was in mid-sentence, Fred interrupted, "Shhh! The Bard is coming on stage!" Fred patted Deirdre's hand.

Deirdre gave Fred a bright smile and turned her chair around to face toward the stage. Lewis saw that her eyes glowed and her lips were parted with expectation.

A young man, perhaps nineteen years old, stepped onto the stage and seated himself on a tall stool. "That's Sir Thomas Forschwynn," Fred whispered to Deirdre, as if she did not already know. "He's the Bard of Bardia." Deirdre nodded.

Sir Thomas had black hair and brown eyes. His happy, sideways smile, dark hair tied back, closely fitting black clothes and boots, and fluid movements reminded Lewis of a lithe, playful otter. Even from his far corner, Lewis could see the sparkle in the bard's dark brown eyes and feel his quiet command over the audience. *I like this guy,* he thought, putting aside his annoyance over Fred and his friends.

The young man began to strum his lute in a preliminary tune-up. The crowd roared and applauded; a table of young women in the front screamed; and some of the men stood up, clapping.

However, for some reason, Sia frowned and left. Lewis immediately took his chair, the one next to Deirdre, before one of the "wallflowers" could snab it.

Now, from his stool, Sir Thomas nodded to the audience. The look in his eyes became one of deep concentration and he drew the lute into position. His fingers rippled lightly over the strings; the music began.

If there's anything spiritual in the universe, Lewis said to himself, *it's this. I've never heard such music in my entire life.* He forgot everything else, the conversation, the ale, the crowded room, himself, even Deirdre, and fell into the music.

CHAPTER 21
BITTERNESS BEGINS

While the music poured over the crowd, Fred leaned close to Deirdre and breathed in her scent. Her rapt attention was focused on the Bard, so he too closed his eyes to drink in the sound. The Bard sang so that Fred clearly discerned all the words. He played his lute without a sound system except the admittedly well-designed acoustics of the stage. The beauty of the technologically simple concert almost brought tears to his eyes.

Plus, Deirdre moved, brushing Fred with her arm. *She did it on purpose! Yo, Louie, she's going to be mine!*

The music reached into his soul. The whole evening swelled fantastically, and he felt like a king—no, like the emperor of the universe, the ruler of a hundred billion worlds with Deirdre at his side.

When Fred opened his eyes, the bard paused and seemed to look directly at him. *That's right, Bard, give me manna!*

The new round of music was harsher, with a strong driving beat and a more metallic sound. Fred grooved with it immediately. *Yeah, yeah, this is creative stuff!* The Bard's chorus, embellished in a variety of beats and tunes, was:

> *Turn away and die.*
> *Face me and live.*

Fred turned toward Deirdre, hoping to catch her eyes, but she was looking at Lewis who now occupied the chair next to her. *Hey, buddy, you're moving in on me!* Then, Deirdre pulled away from Fred and slipped her hand into Lewis's, grasping it tightly with joy on her face, as if they were parachutists exulting at their flight over the world.

Fred's sphere of happiness shrank like hot plastic; it lay in his stomach smoking with a nasty burning odor. He stared at a knothole on the floor.

Then an angry flame leaped through him as if a wasp had stung his psyche. All his muscles tensed, and his head jerked up. Once more the bard's eyes seemed to meet his over the crowd. The young man sent him a warm smile as if to say, "You are a treasure, Fred."

Hey, Tom, Fred thought, how you lie, telling me that I'm a treasure! Me—fat Fred? I make gadgets and drink beer. Liar ... you lie like a rug!

Ripping his gaze away from the bard, Fred eyed Lewis. His friend's brown eyes had that dreamy puppy expression that women couldn't resist. Lewis's hand lay clasped under Deirdre's, his other hand moving to cover hers as the Sir Thomas's music now evoked tenderness. Fred saw the exchange of deep, warm looks; he sensed the current of arousal they shared but that was denied to him.

Fred writhed inside. He had felt the pang of jealousy before, but this one was awful, like all the coat hangers in the world tangled together. *She gave me a sisterly hug—but she gives him her passion.*

A thought slashed through his mind: *Suppose something happens to Lewis to get him out of the way? Then Deirdre will come to me.*

This one made Fred sit up. Out there Sir Thomas still performed, but Fred tuned out and listened to the thought instead. It burned him in a steady lift-off.

If Lewis gets out of the way, you will be the talented hero.

Oh, how Fred liked that thought! Wonderful pictures flowed through his brain. He imagined Deirdre turning to him tearfully because Lewis was gone. He'd put his arms around her until she felt better. Then she would rise on her toes and give him a long, deep kiss. And … and after that, they would—

Fred took a deep breath and shifted in his chair. Something was stirring that shouldn't be stirred—yet.

Next, he imagined the situation at the lab if Lewis weren't there. *Lewis isn't the only genius around here!* Fred imagined Dr. Zadok's big, hairy ear incline toward him as he listened to Fred's ideas.

His imaginations became more and more vivid. *If Lewis were out of the way, I could have his family, too!* Fred imagined himself finding a way to help Gracie and Patrick return to their parents. He, of course, would receive tearful thanks from Cora and Frank Brahmindura. They

would invite him to dinner every night, and the kid's faces would glow every time they saw him. He'd never be lonely again.

Once he was established in Dr. Zadok's lab, he could open the forbidden connection and pass through, becoming the liaison between Lanthra and Earth. Fred imagined government and corporate executives on Earth competing to give him positions with a nice fat salary. He'd be on the front page of all the news magazines. On Lanthra, Dr. Zhartha would recommend him as one of the indispensable people on his projects. Women would melt when he walked by. Men would talk behind their hands, jealous because he had achieved so much.

Dream dust sparkled in his mental sky. The bard played on. Lewis and Deirdre leaned close together, their hands so interwoven that they were about to meld into one solid object.

Fred thought, *I hate you, Lewis Brahmindura. And I will find a way, my friend, to get what I want.*

CHAPTER 22
ICE STORM

Pacing—almost floating—in the candlelit scholar's nook of his dormitory room, Lewis savored his memories. Deirdre and he had been so—what would the French call it? Ah, *tres sympathique*—that's the expression. They had held hands. They had talked, so close together that their foreheads touched, and he could smell her hair, sweet, smooth, and golden. Deirdre and he shared a sweet kiss. She had such an exciting tongue!

Ah, not only had he found a beautiful woman who loved him as much as he loved her, he sensed that she wanted to continue into a committed relationship with him—even marry and have children!

Well … there were the "excepts." Lewis knew that were big rocks under the surface to prevent the relationship from going forward. For instance, she and the rest of the Lanthrans viewed Earth as "the Planet of the Curse." Was he accursed? *Yet,* he thought, *isn't Earth also "the Planet of the Treasure?" Do I have to prove I'm a treasure before I can marry Deirdre? Why is God in the muddle? Deirdre believes in God and Jesus and all that. I don't. How much would religious differences affect our future?*

He began to feel a little sleepy. Lewis settled down into his bed and curled up in the covers. Outside, wind howled and squealed and roared, and freezing rain splattered against the window with sharp, cutting noises.

He liked his simple but elegant room, with a large, diamond-paned window and beautiful hardwood floors, and it smelled of polished wood and candle wax. The Shaker-style furniture included two beds, two desks, and two built-in wardrobes for Fred and him. If one had to be marooned on an alien world, this was a very decent place for it.

One didn't count the chamber pots under the beds, of course, as furniture.

Scrunching the blankets around his chilly feet, Lewis smiled. He drifted to the day when he'd first met Deirdre. Under those drowsy thoughts, however, the great dragon that inhabited his soul shifted. *If you want Deirdre, you're going to have to face God,* the dragon said. *There's no ambiguity about that, at least if you really love her.*

Lewis brushed the thought away.

The warm evening wind that had charmed him and Deirdre roared, an icy gale. Freezing raindrops splattered against the diamond-paned windows. They sparkled in the lamplight that shone outside: topaz, amethyst, sapphire, and ruby. Away in the park, whipping tree branches began to glisten brightly. Spring had brought a late ice storm, a wondrous, magical moment when the world seemed completely transformed. During a tiny instant of time, while the lamps shone brilliantly in the College Park outside and the ice sheathed the tree branches in a glittering rainbow of jeweled colors, Lewis could truly believe in a magical, fantasy world.

His dragon murmured, *King Arthur, hobbits, ghosts, and unicorns—they are all real, in a way. They hint of the reality beyond the physical world.*

Lewis dismissed the thought. *No, those are just mythical entities. The supernatural is only a construct of the starved soul.*

Bam! The loud shock broke Lewis's dreamy thoughts.

"Ooww!" I hit my toe!" Fred lumbered into the room.

Lewis caught a strong whiff of stale ale and rancid smoke. "Hi, Fred," he said, trying to keep irritation out of his voice, "where've you been?"

"Oh, hello, Louie," Fred replied. Lewis winced at the nickname. Fred's voice was thick; he was drunk. "Thought you'd be asleep by now. Mind if I turn on the light?" The big man fumbled on the wall for a light switch.

Lewis told him, resigned to noise and optical pain, "There's a lamp on your bureau and matches in the desk drawer, on the left."

Fred bumped around until he found the lamp and the matches. Soon Lewis shaded his eyes with one hand as Fred peeled off his clothes and kicked them into a pile on the floor. "Back in a minute, Louie," he mumbled and tottered down the hall naked toward the lavatory.

"Fred—!" Lewis called, but his friend did not hear him. Lewis finished uselessly, "Fred, it's a co-ed dormitory!"

In the hallway, he heard a sharp female exclamation and a muffled apology.

Fred zoomed back inside. He put on Bardian briefs from his pile. The big man went out again, forgetting to close the door. Lewis was treated to the heavy tread of several late-retiring students, the flickering lights of their lamps, and the thud of somebody stumbling into somebody else. He heard an "oomph!" a crash and thud, and the lights in the hallway went out.

Sitting up, Lewis groaned.

After a while, Fred returned. He sat on his bed across from Lewis, and began to talk, belching clouds of beer breath. "After you and Deirdre left ..." Lewis heard a snarl in Fred's tone, "I met my friends, and we went to another bar in Forion. There was live music there, too, and the gals love to dance. Oh, sorry I came in so late."

Lewis waved away the apology. "Aren't you an adult? You don't need my permission to stay out late!"

Fred's head swung up. "You don't have to laugh at me."

"I'm not laughing, Fred," Lewis answered.

"It wasn't like that, Louie," The big man sounded hurt.

Fred's talk didn't make sense to Lewis. "Like what?"

"I'm not drunk," Fred continued. "Sure, I had some ale and some beer—the Staggering Dragon's got really good beer—but I can hold my liquor. I'm not even tipsy!"

That statement struck Lewis like a blow to the funny bone. He held his pillow over his mouth, but it could not stop the sound of muffled chortles.

Fred added, "You and Deirdre … I don't mind, I really don't mind!" His voice sounded insincere; Lewis detected an undercurrent of resentment in it.

Lewis whispered, "Yes, Deirdre and I love each other."

"You might as well enjoy your new girlfriend. Hey, the Gregorys are taking good care of Patrick and Gracie. You're Dr. Zakok's brightest star. The magi and the people on the street think you're perfect; even Deirdre thinks you're the cat's meow. Why should you care about a piece of trash like me?"

Lewis could not answer. Fred's last words hit him like a kick in the stomach.

Fred belched heavily and alcohol fumes rolled over to Lewis's nose, "Don't you know what it means to be praised by Dr. Zadok in the College of the Magi? The College only admits people who are likely to become world leaders—and they want you. Lucky you!"

Lewis felt furious. *Is Fred saying that only I get all the attention? After all, he works there, too! Damn him! I hate feeding his deflated ego!*

"What do you want to do, Fred?" he asked, trying to keep his voice cool.

"Can you imagine me running a tavern, maybe? I'm no magus material. Neither are Dale and Barth—they enrolled in the University and learned English 'cause they wanted to become magi—but the elite College of the Magi wouldn't accept Sia's application, and Barth was dismissed. Barth says you have to be related to the right people to get in. His older brother and he both tried but got pushed out because they're related to the wrong people. Like me."

Lewis hated Fred's dripping self-pity.

"Fred, that's nonsense. You remember—We *both* work at the elite College of the Magi. We *both* have access to Lanthra's best technology. Daniel and Zakok intend to train us *both* as magi at the College-in-exile. Dr. Zadok said that—"

"And there's Tom. You know—the Bard of Bardia." Fred was on a roll and wouldn't shut up. "Didn't you hear him tonight? He's spectacular, Louie—like you. He's still a kid, but he's dark, handsome, and real polite, like an aristocrat, you know? Not as skinny as you, and shorter, but, like you, he's a whiz—only at music instead of physics."

"Fred, you are a great engineer and a good musician yourself. I really enjoyed your warm-up for Tom's concert. So did Deirdre!"

"Mmph. Tom can play that lute and sing like you wouldn't believe! It was magic—the way it made everybody feel. Not like me. Just call me flat-note Fred."

His voice still whined. Lewis tried to cut off the alcoholic misery. "Fred, you'll feel better in the morning. Turn off the lamp. Let's go to sleep."

However, Fred sniffled, and his voice dropped to a hushed whisper. "Wanna know something, Louie?"

Lewis restrained a sharp, *No!*

"Back home, what have I got? My Mom lives in a trailer dump with her umpteenth boyfriend and uses heroin. I spoke to her only twice last year. She was high both times when I called her, and she hung up before I finished talking. My real dad was a crackhead, too, but he's dead now. My foster father's dead, too! How do you think it feels, Louie, to be alone? You've never been alone. Can you imagine—my foster Dad died on my college graduation day! Did you know that, Louie? I loved him more than my real parents …"

Lewis felt a twang of compassion for his friend. "I didn't realize—"

"Of course! You don't realize anything!" Fred's eyes, visibly red-streaked even in the lamplight, narrowed, cold and accusing, "Whose fault is it that we're stranded here? Yours! Who played the hero? You! You're the leader in the wilderness! You are the genius who figured out the hot marble! You are the perfect, loving big brother to the kids. Then, as if you don't have enough glory and talent and … family to satisfy any normal human being, you've gotta have more, don't you! You suck up to His Excellency and Dr. Zakok and Deirdre!"

Lewis felt an invisible prowler with metal cutters twist the wires of his fences. His strained self-control snapped. "You won't even try being the hero!" he jabbed back at Fred. "I've always had to bolster up your shaky self-esteem, build you up, encourage you, avoid criticizing you so you could perform up to your best level. Well, I'm tired of it. You need to stand up for yourself, for once, and quit whining! Get some sleep! You'll feel better in the morning."

Fred did not answer, but he turned out the light. Lewis heard him stretch out under the covers, and the bed groaned as he rolled over to face the wall. Soon, snoring buzzed like a ticked-off bee. Lewis, too, lay back and tried to relax. Maybe he'd get a full three hours sleep before work tomorrow …

Immediately his conscience alarm went off. He shouldn't try to prick Fred, even if was drunk. Oh well … everything would get back to normal soon, as normal as anything could be while packing up the lab.

Outside the storm blew violently, ice rattled hard against the windows, and inside Fred emitted snorts and puffs. Lewis imagined Deirdre's warm touches, and they lulled him to sleep.

CHAPTER 23
THE DIPLOMAT FROM SMYTHE

On the morning after the ice storm, Daniel Higgins stood at his window. The ice sheathing on twigs and branches looked magical. Sunlight glittered off the red-budded maples and gold-tipped willows down in the riverbed, making a bold, sparkling strip of color against the gray and russet of the slow-to-awake trees on the mountain slopes. At the window, sunlight soaked his face and warmed his spirits. Daniel's eyes drank of the sky, which was a clear, celebrative blue.

He wished he were outside taking a walk. However, this morning, he had several important appointments, and this afternoon he had a heavy load of papers to review and sign.

Today, over his fine brown suit and waistcoat, he wore the gold robe of the High Magus. The robe made him feel too warm and bulky; however, he had official duties as High Magus as well as Viceroy, so he must endure the robe.

His first appointment was with Robert of Smythe. Daniel usually looked forward to that. Robert was a leader of the Council of the Magi, an ambassador for the Queen of Smythe, and an old friend.

His secretary spoke through the doorway. "Your Excellency, Robert Wrighthaven of Smythe is here."

"Thank you, James." Daniel turned from the window to face

his colleague.

Robert, in his magus robe with the tawny lining of his country's executive circle, swept athletically into the office. He was about Daniel's age, intelligent, with good integrity, but—as Daniel had experienced too many times—dogmatic and single-minded in a conflict.

Daniel smiled in greeting and presented his right hand with the ring of office. Robert took it, held it briefly to his forehead, and they exchanged the ancient blessing: *"Baradyah etoy."* However, Robert's face glowered, and Daniel wondered why.

He waved Robert to a seat on the couch and took a seat on the chair. The man's

close-set eyes narrowed and a muscle in his jaw ticked. "We heard about that matter in Skye country."

"What matter?" Daniel asked. He felt his heart quicken and leaned forward to hear what Robert had to say.

"There was a massacre at Standover in Tiorpatath." Robert glared at him. "All of Standover's citizens, including the women and children, were slaughtered, hacked to death. No one claims responsibility. However, we know that *your* people had crossed the Winerush into Skye country about the time of the massacre. People are saying that you, the High Magus, ordered it as a power play, to make the Torish look evil."

"*What?*" Anger stabbed Daniel and he jumped up. "Who in the *szttit Ta* has done this? And how can you believe that I had anything to do with such a crime?"

"I don't know that you had anything to do with the massacre; I'm just telling you what people are saying."

Daniel was about to explode when a horrible idea came to him: *Charon ordered the massacre himself! This is his trigger: he will blame it on the Bardians and use it as an excuse for war.*

Daniel calmed himself and spoke carefully, "This is the first time I've heard of the matter."

"You did send an expedition into Smythe." It was a

statement, flat and hard.

"I did," Daniel acknowledged, although he would have preferred to deny it. "To the upper reaches of the Skye River."

"Which is in the direction of Standover," Robert thrust.

Daniel thrust back. "It was an illegal entry, yes. However, so was the vicious attack against my people at the ford of the Winerush River and the torturing of some magi that they took captive. We did not go so far as Standover. Those innocent people were not murdered by us nor by any Bardians."

Daniel saw that Robert wanted to believe him. He also saw doubt on the other man's face. He sensed that the more he tried to defend himself, the more the other man would doubt him. He let the pause fill the office with silence, let his anger ebb, and waited for Robert to make the next move.

"Daniel, High Magus of Lanthra, I have another matter. You can expect trouble this summer in Moorway at the Council," Robert stated. "Although I dissented, the executive committee listened to Charon's people and *moved up the schedule*—without informing all of us!"

Daniel felt his whole body stiffen, if it could get more rigid after the faked news about his role at Standover. "Are you sure? No one informed me!"

"Yes!" Robert's tanned face reddened with anger. "What a ploy, and so typical of the Horned Edge! You can be sure they're planning to shove something up our—"

"Very likely," Daniel agreed.

Robert closed his eyes, apparently counted to ten, and his face softened. "All right, I believe you. Bardians did not massacre Standover."

The diplomat from Smythe went on. "However, I have yet another matter to bring up which concerns you deeply. Her Majesty Margaret tells me that your family is going to stay at Deirdre's estates in Smythe for a while. Why aren't you going with them?"

"I plan to join the celebration in the Forschwynn Province until it is time to lead the Council in Moorway. I can leave in less than a week, once my daughters and Patrick and Gracie Brahmindura are safe in Smythe."

Roger raised an eyebrow. "Is that wise?"

"I believe it is."

"Hmm. I disagree; I don't think you should remain here even that long." Robert frowned. He went on, "On top of everything we've talked about so far, the Queen sent me with a message solely for you." He handed Daniel a parchment which had been sealed with a raised gold and scarlet floret.

Daniel broke the seal and handed the parchment back to Robert as custom suggested. The diplomat read the letter from the Queen of Smythe out loud.

I, Margaret, *Thamaon* of Smythe, greet you, Daniel, High Magus, the Viceroy of Rockeerie, and my dear kinsman through marriage. We are always happy to receive my Lady Deirdre and you and your family and guests in Smythe. However, let us remind you that Smythe remains neutral in any disagreement between Tor and Bardia. As a neutral nation, we will not allow the Torish to send any armed force into our country, and neither shall we allow any Bardian armed forces across our borders, except what are needed to accompany Deirdre to her estate. Even so, I wish you well regarding your negotiations with Tor and with the Council of the Magi's resolutions this summer. *Radyah getlueoye.*

Daniel felt growing tension in his back and neck. "In other words, if we are attacked, we're on our own."

"Yes."

"There is another letter to both of us," Daniel said. "It came from Poiemana, which is surprising. Our gentle, old friend

Bogoswega initiated it and asked that it be read and voted on at the Council."

Robert crossed his legs and arms. Daniel felt a headache coming on. "Here it is:"

> Let the College of the Magi remove the sect called The Horned Edge from the body of the magi. The Horned Edge has chosen to worship the god Saoma, and their actions are no longer worthy of the office that they have been given. I do not submit this resolution lightly. I hear that the Horned Edge commits human sacrifice, even though they claim their victims, the *homo azure,* are not human, and they abort their offspring to force population control. Their Order can no longer be called magi at all, for they have abandoned wisdom.

Robert shouted. "How can you and I possibly present this letter at the Council? Where do you recommend that you and I hide when the missiles fly—considering that we'll be presenting the issue on the Horned Edge's home turf?"

Daniel shouted back, "We can't hide! This huge pimple must pop, or it will infect all of us!"

Both he and Robert stood with fists clenched, until Daniel took a deep breath. He prayed out loud, "Help us, *Radyah.*" Then he made himself sit down. Silence reigned in Daniel's office for many minutes. When the ambassador from Smythe leaned forward and put his head in his hands, Daniel spoke in a quiet tone, "Robert, "I need your help."

Sunlight poured into the office; yet it seemed that there were shadows everywhere.

Daniel said, "At times during this Council, I may appear to be supporting Charon and the Horned Edge in their discussions. However, that will be only a strategy, not a change of heart."

"*What?*"

"I need you to trust me, my friend. That's all. Just trust that I serve *Radyah*."

CHAPTER 24
ROMANCE

Early in the morning after the ice storm, Lewis walked with Deidre in Nutman's park. In three days, she and her sister Myra would leave for Smythe, along with Patrick and Gracie and an escort. However, … he had to go to Kingsport. He cherished this time with Deirdre; he held her hand and looked at her lustrous eyes, her poise. Around them, the trees were kings and queens that rose majestically from the mountainsides, and each sparkled in the sun.

As they strolled, Deirdre talked: "On my estate, there's a secret place, a ledge shaped like a saddle high on a forested hill. When I sit there, the height is scary, but I can see far, far into the distance. My heart lifts; it's my happy place!"

Lewis thought about Deirdre's "happy place." *Where is mine?* His heart said, *It is with her.* Looking around at the ice-glistening trees, he asked, "Why is Lanthra so much like Earth? And it's so beautiful here!"

Deirdre squeezed his hand. "Good question! Lanthra and Earth follow the same template, mostly, but Earth's been more trampled."

"Then," he asked, "what about the Blue People?"

Deirdre explained, "Humans on Earth and Lanthra are called *homo sapiens*," according to your classification system. The Blue

People were imported from a planet that was made on a different template, and we classify them as *homo azure*."

"Which means 'Blue People,'" Lewis tried to absorb that. The information was hard to understand, and despite his pleasure in Deirdre's company, he felt a sudden emptiness in his chest. *I am so far from home! And how can I believe that idea of "created on a template."*

When they paused on a small bridge that arched over a stream, Lewis enfolded Deirdre in his arms, and she laid her cheek on shoulder. The tree branches above made a gazebo of ice. He felt her closeness, her warmth. "You are leaving for Smythe, and it won't be long before I have to leave Nutman, too," he said. "Fred and I are helping Dr. Zadok pack up the lab, as you know. You and I may be separated for a long time! But I promise to find you, wherever we shall go."

Her eyes met his, and he saw a glint of moisture. One jewel of a tear ran down her face. "*Forya yo-on, plaitha la-oya, ti ditla foroya.*"

His hand came up and smoothed away the tear.

"We push onward; we reach for life, while death follows behind us," she translated.

He bent down and let his lips brush hers. For a long moment, they shared touch, shared breath. She tasted sweet and warm, like sunlit honey. "*Plaitha la-oya pim!*" Lewis whispered intensely. "We reach for life!"

For a long time, they memorized one another with their eyes, hers gray, his brown. Then they embraced one another again and, as his lips moved to hers, his hands treasured her satiny hair.

CHAPTER 25
A SCOLDING

Daniel looked out his window, watching sunlight sparkle on ice-coated branches. He wanted very much to be outside, but he had many meetings scheduled for today. *Sigh.* His stomach growled. At least breakfast was here.

He had just taken a soothing sip of particularly good hot coffee and was about to bite a warm, freshly baked cinnamon roll when a bustle outside of his office told him that one of the day's challenges had arrived. Dr. Zadok was first.

The old scientist entered his office with a complaint on his lips.

"I have a serious matter for you, Your Excellency," he began in a prickly voice.

Daniel set down the cinnamon roll and hid the rolling of his eyes at the old man's tone. Hopefully Zadok's "serious matter" was not as serious as Robert's report about the massacre in Standover.

"That young man, that Frederick Jontz whom you brought into my department, is very bright, but he is becoming a big problem."

"How so?" Daniel inquired, thinking instead about the massacre and whether Charon had truly murdered the people himself as his pretext for war. *Somebody* had murdered them, and it wasn't Bardians.

He took a precious sip of the glorious coffee, while Zadok griped about Fred. This took a few minutes, ending with "… and he will not take the time to plan properly while we are organizing the disassembly. Also, he is flippant when I try to give him instructions." Zadok paused for breath.

"Sit down, Dr. Zadok." He indicated the cherry settee and seated himself in his favorite gold-covered chair where he could see both the scientist and the sparkling view out of his bay window.

Zadok sat stiffly. His bushy eyebrows had drawn together, and his moustache bristled. Daniel prepared for another onslaught of emotion. "This morning, when I checked the sonic computer— it's the last thing we will take down—I noticed that some of the most important files were erased—gone! These were all concerned with the *noretha* and its coordinates to Earth! To Earth, Daniel, *to Earth!*"

"Are you sure it was Fred who did this?"

"Yes! He admitted that he had been in the laboratory last night. The magi on the third shift noticed that he played with the equipment. Heaven knows what else he may have been doing and for how long!"

Daniel said, trying to sound reasonable, "Isn't Fred given clearance to get into the laboratory whenever he wishes? Didn't you want him to learn as much as he can about the locating technology?"

The old man exploded, "During the appropriate hours, yes! But not anytime he feels like it! Besides, this morning, when I asked him what he had done, he was insolent like a rebellious child!"

Daniel thought of about six replies, none of which would help solve anything. He held his tongue while his lead scientist waved his arms.

"You bring this unknown from the forbidden planet to work

with me on a highly sensitive project, and he wastes our time with his … his free spirit. I call it a lack of self-discipline! That other man—Lewis Brahmindura—has a fine, scientific manner, but this Fred! Spontaneity can be destructive as well as creative! Plus, lately he has been spending too much time with some men I do *not* respect—you know that idiot, Dale of the family, Nototnoreth; they always were troublemakers. Sia is a notorious womanizer and a suspected accomplice in several armed thefts. And that new companion of his, Barth of the infamous Layhew clan—he was my assistant for a while but missed the mark – could he be a secret supporter of the Horned Edge? Who knows what could happen if Mr. Jontz does not bridle his tongue with those people?"

Daniel winced. Zadok certainly had a point. He had assessed the big man from Earth as a talented, boisterous, and basically a gentle character, but with a very vulnerable dent in his self-esteem. The lords of space were at work on him, gnawing at him, trying to use Fred for their goals. The man was in a position to do them much harm.

He would have to bring Fred in immediately and talk with him.

*　　*　　*

"Your Excellency!" His secretary James's balding head popped through the door. The expression in his kind but diplomatic face was neutral, but Daniel saw that trouble was coming.

"What is it, James?" he asked. Problem after problem had come at him this morning. His stomach had gone rancid.

"Mr. Jontz is here as you requested. I can tell him to wait—"

"No, let him come in."

*　　*　　*

Fred waited in the vaulted hallway to be called into the High Magus' office. It seemed symbolic that he now sat on the same bench by the same pillar where he had sat on his first afternoon in

Nutman. Both days were sunny; birds sang; the mountains rose in splendor. However, although on that first day he had felt joy at the beautiful new world, today his mood was foul.

Is it worth it, trying to reason with a little local despot? He heard the oak door open with a smooth rush of air, and the Daniel's secretary in his ruffled white shirt and fancy suit came out.

"His Excellency the Viceroy of Rockeerie and High Magus will see you," James said.

"Fine. Thank you." *What a pompous stereotypical butler,* Fred thought, with disgust. He let the other man usher him forward. As he passed the secretary's antechamber and entered Daniel's office, he found himself thinking, *Last time I was here, I thought that Bardia was the ideal place to be. It has unspoiled nature, a simple, scenic life; I thought it was a place where I could make a clean start. However, it hasn't worked out that way at all. I guess I don't fit in—here or anywhere.* He steeled himself to meet the kingpin of the magi.

Daniel greeted him in a pleasant tenor and offered him a chair. His Excellency opened the conversation. "I heard that you and Dr. Zadok had an argument this morning. He came to me earlier. However, I would like to hear your side of the situation."

"First of all," Fred began, "he accused me unfairly of breaking into the laboratory. I didn't break in. I just went in the normal way—if you can call speaking to a vanishing door normal." He went on, in a long string of excuses. "Okay, it wasn't my shift. But I'd had an idea about how the coordinates are stored in the marble, and by the time Dr. Zadok's so-called regular hours would have come up again, I would have lost all my momentum. Besides, I didn't want the Toy to get all packed up before I could experiment. So, I just let myself in—it was after midnight—and got to work. The people on duty didn't notice me right away because their work was in another room, and I was quiet. I used to do work independently after hours all the time back home. No big deal."

"I understand your need to follow through a productive train of thought," Daniel interrupted. "Creativity does not always conform to a rigid schedule."

Fred felt himself relax a little. *Should I show him what I did?* Basically, he wanted to like the elegant little man who should have been a ballet instructor, the way he moved around. However, he'd been screwed by likeable people before, and he knew that Daniel's mind was as sharp as a guillotine.

He carefully continued, "Now, this is my side of the situation: I thought the good doctor would be happy, but this morning, all Zadok could see was that the sonic computer had some problems. He insinuated it was totally my fault. He acted like I deliberately tried to mess up the machine."

"I'm sure that was hard to take." Daniel sounded empathetic.

"It sure was!" Fred emphasized. "I did nothing to the computer! Sure, I played with it—but I didn't wipe out those files!"

Daniel's posture was open, listening. Fred wanted very much to tell him what he had accomplished. He wanted to hear the warm note of admiration in the man's voice, see the surprise and approval flowing across the authority's features. He opened his mouth; he reached into his pocket …

But then he wavered. *Okay, I probably did screw up the computer. Will I get a reward for what I learned, or will I get in serious hog-muck? Nah, they think I'm a screw-up. There are no rewards for screw-ups.*

Then Daniel shifted slightly on his chair, and when he crossed his legs, Fred's stomach knotted tightly. He blustered, "I came up here to tell you that I haven't done anything wrong! Yes, I did some experiments, and they may have messed up the computer, but I only did it to try to help!"

Daniel put his hands on the desk. "Fred, you are a talented scientist who can see and solve problems in uniquely creative ways. Even at his grouchiest, Dr. Zadok cannot deny this.

However, Dr. Zadok doesn't trust you. He is concerned about the character of some of your friends. They might manipulate you for, let me say, unhelpful purposes."

Fred felt his face flame up. "Aw, come off it, Your Excellency. You monitor my job, my housing, my friends, my whereabouts … Your people treat me like an adolescent on probation."

"Perhaps because you behave like one!" Daniel commented sharply. His eyes examined Fred with surgical precision. "You are entitled to own dissident opinions. So do your friends. However, do you really know who they are? Do you know their intentions? And do they know who *you* are?"

Against his will, Fred had to admit that Daniel had a point. Actually, so far, there had been precious little self-disclosure among Sia, Dale, Barth, and him—they always joked around and made jabs at the Bardian magi.

Daniel continued, "You, Fred, are very important. First, you are from Earth. Second, you have much more power than you realize, to help or to harm my people and your friends."

"I won't harm anyone!" Fred shouted. *Although … it would be nice to get Lewis out of the way …* "What a laugh!" He stood up and thrust his face forward. "You think I'm associating with the 'commies'; is that it? You know what the commies are, don't you, from your precious Earth studies? You remember the McCarthy era?"

Daniel leaned forward, and there was steel in his voice. "Understand," he said evenly. "Understand that you don't understand everything that is going on." His voice got deeper, sharper. "Why do you think we've been disassembling the 'Toy,' as you call it? Don't you think that Charon could use it—and you—to destroy us?"

Fred rose, anger rising, swelling in his chest, arms, and legs. He loomed over the shorter man, his big shadow obscuring Daniel's face. "Perhaps, since I'm so stupid and my friends are such jerks, I should just get out of your way!" Bitterly, he thought, *You don't need me, anyhow. Lewis is doing pretty well by himself.* He started to turn and walk out, but the High Magus' firm voice pulled him back.

"Fred Jontz!" Daniel snarled, "you will go back to work and help Dr. Zadok restore the computer files. You will present your research findings to him, and to no one else. From now on, you will have no further contact with your tavern friends. As soon as our locating system is disassembled, I plan to move you and Lewis out of my province into a safe place. See that you follow through with these orders."

Fred glared and stomped toward the door, his boots sounding very harsh on the parquet floor. As he reached the mammoth brassbound portal, he heard a bell ring, and the door opened smoothly to show the balding, unobtrusive secretary.

"Call an escort for Mr. Jontz," Daniel said, with a flat voice. "He's going back to Dr. Zadok's laboratory."

"Yes, Your Excellency," James said.

Steaming inside, Fred fumed his way back to the locating chambers. *I'm done. I'll fix those effing files, but I won't show Zadok what I've really done, and when he asks, I'll lie about it. After today I will have nothing more to do with Dr. Zadok and his precious laboratory. In fact, I'll go to Tor and volunteer to work for Lord Charon. At least there I'll feel appreciated.*

CHAPTER 26
DENIAL

For a moment, before his next appointment before noon, Daniel turned back to the view from his window. Now, the ice was melting from the trees. It was getting very warm—a gorgeous day to be outside.

Daniel thought of the budding romance between Deirdre and Lewis. She had told him that she loved him. He hoped the relationship had not gone too far at this point. He trusted his daughter to be sensible—this was no time to make major commitments such as marriage.

For a moment, he imagined a wedding between his daughter and the young man from Earth. What a beautiful image! Lewis was a good match in personality and kindness. But he was definitely not a good match spiritually. He trusted no one except himself. This young man had major choices to make. Could he change? He would rather Deirdre wedded to someone who knew himself, who had fought with the bizeor so that Radyah could lead him, a man who knew *victory*. However—Daniel grinned—he was not going to give orders to a headstrong *faetha,* a baroness of Smythe and in the line of succession of that throne.

It comforted him that in Smythe, marriages for the faetha were decided through the Thamaon, the Queen. Of course, Deirdre would have much influence on her own marriage—but nothing could be decided until her third year of service, which was coming up next year. By that time, he supposed she would have a good idea whether Lewis Brahmindura was the proper choice for her.

He had only a few minutes before his final morning appointment. Still deep in thought, Daniel nibbled at his cinnamon roll and sipped his water. *Yuck! Tepid water!* Daniel's soul felt tepid, too, because he was about to get a report from Howard, Nutman's city manager. Unfortunately, Howard was a … he tried to suppress the thought but failed … *blockhead.*

Howard entered and bowed deeply. Dressed in a rather tight brown herringbone suit, he was a thick man who had thick lips, a thick forehead, and small deep-set eyes. Today, he smelled funny, like food burned on a stove. Appointed by the king of Bardia with close connection to the king's advisors, he was an institution in Nutman, and there was no way Daniel could get rid of him.

Daniel gestured politely, "Have a seat."

However, the city manager remained standing, folding his hands respectfully, although Daniel knew the man was probably thinking, *Whatever you want, I'll do the opposite.* Howard reported, "The city is quiet. Most of the people have left for the Quincentennial. Surely Nutman and the Rockeerie province are secure! There have been no attempts to harass the troops stationed at the fords of the Winerush since that so-called attack several months ago. We don't need to mandate this emptying of my city."

"So, you say," Daniel replied, trying to hide his irritation. Howard was full of misinformation. "But I do not agree. Captain Gregory tells me that Lord Charon's Eagle forces and Baron Layhew's Wolf Riders are building up large forces on their side of the river. There was a horrible massacre at Standover in the Skye country which has been blamed on us, but we are innocent. When do you think they'll invade and what are you doing to protect the city?"

Howard hesitated. "Your Excellency, reports say that you are about to invade *them* and that the Torish have to protect themselves. I heard about the massacre at Standover and that you may have ordered it!

Daniel stated, his voice icy, "You heard wrong."

"Well," Howard dithered, "I got word from our king himself to leave Tor alone. If you get a rebuke from Kingsport next week, then you may be sure that King Norhe believes that the aggressor in this standoff is *you*."

Daniel snapped, "You did not answer the question! Whatever His Majesty Norhe Reynolds thinks, I *know* that Charon intends to invade this province. In fact, he plans to conquer all of Bardia! I want the city to be prepared. I want minimal loss of lives and property. Now—when do you think they'll invade and what are you doing to protect it?"

"Well, I don't they'll invade us at all. What would they get for it? After all, Nutman's population is leaving in droves to go to the 500th celebration of the founding of Bardia. They'll all be housed in the Forschwynn province—so how could we pose a threat to any of the Torish? There's no reason for Charon to bother us—unless we somehow provoke them."

The man is incompetent, Daniel thought to himself. "All right, you don't believe that Charon will invade the city. Even so, can you make sure we're as prepared as possible? Food, water, medicine? The Torish forces are not known to be kind."

"Well, Your Excellency, I don't see how to move along any faster. I'm doing my best, you can be sure."

Abruptly, Daniel dismissed Howard. Hurrying to the window and opening it to remove burned-egg fumes, Daniel calmed himself and talked for a while to the Master. "I wish I could go outside and take a nice, long walk," he said aloud.

The Master sympathized but did not give him the go ahead.

"All right, then what do you want me to work on next?"

Fred Jontz. He's a great danger to himself and to you all.

"James," Daniel called.

The secretary came in and waited for the High Magus to

speak. Daniel knew that the other man was unruffled, competent, and extremely intelligent under that bland exterior. He wished James might give him a reassuring hug. However, the leader of all Lanthra's magi did not cry on his secretary's shoulder.

"Someone has got to peel Fred away from his cronies before he causes serious trouble." he said gruffly.

"Yes, Your Excellency," James gave him a low, respectful bow. "What do you want me to do?"

"Send me Sir Thomas Forschwynn right away. And then, send me Hermann. As soon as possible."

James hesitated. "Who is Hermann, Your Excellency?"

"He's my special agent, a spy, so to speak. You'll find him with the city police today."

"It shall be done, Your Excellency." James bowed low and left.

CHAPTER 27
BETRAYAL

The Lanthran sun was setting with a glow of optic purple when Fred returned to his dorm room. He stood for a moment, head drooping. Stripes of sunlight glowed on the walls, with rainbow areas where the light angled through the diamond-paned windows, but the beauty didn't make him feel better. "I suck!" His curse filled the room. "I'm a loser, a total moron. My name should be Frederick Stupid Jontz."

A heavy sullen weight filled his insides like a ball of undigested dough. He took off his smoky-smelling pants and shirt, flung them onto the floor, and stood in his undergarments—more like Egyptian loincloths, he thought with disgust. He missed his briefs and T-shirt from Earth.

Suddenly, he exploded, "Crap! My truck's probably been repossessed! My apartment is re-leased!" He pictured the apartment manager and a cleaning lady going through his possessions, bagging up the hobby materials, cleaning out the refrigerator, throwing away the dirty laundry, putting his sound system and television and computer and other stuff in a storage unit …

Intense anger bit his gut, and Fred kicked the bed.

Then he realized that Lewis's car had probably been repossessed, too. Even the fancy Mercedes with the bio-fuel engine—that car might be towed to a impound lot. Lewis would have to pay a fortune to get the car out. He let out a malicious chuckle.

However, it now occurred to Fred that Lewis had a family to help him. Lewis's parents had probably rescued his things, hoping their kids might be found someday. The itch of jealousy came back worse than ever.

He tried to submerge the feeling, but instead it flamed hotter. "To hell with Lewis! I've got to get cleaned up for dinner with my friends at the Red Oak Tavern." He peeled off his Bardian undergarments and reached for a robe so he could respectfully walk to the bathroom, but just then the door swung open, and Lewis walked in.

Fred's hands zoomed down to cover his privates.

"*Lewis!* What do you think you're doing!" he bawled. "Crap, Lewis! Do you have to stand there and hold the door open?"

Two female university students walked by at that instant, and their eyes went wide. They covered their laughter and hurried past, emitting muffled tittering noises.

Red-faced, Lewis closed the door too hard. It shut with an explosive *bang,* failed to shut properly, and bounced open again. From the hallway drifted raucous laughter.

Wrapping up in his robe, Fred very deliberately closed the door. He turned to face Lewis, feeling rage pour through him, flaring like a supernova.

"I'm sorry," Lewis said sincerely. "I didn't realize you were here. I should have knocked."

Lewis's apologies registered nothing to Fred's burning brain. *And he's trying to be nice. Maybe he's trying to make up for slamming me last night, saying that he's always had to bolster up my shaky self-esteem ...*

He wanted out of there, as fast as possible. Sweeping up clean clothes and toiletries, Fred threw them into a bag to take to the washroom. Meanwhile, he saw the hurt look that Lewis gave him with those big brown eyes that all the women swooned over. He hated those brown eyes.

Lewis neatly bundled up his own soiled garments into a canvas bag and slipped in an envelope. "What's the envelope for?" asked Fred. "Aren't you afraid that it'll get washed with your clothes and leave little shreds all over the place?"

"Fred, this is money for the Blue Lady who does laundry for the dormitory residents. She does an excellent job, and I wanted to let her know that I appreciate it. Who knows what her income will be like if she stays after we all evacuate?"

Fred shut his mouth, but his jaw clenched hard. *So, he's the considerate one, and I'm the ingrate.*

Either unaware of or ignoring Fred's hostility, Lewis asked, "Hey, Fred! Can you hang out with Patrick and me tonight?"

"Huh?"

"I was really hoping you would, Fred. Come with me to supper at the Gregory's. The kids are leaving day after tomorrow, and I promised a brother-brother night with Patrick before they go. Deirdre is having a spend-the-night for Gracie and Myra. I've already made plans for Patrick to stay with me here in the dorm. We'll play games and share stories, and maybe even sneak some goodies from the kitchen. The Blue Lady showed me a pie we could have if we wanted. After all, they have to clear out the inventory before the move."

Stupid kid stuff, Fred inwardly sneered.

"I really want you to come. You've been like a brother to Patrick and Gracie."

Like a brother? Fred's nostrils flared and he wanted to spit in Lewis's face. *Who was the so-called "brother" that took us on that stinking picnic? Who was the great Daniel Boone that got us lost in the wilderness, where Patrick and Gracie could have gotten killed? And who was the hero that let Patrick's ankle get sprained—the kid still hasn't gotten over it. Haven't you noticed that he still limps?*

"Would you like to come?" Lewis repeated.

"I'm busy. Have a good time," Fred answered shortly.

Lewis wasn't so easily brushed off. "Sadie specifically asks that you come tonight, at least. She really wants us all together, because soon we must split up. Patrick and Gracie will go to Deirdre's estate in Smythe with Deirdre and Myra. You and I will go to Kingsport. All of us would like to see you."

At the thought of seeing Deirdre mooning over Lewis at dinner, Fred's insides crushed. "Nope. I have plans."

Lewis stared at Fred perplexedly. "What is *up* with you?"

"You don't know when to quit, do you?" Fred snapped. "How long do I have to wait before you either shut up or I hit you in the mouth!"

"What is the *matter with you?*"

"Aw, knock it off, Lewis! This whole establishment is stuck-up, with their noses in the air, led by that little dandy Daniel. The Gregorys and even your new girlfriend are all in it. You think that's where you fit in—the socially acceptable club? You want to be part of the aristocracy? Their whole thing makes me sick."

Lewis's eyebrows drew together, and he dropped the bag that he had been holding. His voice low and almost dangerous, he began, "Now wait a minute, Fred! I don't know where this is coming from—it sounds like Sia, Dale, and Barth talking, not the Fred Jontz I know."

Fred felt his fists bunch. His inner core contracted even more into an impenetrable dark mass. "There's no point in continuing this discussion," he said. "I won't be patronized. I'm staying with Dale tonight, so Patrick can use my bed. Have a nice weekend."

Grabbing his satchel, he blew out of the room.

*   *   *

An hour later, Fred sat in the Red Oak Tavern with Dale, Sia, and Barth. He downed his second pint of ale and doodled in the rings of moisture on the table, and he didn't make eye contact with his friends or join their banter. Even the dulcet folk music from the stage sounded like a droning housefly, like the one he'd been trying to vaporize with his laser the night Lewis had called him, the night which had started this whole mess.

"What happened to you, Fred?" Barth asked sarcastically. "Did you win an award? Get good news? You look so happy!"

"Go smell your own tail," Fred replied shortly. He stared at the foam on the third pint that the waiter had just brought him.

"I heard you had a confrontation with Danny boy the viceroy," Barth continued unrepentantly.

Fred felt an invisible arrow of hatred in him shoot toward Daniel, the arrogant prick. He heard a long silence from his friends and realized that they wanted him to answer. The silence stretched and stretched, like a tug of war game between the four people at the table.

Maybe it was the ale, or maybe his black anger, but Fred found himself recounting his interview with Daniel, a highly colored story that painted himself as the brave defiant rebel making a stand for freedom. He summarized, "The dude told me to go back and work with Dr. Zadok. I said no—not unless they treat me better."

"Whew!" said Sia, smoothing the white ruffles of his collar and cuffs. "You've got nerve, Fred."

"Imagine you, standing up to Dancing Daniel, Viceroy of Rockeerie and the High Magus," Barth drawled. He had tilted back his chair; his long legs stuck out to one side, and his ankles were crossed. Apparently changing the subject, he asked, "Lewis Brahmindura … he's your roommate, right? Where did you say you two came from? You have the same, unique accent; you mostly speak English—

"Yeah." Fred decided it was wise not to let these people know that he and Lewis were from Earth. "I'm from …" he thought fast to invent something, and finished, "Polunking."

"Hmm." Barth's blue eyes pondered. "And Lewis?"

Fred shook his head. "He's not from Polunking. He said he grew up somewhere further north." That was true enough, using Earth geography.

He felt his mouth grimace. What was the best way to persuade them to get rid of Lewis and glorify him instead? Dale and Sia would be easy to manipulate. They were only sycophants. However, Barth was deeper, more intense, and he also sensed that Barth was not all he appeared to be. The man crackled with energy, something hidden, something powerful. Who was Barth Layhew, really?

At once, he saw Barth in a whole new frame. He reviewed what he had picked up from small talk.

Barth had grown up in Tor. He'd mentioned a brother there that he didn't like very much. Also, from comments here and there, Fred knew that about seven years ago, Barth had graduated from the University of Nutman, a less eclectic group than the College of the Magi, but still very prestigious. He was a very talented engineer, and Dr. Zadok had taken him under his wing and taught him about the locating system. However, after a few months, the two had parted ways. Barth's comments revealed a carefully controlled resentment but no details of the split. *Funny: Barth seems unemployed but always has money. Why would a man of Barth's talents be hanging around Nutman with these idiots?*

In this new frame, all the pieces came together. Barth used to work with Dr. Zadok's locating system; *Charon needs repairs to his locating system in Tor. Barth must be working for Charon—I bet he either wants to sabotage the Bardian equipment or to steal it!*

Drawing triangles in the mug condensation, Fred prepared to launch into his attack to destroy Lewis. *I'll play up Lewis as a "gateway" to steal the goodies. I'll present myself as the indispensable asset to set up and use the Toy in Tor.* He chuckled at his private pun.

"What are you laughing about, Fred?" asked Sia.

"Physicists versus engineers—a very old rivalry."

"So?" Barth asked.

Fred smiled triumphantly. "Lewis can think, but I can make things work!"

"Okay. What are you getting at?"

"I can understand Lewis's ideas about identifying gravitational signatures and initiating the resonances so that you can connect between here and, say, one of your moons for mining—or even somewhere across the universe! You probably know, Barth, that, at certain stations like here and Whitehall in Moorway, the Toy can tap into the singularity at the center of Lanthra's gravity to produce power. Now, that's plenty of power for the connection job—unless you wanted to move a whole planet." Fred knew that Sia and Dale had no idea what that meant, but he had a suspicion that Barth did understand. *Now to jiggle the hook.* "Remember the One Law? 'You can look at Earth, but you can't go there!'"

Barth rolled his eyes. "I worked with Dr. Zadok. How could I forget?"

"Well, as you know, the system always had the ability to connect apparently discontiguous points; that is, the College's Toy already connects Point A to Point C without passing through Point B—except it's not exactly like that, because the universe doesn't have lines and points but everything's in a fluid matrix— but it's a predictable matrix ..."

"I'm completely lost," Dale said, yawning.

"That's nice," Barth said to Dale, and yawned, too. Fred, however, saw a certain tension in his muscles and sparks in his eyes. "So, Points A and C can virtually connect. Big deal. Tell me something new."

"Listen!" Fred leaned forward. "I can make the Toy connect to Earth! Physically, not just virtually!"

"Whew, Fred!" Dale exclaimed, sitting up.

"Does Dr. Zadok know?" Barth asked casually.

"Nope."

Despite the music and much conversation in the Red Oak Tavern, their area seemed intensely silent.

"The key," Fred added, "is this: I, the lowly engineer, learned everything there is to know about The Hot Marble, the *noretha*, the guidance tool that connects Lanthra to Earth. I even know how to make a copy!"

There—a definite attentiveness from Barth. The long legs drew up and the big man sat forward. Dale and Sia's mouths hung open at the mention of the forbidden planet.

Sia whispered, "Is His Excellency is planning to get help from Earth? Is he out to conquer Lanthra with Earth's weapons or something? After all, Earth people don't have those stupid controls on technology."

"Sounds right!" Dale said, looking from side to side to make sure no one was listening. "Our High Magus's new slogan: Down with the Horned Edge and every upstart that doesn't recognize him as the supreme authority! All power to the Old Order of the Magi!"

Barth leaned forward and spoke in a soft voice. "Can you show it to me?"

"What?" Fred played stupid. "Uh, the hot marble?"

Barth's eyes glinted. "Not only the marble. The thoyo-on—the sonic computer, the whole system."

Fred decided to divulge some little-known information. "The Toy? They are taking it apart. It will be shipped to Kingsport, in just a couple of days."

"Really!" Barth considered. He said softly, "So soon ..." Obviously thinking hard, he tapped his mug rhythmically. "Fred, can you get me into the laboratory? Tonight?"

"Uhhh, no, I can't." Fred made his eyes look round and innocent. "Dr. Zadok says that I'm *persona non grata* outside of my regular day shift. But Lewis can."

"Hmmm," Barth leaned back, still twiddling the mug.

Fred shook his head slowly. He said, "The door's been re-coded. *True.* They don't trust me enough anymore to put my face and voice on the 'open' list at night." *False, but Barth doesn't have to know that.*

"Yes," Barth nodded. "I understand. My face and voice used to open it before …" His eyes gleamed with an old memory and narrowed with anger.

"Yep, Lewis can open the door." Fred drank more of his ale. He was beginning to feel light-headed. Getting drunk felt good. Getting rid of Lewis would feel good. He even imagined Barth killing Lewis once he was no longer useful.

"So, where do I find him?"

Impulsively, Fred pulled out a key. "Here—this is the key to our room in the dormitory. Lewis will definitely be there tonight. You can ask him to help you get into the laboratory and do whatever you want to do. Later, though, I want to go with you wherever you take those parts."

Barth took the key and nodded. "Sure," he said with a red-lipped smile, "you can come with us to Tor."

"Hey, there's the waiter over there, if you're ready to order food," Dale said. Fred nodded, and Dale held up two fingers, catching the eye of a waiter across the room.

Fred belched.

CHAPTER 28
KIDNAPPED

As he and Patrick left the Gregory's house after dinner, Lewis said, "When we get to the dorm, Patrick, we'll have time for a round of *Ta-on Cilathanx-boz* and then we'll tell ghost stories." He felt a smile in his heart.

"Wildcats and Wolves!" Patrick's eyes gleamed behind the new glasses. "You have the cards for that game?"

"Sure. I bought them so you and I could play tonight."

"Wow! That's great!"

The lane turned into the main street. In the moonlight, away down the hill, they could see the whole scenic Loudmouth River valley. Silver mist draped the pasturelands, rising, thickening; cool, moist air settled onto their clothes and skin … Lewis was glad that he and Patrick wore their cloaks. Clopping on the pavement in his sturdy boots, his new green cloak flapping, Patrick chattered happily. "Mackerel sky, mackerel sky, may be rain, may be dry," The boy knowingly pointed upward. Lewis followed his gesture and saw fish-scale clouds shining under the bright moons, one full and the other half-full. Stars peeked in and out through the exquisite silvery patterns. There was a shining halo around the brightest, orange-tinged moon. *"Lanthrin e' sewega,"* Patrick said in the Lanthran language. "I see a ring around the moon. The clouds, the ring around the moon, the mist—they all mean it's going to rain tomorrow."

"For a ten-year-old kid going on thirty, you're an excellent weather scientist," Lewis said, impressed. In the lamplight he could see his brother's wavy dark hair, level dark brows, intelligent brown eyes, and rounded face. Patrick hopped from topic to topic, and the whole picture he painted was "I'm excited and happy."

"Mark talked about a magic cave …" Patrick was saying. "Honest—it's magic! He wasn't joking!"

"What cave?" Lewis asked. "The *last* thing I want is for you to wander into a cave—magic or not!"

"Well, here's what Mark says: The cave has passages right under the city. There's a way to get in somewhere inside the College, and Mark says that you can travel in secret for miles and miles under the mountains."

"So, what makes it magic?"

"He said that it's a 'good' place. Bezubs have never been in there, and people who go inside are always safe. Hey, Lewis, do you believe in magic?"

"Uhhh," Lewis said. The question caught him off guard. His brother looked at him, waiting for an answer, and to his surprise, Lewis found himself revealing some very personal thoughts.

"I truly don't know if a hidden, spiritual world is real like atoms and stars, rocks and trees. Maybe religion and magic are just fantasy, a construct for fun or even comfort. Maybe it's like the dragon trapped inside my soul. Okay, *that* sounds like magic, but it's not exactly. It's just a strong desire I feel in my heart that won't go away. My mind says it is impractical, a waste of time and effort, but the dragon twists and struggles, fighting to spread its wings and fly."

The boy's eyes widened even more with bewilderment. "A dragon in your soul?" he exclaimed.

Lewis had an "oops" moment. *My secret is out.*

"Yes, Patrick," he said, fantasizing a bit, "I have a big dragon in my soul. It's gold with red and blue scales on its underside. It sleeps inside me like it's curled up on a treasure, and it breathes fire at me when I try to make it go away."

Patrick looked up at him, cupping his chin, trying to understand.

Lewis saw Patrick's round-eyed joy and amazement, and, for this brief moment, Lewis felt that the relationship between himself and his brother was in perfect harmony. "The dragon," he said, "is time-travel."

*　　*　　*

"We're here," Lewis said. They had come to the university gate. "*Bimi*; may we pass?"

The owlish young woman magus on duty in the lighted stone booth looked up from her book. She waved at them to pass, and answered, "*Forallanoye!*"

Lewis said, "*Golanoya.*" He heard the chiming of small bells, and again, as always, he felt amazement as the hard stone under the arch of the gate vanished. When they entered the passageway through the thick wall, Lewis breathed deeply, enjoying the moist odor of ancient stone and damp moss.

Patrick whispered, "Would the gate open for me like it does for you and her?"

"No. It only opens for authorized people. My voice—my very being—tells the gate that I'm here and that it's okay to open up."

"So, it can smell you," Patrick paraphrased.

"Something like that."

Coming out into the university grounds, they followed the paved road unto the venerable park. The air was still, but frost fell, and they shivered. "All right, bro', let's get inside and have fun." As they approached the dormitory, the lamplight showed Patrick looking at him with merry, sparkling eyes. He teased gleefully, "I saw the way you and Deirdre looked at each other, Lewis. You've got it bad. 'First comes love, then comes – '"

"Cut it out, Patrick," Lewis interrupted, "We're not to that point … yet. Besides, wait until you're twenty-something and an amazing, beautiful woman comes your way!"

"Me? Kiss girls?" Patrick said with disdain, wrinkling his nose. "Yuck!"

They took the path to the right, past a row of hawthorns, toward the dormitory buildings. A bell rang solemnly four times, the clear, deep tone rising from the chapel below the university campus. "It's the fourth hour—about ten o'clock, Earth time," Lewis said.

"I'm hungry," Patrick complained as they neared the dormitory where Lewis lived.

"Already?" Lewis said. "All right—we'll stop by the common room."

"The common room? What's that?"

Lewis answered, happy to share this part of his life with his brother, "It's like a medieval dining hall. The common room is a long, vaulted-ceilinged place with huge wood beams and hanging lights. The people at the college eat meals there, or play games, or just talk. There's a fire going night and day with a big kettle of hot water to make tea and a small barrel near the hearth that's always full of crisp crackers. We'll stop there, get some crackers and tea, hang out, and then we'll go up to my room and play games. If you're still hungry, we can go to the kitchen and sneak a pie."

"Will Fred be there?"

Lewis felt a jolt in his heart. He had been so happy that he had forgotten his argument with Fred. "Not tonight," he answered. The boy looked disappointed but did not ask questions.

The path led around the side of a long brownstone building. Ahead, lighted by the entrance lamp, they could see the building's welcoming porch. "Hey, Lewis, this is really great! Thanks for bringing me here!"

"Well, yeah! I'm proud to bring my brother to my castle."

Under the porch's eaves were rocking chairs and a large

white bench swing, ready—once the weather warmed—for students to enjoy conversation and laughter. Already many daffodils and narcissus were poking up in a garden planted with flowering azaleas, lilacs, and rhododendrons. Tonight, the rhododendrons seemed very dark, and even the daffodils looked gray and hard to see because the mist had thickened, blurring outlines and diffusing the moonlight.

As he and Patrick neared the front door, Lewis heard a friendly shout.

"Hey, Louie!"

Surprised, he and Patrick stopped. Lewis looked around. "Fred?" he called.

A motion caught his eye. Around to the right, near the rhododendrons, he saw a big man, Fred's size and shape. His bulk was barely visible at the edge of the lamplight. *Maybe he's gotten over his grudge,* Lewis hoped.

At his side, Patrick whispered playfully, "This mist reminds me of a story from Sherlock Holmes or Fu Manchu … The evil assassin lurks in the darkness, preparing to pounce on his victims."

"Hush, Patrick," Lewis said, and he shivered.

They heard again the friendly call, "Come on over! I've got something special to show you!"

"Hey, that's great!" Patrick exclaimed. "Maybe Fred can play Wildcats and Wolves with us!"

As he and Patrick walked around to the side of the dormitory, Lewis remembered Fred's belly laughs, the way he made the whole room feel bigger and brighter with his humor. *Yes, it would feel good to have Fred with Patrick and me.*

Parked by the laundry entrance stood a high-walled cart. A large, patient horse with wispy fetlocks like a Clydesdale stood in the cart harness, swishing its tail. "Maybe Fred's planned a midnight ride!" Patrick exclaimed. "It's just like Fred to think of something fun like that!"

"Maybe, bro'," Lewis answered. However, the whole scene

made no sense. In the daytime, perhaps, the few students who were left would be hauling their stuff out of the dorm, preparing to go home or to Bardia's quintennial celebration, but not on this cold, misty night. He and Patrick walked closer. Lewis saw no hay in the cart, only a large canvas stretched over the top. It occurred to him what Fred was doing, and his happiness vanished. He thought, with a surge of anger, *Fred, you stubborn ring-tailed bandicoot! You don't care about Patrick; you're still angry and you're moving out! You are such a jerk!*

Patrick exclaimed, "Fred! I was hoping to see you!"

Patrick's joy only reinforced the anger spreading through Lewis's chest. "Say, Fred!" he demanded, walking up, "What's going on? Because Patrick and I—"

He stopped. "Oh, hello," he said uncomfortably. The big man was Fred's friend, Barth Layhew. No one else in Nutman had forearms the size of tree trunks. The wiry dark person in a tall, shapeless hat must be Sia. The other two men, one tall and lanky, the other tall and broad, were people he had never met before. They loomed in the darkness. Alarmed now, Lewis put out his hand to slow Patrick.

"Stay, Louie; we'd like your help tonight," Barth said.

Squirming inside, like he'd reached into the cookie jar but felt something slimy instead, Lewis asked, "What do you want?"

Barth's heavy hand clapped him on the shoulder. Lewis could smell liquor and smoke. He tried to brush off the unwelcome touch, but the other man's hand gripped tighter. "Who is the boy, Louie?"

"My brother, Patrick," Lewis snapped. "You already met him at dinner at the Gregory's. He tore his shoulder out of Barth's grip. "Sorry, we can't help you. 'Bye."

Putting his own hand protectively on Patrick's shoulder, he steered his brother around Barth and toward the door. However, with every step, the air felt colder and colder. *Why is it so hard to walk forward?* An unfriendly, invisible presence blocked him and

Patrick from the shelter of the building. *What is this?* Lewis's stomach wrenched, then tightened, ready for danger.

A grip like a giant lobster claw seized his right wrist and pulled it behind his back, and a big, hot hand clamped shut his mouth. Yet, after the first panic, Lewis compressed his fear. Time slowed down. Every second became a millisecond. He planned every move, and very coldly, he pictured: *First, I will jerk backward and break Barth's teeth with my head. Then, swiveling to the right, I'll crash my free hand into Barth's nose. Meanwhile, Patrick can run.*

However, Barth whispered curtly, "If you make one move, we'll cut the boy's throat."

Horror broke the ice in his heart. With great effort, he slumped submissively into Barth's grip.

Still holding Lewis's mouth tightly so that he could hardly breathe, Barth swiveled him so that he could see Patrick. The lanky man held a long, gleaming fillet knife under the boy's ear, and with the other hand, stifled the boy's mouth. Lanky Man hissed, "*Vitya e'gola famor ea.*"

Although his body was gripped fast by Bart's arms and his heart was racing, Lewis's mind became cool again. In a flash, he calculated his options again to rescue Patrick. *It still might be possible ...* He could kick the knife out of Lanky Man's hand ... He might be able to shove his fingers up Barth's nostrils and tear his nose off his fat face.

No, I can't let myself do that. No matter how hard I fight, I cannot stop Lanky Man's knife before its sharp edge slices Patrick from ear to ear. Lewis's heart was forced open, terror flattened his mind into a screen, and an evil controller played a horrible movie that he could not block out as, in slow motion, Lewis pictured the knife blade razor through Patrick's windpipe. Blood spurted out of the boy's mouth; he struggled; the light faded from his brown eyes.

Chuckling as if he knew Lewis's thoughts, Lanky Man bared

his teeth and flicked the knife just enough back and forth against Patrick's throat so that Lewis could see light reflecting from its sharp blade.

In that instant, Lewis's self-restraint snapped. He leaped backward, bucking against Barth's control. His head banged Barth's jaw with a loud thud. Barth roared but held on. Lewis banged Barth again, twisting like an angry bull in a rodeo stall, kicking at Barth's shins with his heels, dislodging the grip on his mouth and arm.

Barth stumbled. Big Fellow snarled. Sia leaped to the cart and grabbed a length of rope. However, Lanky Man with the knife merely sneered, and Barth quickly recovered. "So … you want to kill your brother?" Barth asked, breathing hard.

Lewis felt every muscle tense, taut as a bowstring, but there were no new options. Taking a deep breath to steady himself, he forced himself once more to relax. Coldly and quietly, he said, "In this case, it appears courage means keeping still. All right. I won't fight."

"Good, good," Barth breathed, frosty puffs coming out of his mouth. "Now maybe you can keep your brother alive."

Lewis saw Patrick looking in every direction, wide-eyed, hoping for help, but they were alone in the misty night with these violent men and the thick, malignant cancerous presence. Lewis sighed deeply. "Patrick, calm down. Just … rest. You'll be okay."

Barth gripped Lewis's arm. "Help me control this guy, Jack. He's a smart guy, but he still might be stupid enough to fight." Big Fellow Jack added his considerable weight to pinion Lewis, while Kut pushed a gag into Patrick's throat, tied his hands and feet, and tossed the boy into the cart under the canvas.

"This is what you have to do," Barth said, after Patrick was hidden. He and Jack let go of him, and Lewis stepped away, breathing hard. Even though his insides wanted to lash out, he made himself relax. *I will not fight. Patrick must be safe.*

"You and Sia and I are going into the locating chamber," said

Barth. "You will open the door. You will help us pack up some select parts."

"And then?" Lewis asked, trying to keep his voice from shaking.

"And all the time we're inside, you'll mind yourself, because if we don't come out with the right materials, Kut will cut your brother's throat." Barth chuckled. "And, because you've been working with the whole system, and I did work in the laboratory, we'll know what to get."

Stiffly, Lewis jerked his head in acquiescence.

"Louie Boy, get up with me on the front, and we'll head for the laboratory building," Barth ordered, breathing a noxious cloud of ale-breath into Lewis's face. Jack asked a question in Lanthran, and Barth replied slowly and nastily in English, "Yes. Saoma can have him later."

Lewis breathed hard, guessing what that meant. It sounded horrible. *Human sacrifice to a demon?*

Lewis climbed onto the cart. Barth and Sia joined him so that Lewis was squashed in the middle of the buckboard between them; Jack and Kut got under the canvas with Patrick. Sia clucked to the horse, and the cart moved forward.

CHAPTER 29
DEATH IN THE DARK

Nine people are dead because I opened the door, Lewis screamed to himself.

As Barth drove Lewis and the others away from the College of the Magi, cartwheels creaked, and the hard-wooden floor bounced. Lewis sat up front, and Patrick lay tied up under a canvas in the back, along with stolen parts of the magi's locating system and a homicidal manic with a sharp knife.

I could have refused to help the enemy. That's my noble, patriotic duty. But then these vermin would have killed Patrick. Instead, I chose to aid and abet the enemy, hoping that Patrick will live.

Although his body shook with suppressed rage, he could not change anything. He been had caught in a double bind: Damned if you do, and damned if you don't. And now he was nine times damned, plus a traitor.

"Bless you, Saoma," Barth said reverently once the cart had pulled over into a dark side street. "Let me give you gifts." His voice changed to sarcasm. "Now, Louie boy, let's get you into the cart with your brother and Kut."

This time, Lewis could not control his fear. He shook all over. Sia and Jack bound him with cord. The constraints on his body fed his fear. Sia forced a handkerchief into his mouth, and he was so ashamed of himself that he was ready to vomit or pee. For the first time in his life, his knees turned to jelly as Barth and Jack shoved him into the cart and covered him with the canvas.

Meanwhile, the evil in the night only escalated as Lewis felt a pocket of invisible, purposeful malice envelop him. Its unwelcome touch chilled his very bones, promising more horror to come. His shaking got worse; his body literally rattled.

At first, his mind was paralyzed. But, after too short a while, it wheeled too fast. Silently, Lewis shrieked at God or whoever else was in charge of the universe: *Why did you let this happen!*

No answer. He pictured what had happened after he'd spoken the words that opened the laboratory to these men. Lewis did not want to remember, but he did anyway. Surrender. Bondage. Sliced throats. Nine people had been murdered, and the consequences were unforgivable.

*   *   *

Pain began. Sia's hankie in his mouth tasted sweet and slimy; it drew saliva, and he couldn't stop that any more than he could stop the cart or untie himself. Regurgitating, Lewis swallowed over and over to keep from choking, but there was no release from the gag. The cords on the hands and ankles dug into his skin. Every bump of the cart knocked his left thigh into a sharp edge of a stolen sonic computer part.

Also, he could not sense any presence of Patrick. *Oh, God! Is Patrick dead?* He kept picturing Lanky Man's knife slicing his brother's throat, then dumping the body somewhere. *God, no! Don't let Patrick be dead! Kill me; send me to hell—but let him be alive.*

Lewis's nose itched. He smelled dusty crates, a hint of farmyard, a reek of fear, a tang of sweat, plus one of the captors stank, probably Kut who lay near him in the cart. The man smelled as if he had forgotten to wipe himself.

Second by second—after railing at God, he began to feel in

control again.

And he got an idea.

Their first stop would be at the university gate. Lewis knew that Barth would ring the bell for the magus gatekeeper—Neah had this shift—who could speak the night password for them … or she could also call the College militia. This would be a good time to make a little "accidental" noise. *A muffled bump from my feet or head should be enough to startle her. If I can get her suspicious enough to report to security, it's possible that the city guards will stop these creeps before we get out of the city.* The idea filled him with hope.

As he expected, when the cart stopped, Lewis heard the bell ring for the gatekeeper. He heard a routine "*Golanoya*" from the other side of the thick wall. Yes, it sounded like Neah, distracted. When he smelled the cold, moist stone as the cart passed through the gateway, he decided, *It's time to make the noise.* With a thump, his boots beat on the cart's floor.

Get suspicious! He tried to urge telepathically. *But hide it, or they'll kill you!*

"*Te forabag e'oy?*" he heard the young woman's voice call.

Barth's confident reply chilled him again to the bone: "What are we hauling? Come and see."

Don't get out of the gatehouse, Neah!

However, Neah's soft footsteps approached the cart.

"Come and look," Barth's smooth voice enticed. "Inside is a bitch with puppies. They're just a few weeks old."

Lewis groaned. One of the oldest tricks on Earth for molesters to use was the "come see the puppy" trick. Had no one ever given this woman any personal safety training? *No. Lanthra typically doesn't have molesters—that's an Earth thing.*

The cart rocked as Barth descended. He heard footsteps coming around toward him, Barth's heavy and Neah's light and quick. Barth happily described the puppies—six of them, fluffy and roly-poly—and he heard a pleased anticipation in the young woman's voice when she began to raise the tarp. Suddenly, her voice cut off, immediately followed by a horrible choking noise.

Oh, God, no! Barth's killing her!

There was nothing Lewis could do. Choking noises continued, followed at last by a crack and a thud. Once again, cold terror set in. He desperately tried to control his bladder and his bowels.

That scraping ... he's stuffing her body back in the gatehouse, no doubt arranging it so that she looks like she's still reading her book.

The cart swayed as Barth mounted once more. Barth's cold voice punched down in a nasty tone, "I know that noise came from you, Louie Boy. You made me kill that innocent woman. And you made me kill those magi when we got the parts out of the laboratory. They would have thought we were just helping them dissemble the system like Dr. Zadok ordered, if you hadn't tried to warn them. If it weren't for you, those kids would still be alive. Don't make a noise like that again, stupid, or your little brother will be next."

The cart bumped and rattled down Nutman's steep hill until it reached the city gate. Lewis could hear Old John's voice grouching at having to open the gate this late at night. With all the strength he had, Lewis tried to keep still; however, he mentally pleaded, *Please stop this, Old John! Complain, old man! If ever there was a time to be obstinate and suspicious, it's now! Oh, please, please, ring the alarm, call the garrison; send up a flare— just help Patrick and me, for God's sake!*

But Old John opened the gate. Soon the squeak and groan of the portcullis raising came to Lewis's ears. *Old John, what's the matter with you? You're not supposed to let late-night travelers in or out without informing the city guards ... Or are you somehow involved with these people?*

The cart swayed as they started off again. With creaking and clattering, the gate lowered behind them. The horse clopped and the cart thumpty-thumped across the bridge over the gurgling Loudmouth River and headed on into the night.

CHAPTER 30
FRED IS ARRESTED

There was one, just one more concert before the city was emptied. Fred leaned on the leather-covered round table in the Red Oak Tavern and listened to the conversation buzz. He saw that there were many empty tables compared to the usual crowd, but everyone was eagerly awaiting the Bard of Bardia's final performance in Nutman.

Fred bent his head to sip his beer. *When will Barth and Sia come and get me? Surely, they're done raiding the laboratory now. I hope that they used Lewis; I hope the guy is dead! But Barth said he'd be here by midnight. Where is he?* His head felt light and filled with fuzz—maybe it was just the beer. He wasn't drunk yet, but he planned to be quite drunk in a few hours if Barth didn't show up.

Already slow and uncoordinated, his friend Dale waved an unsteady hand in the air at Fred. "Hey, you *Cilanthoon*! You almost knocked over my mug! You're supposed to put the drink to your face, not your face to the drink!"

"Just my Jolly Jontz nature," Fred replied amiably with artificial good humor. Inside, he felt poisoned daggers barbing him from within. He wanted to use them to prick Dale, but then he'd lose an important ally, so he squashed his vindictiveness and took another drink to try to dull the pain. "Which reminds me …

How many Polunks does it take to change a light bulb?"

Dale shook his head, which wobbled on his neck like a gourd on a stalk.

Fred belched, grinned, and pulled out the punch line: "Five. One on the ladder, and four more to turn the room around." He laughed merrily at his own joke.

Dale looked puzzled. "What's a light bulb?"

The joke fizzled and died.

"You don't know what a light bulb is?" Fred asked incredulously. He made his voice dark with sarcasm, to make Dale feel as stupid as possible.

"Sorry," Dale replied. "Never heard of one."

Fred remembered belatedly, *Oh yeah, this stupid world has a ban on electronic technology—except for the precious magi.* He fell silent and tossed back another long swallow of beer. Now his head was buzzing like a hive full of bees. Was it just the many conversations around him?

"Why have a concert when the city is practically empty?" Fred asked. "Is the Bard crazy?"

A grizzled bearded man nearby leaned close. In heavily accented English, Grizzle Face—*the old coot!*—answered, "Sir Thomas follows us like a shepherd. I'm going to the Forschwynn province tomorrow to celebrate the founding of Bardia! How about you?"

"I'm going to Kingsport." Fred's answer was curt and rude. He craned his neck to see over people's heads to the stage. Two women placed stools on the platform, set up the sound panes that they used for amplifiers, and hung extra lamps on the Shaker style pegs that lined the walls near the stage.

"Finally! Is the Forschwynn boy performing at last? No more warm-ups?"

"Dunno," Dale said.

Fred caught a glint in the man's eyes that caused him to wonder if the man was as drunk as he appeared to be. He didn't want to meet Dale's gaze, so he stared into the circular maw of his mug, swirling the gold-brown liquid around, thinking, *I wish my head would quiet down. What does Dale think about me? Is the man laughing at me?*

Bringing his buzzing head up again, Fred carefully surveyed the room. Barth and Sia were nowhere to be found. *Never mind—they are probably still raiding Zadok's laboratory. In another hour, they should be here. By tomorrow, I'll be well away and off to Tor!*

Slowly, so not to attract attention, he slid his hand down into his pants pocket. Yes, it was safe: He felt the hard little object wrapped in a handkerchief—a new hot marble. This one he had made himself. It was a duplicate of the one that opened a corridor to Earth, a beautiful amber nugget that would lead him to fame and fortune.

Fred thought wistfully, *It could have helped Gracie and Patrick get home, but it's too late for that now.* Tossing away the loneliness, he ruffled through his plan. He would go to Tor. In Moorway, he'd show his amazing exhibit to get into Lord Charon's good graces and become the master engineer for his locating system. Then, he'd become a liaison from Charon to Earth—and maybe other worlds, too. He'd be important. He'd get glory. Maybe, if everything worked out right, he could get Patrick and Gracie safely back home.

The sound of skilled music cut off his reverie. Tom Forschwynn was up on the stage. *Imagine, all that talent, and the kid's only nineteen,* Fred thought jealously. The lanterns around the platform favored Tom's black hair and happy smile. *He is a handsome guy, too. I bet all the girls go ga-ga over him.*

Tom led them into songs about Bardian history, and soon a crackle of national fervor filled the tavern. Even Fred got caught up in it. After a while, Fred came back to the present and noticed that his mug was dry. Dale had drunk, not only his own beer, but the rest of Fred's—*the jerk!*

During a lull in the singing, Grizzle Face leaned toward him again. In Lanthran he began a conversation, as if he were a self-appointed teacher of the ignorant. Fred despised being singled out as a foreigner, but he could not hide his poor Lanthran nor stop the other man from talking. Some of the sentences among the garbled flow that he understood were: "Tom Forschwynn is the direct descendant of The Bard that founded Bardia. He's the heir of a very wealthy family, but he's chosen to perform the Bard's magic."

"Yeah, I already heard that before," Fred answered callously in English. He didn't care if the man understood him or not; in fact, he wished the old guy would shut up.

Instead, Grizzle Face leaned closer. He lowered his voice and said in very good English, "He's holding the *biliterad,* the original lute. There are some that say that as long as there is a Bard to play the lute, his Spirit heals Bardia."

Oh, really? Fred thought, disgusted. *Spirit? There is no spirit. You're all deluding yourselves, mates. Bardia isn't protected. The ceiling is going to fall on top of you when the Torish finally invade, and I won't be around to see it.*

He stood up, ready to go. To Dale he said, "I've gotta make a trip. Be back later."

Dale waved a casual hand at him. On the stage, Tom started a new song.

Fred pushed his way through the crowd. Looking back, he saw that his empty seat had been snatched by a dark-haired woman in a frilly red dress. His so-called friend Dale eyed her speculatively. His fingers began to smooth his moustache and straighten his collar. The chick's bosom swelled prettily, and her hand already lay on his arm.

Fred turned and made his way toward the exit.

At that time, Tom briefly adjusted the tuning of his lute, and began to improvise.

Despite himself, Fred stopped to listen. The sound was

mellower and deeper than he had ever heard it. He felt wonder that the kid could make the instrument sing with so many voices. *Mellow as a cello,* he thought to himself. *But spirit? Healing? What in the heck does that mean?*

Tom looked up, somehow caught Fred's eyes, and smiled. Fred started. *How did he pick me out of the crowd?*

Fred turned to leave, but stumbled over somebody's foot, and knocked over a dish of nuts, which scattered all over the floor. Grumbling an apology, he righted himself. A new, large group of people came in, blocked his way, and there was no way he could get to the door. Fred was trapped until the bard finished this number and people began to move around a little bit.

Although the Tom's song was in old Lanthran, Fred found that he understood every word. Somehow the meaning cut through the buzz in his head and sank deep into his mind.

> *Dry, as withered as the blasted fig tree,*
> *I bear no fruit for hungry travelers.*
> *How can you, when I am so utterly empty,*
> *Command I feed your winter followers?*
> *"Rise up," you said. "In season, out of season,*
> *Produce fruit."*
> *I'm out of season, Lord.*
> *My leaves are curled, brittle; my sap is stilled in its*
> run,
> *I cannot force my natural cycle forward.*
> *If my withered roots are in the water of your well,*
> *Deep Spring, will you, eternal living drink,*
> *Refresh the dead? Can you this cursed tree renew*
> *And make parched limbs their benefactor thank?*
> *Unseasonably my fruit shall give someone repast*
> *Should it be done to me as I have asked!*

All at once, like ice evaporating in a blast of steam, the buzzing in his head left him. Oddly, he remembered himself as a young boy, fighting with his mother who was trying to force a coat on him and slapping him in the face, while her current boyfriend yelled and swore at him in the background.

Then a voice deep in his head told him. *It's not over. You are only beginning to feel your place in this story.*

He snarled at the voice, *Get out of my head. I'm leaving. I'm going to Tor, and you can't stop me.*

You will go to Torpatath, the voice replied. *But not the way you have planned.*

He suddenly felt confused and afraid. Suppose his plans went wrong and he missed his ride with Barth Layhew? He had burnt his bridges in Bardia—he'd have no place to go! He'd have to hide out here and probably get caught in the invasion. Or, he'd have to scramble to some other country where he didn't know anyone. He should run right now. The hell with Barth.

Why don't you quit fighting me? said the voice. *Wouldn't you like to have something to hope for?*

"I am the way I am," Fred replied out loud.

Suppose you could believe that you are loved through all your anger and your failures? the insistent voice continued. *Suppose you could let me make you a new person?*

"Not me," Fred sneered. "Besides, what do you mean by 'a new person?'" A woman with a sharp nose turned around to look at him, so he quit talking aloud.

The bard's song ended. Generous applause filled the room as Sir Thomas stood up and bowed.

With a vast sigh, Fred turned away and shoved his elbow through the crowd to make his way toward the door. He gave the doorman his chit from Daniel. "Here, take it. Pay for drinks around the house. One drink—no, two drinks for everyone."

The doorman looked surprised, then pleased, and accepted the piece of paper.

Outside the tavern, the night air was cool on his face. More people were headed in; he was the only one heading out.

"Fred Jontz?" asked a man with a deep, sinister voice.

The stranger who confronted him wore a black cloak. He had very prominent front teeth, side-whiskers, and big ears. Fred thought he looked like a great bat.

"Yeah," he answered roughly. "Who are you? What do you want?"

"I'm Hermann, an agent of the military magi, a servant of the High Magus, and you are under arrest."

CHAPTER 31

CONDEMNED

Fred halted in the circle of light under the entrance lantern. Behind Big Bat were four other men, Very Large Guys. They had their hands on the hilts of their swords, and they carried clubs at their belts. He saw from their brown uniforms and oak leaf insignia that they were indeed the military magi. His stomach sank. *I'm screwed.*

At that moment, Tom Forschwynn came out of the tavern, his lute in a case slung over his shoulder. With a sharp look at Fred and the men surrounding him, he asked, "*Unsaoye, Hermanne?*"

Hermann replied in Lanthran, with deference in his voice, that it was none of the bard's business.

"Let me come with you," Tom said in clear English.

"*Vina?*" asked Hermann, his hands rising in exasperation.

"Because His Excellency has requested that I talk to this man, and this is my first opportunity," the bard replied. Turning to Fred, the kid said, "We've met, I think. I am Sir Thomas Forschwynn—"

"So I've heard," Fred growled. "In fact, you let me do a prologue performance … never mind."

"I think I can help you," Tom said. In the yellow glow of the lamplight, he looked like a college student at a trendy coffeehouse: Medium height, medium build, good-looking innocent face, and the graceful posture of long-time aristocracy.

"No thanks. I don't want help from nice rich boys."

However, when Herman and the uniformed quartet of guards marched him off, the kid followed in smooth andante.

There seemed to be a furor at the university gate. Fred saw the taut jaws and the lowered eyebrows of the guards surrounding him and wondered what was going on. A cluster of lanterns illuminated the entrance more than usual, and at least a dozen military swarmed around the gatehouse. Fred saw them lift a body wrapped in a black cloth. They laid it onto a stretcher. Its arms and legs hung limply like a scarecrow's, showing slender wrists and ankles. When a fold of the blanket fell away, Fred saw a woman's face. "She's Neah! What happened?" he exclaimed. He knew Neah; she was the campus night gate guard, the one who studied all the time. Her puce complexion, bulging eyes, and swollen purple tongue told him that she had been strangled. His gorge rose, and he swallowed back the harsh bile.

Oh my God, he thought. *Did Barth do that to her?*

He felt sick to his stomach. *If Barth did this, then I'm in deep doo-doo.*

*   *   *

The guards pulled Fred to a stop at the High Magus's oak door. One rang a bell. Its solemn *dong* slowly faded, and they waited for permission to enter. *This is it,* Fred thought. *This is where I get what's coming to me.* Afraid he was going to retch, he twisted, and seeing his movement, two of the guards clamped their hands on Fred's arms, restraining their prisoner as if he might become violent. *At least,* he thought, with a splash of shame, *they haven't used handcuffs or chains on me—yet.*

An answering voice sounded from Daniel's office, so they entered the anteroom. Like monsters, their huge shadows sneaked across the walls.

Through the doorway into the office, Fred saw His Excellency. The little man sat at his writing desk. A candle lamp burned at his left, and behind him one lamp in a sconce backlit his hair into a golden halo. Daniel wrote, his pen scratching on paper with large, fluent movements. He did not raise his head when Hermann cleared his throat to announce their presence.

"I have the prisoner, as you ordered, Your Excellency," the vampirish Hermann said in Lanthran. He used a hushed, museum voice.

Fred winced as the guards' hands gripped him tightly.

"Bring him inside." Daniel waved his hand slightly without looking up.

Surrounded and clamped firmly by guards, Fred stood in front of the viceroy's desk. The Forschwynn kid entered the office, but stood in a corner, his face shadowed. A sickle of moonlight shone through the great bay window. It looked like the scythe of Death.

"Hermann, leave Fred here. You and the guards will wait just outside, in the secretary's office," the Daniel ordered.

Reluctantly, the guards' hands released Fred's arms. Hermann bowed. Giving Fred a distrustful glance, he and the guards filed out again.

"Close the door, Hermann," called Daniel. He did not look at any of them.

Hermann threw a troubled and suspicious look at Fred.

Go hang upside-down from a ceiling somewhere, you ugly rodent, Fred thought nastily.

The black-robed, buck-toothed man slowly pulled the door shut, leaving the High Magus, Fred, and Tom alone. A few muffled noises from the anteroom told Fred that Hermann and the guards planned to stay near at hand in case the prisoner got unruly.

Fred shuffled his feet, his stomach crawling with fear, but Daniel still did not look up. The candlelight showed that his mouth was set in a grim line as he wrote. A muscle worked in his temple. Tom stood quietly in his corner, lute over his shoulder, a dark silhouette. No one spoke for a long time.

Fred waited, a tide of fear rising. He tried to swallow, but his throat was tight. Finally, Daniel scrawled a signature on a letter. The little man's cold gray eyes met his.

"Who have you been talking to, Fred, and what did you tell them?"

"What do you mean?" Fred began to bluster.

Daniel's eyes were so cold and angry that Fred stopped, mouth open. A cold prickle started up his spine and continued into the hairs on his neck. "What …" he licked his lips, "happened?"

The terrifying sub-zero aura around the High Magus scared him to pieces. This man could order his execution, and there would be no appeal. That letter might be his execution order. They could hang him tonight, right here in this building. No wonder the shadows were full of whispering spooks. He could imagine the ropes binding his hands, a noose tightening around his neck. He gulped. Cold sweat dripped from his brow, but he was afraid to wipe it off in front of those chilly gray eyes.

"Ten people have been murdered, including the young woman whose body you no doubt noticed when you came in the university gate," Daniel said.

"Ten!" Fred licked his dry lips.

Daniel's back was straight and tense as the blade of a knife, and his voice had a cutting edge. "Someone broke into the locating chamber. The recordings show that Lewis opened the chamber, but the tension in his voice indicates that he did it under duress. The monsters who entered bound and slit the throats of nine student workers who had been dismantling the locating system. They stole essential parts from the locating apparatus. Apparently, Lewis disabled the alarms for them, again, under duress.

Daniel folded the letter. It lay in his right hand like a loaded pistol, and Fred could not take his eyes off it. "Since the robbery and the murders," Daniel continued, "Lewis and Patrick have disappeared. We have not found their bodies, so there is still some hope that they might be alive."

Fred could hardly breathe. A dreadful voice in his mind said, *You are an accessory to murder, kidnapping, and grand theft, Fred.*

The High Magus minced no words. "I know that those people had inside help. That help was you. You have betrayed your own friends."

Fred's hand jerked toward his pocket. His fingers met the round, smooth surface of the *noretha* he had made—a perfect copy of the hot marble that had brought them here. He'd entertained the idea that he could supplant Lewis, get the kids safely back to Earth, and be their hero. But instead of helping Gracie and Patrick, he'd smashed them with an unhealable wound.

His stomach clenched when he saw Daniel's eyes follow his hand. The ruler continued, his voice even, the words measured and restrained, "What do you have to tell me?"

Fred stuttered, "Y …Your Excellency, I … I didn't know; I mean—I'm sorry—" He wished he could sink into the floor or evaporate like fog.

The curl on Daniel's lips showed his contempt.

Fred swallowed and tried to pretend ignorance, knowing that it was futile. "I heard that Patrick was spending the night with Lewis. I … didn't feel good, so I didn't join them. Aren't they at the dorms?"

"No. Do not pretend you are innocent. Their disappearance, the murders, the stolen equipment, even your betrayal—all these events are part of a well-coordinated plan. I want to hear the truth from you!" The High Magus spoke softly, but the menace in his voice was worse than with shouting. He still held the letter, but Fred saw the man's knuckles whiten with tension.

Fred stared down at the floor, his hands clasping and unclasping. He opened his mouth again, but only the word, "Rats," came out. His inner critic commented, *You are describing yourself. You're a big rat, a nothing, a zero multiplied by zero.*

The silence stretched out, and Daniel waited for him to

answer.

Fred wanted to talk about anything but the poisonous truth. Was there any way, even now, caught in the glare of those ice-cold eyes, that he could squeak safely through this?

He took a deep breath, preparing a lie.

A little voice in his mind whispered, *Don't.*

But I'll die, he inwardly told the voice. *I'm guilty—They will kill me!*

Tell the truth, the voice said.

Fred opened his mouth. He talked. Out poured all his thoughts and actions that had led up to this moment, as the High Magus's cold gray eyes fixed on him.

"Back home, Earth home, I used to feel jealous of Lewis—but only once in a while. I hid it. Then, when we came here, Dr. Zadok was all over Lewis, but I was always the bad guy." Fred gulped, but he continued. "Then … there was Deirdre. The way she looked at Lewis … the way she never looked at me … One night, Lewis brought Deirdre to the Red Oak Tavern. The two of them looked so close, so intimate—that's when I knew that I hated Lewis. The clencher, however, was on the night of the ice storm when Lewis said …"

He closed his eyes tightly and the remembered words ripped out of him verbatim: "Lewis said, 'I've always had to bolster up your shaky self-esteem, build you up, encourage you, avoid criticizing you so you could perform up to your best level.'"

God, he thought, *this is horrible. I've spent my whole life whining.*

His mouth felt dry. He felt like a fish trying to breathe air. But Daniel waited, projecting anger like a towering thundercloud, and Fred kept sweating, shivering, talking, driving nails into his own coffin. "I knew his words were true, so I hated Lewis even more. From that time on, I decided to get even."

Fred stopped and gulped. He remembered how he had been happy to imagine Lewis hurt or dead. Now Lewis and Patrick were missing, and ten people were dead—because of him.

Fred's stomach swooped. *I might as well spill my fat guts.* "I knew Barth was up to something, probably espionage, so I set Lewis up, hoping that Barth would find a way to use Lewis to do his dirty work or even do him in."

"How?"

"This is the strategy that I used: I said that I had figured out how to make your Toy, er, *thoyo-on* connect to Earth, but …" Fred swallowed hard, "I also let Barth know that you are dismantling the Toy and moving it to … Kingsport. I wanted to be indispensable."

Coldly, Daniel said, "Continue."

Fred wished that he could sink through the floor. He had never seen anyone so angry, not even his drugged-up mom. "Er …" he gulped, "I figured that Barth probably intended to steal essential parts before the Toy was packed and gone. I decided to make it easy for him. That way, Barth would be so grateful that he'd take me with him to Tor where I'd be important; I'd get recognized; and I could get rid of Lewis."

"How?" Daniel continued inexorably.

The words croaked out, each an evil frog. "I lied. I said that that my voice couldn't open the chamber door, but that Lewis's voice could. I insinuated that Barth should force Lewis to help him steal the Toy's parts *and* the hot marble, before Zadok could finish packing. I knew he would intercept Lewis. But I forgot that Patrick …"

Fred choked. Tears started in his eyes. *I've murdered them,* he thought, *as sure as if I had slit their throats myself.*

"Thank you so much, visitor from Earth," Daniel spat. "You've not only caused your friends to disappear and ten magi to die, but you've also made it far easier for Charon to invade my province. And how many more innocent people will die after that! Now," he growled, low and soft, "Is there more?" He looked pointedly at Fred's pocket.

Snuffling back tears, Fred drew out his copy of the hot marble. It glowed like an amber jewel on the palm of his hand, and its image reflected in the High Magus's ice-cold eyes.

He blubbered, "You remember the last time I was here in your office? I was too sneaky to tell anyone that I had made another 'hot marble'—but it looks like you guessed anyway. What is so significant about it is this: The very fact that I was able to make the marble means that your system wasn't all that 'legal'; with some adjustments it could have connected to Earth. If your stupid One Law hadn't forbidden you to even try, Lewis and Patrick and Gracie could have gone safely back home by now!"

The reflection of the amber marble jerked upward as Daniel started.

In a controlled voice, each syllable pushed out, Daniel asked, "Does this mean that the *thoyo-on* here in Nutman can—could have connected to Earth?"

Fred nodded, cleared his throat. "Well, right now you can see light and hear sound, but ..." He swallowed, trying to control the hard knot in his throat, suddenly remembering how important it was to these people that their machine *not* connect to Earth. "To transfer any matter the system just needs some resonance tuning. Then it could accommodate the gravitational wave functions of complex subatomic entities, and allow, uh, people and materials to cross over. I just found that out when I made the copy of the marble—and I didn't tell anyone. I wanted to give my knowledge to people who would appreciate me. I planned to take my know-how to Tor, and ..." he swallowed, "the hell with Bardia."

That was it. The truth was out, in all its filthy glory.

Now he would receive whatever punishment the High Magus decided to mete out.

As he fell silent, shaking, Fred counted the many people he had harmed: Lewis, Patrick, Gracie, Deirdre, the Gregory family, the Brahmindura family back on Earth, Neah, and the magi who had been murdered, and their families, and whoever got killed in the future because of his stupid attitude.

He looked at Daniel. In the flickering candlelight, the man's fair, curly hair shimmered in an icy halo. Fred thought the man looked like a smaller version of the angel of death: death in the moonlight, death in the room light. *Now what?* He closed his eyes, waiting for the pronouncement of doom.

A few feet from his right ear, a clear voice said, "May I speak, Your Excellency?"

Fred started, almost falling over. The marble fell out of his hand and rolled to the floor.

In two steps, Sir Thomas Forschwynn drew into the light. Catching up the marble, he bowed low to Daniel. "Viceroy of Rockeerie, High Magus of the Council, may I speak?"

Daniel turned his face toward the young man and gestured. "You may speak."

"Your Excellency," Tom said in a calm, strong voice as if he had been hobnobbing with viceroys and elite magi all his young life, "Breaking the One Law—with all its evil consequences—deserves death."

"Yes."

"Yet, it is possible to redeem the consequences."

Daniel blinked, as if briefly surprised. "True. The consequences can be redeemed, although they cannot be undone."

Tom said earnestly, "As the direct descendent of the Bard of Bardia, it is my task—my whole life's endeavor—to proclaim the redemption of the damned."

Fred saw anger in Daniel's eyes, like the glare at the center of two diamonds. "Look at this, young bard," Daniel said. He snapped his fingers, and Fred nearly jumped out of his skin.

Above them, two small planets shone in the air as one might see them, from orbit: Two spectacular blue jewels wrapped in white clouds. In miniature, Fred watched Lewis, Patrick, Gracie, and himself flowing through a bright fluid from one to the other, and he realized that he was looking at a clip of them being transported from Earth to Lanthra.

Daniel said, deadly serious, "You cannot see them, but the Lords of Space—so their hierarchies are named—also came through that nexus, many of them following you, Mr. Jontz! The *bizeor* live in relationships. Wherever they reside, they stir up every kind of perversion, cruelty, deception, rage, murder, war ..."

Fred saw the bard's hands tighten on his lute. Tom whispered, "I know. But I live to tell about the power of God, not the power of demons." He regarded Fred carefully, just as a doctor might examine a patient with AIDS. "What are you going to do with him?"

The High Magus held up the letter. "This is the order for his execution."

Fred gulped.

"Will he die tonight?" the bard asked.

"No." Daniel put down the letter and rested his hands once more on his desk. "The One Law allows for three days' stay of execution."

Fred's knees wobbled, and he was afraid he might collapse on the carpet right in front of them.

Daniel rang his bell; Hermann and the guards entered his office. They had brought handcuffs. His head drooping and his knees wobbling, Fred submitted to having his hands secured behind his back. The guards took his arms and led him out of the office.

CHAPTER 32

SAOMA'S SHRINE

Much later, Lewis's discomfort level had increased from intolerable to hideously eye-popping horrible. His arms and legs were completely numb. The nasty gag and Kut's butt perfume revolted him so much that he had continually swallowed to keep from vomiting, and now his throat was on fire. Besides that, during the long, bumpy ride, a strand of Kut's long, greasy hair had slipped into one of his nostrils and tickled madly.

The cart stopped. Lewis heard the whir of an owl and the warble of a nightingale. Far away, probably near the Winerush River, a wolf howled. There were other sounds in the forest, rustles of undergrowth, an animal growl and cough, a distant yowl like a big cat in heat. During this time, Lewis's mind surged with pent-up, useless energy, while his body felt galled to a frenzy. He mentally shook a fist at God. *You cannot let them kill Patrick!*

There was no answer.

He called with his mind, feeling a cynical stab in his belly, *Where are you now, God? Don't you have any miracles left in you? Why can't you help us? Do you exist? If so, did you set everything in motion only to withdraw to a distance and watch the universe run? Or, are you cruel?*

The cart rocked as Barth, Sia, and Jack got off. The tarp peeled back, and Kut slid out. There was just enough moonlight for Lewis to see Barth's tall figure standing at the foot of the cart, helping Kut stand up.

The man cursed and complained, but Barth cut him off. *"Bifortil, Cilanthoon. Dit dileh."*

Lewis knew that meant: "In a little while, Jackass. Not here." *They're going to kill us soon, he realized.* He began to shiver.

Barth gave orders, and Jack and Kut hauled him and Patrick out of the cart. When Jack removed the gags, Lewis knew that they were indeed beyond hope; there was no one around to hear them call for help.

He and Patrick stood where they were, partly because no one ordered them to move, and mostly because they were so wobbly that they could not yet walk. When his eyes adjusted to the moonlight, Lewis saw that they were on a deep cloven track amidst the mountains. One shining moon shone above, outlining fleets of glimmering clouds.

While they stood, Barth lit a hand lamp. Lewis saw a small sphere of eerie red light around them while the forest darkness intensified. He heard the horse swish its tail.

Even though he wanted to be the brave big brother, to hug Patrick and comfort him, Lewis could not; his hands were still tied. Beside him, Patrick shook with major earthquake intensity. Lewis croaked, "Are you okay, Sport?" Patrick mumbled something incoherent.

Despite all his desire to appear strong and confident, Lewis moaned aloud from the pain of the prickling circulation in his legs. He felt deeply ashamed but could not stop.

In a few minutes, Kut's hands pulled them away from the cart and they stumbled after Barth up the track. Jack tailed the end. Lewis heard creaking and groaning and sharp commands as Sia turned the cart around and started back down the track.

Soon, he was huffing because the road became much steeper.

The track was so narrow that it could not be called a road anymore but a narrow path that climbed the shoulder of a mountain. Except for his hard breathing and the intense pain from his wrists, he might have been in a mere bad dream. However, not only his limbs, but his viscera and his thoughts trembled with terror that would not leave.

Barth put out the lantern. A totally illegal flashlight in his hand now showed a tracery of budding branches, but to Lewis these seemed like a tangle of groping hands, ready to strangle him and Patrick.

How long before we die?

They climbed higher and higher. Jack's hand gripped his arm as they walked, but he stumbled many times, and fell once. After a while, to his right, Lewis heard running water. It was easy to guess that their path ran parallel to a cold mountain creek, invisible but noisy, flowing between the mountains to join the Loudmouth River.

Drip! Scented dew from the branches of rhododendrons, laurel, and dogwoods dripped onto his head. In a dim place in his mind, Lewis knew that the scenery was awesomely beautiful, but the aura of threat was so strong that he felt he was walking through a dark corridor in a haunted house. The path went on and on, very steep. Eventually, they left the sound of the creek behind. Lewis's heart beat hard and fast, and he panted. *How long do we have before they kill us?*

Abruptly, Jack's hand pulled him to the right. He stumbled, fell, was dragged for a distance. Jack grabbed the front of Lewis's shirt and hauled him back onto his feet. He heard Barth say the dreaded words, "*Dileh tha,*" and they stopped.

Lewis sensed open space around him. Barth's flashlight showed that they stood on a level area. On his right, a cold breath of air drifted onto his sweaty face from a yawning depth. To the left soared the rest of the dark mountain's cliff face. Here, a little waterfall splashed down the cliff, pooling into a bowl of stone before it burbled off down into the low places.

Kut and Jack made Patrick and him sit on top of a cold, flat boulder. Lewis opened his mouth to say something comforting to Patrick, but no sound would come out. The captors took turns drinking from the spring, then came back to their prisoners.

"*Dedileh, e tha ditla,*" Barth said. He held up the flashlight, and, near the spring, Lewis saw a great cairn that looked suspiciously like a tomb. Its dark opening painted with red slashes and topped with two white horns seemed to pull him toward it. To Lewis's horror, he caught a whiff of corruption coming from the cairn, and malignant, faintly glowing bumps clung to its stones like warts.

His stomach dropped. This was the worst part yet. *Barth and the others intend to kill us here as an offering to their god Saoma.*

Patrick and he had only a few more seconds of life.

Jack grasped his shoulders firmly so that he had to watch what would happen next. Lewis heard the sharp intake of Patrick's breath and saw a glint of light on Kut's blade at Patrick's throat.

In between one heartbeat and the next, time seemed to stop; the universe gathered around this single instant. Inside Lewis was screaming, but outside no sound would come out. He felt as if an invisible hand had stifled his mouth, pushing back his words as he tried to speak.

The evil presence whispered in his thoughts, *I have trapped you in this hideous instant forever. Your dying memory will be of Patrick's white face, eyes round and terrified, mouth open, blood gushing out, and then the light in his eyes fading, the little movements of life stilling until your brother is no more than a heavy human bag.*

The sharp blade reached Patrick's ear. Lewis could see a trickle of blood start from the boy's neck. *Help, help! Oh my God, they're cutting Patrick's throat!*

CHAPTER 33
A LITTLE GIRL'S POWER

The morning after Gracie's brothers' kidnappings brought a gray, cold rain. After a breakfast she could hardly eat, she stood near the window in the Gregory's kitchen, waiting. Normally she enjoyed rain, enjoyed the chance to eat meals with Sadie. However, today, all the good things felt and tasted like dry dust. Her brothers might be dead; people had been murdered, and Fred had helped the enemy who had done it.

She saw someone coming, a vague figure wrapped in a cloak because of the rain. Soon there was a knock on the door, and she shivered. *What now? Are Lewis and Patrick dead?* When Sadie opened the door, Gracie saw that a Bardian soldier had arrived with a note. "What does it say?" Gracie cried.

Sadie scanned the note and answered, "Fred has asked for one final request before his execution: He wants to apologize in person to the people he betrayed, especially to you, Gracie."

Gracie wanted to puke up her breakfast. *Oh, Fred! How could you do such a thing!* Her insides knotted.

Sadie hugged her. "You don't have to go, dear one."

But her soul felt a strong nudge. *Go see him, Gracie. This is important.*

"I'll go," she said in a tiny, dusty voice.

*   *   *

Captain Gregory and some guards brought Gracie to a room

in the prison. It had no windows. A smoky, smelly lamp illuminated the stone walls and Fred's unhappy face. Her brothers' friend sat on a bench in gray prison clothes, his hands cuffed behind his back and his feet chained to the floor. Gracie could hardly bear to look at him, much less meet his eyes.

The guards brought in chairs for them, flanking their prisoner to protect Gracie. She gulped. *I feel like such a baby. I can't do this.* Her knees shook a little.

An aching silence dragged on, and Fred's chains clinked as he shifted slightly. However, no one spoke.

He called me here. He should speak first, Gracie thought. Anger exploded insider her. She felt more furious than she had ever felt in her whole life! A stinky ball of bitterness began to sink into her heart.

Finally, Fred opened his mouth. Only a dry croak came out. He coughed, cleared his throat, and began to talk. "I want to apologize to you, especially you, Gracie," he said at last. "I've hurt everyone, including you, and you are like a sister to me."

Gracie gave him only a tiny nod to continue. *Sister?* her mind spat. *And you let my brothers be kidnapped and probably murdered, even tortured?*

Fred closed his eyes, let out a deep breath, and spoke again. "I set up Lewis to get hurt because I was jealous of him. I made *him* the means for spies to get into the locating chamber and steal equipment. I didn't care if anyone died because I hated everyone. I even planned to defect to Tor."

Gracie looked up. She saw the agony on Fred's face, the white of strained muscles, the red flush of embarrassment, the gray haggard look of a prisoner. It did not move the disgust that filled her.

Fred had more to say. "I played with the locating equipment myself, and made a copy of the marble, the locator of Earth for the Toy ... the *thoyo-on.* Anyway, I ..." his voice broke, "I was planning to take it to Tor and help Lord Charon connect to Earth.

It didn't matter to me what he did after that. I wanted to show everyone I was as smart as Lewis, that I could work the technological magic as well as he could."

Fred breathed in, sighed, and stared at the floor. "What's the worst of all, I think," he continued, "is that I didn't care anymore about your family. I was so full of hate that I couldn't think straight. The bezubs got their claws in me."

Gracie sat glued to his chair. Her eyes swept over Fred's chained feet and hands, his corded neck, but pity would not rise from her soul. Words, when they came, croaked out, "What do you want now, Fred?"

He shook his head miserably. "I don't know; I don't know. Okay, I do know. I want you to forgive me. I wish I could undo the harm I've done. I wish I could go back and start over, but I know that what has been done can't be undone. I deserve to be punished! Gracie, I want to say, I'm really, really sorry. Forgiveness: That's what I want. That's what I want more than anything else in the world."

Gracie felt Captain Gregory's hand on her shoulder. She reached up and clasped it, feeling the comfort of his warm skin and the aura of his care.

When Fred and her brothers and she had arrived from Earth, she had seen the bubbling spring of celebration in him, had felt his goodness. But, when Fred had begun to hang out with his sordid friends, just at the time when Gracie was so glad to have a new family, her happiness had been spoiled. She had sensed his spirit shriveling and had felt his love fade. It hurt. It hurt!

Can I forgive him? No! It's too late! He won't change.

Gracie took a deep breath and held it for a moment. In her mind she saw images where spirits fought, bezubs against the Radyah and his *foraya*. The bezubs clutched Fred, their hideous forms laughing, ready to snatch him to Hell. Radyah, her Jesus, glowed with power and goodness, but he sat on this throne, silent, sad, waiting.

How can I forgive him?

Gracie's choice was solely up to her, she knew. *Fred's going to die—and the bezubs will take him,* she thought. *He deserves it. I should just let him go to hell where he belongs.*

She collected saliva to spit at Fred.

However, when Gracie looked Fred in the eye, ready to spit in his face, what she saw there made her pause and her mouth to dry. Fred wanted to undo the wrong he had done, but he couldn't. He was a prisoner, not just in his body but in his soul. At that moment, Gracie sensed that she had far more power than she had ever realized. Somehow, giving her forgiveness or holding it back would empower one side or the other in the battle for the universe.

Could she forgive Fred? Not without help.

Lord God, Gracie prayed, *I can't do this. You are going to have to do it through me.*

She swallowed. Captain Gregory's comforting hand stayed on her shoulder, and she took a breath. "I forgive you," she said.

CHAPTER 34
A HANGING AT DAWN

What a beautiful dawn after days of rain!" one of Fred's guards coming on duty said to another in the Lanthran language. "Every star is a brilliant lady, shining at her wedding."

"*Harethlu e'Ba,*" the other replied.

"Truly!"

Fred slowly got up from his bed. In his prison there was only lamplight. He did not want to hear about the stars. In two hours, once the stars cleared and the horizon began to glow rosy pink and peach, he would be hanged by the neck until dead.

He groaned. They expected him to wash up, dress up, brighten up, as if being hanged was an occasion to celebrate. *Why not just come in my cell and string me up? I could do without all the fuss.*

Pulling on prison clothes, he thought about his execution. Would death be quick, or would the pain go on for a long time? Suppose he had to pee? Would his bowels relax and release their contents? Suppose the rope broke and they had to hang him all over again. Would he scream and cry when they were putting the rope around his neck?

When he had finished dressing, the guards came into his cell. Both were very tall, broad, and strong. They searched him, as if he could have hidden an escape tool in his prison shirt or pants. The shirt reminded him of one of those abominable hospital gowns. It was too tight in the chest and too loose about the neck. The stupid pajama pants closed with a drawstring. *I'm already strung up,* he thought hysterically. The guards were thorough. After their inspection, they cuffed his hands behind his back and led him out.

Fred wanted to blubber and plead. However, his eyes felt dry; he could hardly blink. He walked between two guards to the inner chamber where his hanging was to take place. Of course, they had to have some ceremony before they did it. Most likely, they would read the charges, pronounce the sentence, give him time to commit his spirit to God—Lanthrans, or at least Bardians – did the God thing even more than Earth people. And then …

The hanging chamber compared in appearance to a college classroom. It was furnished simply with a podium and some hard-backed chairs, except that the back of the room contained a wooden platform and gallows.

The guards walked him toward the gallows. Fred smelled wood, all polish and wax. But he shuddered when he caught a whiff of old urine, as if they had not been able to completely remove the liquids released from the last prisoner to die here.

Daniel stood at the podium. He looked stately in the gold robe that was the prerogative of the High Magus, but his blond hair looked frizzy this morning and there were deep violet shadows under his eyes. Two magi stood at his right and left sides dressed in plain black robes. One was Dr. Zadok; the other was Mark. Seven other blacked-robed men and women sat on chairs; their hands folded. All of them pierced Fred with their eyes.

The guards led Fred to the gallows. To his shame, his knees melted like warm toffee, and they half dragged, half carried him up the gallows steps.

Daniel stood, and so did the other magi. Mark handed Daniel a ceremonial parchment. He read the One Law while Fred stood by the noose, head bowed, staring at the floor.

> *One God, one Lord, one History.*
> *People of Lanthra, see His story from afar*
> *But do not go to the world of the curse,*
> *Or you will bring it upon you.*

Daniel laid aside the parchment with a slight rustle of leather and robes. He cleared his throat and spoke again. Fred did not look up, but he could hear by the change in Daniel's voice that Daniel was addressing him personally.

"Lanthra has only One Law. This is your part in breaking that Law: Frederick Jontz, you aided the Horned Edge who will connect to Earth to exchange Lanthran technology for weapons. They intend to conquer both Lanthra and Earth." Daniel paused. Fred nodded slightly. He was beginning to understand, although he wished he didn't.

"The Horned Edge wanted our system's hardware to repair their burned-out *thoyo-on* for the exchange, and *you*, Fred Jontz, made that possible. You deliberately incited the Horned Edge to kidnap your friend Lewis Brahmindura whose command could access the laboratory that contains the system. With Lewis, the kidnappers took Patrick, your friend's brother and an innocent child. Also, the Horned Edge persons murdered ten of our scientists, and it is probable that Lewis and Patrick have also been murdered. Note: Breaking the One Law leads to breaking all laws."

Fred could not bring himself to look at Daniel's face. He stared at a knothole on the wood platform near his left foot. At first it incongruously looked like a squirrel eating an acorn—a silly, happy squirrel. However, as he looked, the image changed. It looked like a sneering mouth under demonic eyes. He startled and the guards at either side tightened their grips on his elbows.

The High Magus carefully enunciated as usual, but his voice sounded especially sharp as he continued to speak to Fred. "Because you have enabled a dangerous plot, the fruit of your choice will lead to many more deaths and much sorrow—perhaps even to a second Great Rebellion that may encompass your world and mine. Your actions have already resulted in kidnapping, theft, and murder."

The evil face in the knothole appeared to laugh. Fred was scared to look down any longer, so he looked up. Daniel met his eyes. The High Magus looked stern and sad. Fred could not stop trembling.

Daniel said, "The Lanthran punishment for breaking the One Law is death by hanging. By the Law that was given to Moses on Earth, cursed is anyone who hangs on a tree—and this gallows is made of wood. However, remember that the Lord himself was hanged on a tree!"

Fred's mind locked in fear.

"Let the sentence be carried out."

Fred's knees buckled again. The two guards propped him up and he was so ashamed he wanted to sink through the floor. *Can they smell my fear? I can!*

"Frederick Jontz, will you entrust your soul to him who was hanged, died, and rose from the dead, who lives and can save you from eternal death?" Daniel asked solemnly.

A long silence hung in the air. Fred's own breath sounded loud and harsh, but each inhalation felt infinitely precious.

He answered, hardly knowing what he said, "Sure, I will."

The short ceremony was over.

Fred mounted the platform. Somehow, he found the strength to stand upright while they put the rope around his neck. There were a few more seconds to breathe while they carefully examined the knot.

This was it. Time to die. Fred inhaled one last time.

A newcomer banged the door and rushed into the chamber. She was thin as a stick, gray-haired, and wore the black robe of a magus. The woman handed Daniel a note and then, covering her beaky nose with one hand, said something in a low tone. Daniel nodded.

"Wait," Daniel said, holding up one palm. He opened and read the note.

Fred stood on the platform, if a trembling mass of jelly could be said to stand. The scratchy, thick rope encircled his throat; the trapdoor was ready to drop.

For a long time, nobody talked. Nobody moved. The magi and the guards waited, and Fred inwardly groaned, *Just get on with it! Don't give me time to imagine what's going to happen to me.*

"We have reason to delay the execution," Daniel said at last. "Take the prisoner back to his cell."

CHAPTER 35
RED SUNRISE

In dim, grainy light before dawn, with Barth's flashlight focusing on the show, Lewis could not look away from Patrick's murder. He saw Patrick, immobilized, eyes wide. He saw Kut's knife. Along with the distant cooing of a dove and a twitter of finches, he heard the boy's desperate voice pleading for them to stop.

Lewis knew that the knife would soon lick his own throat with its sharp tongue. He would feel the intense deep pain, then choke on the flowing blood when he tried to take a breath through a severed windpipe. But that was nothing compared to seeing Patrick die.

Barth's hand stayed Kut's knife. "*Y'dit toma.*"

The would-be murderer drew back the knife a few millimeters. In a surly voice, he asked a question.

"I've changed my mind," Barth answered in slow and deliberate English. "Louie let something slip. He said that they 'got moved from Earth to this crazy planet.' I didn't know before now that they were from Earth. That changes *everything!*"

Kut began to argue in Lanthran, but Barth's huge hand swept up and slapped the man's face. In a slow, insolent tone, Barth said, "I happen to know that Baron Nargoleh Layhew is obsessed with Earth. I want to take these people to him at Torgard. We will get a big reward, and the baron will enjoy hearing first-hand about his favorite planet."

The roaring sound of his pounding pulse filled Lewis's ears. His vision faded; he began to faint, but Barth and Jack hauled him to his feet. One of them cut the cords away from his wrists. Through a brown haze, Lewis saw that Kut had freed Patrick also.

"Put them over there," Barth ordered. He pointed, not to the garish Horned Edge cairn, but to a small stand of pine trees with a view over the mountains. The big man grinned, and Lewis realized he could see the man's oddly red, effeminate lips in the light of dawn. Their captor seemed elated, but Lewis had no idea why.

He and Patrick sat close together. Slowly, like an old and sick person, Lewis fumbled to grasp his cloak. Holding the cloth in his trembling hand, he wiped the blood off Patrick's neck. Inside, he felt as numb and cold as a block of concrete, too torpid to think or even enjoy affection as Patrick, sweet as a young child, began to relax against his side.

Meanwhile, the moons set behind the gnarled conifers and dawn grew over the mountain ridges. Up rose the sun as a violent red streak on the horizon, then it glared, a huge burning ball. A procession of flat purple clouds drifted closer from the northwest.

As he lifted his head, Lewis saw blue ridges and peaks. Birds sang in fortissimo. The beauty could not reach his heart, however; it seemed dead.

After a time—it might have been as little as fifteen minutes, or as much as an hour and a half to Lewis's distorted senses— Barth brandished a pouch from a bag slung over one shoulder. "Time for breakfast!" he called cheerfully, as if they were all merely on a campout.

Kidnappers and prisoners alike were handed bread and apple chips and thick wads of greasy meat. Barth filled a large tin cup from a flask and passed that around also.

When he looked at his food, Lewis's lip curled. It was a

morbid fellowship meal, and he did not want the bond of breaking bread with his captors. But when he saw Patrick eating, he bit into a piece of dried apple. The first few swallows of food sent such a burst of strength into his body that he straightened up his sagging posture. His hands and knees stopped shaking. Like water in an unclogged drain, Lewis's thoughts began to flow again. He noticed that Patrick, too, had brightened up considerably as well, although his brother said nothing.

For a while he and Patrick munched, looking around. In one direction, the little waterfall splashed into its fern-laced, pebbly pool; in another he saw the horrible cairn. The sliced cords that had bound them still lay on the ground.

Lewis shuddered. He forced his eyes away from the Horned Edge markings around that nasty hole, even though he could not help but smell its putrid air. Determinedly, he focused on the awesome view to the northeast. Below them lay the deep cleft of the Winerush River. Beyond, layers and layers of blue-forested mountain ridges spread onward. Behind those was a red, rising sun under approaching purple clouds.

He still felt numb ... the beauty could not enter his emotions. Yet, cool analysis cranked again in his brain until its function became a smooth, mechanical flow. Lewis looked down. Could he and Patrick escape that way? *Not a chance,* he decided. *It's a sheer cliff with an overbite. We'll fall onto the rocks.* The only way back to Nutman was the way they had come.

When the tin cup came around, Lewis took a cautious sip. *Definitely not water,* he thought, trying not to embarrass himself by coughing and wheezing. *More like firewater. Just what I needed after getting a stay of execution!* He was dreadfully thirsty, and he didn't want to go anywhere near the Horned Edge altar to get to the spring, so he drank before passing the cup to Jack, who leaned on a rock nearby.

Now that it was light, he could examine his captors' features. Barth, of course, he had seen before too often. He had blond hair like Fred but a taller and thicker body. His confident gestures, swaggering walk, and the insolent expression on his face sickened Lewis to the point of nausea. Kut, however, Lewis merely despised. The knife-happy killer was thin, rangy, dirty, and pinch-faced, with a scraggly dark moustache. The third man, Jack, kept aloof from everyone. He was tall and square and balding, with sad brown eyes. Lewis despised him, too, except that he hated him less than Kut because Jack had treated Patrick more gently.

Now that Lewis's mind was working again, he wondered why they were all lounging around this horrible place with the gorgeous view. *Where did Sia go with the stolen equipment?* he asked himself. The answer came easily: *Most certainly to Lord Charon's locating system in Moorway. And, how does Barth plan to get us down from these heights and across the river, with its Class V and VI rapids and no bridge? Barth said that they're taking us to Torgard ... and Baron Layhew has a reputation as an evil, evil man.*

He looked at Patrick, who nibbled cautiously on some of the greasy meat. Lewis softened a little to see his brother's rounded features. His hair, dark like Lewis's, looked scruffy. There was a big dirty spot on one cheek, and pieces of straw stuck out of his wrinkled cloak. Somewhere in its numb core, Lewis's heart wrenched with both affection and pain. He thought, *I could bear this if only I knew that Patrick was safe.*

Turning toward Lewis, Patrick's brown eyes twinkled a little. His young, still pudgy hand gestured toward the last red streak under gathering clouds. He quoted, "Red sky at morning ..."

"Oh, yeah. My brother, the weather prophet. It's going to rain." *And, rain or shine, I've got to get him out of here before they take us to Torgard.*

Now that he had eaten, his brain was spinning with thoughts and ideas of escape. Lewis sat quietly, meekly, and he looked intently at Patrick, who looked at the view.

Mountain ridges faded and the horizon turned dull gray as

the low clouds spread over the landscape. Lewis suddenly thought of Deirdre. *Thank goodness she was not with us when we got ... when this happened.* The early morning air now penetrated the sleeves and neck of his cloak with a moist chill.

"How're you doing?" he asked Patrick. His voice felt rusty.

"I feel like I was captured by aliens in a flying saucer and dragged around behind them on a cable," Patrick said. He grinned, trying to be funny, but the joke fell flat.

Lewis cleared his throat. He looked carefully at Patrick's neck and saw dried blood clots where Kut's knife had sliced the skin and ugly blood smears where Lewis had wiped the cut with a corner of his cloak. But the color had come back to the boy's cheeks.

"I'm fine," Patrick answered, touching his neck. "My head is still attached." A lop-sided smile spread over his face as if he guessed what Lewis wanted to do. "Suppose we could fly away like birds?" He pointed to the cliff below where two optimistic buzzards circled.

Just then, a cup of the fiery drink was passed to Lewis again. He looked at the full cup and then at the men in their circle. He glanced at Patrick, and inspiration struck. He had thought of a way of escape—that is, for Patrick.

It might work, it just might, he thought. Excitement and fear bubbled up together.

He felt a contradictory tug in his stomach. An inner voice said, *Don't do it, Lewis. Barth doesn't plan to kill either of you now.*

He argued: *If we stay here, we are completely in this madman's power. Barth has already killed innocent people. There's no certainty that he won't change his mind about us. Patrick can escape. I can handle the brunt of whatever evil these goons have planned for me.*

The inner voice argued back: *Do you think that you are strong enough to handle the consequences if your plan doesn't work?*

Lewis stubbornly dismissed the voice. *My plan will work,* he thought confidently. Inside, he still felt a check, a small tug at his decision. He shook it off.

Calculating, he thought: *We're five or six hours away from Nutman. That's not too far for Patrick to walk in one day. The path seemed clear. Once he gets to the city, he'll be fine. Even if I die, Patrick will be safe!* He sipped more firewater, considered his plan a little longer, and then decided to act.

First, he caught Patrick's eye. Meaningfully, he inclined his head toward the path down which they had come and used the eye contact to move Patrick's gaze in the same direction. He looked down and wiggled his feet to imitate running.

An alert, attentive look sharpened Patrick's features. His eyes glowed and he nodded slightly. Shuffling his feet, he got up, and stretched. "I've got to go lose some booze," he said loudly, and ambled toward the trees near the trail. No one stopped him.

While Patrick walked into the gloom under the trees, Lewis took one more slow sip of firewater. He looked around at his captors. Barth was occupied with pulling something else out of his bag and talking to Jack. Kut stood close by, waiting for his share of the booze.

With a jerk, Lewis dashed the contents of the cup into Kut's face. "Run!" he yelled. He caught a glimpse of flying leaves as Patrick vanished into the forest.

While Kut sputtered and cursed, Lewis flung himself onto Barth's back from behind, locking both arms around Barth's solid neck. "Run, Patrick!" he bawled one more time. He squeezed Barth's neck hard. Barth flung himself forward to dislodge his attacker, but Lewis savagely kicked the back of his knee and the big man collapsed. Gasping, the heavy man fell face down on a jutting stone while Lewis jumped away.

Jack did nothing. The bald man stood with his arms dangling loosely, his mouth gaping.

Lewis dashed to follow Patrick.

Despite his long legs and his fear, Lewis ran more slowly than he could have. Intentionally, he kept looking back. *Come for me, you dirt-brains, and leave Patrick alone!*

Jack, faster than expected, caught up with Lewis. The balding man grabbed at Lewis's clothes. "Don't wait for me, Patrick," Lewis called. "Keep running!" He put on a burst of speed that dislodged Jack.

In a minute, he stopped and turned around, stooped to grab a thick, solid branch on the ground to use as a weapon, and, turning at bay, he held out his improvised spear. *I will fight—no rules, no mercy—until Patrick escapes.*

Jack held off until Kut caught up with them. Kut drew his knife. The two men circled Lewis cagily. "Come on," Lewis taunted, baring his teeth. "Aren't you afraid of a desperate man with a big, sharp stick? Let this rip up your skin if you try to touch me!"

"Oh, we'll get you, all right," Kut promised. "You'll be a carcass soon."

Jack found his own big branch. He and Kut attacked Lewis at the same time. Kut's knife threatened to slit a nice space between Lewis's ribs. Jack's branch whooshed as it tried to brain him.

Swerving and ducking at the same time, Lewis began to feel afraid. They seemed quite willing to kill him despite Barth's reprieve. He shoved his fear aside and aggressively attacked the two men with his stick. "I'll kill you both, if I have to," he panted.

CHAPTER 36

THE BARD'S ASSIGNMENT

The morning dragged on. Fred slumped on his bed, staring at the floor. At noon, the guard brought Fred a lunch, but he could not eat it. Bread and soup sat untouched, getting stale and cold.

Later, about mid-afternoon, a guard came to remove the tray of uneaten food. Fred, in a state of shocked blankness, was hardly aware of him.

Then another guard opened the door of his cell, and Fred slowly lifted his eyes. His head seemed to weigh a thousand pounds. It was the fellow who had commented on the stars. "You have a visitor," the guard said.

He tried to focus. He had been staring at the ground so long that he could hardly see, but framed by the bars of his cell door stood a young man with dark hair. Fred's heart leapt in amazement, and he exclaimed, "Lewis! "You're back!"

The young man stated, "Lewis is kidnapped or dead. Look again."

Blinking, Fred tried to get his eyes back in focus. The fellow looked somewhat like Lewis, but he was shorter, broader in the shoulders, and only a kid, perhaps nineteen. He looked very familiar. "Oh, yeah, you're the bard." Then it occurred to him what that meant.

Lumbering, clumsy as a bear awaking from hibernation, Fred rose to his feet. He bowed deeply. "Sir Thomas Forschwynn, Bard of Bardia, I am at your service," he said formally, as if he were in an old movie. To his own ears, his voice sounded flat.

"*Alor etoye*—I have a purpose which concerns you," Sir Thomas said while the guard locked the cell door again. He made an imperious motion and the guard bowed and left.

Sir Thomas got to the point. "I intend to pay the ransom for your life."

Fred's knees gave way and he sat quickly on the bed with a thud. "*What* did you say?"

The young man's eyes, dark and proud, showed no warmth and he did not smile. "The night you were arrested, I sent a message to my parents. I asked them for my inheritance; and their reply arrived this morning. Since the High Magus has agreed to accept the ransom, the next step is your choice: You may allow me to buy your life. Or you may refuse to belong to me and hang."

Fred felt his jaw drop. "You mean, the hanging's *off*?"

"If you are ransomed, you are my *subua*—my possession from now on. If I die before you, you will belong to my heirs or to my younger brother and his heirs, or any other family member who remains. There is no release."

"And I don't have to hang?" The dim, square gray cell looked ten times brighter.

"Yes," the bard said. "The ransom is the only way to save your life."

Fred felt giddy. He swayed and had to hold onto the wall.

"You have a pardon—probably the first person in Lanthran history to have one for accessory to murder and kidnapping, not to mention violation of the One Law. The High Magus asked the Master for you, and His answer was yes. Then the magi who are still at the College voted, and they agreed. You may live the rest of your natural life—however, you must be a slave to remind you what has been done for you."

Ashamed, looking down at the cold cell floor—which at least did not look back at him with scary, evil eyes—Fred asked, "Why would you do that for a nobody like me?"

Sir Thomas answered, "Look up at me, Fred."

Fred looked up.

The kid held himself like a king as he said, "You are a treasure, Fred. The Master loves you. He wants to enjoy your funny sense of humor, your ability to appreciate all kinds of sounds, your premature bald spot, and even your taste for busty women. He can't do that if your soul is dead, and—believe me— your soul won't survive long without his help! Besides that, the Master tells me that you have an essential place in his story. He – and I – want to see that fulfilled."

*　*　*

After Sir Thomas left, events moved quickly. The guards let Fred out of the cell. Through it all, he moved like an automaton, his mind stunned. *I'm alive! I'm alive!*

"Come with us," the guards said. They did not bind his hands. "You must bathe before you present yourself to the Bard of Bardia, your master."

In the staff's washroom—not the dank little prison privy – he bathed himself. The guards gave him new clothes. After he dressed, he looked at himself in a full-length mirror.

On the positive side, his paunch was much flatter. In fact, since arriving in this world from the blasted picnic, he had done nothing but walk up and down hills … well, and sulk in bars. He was tall and healthily broad in the cream and brown pants, shirt, cloak, and knee-high boots. The Forschwynn uniform looked good on him. His clean blond hair curled nicely. Yes, he still had the balding spot at the crown of his head; however, they had given him one of those neat hats. Like many of the Caucasian-type men around Nutman, he had grown a full, red-blond beard.

On the negative side, his eyes looked like bloodshot blue marbles sunk into gray sockets, and there were pouches under his eyes. In other words, not counting the fancy clothes and healthy body, he looked like a homeless bum. *Not bad, Fred,* he told himself sarcastically. *You will make a spiffy slave.*

Everything seemed surreal. He was going to live. He was ransomed.

What next? From the washroom, the guards led Fred up many stairs. His head seemed to float over his body. They reached a wide hallway. *What a gorgeous office corridor!* On the left lined a row of fine oak-and-brass doors. On the right were arching windows that looked out over the city. Fred blinked in the strong morning sunlight.

"Sir Forschwynn," the guards called at the door. "We have brought your *subua.*"

"Bring him inside," the bard's mellow baritone voice ordered.

Oh great—after thirty-two years, I've become the slave of a nineteen-year-old.

The guards escorted Fred into a sunny residential suite. Sir Thomas, sitting on an elegant cherry wood chair, wore a well-tailored suit, cut rather like late 18th century (Earth time) suits, and his knee-high boots were perfectly polished. Plain white cuffs showed at his wrists; Fred noticed that he had sapphire cufflinks.

To divert his nervousness, Fred admired the view of the Rockeerie Mountains. Afternoon sunlight highlighted every new green leaf and poured through the diamond-paned windows like golden emollient. The spring sky over the mountains was deep blue with a faint rainbow tint. Birds sang like crazy outside.

"Leave us," Sir Thomas commanded. The guards bowed and left.

Fred wondered what to do, what to say. *How does one behave toward a kid who has spent his whole inheritance to rescue a slob like me?*

Sweeping off his hat, he knelt. However, Fred suddenly realized that his bald spot was pointed toward the young aristocrat, and he felt so ashamed that he could not look higher than the bard's boots. "Thank you, Master," he mumbled.

"Get up, Fred," Sir Thomas commanded in English. "I *am* your master, but both of us serve a greater Master, *Radyah,* the Lord of Rest."

Fred didn't know what to say, so he stood up straight.

Sir Thomas said, "You are my slave, but I don't want to make that public. To other people, you are my assistant. From here on, call me Tom."

Fred stood, still looking down. He restrained an urge to touch his rope-free neck. "How can I call you 'Tom'? You're, like, the hero of a whole country!"

The kid lifted a big leather instrument case. "Yes, I'm the direct descendant of the Bard of Bardia, and I am this era's Bard, also." His voice was serious, but Fred could hear that wonderful lilt that graced the kid's singing. "Yes, I'm the Forschwynn heir. And I command you, call me by my first name."

"Okay, er, Tom."

"I have an important concert to do this summer in the Torish capitol, Moorway. It was arranged last year by the Council of the Magi, and, although the High Magus Daniel warns me that I will be in danger, my heart says that I must fulfill that commitment. In a few days, I'm leaving Nutman to travel to Tiorpatath until I reach Moorway."

"Okay," Fred blurted, "You're going to Moorway? To Lord Charon's capitol and the home of bloody *Saoma* worshippers?" *The kid's insane; he's going to commit suicide!* Fred steadied himself. Straightening, he glared at Tom in the eyes, "Am I coming with you?"

Tom pursed his lips. "No. I'm sending you to my family's estate in the Forschwynn Province. There, you will present yourself to my father and serve him in any way that he asks in the upcoming huge Quincentenary gathering. There will be possibly a million Bardians there! He can officiate, since he was the Bard before I was, but you will represent me—and play in some of the events."

Fred imagined himself in the Forschwynn province, smiling and entertaining thousands upon thousands of people. He gulped.

Tom said in a final order, "My personal attendants already wait outside the Nutman gate. Get your mandolin and any other possessions you have and go with them."

It took several moments for Tom's words to sink into Fred's battered brain. "Uh, I'm supposed to go ..." Once the words processed, his chin lifted sharply. He blared out, "*Why* can't I go with you? You're just a kid—"

A shadow crossed Tom's face. He retorted, "The bizeor tempted you once and look what happened."

Fred's insides flared like hot lithium. He bellowed so loudly that the windows rattled, "Do you think I'll betray you, the person who saved my life?"

Tom did not flinch. "Fred, shut up! My concert is in Moorway, the capitol city of Tor, the headquarters of the Horned Edge who worship the devil Saoma. Don't you realize—the demons of Earth have captured you once. Suppose they seize you again?"

"Oh, come on, Tom! You are going to need help! I won't betray you or anybody, ever again!"

"Stop—"

Fred shouted, "The bezubs would get me but they'd leave *you* alone? Get real!"

"Be quiet!" Tom ordered, his eyes snapping mad.

Pressing his lips together tightly, Fred stepped back. He thought sarcastically, *Yes, master, I hear and obey.*

Tom placed the large lute case on his knees and his hands smoothly unlatched the clasps. Carefully he took out the ancient lute—the one people said was magic. The lute's wood shone deep red when the sunlight played over it, and its great body swelled lusciously. It was different from Earth lutes in that it did not have a kinked neck, and it could also be stood upright and played like a small cello. Even the tiny draft of air in the room made the lute's body resonate at the very edge of audible sound, as gentle as a butterfly.

Relaxing, Tom waited until Fred controlled himself into compliance. Then, Tom's strong, long-fingered hand strummed the lute lightly.

Calm slowly eased into the atmosphere. Under the spell of the music, Fred's tense muscles loosened. He remembered what he was now, *subua*. With one hand he felt the collar of his new uniform. *Instead of a hangman's rope, I wear nice clothes. Thank you, Sir Thomas, er, Tom.*

At first, while Fred continued to stand, Tom picked a simple tune. After a while, the melody glided into a brisk pace like a mazurka. Immediately the whole room quickened. Lively sunlight danced on the walls. Away out the window, a breeze stirred up new green leaves. The world outside looked fresh and beautiful as the Garden of Eden.

Fred cleared his throat and the bard stopped. "Tom, I have something to say."

"Go ahead."

Fred asked bluntly, "Are you trying to be like the original Bard of Bardia who roused the people to fight their evil rulers? Is that your mission?" Strings twanged as Tom's hands jerked, and Fred knew he was right on target. "I won't let you go to Moorway alone! You're only nineteen, and I do remember the screaming horde of Torish bushwhackers I rode through when I first came to Bardia."

Tom's dark eyes flashed. "That's not what the Torish people are like. That's what people who serve Saoma are like. Remember that distinction, Fred! Even in Moorway, Radyah has many people."

"But – will you have some sort of entourage to protect you?"

"No. Until the time is ready, I don't want the public to know my *real* business. Can you imagine? 'I'm here to play in the big concert for the Council of the Magi this summer … but I'm really here to start a rebellion.'"

Fred pushed his case. "You're behaving like some college student kid going to tour a war zone just to get a thrill! This isn't a trip for a travel magazine! What if you get sick? What if you get robbed or mugged, for heaven's sake!"

"Go get your things and eat something, Fred, then wait for me in the common room." Tom broke eye contact and made a cutting gesture. "After that, you're leaving for the Forschwynn province."

* * *

"Your Excellency," James's voice said, arousing Daniel from a nap between morning appointments. Daniel felt a gentle touch on his arm and opened his eyes. His secretary's round, imperturbable face looked down at him. "You have two more appointments before lunch. Also, you have a note from Sir Thomas Forschwynn. He would like to meet with you as soon as possible. Apparently, Mr. Jontz insists that he shall go with him for his Moorway concert. The bard is about to send him away to the Forschwynn province to assist with the Quincentenary Celebration of Bardia, but he wants your opinion."

Daniel's stomach growled. He got up, stretched, and grouched inside, *Master, what now? Fred will be severely tempted if he goes to Moorway. If he falls, two worlds may fall with him.*

The answer came immediately. *Yes, he may fall. Even so, he is my servant. Send him with the bard to Moorway.*

Chapter 37
BOTCHED ESCAPE

Kut dodged the poke that Lewis aimed at his eye. "You're a mean one, aren't you!" the wiry man retorted.

Jack took a heavy whack on his right arm; but the bald man came back with a defensive blow that broke Lewis's stick. Lunging forward, Lewis ripped the branch away from Jack's hand, and punched him in the face with it. He felt a very satisfying crunch. The bald man's nose blossomed into a red gush. Next, holding Jack's big branch, Lewis turned his full attention onto Kut with the knife.

"You *won't* get a chance to use that knife," Lewis snarled. "And I have not one drop of pity for a man who is willing to slit a child's throat!"

So focused with rage that every second happened in slow motion, Lewis swung the branch at Kut. The wiry man's knife went flying off to one side. It stuck in a tree truck, quivering. His mind detached, Lewis watched himself smack Kut on the face, back, neck, stomach, and groin while the man screamed.

Barth hurried over.

With one fist, Barth knocked Lewis to the ground. Instantly, the weird detachment of Lewis's mind ended. A huge feeling of pain, like a truck had hit his face, ricocheted through his nervous system.

Bending over, holding a fistful of cord, Barth quickly tied Lewis's feet, rodeo style. Ignoring Lewis's flailing blows to his face and head, he wrapped him struggling and kicking in his powerful arms and carried him back up the path. At the top, on the flat rock escarpment, he dropped Lewis down by a sticky young pine tree and tied him to it.

Kut and Jack followed Barth. Kut's eyes glared hate and murder. Bruises and cuts covered his entire face. He had his knife again and made a nasty imitation of castration for Lewis's sake before he put it away.

Jack's nose had already swollen huge, and he held a bloodsoaked rag to his face to staunch the red flow of blood. With his free hand, the taciturn man held out a small boot with a dangling lace.

Breathing heavily, a giant bruise on his cheek, Barth grunted, "Yeah, that belongs to the boy." Suddenly, he seemed to grasp the implications of what Jack was saying. His voice rose with anxiety, "Go, you two! Go and get the boy! He could ruin everything!"

Exchanging a wearied glance, the two men ran down the path.

Lewis panicked. He struggled wildly, but, tied to a tree, there was nothing he could do.

All along he'd planned that they would capture him again, but he had hoped for enough time for Patrick to get away. *Suppose they catch Patrick. Suppose Barth changes his mind after all the trouble I've caused and lets Kut carve him up?*

Barth sat nearby, holding a wet cloth to his cheek. He glared at Lewis with furious narrowed eyes and a very red face. Meanwhile, the air grew colder and damper, and the daylight darkened. The birds quit singing. A breathless silence lay heavy around Lewis, the deep breathy yawn of a high place. Low gray clouds moved in, then fog, and the heights gradually disappeared into gray mist.

Lewis leaned back against the pine tree, his heart pumping fast. His left eye swelled, closing shut. His whole head throbbed with pain and his throat burned with thirst. However, now his part was over. He hoped to see Kut and Jack return, their hands empty. Perhaps Barth would shout and kick the dirt. Perhaps in his anger, he would beat him up or worse. *Patrick's going to get away, and I'm going to take my lumps, and that's that,* he told himself.

Too soon, a rustle down the path told him that the two men were returning. When Lewis saw Patrick's body dangling limply over Jack's shoulder in a fireman's lift, a shock of fear clutched his heart. "What did you do to him!" he roared, straining against the cord that held him to the tree.

"Nothing. *You* messed him up with your stupidity." Barth spat savagely.

Lewis shouted more, but the others ignored him. Jack laid the boy down on the ground. Patrick began to moan softly. With hot tears in his eyes, Lewis watched him rock back and forth in the fetal position on the ground.

"We found him by the creek," Kut said. "He was already hurt," he added defensively.

Barth very gently felt Patrick's bared ankle with his big fingers. The boy began to gasp, "Uh, uh, uh, OW!"

"You broke your ankle," Barth told him. "And then dislocated it. And on top of all that, your skin is torn in a deep, dirty cut, so you're in risk of an infection. How'd you do that, kid?"

"Caught … my foot … in a root."

Turning from Patrick, Barth scowled at Lewis. "That was a stupid, stupid thing to do. Did you think your brother would get away? Or that he would be okay if he did? It's further back to Nutman than you think, and wilder, too. Do you think the beasts would let him alone? I know of one or two out there that have a liking for human meat, and your brother would make a plump, tasty meal."

Barth spat on Lewis, then turned back toward Patrick. He got a leather wallet out of his pocket. "Here, kid, bite on this, or yell if you want. I'm going to manipulate your foot, so at least the bones won't rub together. And I've got to clean the cut."

Patrick accepted the wallet between his teeth, while Barth used his huge hands to manipulate the boy's ankle. With a scream, Patrick fainted.

"Brave kid," Barth commented. He got a blanket out of his bag, wrapped the boy carefully to keep him warm, gently washed the wound, and used a stick and his own big, red handkerchief to immobilize the ankle. When the ankle was stabilized, Barth elevated the boy's foot with a rolled-up cloak. Patrick stirred, and Barth muttered, "Got to prevent shock. That would be more dangerous than the fracture." He added another blanket.

Jack sat on the ground passively, eyes closed, but Kut watched his leader with amazement. In his own language, he said something Lewis couldn't follow, and Barth answered sarcastically, "I can kill them, and I can heal them, too. My daddy was a doctor. My brother and I used to help him with his patients when he was drunk."

Lewis sagged back against the sticky pine bark. He felt angrier than he had ever felt in his life as Barth mocked him, "For someone so smart, you're pretty dumb. Your great plan almost killed Patrick."

Shuddering, Lewis said nothing.

Barth laughed.

Lewis wanted to jump up and pound Barth into pieces. Insane tri-tones of demon laughter filled his mind. *Where was God for that little boy?*

I don't know!

Sure, you do. Lewis. There is no God.

The torture of his fear was horrible. He could not escape— there was only one active thing he could do: Quit feeling.

His physical sensations began to shut down first. Lewis could hardly feel the pain in his bound arms or the bruises on his throbbing face, even though he saw his brother's pale face and heard Patrick's soft moans.

Next, his emotions shut down. Lewis felt his anger coalesce into a hard, bitter ball. Memories withered: his happiness at Patrick's excited face, Gracie's hug, Deirdre's soft kiss in the moonlight, and the future of building new friendships, new achievements, and perhaps even a marriage with children of his own. Other memories rose and soured: Lewis saw his mom smiling at him; he felt his dad's proud handshake at his college graduation. That graduation Rolex watch, the symbol of his family's love for him, was gone, probably ripped off the wrist of the Bardian soldier who had traded clothes with him, the man that the Torish had tortured to death.

Last, as Lewis blinked and shifted to sit up straight, his environment seemed to fade. Their little area became a shadowy island in a grim, gray sea. Everything smelled damp, but that sense lessened. Even the cairn stench faded. Nearby, Patrick moaned; Barth, Kut, and Jack idled by the waterfall's pool. Lewis's brain detached until he floated in a Zen world.

His calm shattered when, Lewis heard the weird closed-in clopping of hooves. *Rescue?* Detachment broke; hope blazed in his mind. He saw cluster of cloaked soldiers on mounts coming out of the mist. *Bardians?* When the company stopped, crowding the ledge and filling it with the smell of horse, Lewis saw them stare at him tied to the tree and at the boy lying wrapped in a blanket on the ground.

One of the new arrivals, whose drawling voice gave him away, was Sia. Lewis's hope imploded.

"Ready to go to Moorway?" Sia asked Barth impatiently. "The new bridge's cable system you designed is good—I crossed the river with the stolen equipment. No trouble at all."

"We're going to Torgard," Barth stated.

Sia exclaimed, "But we planned – "

"The plan has changed!" Barth snapped. "Yes, the equipment goes to Moorway with you. The rest of us, however, go to

Torgard. End of discussion."

It started to rain, hard. *Perfect weather,* Lewis thought. His eyes closed and his chin sank to his chest. He was getting soaked.

Jack and Kut mounted spare horses. Barth set up a blanket hammock on one horse's side to carry Patrick. When the soldiers began to file from the ledge, Barth bent over to slice the knots on Lewis's hands and feet. "These are Baron Layhew's Wolf Riders," he boasted. "They are the strongest, most vicious of all Lord Charon's servants." He saw Lewis's horror and laughed. "Soon they'll take Nutman. The precious Bardian College of the Magi is going down and the High Magus is going over to my Master. We'll start our own College in Moorway, and after that everything will change—a new beginning for our world with Samoa's people in charge. Including me." For an instant Barth's eyes glowed as he looked far away into his dream.

When Lewis gaped, the big man laughed, "I forgot—you don't know who I really am. I'm a high-ranking disciple of the Horned Edge and a priest of Saoma. I am the right hand of the ruler of Torpatath that you call Tor, the *true* High Magus, Lord Tahei Charon." Barth proudly held out his right hand. His middle finger sported the Horned Edge ring, which was large, gold, and had a black stone. "Here's something else you probably didn't know, Louie Boy," Barth continued, helping Lewis to a wobbly stand. "I'm the brother of Baron Nargoleh Layhew. He and I are Lord Charon's strategic commanders for the invasion of Dancing Daniel's province."

Lewis fought despair. *What will happen to Deirdre? To Gracie?* But he said nothing while rain streamed over his head.

Nettled by Lewis's silence, Barth let him go and hissed, exuding sour breath, "None of this had to happen if you'd bothered to take our side. The whole city of Nutman would be better off if you hadn't trusted that silly little dandy of a High Magus, melting like a fool over that fat daughter of his, you egotistical … you … *zatha* from Earth!"

Lewis caught a glimpse of scathing hate in Barth's eyes and beyond that was another, sicker emotion. *What? He's envious of me?*

Wolf Riders brought up horses for them. When Barth helped Lewis struggle onto a short bay gelding, he leaned close. Each word was corrosive acid dripping from his red lips. "As I said, we're going to Torgard. Your brother whom you so stupidly tried to slingshot away must now go to the nearest hospital. Not you get to visit *my* brother. I'm sure he'll be pleased; he's always wanted to meet an alien from Earth."

They rode off together into a downpour. A huge wet leaf smacked Lewis in the eye.

CHAPTER 38

GOOD, SWEET WATER

Dawn began, an optic orange streak on the horizon as Fred and Tom left Nutman. Both carried large packs on their backs, and instruments in cases hung over their shoulders. In half-light, they passed through the city gate onto the westward road.

"Why are we going toward Smythe to get into Tor?" Fred asked. "Isn't it the wrong direction?" He knew he was whining and despised himself.

Tom replied, waving to Old John the gatekeeper, "The best crossing is there. Plus, Bardia is almost at war with Tor, and Smythe is neutral. Anybody from this area who wants to get into or out of Tor will cross the bridge at Turnup on the Winerush."

Fred felt numb and stupid. His hand crept to his throat as if a rope were still squeezing it. Glancing down, he saw that, below the bridge, the Loudmouth River's clear water burbled happily over pebbles, but that sight couldn't gladden his heart.

He jumped when Tom nudged him. The bard's eyes sparkled with mischief. "I saw you perform at the Red Oak Tavern. You play the mandolin well, and your voice is good. Fred, you will open my concerts from here on."

Panic and desire at the same time had made Fred's stomach

jump. "I'm not that good."

"Sure, you are."

"Well, I'll think about it."

And he did, over and over and over as they slogged on.

Neither Tom nor he talked much as the day broadened. All morning, blue sky soared overhead punctuated by white puffy clouds. The going was easy.

They came to a crossroads, Tom stopped. "Let's take the right fork."

"But the straight road goes directly into Smythe and it's nice and level," Fred disagreed. "I know my geography."

"Aye, but it's the longer road. Also, I have a purpose!"

Tom proceeded to the right. Fred sighed and followed. *I know who's giving the orders, and it ain't me.*

* * *

The first mile rolled through bucolic pastureland. They climbed a rise, turned past a cluster of pine trees, and saw a long horizon of high wooded peaks ahead. Fred pulled his hat brim up to see better. "We're going into the beauteous Rockeerie Mountains," Fred commented. "The steep road."

Tom nodded. "The short cut. The road gets wild and it's all uphill. But it saves us a half day of walking."

"Oh, great," Fred said. Pack, cloak, hat, and mandolin weighed his body. He sweated, but Tom seemed tireless.

Soon, the road negotiated steep curves under a canyon of great trees. A mountain brook burbled beside the road, but Fred plodded and generally felt miserable. Around noon, Fred experienced about two minutes of a glorious view, but then fog rolled over the landscape. It started to rain profusely until muddy rivulets ran on the road and gusty wind kicked up a spray.

Beside the bard, Fred slogged along, puffing, sweating, his hat dripping, and his pack got heavier with every bend in the road. *I will not complain,* he thought determinedly, *I will go just as long as Tom does.*

Soon Tom shouted through the pounding rain and pointed toward the right. "We're on the watershed of the Winerush. See? A lovely waterfall leaps down from this slope toward the Sapphire Lake."

Fred looked. He squinted and tried to x-ray through the dense mist to see the waterfall. However, all he could see were gray trees and muddy road.

"Wonderful view, absolutely gorgeous, full of gorges," he commented dryly. His stomach told him that it was time to eat. *Why can't a lordling like Sir Thomas Forschwynn travel in a carriage? A walking tour for the Forschwynn heir sounds ridiculous.*

Fred reached his limit. His legs turned to lead, and his body sagged. At the very instant that he opened his mouth to beg for a halt, the rain stopped. The dark clouds quickly blew away.

"I have something to show you," Tom said.

"What?" Fred complained, holding back a temper tantrum. "Does it include lunch and a rest?"

"Turn here, off the road to the right."

Fred forced his body to follow Tom up a leafy, slippery slope, holding into saplings and roots. His boots and clothes got filthy. He got leaves and dirt in his beard. Sweat dripped down his face, and trees dripped on his head. However, when they reached the top, the air cooled. Birds began to call again.

"I'm hungry!" he complained again.

Tom ignored him. He pointed to a sunny spot through the trees. "We're nearly there!"

"Where there?" Fred stood up straighter, anticipating a great view or maybe even a hospitable mountain cabin with a well-stocked pantry and the table set just for him and Tom.

When they broke out of thick undergrowth into a highland bald, the change in light was so intense that Fred shielded his eyes with his hand. Across the green meadow stood farm buildings and a sturdy log cabin. Smoke curled up from its chimney. There were several rocking chairs on its shady front porch, one of them moving as if the rocker had just gotten up for lunch. Fred smacked his lips. He could taste cold beer already or maybe sweet tea. And meatloaf with mashed potatoes. And – *yummy* – apple pie.

Instead, a powerful smell assaulted Fred's nose. He covered his face with his sleeve. "Phew! Disgusting! That stench is enough to knock a man down!"

A few yards away, pigs grunted and rooted the muddy ground in their pen.

Fred backed away. His feet tripped up on a stick and he dropped the mandolin with a *clang*. "Are we supposed to eat one of these for lunch? Or is one of them a special pig with a genius spider friend? Can't you *smell* that fragrant odor?"

The pigs screamed as if they hated Fred at first sight. "Whoa!" he shouted and jumped back a dozen feet. The filthy animals assailed the fence, and a fresh wave of pungent stink arose from the mud. Suddenly an ugly hairy boar with an evil snarl crashed against the pen's fence so heavily that Fred yelled, "Let me out of here! These pigs are trying to kill me! Is *this* what you wanted me to see?"

Meanwhile, Tom sauntered past the snorting violent pigs, not to the cabin but to the woods. He ducked under lush, wet leafy branches and disappeared.

Fred's stomach clenched and he shouted, "Where'd you go? For heaven's sake, Tom, don't leave me here alone!

Tom, voice, muffled by the woods, commanded, "Follow me!"

Fred groaned and complied.

Under the trees the gloom was so intense that Fred could see nothing. In a few seconds his eyes adjusted and – *thank goodness* – his nose felt well clear of the stench. Not far ahead, he saw that Tom squatted by a hunk of gray rock, his pack laid behind him on the roots of a truly impressive tree.

"Hey," Tom called, waving his hand. "When you get here, look down. You'll see. It's good."

His stomach growling, but Fred dropped his pack next to Tom's. The two men knelt together on a leafy, muddy area on a flat rock. Fred inquired, "Why are we here?"

"Shhh," Tom whispered, "just be quiet for a while."

Fred waited, gritting his teeth. Silence stretched and stretched. His knees hurt. After a while, however, the air smelled fresh and foresty. Under the trees he saw ferns, glades of pink lady's slipper, trillium, and Solomon's seal.

"Can't you see it?" Tom pointed to a spot near Fred's feet.

"I see dead leaves, mud, a big rock, and some sand."

Tom put his hand on the back of Fred's head and pushed it toward the ground. "Now, can you see it?" Tom asked.

"No," Fred grumped, but then he caught his breath. "Yes!"

He was kneeling beside a pool of water, so clear that he could see every grain of sand in the bottom. Gently, Tom removed his hand.

Fred bent down until his nose almost touched the ground. "It's a spring!" In the bowl of rock was water so clear that it was almost invisible. At the bottom of it, a little whirl-devil of sand danced in a tiny cone. "Is the water drinkable?"

"Yes!" Tom bent to drink. When he came up, he had a goofy grin on his face. His chin was wet – so was his ponytail – and he wiped his face with a linen handkerchief. "It's good, sweet water. Go ahead, have a drink."

Fred put his lips to the pool. The water was cold as ice, and it tasted fresh. He drank deeply. After he finished, Tom drank again. They kept taking turns, letting the sand settle after each turn, until both felt satisfied.

"Time for lunch!" Tom reached his pack and sat on a huge tree root.

"Sure, great!"

Letting his tired muscles relax, Fred leaned against the tree trunk. He chewed a hunk of multigrain bread, ate long strips of dried mystery meat (*don't tell, don't ask,* he thought), devoured a bar of what tasted like chocolate goat cheese, and drank afterward from the pool.

After the noon meal, they made their way back to the road. Fred stayed well clear of the pigs although they screamed porcine threats at him.

For hours they walked in winky-blinky sunshine as the clouds drifted overhead. Tom sang loud verses of his favorite Bardian songs, but Fred mulled over his private thoughts. Over and over again, his hand crept toward his throat where the noose had tightened. *I'm guilty, guilty, guilty.* Underneath the fear, in his memory, the little spring welled. He could even feel its cold, clean trickle in his heart.

Meanwhile, Tom's self-entertainment noises moved from teenage bellowing to artful and (thankfully) quiet singing.

Deep spring, will you eternal, living drink
refresh the dead?

Fred's hand stopped its compulsive trip to his throat. "Tom, sing that again."

"Sure!" Tom began again. Fred felt the poetry sinking through mental topsoil to the bedrock of his heart, even though he didn't understand the words.

CHAPTER 39

TURNUP

In the late afternoon, they reached the final ridge of the Rockeerie Mountains. "Finally," Fred sighed wearily, "A view." From here on, the road descended. Fred shaded his tiring eyes to cut down the intense westering sunlight that glowed on the the Poloughny River.

Tom put down the lute and stretched. "Ahhhh – we've almost reached Turnup."

"Yeah, I *know* my geography." Fred snapped. "Turnip's our destination tonight, the border town in Smythe where we cross into Tor." Fred set down the mandolin and his pack. He plomped his tired butt onto a rock beside the road.

"Don't get too comfortable, Fred. There's a very, very nice inn in Turnup where I plan to stay for the night. My dad took me there when I was just a little kid. It's right on the Sapphire Lake."

Fred thought, *In some ways, Tom, you're* still *a little kid.*

"I ate roasted chicken. They had the best lemon pie . . .." Tom smacked his lips and his face glowed with the deep happiness of someone reliving a wonderful memory.

"Great!" Fred's mouth watered. "Let's go!" He and Tom picked up their gear and went on.

*   *   *

In an hour or so, when long bars of pink sunlight edged blue clouds at the horizon, Fred and Tom reached the main road and joined the traffic. Walkers, riders, carters, truckers—a lot like the evening rush-hour traffic on an Earth highway.

However, a small company of *faetha,* the lady landowners of Smythe, rode in the opposite direction on fine matching chestnut horses. Most were young, and all were beautiful.

Fred found himself licking his lips. *I wonder if any women groupies will show up at our concerts.* He imagined several sumptuous women embracing him, one in each arm—

At that moment, a stray clod of mud hit him on the nose. "Yuck!" he yelled. The faetha looked back and laughed.

"That's what you get, Fred, for ogling the women," Tom joked.

Fred looked away, but not before he saw one of the beautiful women throwing Tom a kiss. He seethed. *What's wrong with me that all the women prefer the other guy?*

Sunset rolled up its glory and gave way to night. The deep blue sky twinkled with stars, three moons were visible, and the air crisped so that dewdrops budded the brim of Fred's hat.

"We're almost there," Tom announced. "Food and bed ahead." Finally, the kid looked tired.

Tom led Fred single-mindedly past storefronts and narrow five-story apartment buildings. At last, they came to a lane where landscaped estates and mansions lined the lakefront. Fred could see the Sapphire Lake glittering in gaps between the big houses. Fred muttered, "The rich get the cream, as usual." Immediately, he felt guilty. *You blockhead! You just insulted Tom!*

Near the Sapphire Lake's edge, they stopped.

Here, topiaries and azaleas and lavish spring flowers that Fred couldn't recognize graced the front of a grand, brightly lit chalet. Fred approached a large sign engraved with flowing gold script. Feeling stupid because he didn't know what it said, he sounded out the Lanthran words, *Tosappa Farel Abag.*

"Here we are!" Tom exclaimed. "I can't wait to go in, put my gear down, eat a delicious meal, take a long, hot bath, and hit the bed."

Fred asked crankily, "What is the name of this place?"

"Oh, the sign says, 'Castleview Inn.' In fact, my uncle's castle is right across the lake."

"English takes less time to say anything," Fred grumbled, but not loudly. "So, who's this uncle of yours?"

"Er, my mom's brother. But I've never met him, and Mom doesn't talk about him."

*   *   *

The Castleview Inn was no shed. In the lobby, great beams supported an age-yellowed ceiling that peaked in a high loft. A grand freestanding staircase spiraled to the upper floors. Deep red leather armchairs and sofas graced the hearths of, not one or two, but four fireplaces. Everywhere stood elegant tables loaded with flowers and bowls of fresh fruit. Fred, who had visited some of Earth's best airports, hotels, conference rooms, and lodges during job-related conferences, gaped with his mouth open.

Fred looked at Tom, eyes narrowed. *Who's paying for this? And why is this lordling wandering around with a bum like me? I can't believe that he ransomed me with his whole inheritance!*

Tom approached the check-in desk. He had a goofy nineteen-year-old expression on his face, eyes shining and black hair straggling around his head. Yet Fred noticed, he moved with a confident elegance.

The hotel clerk, an elderly gentleman with a baldhead and a handlebar mustache, gave them keys and took their gear, including the lute and mandolin. Fred saw recognition and a joyful gleam in the man's eyes. "Shall I send these up to your rooms, my lord?"

Tom nodded. "Yes, thank you."

The gentleman bowed low.

Tom rubbed his hands together as they walked toward the

dining area. "Come on, I'm hungry."

Fred couldn't help himself. He whispered, "How are we paying for this if you gave up your inheritance?"

Tom whispered back, "Bardia, via High Magus Daniel, gave me an expense account."

The dining room was packed, so Tom suggested, "Let's wait at the bar until we can sit at a table."

"Isn't there any legal drinking age in this country? I mean, are you old enough for this?"

"What?"

"Never mind."

Townspeople and travelers filled the bar elbow to elbow. Tom found a tiny space at the counter where they could drink standing up. Fred's feet groaned, and he really, really hoped they would get a table soon.

"I'll have a peach brandy," Tom ordered the bartender.

The bartender, a solid middle-aged man, nodded then turned to Fred. Fred felt his face going hot because he suddenly couldn't remember a word of Lanthran. He whispered to Tom, "What's the Lanthran term for 'beer?'"

Tom told him. Fred complained, "It takes forever to say anything in your language. Why don't you just say, booze?" But he ordered, "*E'yo boonappua sia.*"

The bartender nodded and turned to fill their orders. When the drinks arrived, Fred leaned against the counter. The bar buzzed with a comfortable roar of conversation.

Tom sipped his small glass of brandy, sighing with deep appreciation; Fred chugged his large mug of beer. The dining room was still overflowing with people, so Fred ordered another beer. The cold liquid rolled over his tongue. Its golden color in the clear mug suddenly reminded him of the hot marble. "I wonder what they did with it?" he said out loud.

"What?" Tom asked.

"The marble, uh, copy that I made. The one that connects

to—

"Shhh!" Tom looked carefully around. "I have it."

"What?" Fred exclaimed.

"Yes."

"But—

"Shut up, Fred. The High Magus wanted you to have it. I'll give it to you right now."

"That makes no sense at all."

"Yes, it does. But this is neither the place nor the time to mention … that planet. Here's the *noretha.*"

Tom dug the amber sphere out from an inner pocket. Fred saw rich, golden light glowing through it, but not from it, and when he took it from Tom, it was warm, but not hot. *Thank goodness, no one is connecting to Earth right now.* He was so full of questions that he wanted to burst, but he put it in a deep pants pocket, feeling like a large hobbit with an evil Ring. He thought, fingering the object, but without any pleasure, *Because of me, ten people got murdered, and Lewis and Patrick were kidnapped or worse.*

Suddenly the beer tasted sour. Fred's throat constricted and his hand twitched. He was afraid people in the bar would stare at him, so he slipped the guilty hand into his pocket.

At that moment, a young waiter walked toward them. He was a fuzz-mustached youth carrying a tray of beer for another party. When he saw Tom, he stared. The tray tilted, and all the glass beer mugs fell off with a terrible crash.

Everyone in the bar looked. A lot of people laughed. The young man started off red-faced to find a mop and a bucket, but he turned and paused. His eyes lingered on Tom's face reverently, as if it were a rare postage stamp. Then he darted into the kitchen.

When he emerged, he brought a very distinguished-looking man with him.

"I'm the Castleview Inn's owner, Master Merela," the man said, bowing with a flourish. "And I am so happy to be of service to you, Sir Thomas Forschwynn."

The owner was elegant and trim in a dove-gray suit. His hair ringed his head in a silver wreath, he had a short, neat beard, and his brown eyes showed sharp intelligence. He gave Fred a penetrating look. Fred bowed politely back at him.

"I met you years ago, Master Merela, when I stayed here with my father," Tom said. "You look the same as ever!"

"Thank you! Always at your family's service, Sir Thomas." Master Merela bowed again. People all around them stared. "Please let us know if there is anything at all we can do for you," He flashed his excellent teeth in a smile. "Perhaps you would give us the honor of an impromptu performance at the inn later this evening?"

The unlucky server flushed scarlet as he cleaned up the mess. He kept sneaking looks at Tom. When he finished cleaning up the broken mugs and slopped beer, he squawked, "I saw you, Sir Thomas! T'was at Farleigh two years ago, when I was a'visiting my Gran. Is your lute really magic?"

The owner impaled him with a look and the youth guiltily faded into the utility area.

Tom bowed back to the innkeeper. "Thank you so much, but I must decline the performance."

At least two-dozen people stared curiously at them. Fred felt jitters in his stomach. There would be a series of concerts as they travelled toward Moorway for the Big One, and he would be expected to be the master of ceremonies for the bard. He was sure that all of tonight's people were judging him, comparing him to Sir Thomas, and finding him inferior. He tried to wear a nonchalant expression.

"Of course, Sir Forschwynn," Merela said. "Is there anything special I can do for you tonight? Perhaps a table beside the window?"

He gestured toward the dining room's great window. It had a fabulous view of the moonlit Sapphire Lake.

"I couldn't ask you to move other guests to make room for us," Tom demurred.

"A table will be ready for you in just a moment," Merela insisted.

Despite Tom's protests, a waiter seated him and Fred by the lakeside window. They had to squeeze past a huge pack of fancy, purple-uniformed men, but the view was fantastic. Lights twinkled merrily from mansions nearby and from a mountaintop castle across the Sapphire Lake. Their supper came, a fine meal of pan-fried trout, new potatoes, spring peas, cranberry muffins, more beer, and apple-walnut pie. Fred put his worries behind him and tucked in.

*　　*　　*

"I'm going to bed," Fred said after he had eaten all he could hold. His face cracked open in a huge yawn.

"I'm too full to lie down," Tom said. "I'm going to sit at that nice quiet lounge area by the fireplaces. When I feel sleepy, I'll come up and join you."

Fred climbed the spiraling staircase, and following the balcony, he found his room. "Nice!" The creamy white plaster walls and large beams reminded him of a colonial mansion. On the very large bed—he was expected to share it with the bard— lay a hand-stitched sunshine yellow quilt over clean white sheets and plump pillows. "Ah, sweet sleep," he sighed.

Fred conked out as soon as he hit the bed. However, an hour afterward, he awoke. Comfortable warmth glowed around his body, but the same beer that had made him sleepy also caused him to waken with an urgent need.

He waited as long as he could, but eventually he absolutely had to leave the warm bed. "Now, if I can only find the bathroom," he said to himself. "What did that host say? To the left and down the hall?"

For some reason, the corridor to the bathroom was pitch black dark. Muttering with sleepy annoyance, Fred looked for a lamp or a candle. Finding none, he felt the wall with one hand in the dark until he had found the right place.

A few minutes later, much relieved and still half-asleep, Fred stumbled into a man in the corridor. The man held a small hand lamp. In its flickering light, Fred made out a tall, dark-haired slender shape and a young face. "Tom, is that you?" he mumbled.

"*Dit,*" the man replied. There was a silence. Then the man said in broken English, "You're the fool with Sir Thomas Forschwynn, the Bard of Bardia?"

"Yes," Fred answered with a jolt of anger. *Who is this guy?*

The man socked him on the jaw. Fred toppled like a cut redwood.

Strong arms grabbed him, trussed him until he could not move, and gagged him before he could cry out. Like spiders capturing a moth, several men dragged him into a dark room. A blaring light briefly flashed in his face. "*Subua* Forschwynn. *Unya sa?*"

A sibilant voice answered, "*Alor.*" Someone lit a candle. Once the spots left his eyes, Fred saw that he sat against the wall in a crowded room. Tom, also bound and gagged, sat next to him. Tom's eyes were wide with terror. His lip was split, and a purple bruise colored his cheek.

Fred's heart pounded. Adrenaline yelled at him to flee, but he couldn't. Chest heaving, he turned his head to and fro to see if there was any way at all to escape, but there was none. *Help! They're going to kill us!*

Soon the men in cloaks, hats, and riding boots brought his and Tom's gear into the room, including the mandolin and the lute.

One of them blew out the candle. The point of a dagger tickled the angle of Fred's jaw. *This is it. God rest my soul. I hope it doesn't hurt too much.*

Hot breath tickled his ear and a whisper mocked him in Lanthran, "Be good now, *subua,* or you'll be good and dead."

Fred was hauled to his feet. A thud and a scrape told him that

Tom was also being leveraged to a standing position. His feet were untied, Fred was wrapped in his traveling cloak, and the kidnappers quietly hustled him and Tom out.

The man herded them down the spiral staircase, past the great and quiet lounge, and avoided the clerk's desk by going down a corridor to a side door. One of the men slowly slid back the heavy bolt; Fred could hear the tiniest squeak of metal against metal. *Somebody save us!* However, he was gagged, and nobody had telepathy.

CHAPTER 40
INFECTION

Patrick imagined that he lay in a friendly big bed. Under the covers, it was warm and cozy, and he could rest. But the good feeling did not last long. He lay on a cot. His ankle hurt with a fiery pain with rhythmic throbs. Each throb stabbed all the way to his knee. Fever made his head whirl. However, even as bad as he felt, he was curious. Opening his eyes, he looked around.

The first thing he saw was his brother. Lewis's eyes, one of them swollen and blackened, looked at him tenderly. At once, Patrick knew that Lewis had tried to sacrifice himself to save him. He longed to be gallant like him instead of a lump on a cot. "Thanks, bro'," he whispered.

Lewis gave him a crooked smile. "We'll get you to a doctor, Sport."

Patrick smelled campfires. They were in a Wolf Rider camp. And it began to rain, hard. Big drops splashed onto Patrick's face.

"Over here," he heard Barth grunt. Lewis carried Patrick into a large tent. Inside was a strong smell of disinfectant and a faint smell of mold.

"Patrick, we're at the camp hospital. I'm going to lay you down now."

Patrick screamed when his ankle jarred. Lewis shouted, "Don't you have a doctor here someplace?"

Barth, however, was arguing with one of the gray-uniformed Wolf Riders, an officer who looked high-ranking because of all the medals on his chest. Barth stated, "We're going to Torgard first."

"Why the delay? We could save ten *lantern* and two days if we go straight to Moorway." the Wolf Rider officer said.

"A doctor!" Lewis thundered.

Soon, Patrick looked up into an elderly man's face. The man said in Lanthran, "*Eaye ris'e linath?*"

"*Alor, o alor!*" Patrick answered fervently. He cringed when the man removed the splint Barth had made on his ankle. However, the man was gentle as he examined Patrick's ankle as well as his eyes, face, neck, and armpits.

Lewis asked in English, "What does my brother need?"

Shaking his head, the doctor answered in cultured English, "He has a fractured dislocation of the right malleolus. It may even involve the tibia, and his growth plate is possibly involved. There's a very deep cut, down to the fascia. This injury is unusual for a lad his age."

Lewis lips thinned into a hard line. "I believe it."

Patrick saw Lewis glare at Barth, but Barth smirked. "It was your fault, Louie. You let your own brother get lost in the woods and look what happened."

The doctor asked Barth, "How'd you come by a laddie in these woods, Master Layhew? He looks no older than ten years. And—" He drew in a quick breath. "I say!" He noticed Patrick's wrists. "The boy has been bound cruelly!"

Patrick saw that Lewis opened his mouth to tell exactly what had happened, but Barth interrupted, with a warning look and a movement of one fist. The big man said smoothly, "We rescued them from a Bardian patrol coming back from a border raid. They were incredibly lucky to get away alive!" Barth's eyes looked amused. Lewis's shot angry sparks.

The doctor said, "I've the facilities here to pin the ankle, but we can't immediately because we'll have to stop the infection as quickly as possible! This wound is extremely dangerous."

"What?" Patrick asked. "What's wrong?" His voice sounded like a croak.

Barth answered, and his voice sounded smug to know the technical jargon, "You have a staph infection. The wound is very quickly swelling and getting pus."

The doctor nodded. "I want to get that infection under control. We must keep the boy here for several days, maybe a week, and – "

Barth interrupted, "For security reasons, I'm in a hurry. No, give me the medications he needs, and we'll treat him on the way. The medical people in Torgard can treat the infection and pin the ankle."

"He shouldn't travel!" Lewis objected. "He's close enough to shock as it is, and a lengthy trip with that ankle in wet weather …" His brow furrowed with worry.

Barth ignored him. He turned to the doctor, then shrugged. "Give me the medicine for the infection and some painkillers. We're going to Torgard."

He spun on his heel and left the tent.

"Yes, Master Layhew," the doctor said to Barth's receding back. Patrick could hear a touch of sarcasm in the doctor's voice, but he felt too strange and weak to analyze it.

The doctor went to get the medicine, and Lewis pulled a stool up to Patrick's side. "I'll stay with you, bro'," he said. "I …" His voice broke. "I'm sorry this happened to you."

When the doctor returned, he carefully washed Patrick's ankle, applied some ointment,

and gave him a swallow of some nasty medicine. Lewis held his hand during the treatment, while Patrick cried and groaned. Dimly, Patrick heard the doctor whisper to Lewis, "We've some people in Torgard who can …"

CHAPTER 41

MEET BARON TRAGER

Fred, Fred, wake up, Fred!"

Fred stirred a little, feeling like a block of rock. His nose sniffed cold, damp air and he did not want to get up because his mind felt gummy, and the blanket felt so nice and warm. He opened one eye.

Tom, his lip split, and awful bruises around his eyes, hovered over him, alternately shook him, and pulled on his arm. The kid's long, uncombed hair flew in all directions as he cried, "We've got to get out of here!"

Stupidly, Fred rubbed his jaw. "Ow!"

Slowly he sat up to take stock of his situation. Unhappy, he remembered last night and groaned. "Are you okay, Tom?"

"No!"

With a slow haunting scrape, a heavy wooden door opened to Fred's right. A quintet of men in plum velvet livery pressed into the room. "You're summoned. Get your clothes on," one said in a gravelly voice, like a person who smoked and drank too much. Several of them carried great pikes; the rest carried swords and clubs.

Fred gaped. *I can't believe it. A pack of purple people-eaters.* However, Gravel-Voice snarled so fiercely that Fred jumped up. He pulled on yesterday's clothes in seconds. He grabbed his boots and quickly tried to pull them on. The boots felt weird, kind of hollow and damp. "Oh, shoot, I forgot to put on my socks!"

Gravel-Voice, who was a big man with a handlebar moustache and pouchy eyes, knocked him hard on the side of the head. "Hurry up!"

As Fred trotted fast down and down and down an endless winding staircase, his right heel began to develop a raw blister. Yet, pain had its benefits. Although his jaw ached, his body sweated, and his blister got bigger, his fear-shocked brain began to function.

Guards and prisoners reached a landing and followed a series of corridors, including more stairs. By then Fred could run the good old mental computer with a critical thinking program. In various rooms along the way, he took note of crystal old-fashioned lamps, fine furniture, gorgeous rugs, and various fine paintings. However, jutting out at intervals in the corridor, stone gargoyles stuck their tongues out at him. *The same back at you, butt-uglies!* Besides the fine, expensive accoutrements, Fred noted trash and fresh gobs of phlegm on the floor, cobwebs in corners, and black mold in corners where the roof leaked.

Analysis concluded. *The place is gorgeous and very dirty at the same time—probably like its owner. Good grief, look what they left wide open ...*

"Yikes!" he yelled and pointed ahead to distract the guards. "There's a big rat over there!"

"Shut up!"

They descended a spiral staircase to yet another series of corridors. *We've gone down three hundred and sixteen steps,* Fred figured.

"In here!" Gravel-Mouth growled. The guards stopped. Gravel-Mouth knocked, and a lordly tenor voice ordered, "Bring them in." Tom and Fred walked through an oak door with bright brass bindings. It took a few minutes them to catch their breath; meanwhile, Fred scanned the room. *Looks like a Brothers*

Hildebrandt illustration, he thought.

A large Persian-type carpet graced the floor. There were three stuffed armchairs covered with violet and gold velvet, two quartz-topped end tables, and a sturdy buffet table with glass cabinets, and carved lion feet. From the beamed ceiling hung a large crystal chandelier (with a big cobweb near the top, complete with large spider). Tapestries of hunting scenes covered the walls, many of them showing a handsome blond man killing the boar or the lion or the dragon.

Center stage, attractively illuminated by the glow of lamp and candlelight, sat the blond man. A writing desk covered his lower half, but Fred could see that his puffy-sleeved jacket was black velvet embroidered with gold fleur-de-leis and he wore a large Horned Edge ring on his left middle finger.

Fred's body felt sore, and his brain shaken, but his analysis program was working well. *Meet the owner of this crumbling piece of ostentation. This dude has a problem with narcissism. Fortyish. Elegant. Smart. Ambitious. Probably mean as a snake. Judging by his clothes and accessories—not to mention those cute purple uniforms he puts on his lackeys—he spends money like water and wonders why he is perennially in debt.*

Tom exclaimed, "What do you think you are doing? Why are we here?"

"Sir Thomas Forschwynn," the baron greeted formally, "I am your uncle, Baron Arthur Trager." He did not rise but merely nodded slightly. His cool gray eyes brushed over Fred's and stared at Tom. Fred thought he looked hungry, predator hungry. "My dear nephew. Coming to visit after all these years?"

Tom's eyes flashed. "I would have visited you quite willingly if you had asked. Now, what do you want, *O Lutaya,* my dear uncle, Baron Arthur Trager?" There was an angry edge to his voice. He bowed. At his quick cue, so did Fred.

After that, Fred got lost as Tom and the baron exchanged quick aristocratic niceties in Lanthran, the baron in a barbed tone,

Tom with his mellow voice, but very strained. They appeared to be speaking an older form of the language, with fewer words and more syllables. However, Fred understood when the baron said, "In a little while, I want you to write something for me." He gestured toward parchment on the table and an inkbottle with a quill. "Sit down!"

Glancing at the baron's bullies and their formidable pikes, Tom sat on the edge of an armchair conversationally close to the baron's. Fred remained standing respectfully like the good-boy servant.

The baron ignored Fred. He might have been a piece of furniture in a thrift shop.

Meanwhile, Tom said something to the baron in Lanthran that Fred could not follow. His voice rose and he made open gestures of appeal. However, Trager smiled very slightly, arms crossed, his lips thin.

Once Tom quieted, Baron Trager leaned forward, folded his hands, and let out a long stream of coolly spoken narrative. Fred caught a little of the story. Trager described his dear sister, now Tom's mother, Rachel. There was invective about her ignoble boyfriend from Bardia who was not worthy of the Trager family. Bitterly, the baron described the man, now Tom's father, Edwin, as a base-born farmer, undeservingly endowed with land, Bardian heritage, and excessive riches that he ought to share, since he had married Trager's sister, after all. Not only that, but Rachel had scorned his brotherly love.

According to Trager, the Bardian prick had been a guest at this beautiful Sapphire Lake barony. After many tours, hunts, and feasts, Edwin had "sneakily" proposed marriage to his chosen lady, who accepted. When Trager found out and protested and tried to "protect" her, Edwin had attacked him. The evil villain then stole Rachel away to the Forschwynn Province, leaving Trager bleeding and broken on the hard, cold floor.

Tom stiffened. His face turned bright red. He looked like he was going to either faint or explode. In English, probably for Fred's benefit, he said through his teeth, "You made advances to your own sister to lock up her share of the inheritance; you're angry because my father rescued her from *incest*; and you've kidnapped your sister's child. So, Baron Trager, what are you after now?"

"Only justice," Trager replied, in excellent English. "Besides the political crime of carrying off my sister, who is a citizen of Tor and an heir of Torish land—for as you well know, your grandfather's will passes half the estate to her and from her to you—your father owes me a liability for this."

Trager shifted his chair and drew back his cloak enough to show his knee, which was locked in a flexed position and encased in a leather brace. His gray eyes steadily fixed on Tom's, the baron untied the brace and rolled up his pants to show the scars on his knee.

Tom did not comment, and Fred did not feel it was wise, either.

Rebinding the brace and covering up the leg again, Trager turned to his lackeys. "Bring a lamp. I want my nephew to see clearly when he writes."

To Tom he said intimidatingly, "Now, take up the pen to ink and write what I tell you."

Tom hesitated as if considering whether to argue or fight. Baron Trager waited, the atmosphere growing more and more ominous. Finally, Tom picked up the pen and dipped it in the inkwell. The baron dictated:

> *To Sir Edwin Forschwynn: I am writing you through the hand of your eldest son. He and his servant are visiting me at my castle by the Sapphire Lake.*

The baron noticed that Tom was not writing. "What is it, Sir Thomas?"

"Uncle," Tom said, "Why—?"

"Ply the pen, Sir Thomas," Trager commanded. "Do I have

to repeat what I said, since you interrupted me?"

"No."

Tom scratched the words onto the parchment. The baron waited until he had completed the introduction, then continued dictating:

You will understand the situation when I tell you that neither the lad nor his companion will see the spring turn to summer unless you deliver, in gold, the amount of—

Tom's hand slipped, leaving a jagged mark after the words. The baron took the paper away from him and held it up for examination. "Very good!" he commented. "The splash of ink creates the proper threatening effect. I see that Edwin has his sons trained in penmanship. A fine, artful hand you Forschwynn have, whether for music, or writing—or bashing with the mace."

He pulled away from the table and smiled again. It was not a nice smile. "That'll do. I'll finish it." He put the paper aside.

Fred shuddered. *What next?*

"Currie," Baron Trager turned to one of the younger bullies who hovered in the back of the room. "Did you bring the laddies' gear?"

"Aye, my lord." A weedy-looking young man came forward but not too close, as if afraid of a slap on the face. He held up two bundles and two instrument cases.

The baron stroked his beard, considering. "You travel lighter than ever your father did, Sir Thomas. And poorer." Examining the bundles, he took Fred's first and pulled out various articles, including one round amber object. "What's this? A jewel perhaps?"

Fred felt all his blood rush to his face. He coughed, choked, then sputtered out nervously, "It's … It's my lucky marble."

He glanced at Tom, trying to send the telepathic message, *Please confirm what I said. Please don't let this greedy pervert take away the hot marble, the jewel that can find the way back to Earth.*

The baron held the marble up to the lamp between two fingers. It glowed in the light and looked very pretty. From a drawer in the desk, Trager pulled out a jewel glass and examined the marble more closely. "Hmm, only glass, a common toy. Or," he leered, "perhaps more than a toy." He made a complicated gesture with his left hand and sang out a weird, loud command, "*Noretha, he get!*"

Fred held his breath. The marble had glowed before by science. Could the baron make it brighten again by some magic invocation?

Nothing at all happened. Baron Trager looked disappointed.

"My subua found it along the way," Tom explained, trembling a little.

Thank you! Fred signaled with his eyebrows.

Tom coughed, probably to hide a nervous laugh. Fred felt close to hysteria. He tried not to burst into tears.

Trager flipped the marble toward Fred the way a man might flip a pebble into a creek. "Take it, you lout. And much luck may it bring you."

Fred caught and quickly pocketed the marble, trying to look both loutish and grateful.

The baron picked through Tom's pile of stuff. "And what of yours would your father and mother recognize?"

"My embroidered shirt. My sister made it," Tom said quickly.

Sneering, Trager said, "I don't want your stinking shirt. I want something dearer than that to send with the, *ahem,* note to your parents." Trager found a gold-engraved toiletries box among Tom's personal items. "Ah, this is nice. I'll keep it." He put it aside. Then he put down the bundle and reached over, awkwardly because of his stiff knee, to lift the lute in its case. "I'll take this."

"No!" Tom was agonized. "Don't take the lute. I need it—"

"Need it? For what?" the baron snapped. His gray eyes were cold.

"For my concerts," Tom blurted out. His face had gone from pale to almost albino.

Tom's anxiety pleased the baron. His eyes narrowed and a wicked smile played around his lips. "Do you think, once the ransom is paid, that I'll let you go your merry way? You think I'll settle with your father and mother for one meager load of gold, the price of my castle's stone? No, boy, I'll play you for a kingdom! Your country will trade much for such a fine piece—the very Bard of Bardia. They may even accede your Forschwynn estate to me after Bardia falls to the Horned Edge."

Tom looked sick.

Baron Trager turned to Fred, who wanted to sink into the floor. "You too, *subua e'* Forschwynn. I want something from you to send with the letter." He sneered, "Not your *dittiean* marble."

With a deep sigh, Fred handed over his high school ring with the big ruby. His foster-dad had paid for it, and every time he rubbed the ruby, Fred could remember the dear old man who had taken him in because his drug-addicted mother would no longer care for her son. Suddenly his blood ran cold. He hoped intensely that the baron would not read the inscription on it and start asking uncomfortable questions such as, *Where are you from?*

They were given their possessions minus the lute, the box, and the ring and then were escorted out. The baron's men made them trot up and up the stairs until Fred could feel his heart hammering, his knees shaking, and heat and thirst plus the fear that he was going to have a stroke or heart attack – or both.

CHAPTER 42
TORGARD

Weary to the bone and damp because the weather had sot into a gray drizzle, Lewis bumped along in a caravan of Wolf Riders. They rounded a hairpin curve, and Lewis could see an imposing dark blocky fortress built on a mountain: Torgard. He remembered that Torgard was Baron Nargoleh Layhew's castle. If the baron was anything like Barth, then he was in for a real treat.

Now the fortress gate's maw loomed ahead. As the company passed through the dark gate, Lewis turned around again to look for Patrick's covered wagon. Yes, the wagon entered the gate; however, it then turned in another direction. "Hey," he called to the Wolf Riders around the wagon, "Where are you taking my brother?" But nobody bothered to answer.

Its equine head sagging, Lewis's horse milled around with the others in the fortress keep, which was a wide cobbled area filled with cloaked citizens, dismal tables for vendors, speckled chickens, quacking ducks, skipping goats, baaing sheep, and lots of muck. Lewis and his guards left the keep and turned into an alley, a narrow worm-track. At the end of it, the troop rode through an arched doorway into a stable. Immediately, a strong smell of stable animals hit Lewis's nose. *Whew! Beast, you and your friends stink!*

So do you. The horse shook its mane tartly.

Oil lamps in sconces on the walls showed him very a large stable. Lewis guessed that quite a few levels of castle rose above his head, supported by walls (judging by the entrance) around three meters thick.

His horse came to a stop on flat stone pavement. Its ears waggled and it snorted. It turned its head toward him as if to say, *Get off, knucklehead!*

Lewis eased his feet from the loops of rope that served as stirrups. When he, as limber as a wooden two-by-four, lifted one leg over the back of the impatient beast to dismount, his horse-challenged boot immediately caught in the stirrup, and he teetered and dropped onto the smelly floor.

Someone offered him a hand. *The hostler, thank God, and I hope that he or she is a lot nicer than the other people I've met so far.*

"Thank you!" Lewis sighed, reaching up. However, when he took the hostler's hand, he felt thick, soft fur. His eyes lifted slowly to the hostler's face. "Hello! You are one of the Blue People!" The hostler had a thick walrus moustache, round brown eyes in a blue face, a hat over messy straw-colored hair, and no clothes at all over a blue hairy body. He was very obviously a male.

Good-naturedly, the hostler stuck out his impressively long red tongue and wagged it in greeting. After months of working in Nutman and signing to various Blue maintenance workers or food servers, Lewis understood this Blue Person's nonverbal language: *My name is Gus. Who are you?*

Lewis decided to be bold. He made the hand motions for "I'm Lewis. I'm from …" he paused, took a dare … "Earth." The Blue Person began to sign an excited reply.

However, Barth knocked the hostler's arm down and took Lewis's arm in a mock friendly but overly tight grasp. "Quit playing with the animals, Louie. And do *not* broadcast that you're from Earth. My brother Nark wants you and your forbidden planet all to himself."

"Gus," he ordered impatiently, "Get out of here!"

Obediently, Gus turned and led the troop's horses to their stalls. Lewis suddenly felt hollow as the friendly Blue Person left. Meanwhile, the troop dispersed, but Barth stayed with Lewis.

"Come with me," Barth said. "Up these stairs." He directed Lewis toward a spiraling stairway.

"Where did they take Patrick?" Lewis asked as they began to climb.

Barth flashed him a look of utter contempt. "The hospital, dummy."

His head drooped. His hands dropped limply. Lewis trudged with Barth up the stairs.

Soon, crowding him against the turret wall, a group of males clicked by in black, polished shoes. They all wore short hair and white or blue shirts, bland ties dark jackets, and slacks, like Earth's businessman uniform. Each sported a funky gold ring with a large sparkling diamond. "*Shields,*" Lewis exclaimed, "wearing Saoma-worshippers' rings!"

"Yep," Barth said.

Last, before the hallway ended, came a train of men and women dressed in orange robes with scarlet lining. "Horned Edge magi?" Lewis asked Barth, who nodded. These magi also wore the rings. Some were bald with intentional scars in patterns on their heads. A few looked "normal," but a cold aura about those suggested that these were the most dangerous of all.

Barth directed Lewis through a large, brassbound door. "Wait here. I'll be back in a minute and then we'll see Nark … 'My Lord,' to you."

Lewis found himself in a small domed chamber. Across from him stood two large men, apparently on routine guard duty because they both looked bored. Each was clad in a gray and white uniform with a silver wolf blazoned on the left shoulder and a long sword at his side. Their faces were hard, almost depraved. One gestured at a chair, "*Poth dileh.*"

In a few minutes, he felt a rapping on his forehead. He had fallen asleep in the chair, and someone was giving him a "noogie," rubbing knuckles painfully into his forehead.

"Hey!" he yelled and punched out with his fists.

Barth's arm blocked the blow. His sneering face blasted sour breath at him. "Get up, Louie. My brother's ready to see you."

CHAPTER 43
BETRAYAL AGAIN

When they finally reached the top of the tower and had been forced into their room, Tom flung himself face down onto the cot. Fred did the same, feeling chilled and damp as if he were imprisoned in a tomb. Inside and out, he was shaking.

When rumbles and painful contractions from his stomach reminded him that he was hungry, Fred groaned. He rolled to a sitting position. Straight ahead he saw a drab, gray stone wall; behind him, more of the same thing, above him, a low arched ceiling. On the right was the heavy, metal-bound door. "They don't have any fire code, doggonit." Weak light illuminated the room from a single window to the left. Cold seeped from the window. "Oh, my Lord," Fred declared sincerely, "thank you that it's not winter!"

Tom raised himself up from the cot. The muscles around his jaw clenched with tension and his skin tones had gone gray. In the corner lay a laver filled with clear water. Tom splashed his face and dried off with one of his undershirts. He began to groom his appearance, especially his tangled hair, using Fred's toiletry kit. Under the cots were chamber pots. They both used them. There was, of course, no privacy.

"For a place to board his nephew, your uncle's

accommodations are rather marginal," Fred said. He tried to keep his voice light.

"Better here than the dungeon," Tom countered darkly.

Tom sat on the cot, staring into space, while Fred turned his attention to the window. Several square panes of clear glass were sealed with lead into the thick stone. He put his nose close to the chilly glass and looked out. *No wonder they don't need bars.* His stomach lurched. "What a fine view. I see the Sapphire Lake below, Tom." The bard did not answer. Fred swallowed. "I hate heights."

"Hey, Fred," Tom said at last, "hand me your mandolin." Fred did.

The bard played a flowing tune that reminded Fred of a light glistening on a waterfall. He started to turn away from the window, but a yellow gleam of morning sunlight rayed through the window. The light warmed his shocked body. It warmed his brain. It reminded him that he had been saved from hanging and, therefore, he might be saved from being murdered. Analysis once more kicked in and an algorithm of a possible escape cascaded like magic because he remembered seeing …

"Tom," he whispered. "I've got an idea."

Tom stopped playing. "What?" he exclaimed, his eyes lighting up. "You are serious, aren't you?"

"Oh yes." Fred kept his voice low. Trager might have some of the not-so-primitive Lanthran technology to monitor this room. He doubted it, but he decided to play it safe. "Yes, Trager's made at least two mistakes. Number One: The door to this room opens inward, not out. Number Two: Some slob carelessly left a door open in a filthy cupboard near the staircase, which I saw on the way to our conference with him."

Tom jumped to his feet. "You have a plan! What is it?"

Fred began to talk. But he only told Tom part of his plan.

*   *   *

Fred and Tom spent a long, boring day in the tower prison.

They took turns playing the mandolin, but their hearts weren't in it. In the evening when the room was quite dark and they were very hungry, they heard someone coming. Fred and Tom settled into their battle positions. Fred hid behind the door. Tom sat on his cot. Behind the door, they heard a squeaky tenor say, "I imagine the wealthy young Sir Forschwynn can pay for his supper."

"Aye," said a rough bass. "And we shall find out, if Baron Trager left anything for the picking."

With a noise of boots and keys, the door opened inward. In walked a steward, wearing a white cap over his hair, a starched white apron over his clothes, and a nervous frown. Behind him loomed a very large guard in the omnipresent plum velvet uniform. As the steward carried a large tray with covered dishes, bowls, a tureen, and steaming mugs, he looked around for the nearest place to put the tray. He walked toward Tom. "Get off your cot," he ordered. "I'm about to drop this thing!"

The guard turned his head from side to side. "Where's your slave?"

Tom hurled himself at the steward.

"*Yiii!*" the man yelped. His tray crashed to the stone floor. Hot soup splattered everywhere, scalding the guard, and a muffin flew across the room.

Tom sprang to the door.

"Grab him, you idiot!" yelled the guard, hands covering his burned face.

However, the steward, fluttering with indecision, tried to gather the crockery. "The chef will kill me!"

"You fool! This man is worth more than your effing muffins!" The squinting guard reached out a ham-sized hand and by sheer luck clenched Tom's collar before he could escape.

Just then, as the plan called for, Fred jumped out from behind the door. "Gotcha!" he roared, as if he were going to overpower the guard and save Tom. However, instead, he pushed both the guard and Tom into the room, ran out, and slammed the solid oak door shut. Fred bolted it, imprisoning the three struggling men in the room while he was free in the corridor. This was the part of the plan he had not told Tom.

Through the door, he could hear blows, desperate pounding, scuffling, and shouts, and Tom's outraged yell. "Fred, I thought we were *both* going to escape!"

Fred turned his back on the door. As he trotted to the stairs on the route he had followed, he guiltily remembered Lewis and Patrick, kidnapped or dead, because of him. He remembered Gracie's pretty little face looking at him with deep sorrow. Now he was doing his thing to the bard. *I'm a Judas. I keep betraying people,* he thought.

It's the only way, another voice said in his mind, but Fred's hand slipped up to his throat.

CHAPTER 44
BARON NARGOLEH LAYHEW

Following Barth into a large chamber, Lewis reminded himself: *Barth and Nark want you alive, Lewis. If only you can get some status, get recognition in this system, then you may get enough influence to rescue Patrick, keep Gracie safe, maybe make peace with Fred, and even get us back home!* He decided to be very, very good.

Lewis shrugged off the sense of evil as he smelled the cold polished chamber. The odor reminded him of the inside of a tin can that had not been washed before it had been discarded.

Be calm and carry on, Lewis, he thought.

As Lewis approached the front of the chamber, he noted benches, a dock, a rail, and a tall magistrate's seat. *A courtroom.*

In the magistrate's seat sat Baron Nargoleh Layhew of Torgard. The man wore a filigreed black tunic over a red silk shirt. Lewis got a quick impression of Blackbeard the Pirate: lots of wiry black hair, a huge gold stud in one ear, big threatening yellow teeth, an overly red mouth like Barth's, and calculating dark eyes.

Baron Layhew stood up. He was bigger than Barth, who was a very big man. His great tresses of greasy black hair waved down his back and the black beard covered his entire chest. The baron's narrowed eyes bored into Lewis; his red, sensuous lips curled downward in a contemptuous frown.

Barth walked Lewis up to stand in the dock, then took a seat beside the baron. Lewis felt so tired that he had to lean on the dock. He clutched on it tightly to keep from swaying on his feet. His nose began to run, his throat felt raw, and he coughed.

First, Nark's eyes drifted toward Barth. In very thick, accented English, he snarled, "What kind of trash have you brought to waste my time?" He sneered at his brother, "Look at you, a slathered mess. I'm sure that, if you were in Moorway instead of here, your beloved master, the magician lord, would give you a grand reception. And wouldn't you have cleaned yourself up nicely for him? But, for me, you look like *bizeor* dung!"

Barth's face twisted with anger. He retorted, "I went to a great deal of trouble to bring you somebody from the great planet Earth that you're so curious about. I was planning to give him to Saoma, but when I found out he was from Earth, I choose to bring him to you."

Even through his tiredness, Lewis noticed that Barth did not mention Patrick.

Lewis saw a new gleam in the baron's eyes, but the man growled, "You want me to be grateful? You only stopped here because Lord Charon insisted you not dump some filthy Bardian prisoner in his lap when he's trying to get the invasion started. You're always going out of your way for *him*, lovely Lord Charon, leaving me to do his dirty work."

Barth flushed. Stiff with repressed rage, he got up to leave. Nark's low hiss pulled him back as if snapping a leash. "Sit down."

Barth sat.

While the brothers glared at each other, Lewis shifted to support his tired legs. He felt one boot slip on the stone floor, glanced down, and felt his spine tingle and hair rise. Blood and slime covered the dock's floor. "*What in the hell is this filth!*" Lewis roared.

However, Baron Nark pierced him with a glance. "Shut up. Go sit down."

Lewis quickly exited the gross dock, strode over to the left, and sat down on a bench. While the brothers Layhew picked and bit at one another with words, Lewis wiped his runny nose on his sleeve. *So much for my resolution to be calm, cool, and collected. I blew it. And*—he coughed—*I am getting sick!*

*   *   *

Finally, the brothers' bitter exchanges fell to silence. Barth's lips snarled and Nark's teeth showed. Then, for the first time, the baron fixed Lewis with a long appraising stare, glaring under his black bushy eyebrows.

"Get back to your place," Nark snarled, pointing to the dock, "you stinking stick with the red nose!"

Lewis felt heat rise to his face. He retorted, words boiling out, "And why do you suppose that is, Nark? I've been kidnapped, threatened with murder, beaten up, deprived of sleep, food, water, and rest, constantly afraid for my younger brother Patrick who is so sick that he might die, and you are angry because I'm a little bit seedy?"

Barth rolled his eyes and shook his head slightly, meaning: *You shouldn't have said that, Louie.*

A corner of his mind told Lewis to stop, that he was provoking a very dangerous man, but –

"You!" Lewis spat to emphasize his contempt. "You pervert! You who leave this nasty, slimy mess on the floor in your courtroom from God knows what sadistic amusement you enjoyed—do you dare to insult me because I smell like a campfire and a few days' sweat?"

Nark narrowed his eyes and bunched his fists.

As if in slow motion, Lewis watched a mass of black hair run toward him. He tracked the blur as Nark's fist jolted into his face, right below the already-bruised eye.

Lightning bolt pain … Lewis's knees buckled; somehow the

floor came up and hit him and he lay still for a moment, listening to himself moan.

"Were you somebody important on your precious planet?" Nark stood over him, fists bunched for another blow. "Here you're *subua*. Do you know what that means? You're my property, like a rock in the field or a shirt or a dog. Now, you'll be useful to me, or I shall throw you away, along with your poor, sick brother."

Almost blinded from pain but sizzling with rage, Lewis glared at Nark's long legs, bulging belly, vast black hair, and mean dark eyes. "When I get up," he snarled, "I'll give you a boot in the family jewels! If I had a weapon, you'd feel it crunching your skull!"

Nark bared his teeth, but Lewis continued, "I'll show you 'property!' I can design weapons of war that you've never heard of! Just imagine a nuclear bomb detonating in the bowels of your fortress, the rock vaporizing, this mountain melting for miles into the bedrock, and your atoms scattering into the thick, poisonous mushroom cloud!"

Nark showed his incisors, growled, and drew back a heavy booted foot to kick Lewis in the teeth.

However, Barth spoke up, "Brother dear, if you kill him now, you'll never discover what he has to say about Earth."

Nark breathed hard, but stopped his kick, slowly gathering his rage back into control. "Take your useless 'present' out of here, then, little brother, until he's decided to learn his place."

CHAPTER 45
FRED'S PLAN

Many spirals later, Fred found the little closet. The uncertainty was horrible. *If Trager's people find me here, will they kill me? No, when he finds out what I'm doing, Tom will kill me!* The closet door swung open. With a loud *squeak!* a rat dashed over his boots. "Ack!" Fred cried and fled. Somehow, he squinched up some courage, went back, and did what he had to do.

For once, he was glad he had been fat. He'd lost weight, but his clothes were still large and loose. He stuffed his shirt and pants until he could hardly stand up under the weight of his new treasure. Last of all, he covered himself with his cloak.

Shouts and pounding came to his ears. His hands felt slippery with sweat, and his blood pounded in his ears. Getting an idea, Fred ripped off a button that was already straining from his bulging shirt. As if it were impelled by magic, the button pinged off the floor to the ceiling and bounded away like a 1960's space race Super Ball. It bounced on and on; he could hear it thumping ecstatically down the spiral stairs.

Make them follow the button, please! Meanwhile, Fred crammed himself and the useful find inside the closet.

Eventually he heard a rush of guards storming toward his button. The air vibrated with a bellow as someone found it. Many voices yammered and shouted, and the hue and cry clamored into the distance.

Fifteen seconds after everything had quieted down, Fred squeezed out of the closet and raced upstairs to find the chamber where Tom and he had been imprisoned. *Gotta hide my treasure!*

Fred unbolted the door and slipped inside the prison. Tom, who by his sweaty hair and new bruises must have put up a fierce struggle, lay tied hand and foot to the cot with strips of torn linen. The kid's mouth was folded into a thin, angry line, and his eyes blazed.

Tom snapped, "Of all the ruthless, inhuman things to do, pretending that we were going to escape together and then using me to take your own escape!"

Fred bent down close to Tom's ear and whispered, "We have to hurry! Let me untie you."

"You snake! What—?"

"Shut up!" Fred knelt by the cot, turned it over, and began to work on the linen knots that secured Tom's hands and feet to the frame. At last Tom got up and staggered around, stretching his arms and stamping his feet. He carefully averted his eyes from Fred; in fact, he kept a huge hostile bubble of space between himself and his corrupt *subua*.

"Tom," Fred broke the taut silence. "Tom, please look at me."

Head lowered, Tom only crossed his arms and turned his back.

Fred reached under his cloak and jacket. He pleaded, "Tom, please forgive me. I never intended to betray you. I played Judas once, to Lewis and Patrick, and I'll never, never do that again."

He pulled out the treasure he had gleaned from the closet. "Tom, I wouldn't have left you here even if they had told me to go! But I had to fool you so that I could fool them. Otherwise, if we got caught trying to escape, the baron would have put us in the dungeon, in chains, no doubt, and we'd *never* get a chance to get away again!"

He saw Tom's head straighten up. He slowly swiveled and saw the treasure—a great pile of thin brown rope, woven from siphe, which was probably the strongest fiber on Lanthra or Earth. His eyes went wide. All the tension of the past day broke loose, and tears flowed freely down his cheeks.

Fred got up and put an arm across the younger man's shoulder. Tom took a deep breath. "I thought the bizeor had possessed you. I was afraid that everything you have said and done since … since I ransomed you was a lie."

"It was no lie," Fred told him.

The bard rubbed his eyes with both hands. "When are we leaving?" There were still tear tracks on his cheeks, making him look about eight years old, but he stood with a type of gallant bravery.

"We had better get out *now*, before the purple-people-eaters come back. Although—I have no idea where to go from here. Across the Sapphire Lake back to the inn we left? Or off immediately to Moorway?"

"No! We'll go to Gapstand. That's not among my tour stops, but they *do not* like Baron Arthur Trager. They won't help him if he comes after us."

"We hope."

Fred tried to act calm, but his innards were flopping like a trout that had swallowed a big fly. *If you thought the last part was hard, buck up, because this part is the* scary *part.*

It felt totally weird to be rescuing his rescuer. Fred avoided Tom's eyes as he measured the rope in ells around his elbow. A snakelike voice hissed in his mind, *Do you think you're really a good guy now? Or will you let your friend and lord die if you can save yourself?*

Shut up!

"We've about four hundred *wisto* of rope, but we'll have to knot it," Fred stated, "or we'll never be able to sustain the climb down from here."

While Tom collected their remaining gear, Fred tied large knots in the rope. They had to get *out of here* before morning or the baron's men came back, whichever happened first. Fred felt adrenaline accelerate his heart; sweat tickled under his arms, but his mouth felt dry. When the rope ran out, they fastened the strips of blankets to extend the rope just a little further, adding a primitive platform of broken cot frame. To this, Fred fastened their one remaining musical instrument, the mandolin. For this, he tied slipknots, because his fingers would be sausages by the time he got ready to release it.

"Ready?" he asked Tom.

"Ready," Tom replied, and he sounded shaky.

The two men used a board from a cot to break the window. It made a lot of noise and both Fred and Tom winced. Cold night air poured in.

The mandolin went out first. Tom lowered it, slowly playing out the rope. Next went the platform. "Be careful! Don't tear yourself up on the broken glass!" He padded the sharp windowsill with a blanket.

Fred stuck his head out the window. It was totally dark outside. The air felt cold and damp, and a breeze rustled in the treetops below. "Gonna rain," Fred grunted.

To brace the rope, they securely fastened the rope to the other cot, which would (hopefully) not break and fly out the window. "I'll go first," Tom stated.

"No!" Fred insisted. He gulped, his hands felt horribly slippery, and his courage felt as artificial as tin cymbals. "Me first, m'lord."

"Do you have any gloves?"

"Uh, no."

"Let's wrap our palms in pieces of my shirt."

Tom wrapped Fred's hands and Fred wrapped Tom's.

It was time for the descent.

Fred climbed out of the window, backside outward. At that instant, the hazy moon peeked out of the clouds. "I don't *want* to see where I'm going!" he told the moon. Carefully, he lowered himself, his feet against the wall of the castle, his powerful arms taking part of his weight. At the first knot he rested. The light was brighter out here than in the room. In the east, he could see little blue *Bibo* over the folds of the mountains. In the south, Sapphire Lake glittered with faint blue diamonds. However, the air felt so heavy that Fred knew that a big, wet thunderstorm was approaching. Trembling, he said, "Please, God, no lightning tonight." Then he descended to the next knot.

Fred briefly pictured the ground below where he hoped to eventually plant his feet. That didn't help at all. Imagining the tremendous fall down wall, cliff, and crag had him awash through with fear. His hands got slippery. Trembling, to his horror, Fred barely made it down to one more knot. *Only about eighteen more of these knots to go. Argh!*

After half of forever, a chemical reaction from fatigue began to settle in. The muscles in Fred's wrists and shoulders trembled with spasms. He had to rest … but he had to get going … Soon, he feared, the power would leave his muscles and he would either have to be standing on the platform or on the ground, because then his arms would give out and he would full body kiss the dirt at terminal velocity.

I'm going to fall; my muscles will go dead and that will be it! But he somehow reached the cot-frame platform where he had good support for his feet. The sighing hemlock branches around him made it too dark to see the ground. Panting, sweat soaking all his clothes, he rested. *How far above the ground am I? Seventeen meters? Fifteen meters?*

Then he remembered, *Oh, I've got to get the mandolin off the platform.* His chest heaving, Fred squatted awkwardly, trying to snag the slipknot around its case strap with one hand. After one, two, three attempts he succeeded. *Thank God for Webelo's and basic slipknots!* Now he had to get himself and the mandolin down to earth.

I'm at the end of my rope, he thought hysterically. He had no choice except to fall and hope he didn't get impaled on a branch or broken on rocks.

With a stab of guilt, Fred let the mandolin drop. *Better you smashing first than me.* A complaining twang told him that he was about four meters yet above the ground. He groaned. "Broken leg, here we come!"

But he was exhausted, so he had to finish the descent. Fred grasped the platform with trembling hands. He let his body slowly dangle down. At that moment, the climax of fatigue set in and his muscles could no longer function. His hands let go. Fred fell feet first. *Whumpf!*

He lay stunned for a moment, legs smarting—no, more than smarting, screaming—but after several minutes, he knew that he was still in one piece. *Hallelujah!* Fred found the mandolin. It was intact, even playable. *Hallelujah again!*

Somewhere above him, Tom clung to the rope, probably about halfway down. Heart pounding, Fred waited. No sign of Tom yet. Fred chewed on his nails, ignoring the smell on his hand.

Finally, Tom, too, reached the platform. He dropped just as Fred had done but cried out when he landed with an evil *crack!*

"Tom!" Fred yelled.

Tom tried to speak, but Fred heard only a wheeze.

Fred panicked. He ran around like a terrified dog, yelping for help. In a little while, he realized what a fool he was and returned to Tom's side.

Tom gasped and lied, "I'm fine." Groaning, he pushed himself to a sitting position.

Hope steadied Fred's heart. He took a deep breath. "I was afraid you were paralyzed or broken into bits."

"Me, too." But Tom's head slumped forward.

Fred felt panic rising once more. He was too tired to carry

Tom. Dawn would come any minute, and the baron's men would recapture them. *What am I going to do?*

Tom raised his head. He was shivering.

Is he in shock?

However, the kid said acidly, "Let's get away from this burg. I never want to see it again, not even I inherit it—which is not impossible if I survive." Tom struggled to get up, so Fred gave him a hand.

"Ow!"

"You are hurt," Fred cried.

"All right, a little, but I can walk."

Tom tried to speak again, but instead he coughed. Rain began, big raindrops. *Pat, pat, pat, patta, patta,* and then it was pouring on them. A bird sensed that dawn was approaching and began to chirp.

CHAPTER 46
A VISIT FROM BARTH

L ewis sat in the tower room in Baron Nark's castle. Surprisingly, the room was not dank, dark, or filled with moldy straw. Instead, it had candle lamps that warmed the place with cozy light. It had clean toilet facilities, a decent bed with blankets, a silver pitcher and laver of water, a bottle of wine in ice with fine wineglasses, linen napkins, and a tray of good food: fresh pastries, wrinkled dried apples, whole-grain bread with butter, and slices of cold turkey.

But he didn't feel hungry; he felt sick. *I blew it. Big time. I blurted out that I had my brother with me when we were kidnapped. Now Nark can threaten to hurt Patrick to keep me in line, or even ... he felt sick in a whole new way ... sacrifice him to Saoma!*

His nose was streaming now, and he had developed a small, relentless cough. Wiping his nose on a napkin, Lewis considered his options.

What next? Escape? Har, har—that's not likely. Kill myself? Hmmm. Let Nark kill me? Sounds easy.

A sarcastic voice in his mind said, *Look, you idiot; why did Nark put you in a nice room instead of a dungeon? Because he still hopes you can give him what he wants. Now, if you can't beat 'em, join 'em. That's right, join them. Put your stubborn arrogance to use and negotiate a way to protect Patrick.*

Lewis squirmed inside. *Okay, so how?*

Grovel, you idiot, grovel. Turn yourself inside out—you're stubborn enough to do that! Switching sides will put you in the position you need to rescue Patrick. And if you can do that, you can get him and Gracie home. And save Bardia, too, if you're up to that.

Considering, considering hard, Lewis found himself mechanically eating turkey sandwiches and drinking wine. Like a programmed robot, he took a washcloth, soaked it with cool water, and held it up to his swollen face. And then, he bathed himself. And then, he put on a fresh cotton nightshirt. At last, he crawled into bed. He felt warm. He fell asleep.

*   *   *

Too soon, a squeak of opened door and a strong reek of whiskey startled him awake. "Whozzit?" he groaned, trying to see in the dark. A little light drifted through the narrow slit of a window and his eyes adjusted to see the intruder. Immediately, Lewis regretted deeply the surgery he'd had to restore his near-sighted eyes to a healthy 20/20. Barth Layhew staggered forward and approached his bed.

"Move over, Louie, I wanna sit down."

What the—! Lewis felt cold rage squeezing his insides and he assumed an attack position: hands ready to squeeze neck; feet ready to kick groin. *I will not let this idiot paw me!*

Be good, Lewis, be good, a voice inside told him. *He mustn't hurt Patrick on account of your temper.* With immense difficulty, he forced himself to sit still.

Barth shoved Lewis aside and settled on the foot of the bed, back to the wall, long legs jutting out. Holding a sloshing bottle of booze, he took a long drink and ordered, "Get up, stupid, and light a candle."

Be subua ... for Patrick's sake. Lewis lit the nearest candle with a click-stick. *Maybe I could set this creep on fire – No, no, no, no!* Lewis refrained from deadly tactics. His insides felt cold and murderous, but he used the pain to focus his stubbornness.

"What is it, Barth?" Lewis said calmly, reclaiming a sit-down place on the bed. His stuffy nose ran, and he wiped it on the useful linen napkin.

Barth sighed, a deep, sad whiskey-stinking sigh that made Lewis want to spray the air with a strong air freshener. "I've got a brother and you can see what a demon he is. Yet I serve him. You've got a brother, a real nice kid, a brave kid, and you throw him away."

"*What?*" Lewis nearly exploded, but he quickly bit the anger back. *Cooperate, cooperate ... even if you have to kiss ass; that's the only way to get anywhere with these people ...*

Barth's voice dripped with "poor me." "You've got a family. Fred told me about them, and I saw them at the Gregory's house— such a nice family. I wish I had a family like yours."

"Oh." Lewis wanted to drive Barth away: Barth the killer, Barth the kidnapper, Barth the fanatic Saoma worshipper who had intended to sacrifice him and Patrick on an altar, and suddenly Barth the sentimental drunk.

Allow him to talk, said a thought that cleared his mind like a cool, wholesome breath of air.

I'm trying, I'm trying. Lewis took a deep breath. *But what do you want me to do, hug this brute? Tonight, he's drunk and gooey, but tomorrow he'll punch me bellowing* "Ode to Joy."

What have you learned about Barth in tonight's encounter?

He wants a family like mine. He's jealous of me. So how can that be useful?

How indeed? You will see.

As if Barth had heard the conversation in Lewis's head, he muttered, "Tomorrow, you'll have to behave, or you'll get beaten into bloody pulp. My brother's dying for you to tell him about his beloved Earth. He won't quit until he gets what he wants."

"What does he want?"

Lewis was startled when Barth leaned close to his face, whispering, "I hate you! My brother wants something from Earth! And you're from Earth! He wants you more than he wants me!"

With a big blast of bad breath, Barth collapsed sideways, effectively taking over the entire bed.

Lewis managed to pull a blanket out from under Barth's heavy body. There was absolutely no way that he would touch the man, so he lay down on the floor, wiping his nose and coughing.

CHAPTER 47

GAPSTAND

Several large, gray owls looked down on Fred and Tom from the raftered ceiling over the dirt floor of a crumbling abandoned barn. Beetles scuttled in the corners, mice made little rustling noises, and there were dusty cobwebs everywhere. Fred was grateful anyway. Outside, rain pounded the metal roof. Inside, their refuge was very dim, full of a pungent smell of old manure, straw, mouse droppings, and dust. The kid lay on his back with his damp cloak as a blanket.

"We stink," Fred said unnecessarily.

Tom groaned, and Fred was sure he had broken a bone somewhere. *I have got to lighten the mood.*

Fred began, "Why not stay here a few days? We have a nice little hotel! There's plenty to drink in the water barrel if you don't mind the mosquito larvae."

Bending and wheezing like a very old man, Tom sat up. "You and I are going to Gapstand," he asserted. "Now, before I can't move any longer. Where's that water barrel?"

"You are a stubborn bloke," Fred said admiringly. "Almost as stubborn as Lewis."

*   *   *

A few hours later, the rain slacked off. Fred and Tom staggered from a soggy lane between hedgerows to the broad highway. They could see a thin, red sunset over twinkling lights ahead.

"Gapstand," Tom gasped. "We're here."

Gapstand: The street was not paved, and Fred slogged through dark brown mud littered with horse droppings and crossed by grunting pigs. A mule-drawn carriage splashed past them, covering them with filth. They were too tired to care.

Tom stopped. "I see the sign for an inn."

Fred read, in distinguished letters: Tall Tree Lodge. Over the sign rose a very nice fieldstone building with warm lights inside and, behind it, a hill crowned with tall trees that smelled like pine and balsam. "Tom," he said, "We can't stay here."

Tom gave him "the look."

"I see another sign: Gapstand Inn, 0.1 lantern ahead. Yes, that one—the grubby one."

"But—"

"Tom," Fred tried patiently, "We don't have any money."

Even in the shadowy street, Tom's jaw looked set. "All I have to do is sign my name and they'll charge it to my father ..."

"Trager's going to look for you! We have to hide!"

"I'm so tired, and the Gapstand Inn ... is a dive ..." Tom grabbed his side. He coughed until he retched and vomited onto the mud.

Fred's stomach twisted. *The spoiled little brat wants to stay at the luxury inn. Why stop him? Go ahead, let him get his way and get caught! Let him experience what you felt when you were going to get hanged!*

Clenching one fist, Fred beat himself on the thigh. *No!* He inwardly shouted. *I will not think like that!*

He touched the bard's shoulder. "Baron Trager knows your taste in inns. We have to stay somewhere else."

"No," Tom complained.

"Yes, we are."

Fred dragged him to the Gapstand Inn. The three-story

building was squatty, almost a dirty dump, but lights glowed cozily from many windows. Fred helped Tom use the do-it-yourself shoe-cleaning station to scrape the clods off their boots before entering the building.

As they opened the front door and walked inside, an outrageous idea struck Fred, a lightning bolt out of nowhere. It was so different, so much better than his earlier jealous thought that he laughed out loud. *This ransomed slave will be useful to his master after all.*

"What *e bizeor ditlabath* is so funny?"

"Never mind," Fred chuckled. *Oh, this one's a doozy!* "You'll learn soon enough."

Fred plodded forward. In the big boxy common room, the smoky air smelled of sooty lanterns, fresh beer, sizzling sausages, and warm bread. Fred's mouth watered. Food had never smelled so good. A very nice fire burned on a hearth where a dozen large chickens turned on a spit, dripping juicy fat.

Okay, my plan—how do I start?

Men and women crowded around rows of long tables while servers brought or removed food and drink. The common room was filled with conversation, laughing, the scrape of chairs, and the clinking of crockery.

Tom said darkly, "We don't have any money. We stink! How are we going to get anything to eat, much less a room?"

Fred smiled his best innocent grin. "Follow me and do as I say. I have a plan."

"Oh no," Tom groaned. "Not another plan. Do I have to be beaten and tied to a cot again?"

Fred led Tom to a gap at one of the tables. Patrons gladly moved away. They sat down, and a female server drifted in their direction. Fred watched her with appreciation. She had long curly black hair, a generous bosom, long legs, and fabulous buns. The woman gave Fred a long, knowing look and her little pink tongue stuck out just a little

"Hello, my name is Helga, and I'm going to be your server tonight," she said.

"Hi, Helga. I'm Fred."

Her left eye winked and she tossed back her hair. "Glad to meet you … Fred. Did you and your friend have a good fight?"

Fred remembered his and Tom's multicolored bruises. "It was a *fantastic* fight, thank you."

She laid before them, boarding-house style, plates of well-done sausage and chicken, baskets of warm home-made bread, and a platter of cheeses, dried fruit, raw onion quarters, and garlic cloves. With a saucy smile and a bounce of hip, she laid down a huge mug of beer for each of them, letting her hand brush against Fred's. "Maybe you can tell me about your fight, later."

"Sounds wonderful!"

After Helga left, Tom lifted his mug and groaned with pain, but chugged down the beer anyway. He stammered around a huge chunk of bread, "How do you p-propose to pay for this?"

"You'll see," Fred told him, between mouthfuls.

The men sitting at table next to Fred and Tom looked congenial, so Fred spoke up in his weak Lanthran. "*Dedileh, Boonua. Boonappua sia etaboon e'ya.*" The men near him clapped with approval. A light camaraderie began immediately.

"Fred," Tom hissed. "How are you going to pay for beer for yourself, not to mention for your new friends?" His face looked pale and there were bright pink spots on his cheeks.

"Relax!" Fred told him. He belched loudly.

The men around them received new mugs of beer. Fred joked and ordered more beer when they were done. However, he stayed sober and listened, catching fragments of Lanthran that he could understand. Gradually, he learned that Gapstand was hosting a weaver's guild convention and most of the men and women in the room were members. Fred listened with (apparently) great interest as his neighbors at table discussed dyes for Skye wool, and the justification for a new shipping tax, and a special delivery ordered by the military. It sounded like the Torish government was paying for wool with one hand and taxing the weavers' profits away with the other, and they were feeling very sore about it. He ate and drank and laughed and listened, and then his ears picked up with true interest.

Someone mentioned a large order of the wool from the Steerage Islands, off the eastern coast of Tor. Fred caught the words, *"din Baradyah."* It was to be dyed brown, like Bardian uniforms. The weavers kept talking. Fred ordered more beer for everyone at his table.

Tom watched the beer coming and going. Although he had consumed a great deal himself, he whispered frantically, "Fred! What are you doing? Our bill is going to be enormous!"

And it was. At the peak of the supper hour, when the din of beer-happy voices was loudest, Fred and Tom went up to the cashier's desk. A small man with a shrunken chin and white hair totaled their chits.

The cashier's eyes widened when he finished the tally. His voice rose when he said, "Six thousand, five-hundred, and sixty-seven brot."

In a tiny, private whisper, Tom began, "Sir, we have no money, but—"

The cashier dropped the chits all over the floor. *"Eaye dee ion?"*

Tom murmured, looking like he wanted to sink through the greasy floor, "That's right, but—" He broke off and lowered his brows at Fred, a dark thunderous look in his eyes.

The elderly man looked aghast. "I'm calling the owner." He pulled a cord under the countertop. Also, shaking his white-crowned head, he shifted his eyes toward an ominous large man standing near the door, who nodded and approached as the clerk kept a suspicious eye on Fred and Tom.

His cheeks and ears bright pink, Tom kept his back to the crowd. However, Fred smiled, waved at his new friends, and "hung out" as if he belonged at the cashier's desk area.

In a short time, the innkeeper stepped out from a back room. Fred gasped.

She was taller than he was and almost as wide as she was tall. She had at least six chins sprouting long black hairs, and Fred saw a moustache under her pert little nose; yet she was somehow very pretty. Her body moved powerfully, with a feminine rhythm. Her blouse, with a scandalously low V-neck, complimented her giant bosom. However, there was a steely glitter in her dark eyes.

The innkeeper snapped, "What's going on?"

Tom pleaded. "Please Madam, listen to me." The young man continued in a stream of Lanthran that Fred could hardly follow, except for: "But we want to pay our bill."

The innkeeper set her jaw and gave them a wilting stare. "Likely story." She jerked her many chins toward the hulky security guard, who grasped a heavy club and moved forward. "You two, stay right here or get beaten to pieces." She motioned toward Helga, who had just come out of the kitchen with a tray of beer. "Go get some rope. The little guy looks like a drowned rat, but the big one might give us some trouble. After that, bring the sheriff. Tell him to bring plenty of backup."

"Aye, J.T. Let me watch you tie up the big one first, and then I'll get the sheriff." Helga gave Fred a wicked glance, a ravishing smile.

Fred broke in, "Yes, we spent a lot tonight, but we intend to make it up to you, and we can do it!"

Tom stepped forward. "Ma'am J. T., please … Give us a job and we'll pay for it all."

J. T. folded her heavy arms and scowled. "I've plenty of dishwashers and floor technicians already."

"Let me suggest something," Fred pleaded, hands clasped in the begging position. *Lord, this has gotta work, or we're goners. We'll go to jail for years—or they'll hand us right over to the baron and good riddance.*

Fred said very quietly, for the innkeeper's ears only, "We're musicians. My friend's name is Sir Thomas Forschwynn, the Bard of Bardia. I'm Fred, his servant."

At that, J. T. blinked. Fred saw that name-dropping might be working.

Fred continued, "You *know* his music will be awesome. He can bring in the customers. In fact, allow him to give a performance for your guests here tonight and take up a collection. You won't be disappointed."

Tom opened his mouth, but Fred cut him off, "We'll repeat performances nightly until the account is settled." He didn't dare look at Tom or wait for him to ratify the idea. In an even lower voice, he said, "However, please don't advertise that the Bard of Bardia is here. There are some people who, um, do not wish him well." He fervently hoped that J. T. was one of the Gapstand people who disliked Baron Trager.

J. T. looked Tom up and down. The hard glint in her eyes softened "Well, try it. I suppose ye'll be needing room and board the while until ye've paid up?"

Fred nodded hopefully.

"It'll be tallied up along with tonight's total."

J. T. waved off the hulky bouncer, who went back to his station by the door. Helga showed up with the rope looking rather eager, but J. T. sent her back into the kitchen.

Jaw set, eyes glaring at Fred, Tom collected the mandolin and pushed his way to the center of the room. There was no stage, just the rows between and around the long tables. Tom sat on a bench. Everyone stopped eating and stared.

While Tom got into performing position, Fred took the part of master of ceremony. "*Golanoya ta gella eaye*!" he called. "Hear ye, hear ye!" He waved gaily at the cluster of weavers where he and Tom had sat. Many of them laughed.

When Tom plucked the strings, pain crossed his face. However, he began to play, and instantly the entire room became silent. Fred could feel their awe. His own soul brightened, as if an encouraging spirit had touched him. *Peace be to you.*

After too short a time, Tom clutched at his side; then he dropped the mandolin into its case with a great *bong!*

A horrified gasp came from every throat.

Holding his right side, more than slightly pale, Tom pushed his way out of the center. "I'm done, Fred. Your turn." He slowly and carefully sat down on the nearest chair. "It was your plan, after all."

Fred's big grin froze on his face. His stomach dropped, and he felt quite cold despite the heat in the room. Dozens of expectant faces turned toward him, waiting for some music. He whispered, "I'm not good enough!"

"I don't care!" Tom hissed. "I can't do any more. I'm done for."

Shaky, Fred took the bard's place in the center of the room. The mandolin felt like an alien object. Fred wondered if he could play even three cords. His mind was blank.

When his desperate eyes searched the room for some inspiration, he saw one lamp glowing brighter than the rest, like a full moon over a lake. It seemed to say, *Don't forget—you are on a mission for Bardia.*

Oh, yeah. Fred remembered why Tom had planned the concert tour. *We're supposed to distract Lord Charon's guests while the Patriots take over the creep's castle.*

Strumming on one chord until he achieved an easy downbeat rhythm, he quickly decided to ad-lib a rap song. It didn't matter if the crowd could understand him. They had drunk enough beer to make them happy. All he had to do was play two or three chords, keep talking, and keep the mood going. He began, Arlo Guthrie style,

I'm here to talk about the war,
The war that began in Moorway.
It all began with the barons' greed

And drifted down to your way.

He hammed it up, and the audience roared. After an hour of desperate ad lib performance, Fred halted. J. T. thrust her bulk forward to the center of the room and the crowd quieted. After a short speech, she led applause. The clapping and hammering on tables were deafening; it lasted for a full five minutes. Then J. T. passed a basket around the room. It began to fill with silver *brot.*

In a few minutes, J. T. brought the basket of money to the cashier to be totaled.

Tom and Fred waited anxiously while the cashier shot accusing glances at them and droned, "Sixty, sixty-two, sixty-three brot."

J. T. huffed into her moustache. "Sixty is mine tonight. Give the rest to the laddie here." She gave Tom a long look, and Fred could swear that her brown eyes darkened with attraction and there was a slight, sensuous smile playing around her full lips.

He glanced at Tom to see if he had noticed, and to his amazement, the kid was responding in a way he would have never guessed. Tom's eyes grew soft when he looked back at the woman, and his voice sounded like music at a beautiful señorita's balcony when he said, "Thank you, J. T."

Wow. Now I know the Tom's taste in women. He likes big powerhouses with a touch of sugar. Fred wanted to giggle hysterically, but he controlled himself while the cashier dropped a very small collection of silver coins into Tom's hand.

"We'll see what comes in tomorrow night," J. T. said in a business-like tone. Abruptly, she ordered. "Come along with me to the back, you two. Young man, I saw you a' grabbing your side. Robbed, were you? And beaten perhaps—by the bruises on your face?"

Fred and Tom followed the big woman through several doors into a cozy sitting room that smelled pleasantly of herbs. He saw red-leather bound books on the wood-paneled walls—including sonnets by Shakespeare and Elizabeth Barrett Browning. Three venerable armchairs and a well-used blue matching sofa with plump cushions looked gloriously comfortable, and a warm fire glowed in the hearth. She filled and hung a polished copper teakettle over the fire. *No wonder Tom likes her,* Fred thought. *She's got class under that, um, exterior.*

"Sit," J. T. commanded.

Obediently and gratefully, they sank into armchairs. J. T. sat down on the third armchair. For a few minutes she looked them over, stroking the moustache on her upper lip. Fred saw her gaze x-ray him closely, and he felt pierced by a keen analytical mind. She did the same to Tom, but Fred noticed her eyes darken again when she looked at the bard, who returned her look.

I can't believe it, he thought. *What a pair!*

Finally, she said, "You're the High Magus's laddies, I see."

Fred pretended to know nothing. "High Magus? Who—? What—?"

J. T. leaned forward. "Don't be stupid. I can guess what you're up to. Your song made it obvious." Except for crackling of the wood fire, the study was silent. "Sir Thomas, can anyone make music as magical as you can? So, why might you be in Gapstand covered with bruises? Where is your lute? Why are you not singing for barons, kings, and lords? And, Fred, I've guessed where you come from, since you can imitate songs from You-Know-Where!"

Fred nearly choked.

J. T. rolled her eyes and laughed.

CHAPTER 48

PATRICK AND THE PATRIOTS

Rain pounded on the roof of the covered wagon where Patrick rode. The sound hurt his ears. It was as unpleasant as the hiss of electronic static. His ankle throbbed rhythmically with each bump of the wheels. His mind felt divided into rotating compartments: supernova, black hole, supernova, black hole, supernova. The rotations coincided with feeling burning hot or shaking with chills.

During one of the blazing hot spells, Patrick felt rain on his face. It felt like being pelted with ice cubes. Some gray-uniformed soldiers had lifted him onto a stretcher and were carrying him out of the wagon. They went into a low, grim building.

"Where's Lewis? Where's my brother?" Patrick asked. No one answered him. The Wolf Riders left him alone, on the stretcher, on the floor. Patrick stared at white, bare, cold walls.

An hour passed, and no one came to talk to him. The fever passed into another chill, and he started crying like a toddler. He wanted to see anyone, even a stranger. While the tears were still streaming down his face and he was stifling sobs, a woman with iron gray hair, a hard jaw, and soft eyes came in. "Where's Lewis?" he asked. His throat was so dry he could hardly croak. She shook her head, but she held his hand gently and wiped his face with a clean white cloth.

Two men wearing gray robes, apparently doctors, entered the room, talking to each other in low tones. They called the woman away from Patrick. He clutched at her warm hand that had held his, but she got up. The older of the two doctors bent down. Patrick saw a graying beard, a big nose, and two dark eyes with happy crinkle marks at the corners. The doctor began to remove the splints from the ankle. When he saw that Patrick's foot, ankle, and shin were swollen, dusky, and hot all the way to his knee, he winced.

In Lanthran, he talked to Patrick. "I hear you've been calling for your brother."

"*Alor,*" Patrick said. His voice was a mere croak.

Pulling out a vial of greenish liquid from the pocket of his cloak, the doctor very gently used a cloth to spread the liquid over the swollen area. He said, "Your brother was in this fortress. He was with Baron Layhew, a verra' dangerous place to be. Howe'er, I've heard that he's left for Moorway, to work for Lord Charon." He fell silent for a moment, then continued, "The rumors say that you are refugees. They said the Bardians attacked you."

Patrick stared at him. He burst out, in English, "What? No way! That Barth Layhew kidnapped us. He and his goons got Lewis and me at Nutman University at night. They put a knife to my throat! They were going to sacrifice us to Saoma!" He touched the scab on the side of neck.

The doctor drew in a sharp breath. He looked up at the older doctor and the nurse, then turned back to Patrick. "I'm sorry these things happened to you. Yet, we have a good plan for—"

He broke off abruptly. A soldier, one of Nark's Wolf Riders, entered the room.

The older doctor bent over Patrick's ankle, which felt better already, as if soothed by a cooling, minty bath. He spoke calmly in Lanthran, and Patrick could only follow about a third of what he said. "Give him some *siarela* ... we'll put the boy to sleep before we clean the pus out of his ankle. He hasn't eaten, has he?

No? Good!"

The Wolf Rider looked gruff and frankly bored. He left the bare, white room. As soon as he was gone, the younger doctor gave Patrick a knowing wink.

The woman who had held Patrick's hand went out and came back with a cup Raising his head with one hand, she held the cup to Patrick's lips, and he drank. The liquid was sweet, syrupy, with a sour tang and a bitter under-taste. When he had drunk it all, he lay back and the nurse covered him with a thick, soft blanket.

They left him again. He was in fever mode. The white walls seemed to pulsate when he looked around, so he shut his eyes. Behind his eyelids, he saw bomber airplanes taking off, one after the other, and each exploding in the air. After about twenty explosions, he broke out into a huge sweat. His clothes were drenched. Suddenly, he felt better. *Things are going to be all right.* The thought lifted his soul.

CHAPTER 49
THE BARD RESUMES HIS ASSIGNMENT

After coming to the Gapstand Inn, Tom and Fred worked hard to settle their debt and recover from their bruises. The inn always had a lively business. Its customers – and also the employees who were well trained under J. T.'s management—tended to be messy, loud, and plain folk, and all of them detested their country's Saoma-worshipping controllers. Fred guessed that Baron Trager probably knew that they were there by now, but he left them alone.

Fred was happy. His performance skills improved; Helga was a tasty dish, and she and he flirted constantly. Tom was happy, too. Once he recovered, his music was marvelous, as usual, and J. T. kept a loving eye on him.

Spring passed into summer. Late one humid evening, after the dining hall had closed and Tom and Fred were relaxing with J. T., her sitting room door banged open.

"Help!" Tom yelled. J. T. sprang up with a broadsword.

Fred wrestled himself into an upright position, but the armchair seemed to hold him like a soft octopus. "Huh? Who?" He suddenly recognized this fellow: Big ears, buckteeth, round and bright little eyes that looked like a bat—it was indeed Hermann, Daniel's special agent, the man who had arrested him in Nutman. The ugly sight zapped the cozy mist in his brain. *Oh great, the vampire enters the scene.*

"Thank Radyah that you're alive, Sir Forschwynn!" Hermann cried. He strode in, his black cloak streaming behind him. Spurs clanked on his boots, and he carried an unsheathed bright sword. He bowed low to Tom but glared at Fred. "And, once again, we meet, you fat dirty fuzzball!"

Fred's lips curled in an insincere smile. "Hello, Hermann. And do you not look ridiculous, you flapping bat?"

As Fred rose to his feet, Hermann stepped forward. "'Tis providence for sure that I came tonight, Sir Thomas. I came to protect you from this …" he sputtered, "this traitor!"

"What did you call me?" Fred roared. "You—"

"Stop it!" J. T. ordered. "We're on the same side. There's enough trouble in Torpatath without you snarling like surly dogs!"

Hermann's eyes narrowed into glittering slits, and Fred could swear that his big ears turned toward him like radar dishes. "This big *cilathoon,* the one who betrayed his friend Lewis Brahmindura—I heard how he treated you, Sir Thomas, when you were in Baron Trager's power. How can you trust him? He will only betray you, Sir Thomas, and he will do it again and again, for that his nature."

"*What*" Fred bellowed.

Hermann turned to Tom and J. T. "His Excellency sent me after you disappeared. After much searching, I met a man in the city who is a relative of one of Trager's staff. He told me that your subua had tricked you, tied you up, abused you, and escaped from Trager's castle. I thought you were dead! Murdered by your own subua! So, I tracked his fat feet until I came here, to this Gapstand Inn, and learned that he gobbled much food and beer, made a big noise, and was unable to pay for his presumption!"

Fred felt heat rush to his face. He clenched his fists and leaned forward. "I did not betray Tom at Trager's castle! I played a trick on him, but that was so I could help him escape! I am Tom's servant!"

"A pig can get a bath," Hermann said. "But he remains a pig, nonetheless."

Fred crouched menacingly, ready to squash the smaller man and impale him on his own sword. "So, you're calling me a pig? I'm a boar, then, and you are an ugly rodent! Try anything with that sword and watch me tear off your nasty little head!"

Hermann turned to Fred with an insolent expression and readied his sword; Fred strode forward; but Tom jumped between them.

"*Enough!*"

Fred and Hermann stepped back.

"Our mission is to give aid to the Patriots in Torpatath. My end goal," Tom stated, crossing his arms and glowering like a miniature version of J. T., "assigned to me by the High Magus himself, is to perform in Moorway for the High Council of the Magi, during which the Patriots' revolution will begin. I have chosen to bring my subua Fred as my manservant. He is both loyal and extremely helpful."

"My business, laddie," Hermann snarled, "also assigned to me by the High Magus, is to see that the Bard of Bardia remains safe—that's *you*. And you won't be safe with this buffoon." Sword still pointed toward Fred, he moved to take Tom's arm. "Now, I've heard that Trager-trouble is coming. I'm taking you out of here immediately!"

Tom threw off Hermann's hand. "Do not question my decisions! I am not a child!"

One of Hermann's eyebrows crooked upward, and even Fred couldn't repress the thought, *You're barely an adult, Tom.*

Fred suddenly realized something awful. Talk about being safe … "Oh my God, I've just remembered … You need to know … The weavers …"

"What are you babbling about?" Hermann snapped. "Trager's coming; we have to go!"

"I'm not babbling," Fred insisted. "You've got to carry this observation to Daniel and Captain Gregory: The weavers clued me on what's going to happen! They were talking about a *huge* order for brown wool—"

J. T. roared, *"Shut up and sit down."*

She made a commanding gesture, and each of them sat. Hermann sheathed the sword and sat carefully on the edge of a chair, Tom glowered, sitting on the sofa with J. T., and Fred, on another chair, knew that his own face must be red as a severe sunburn.

J. T. growled, turning to Hermann. "Listen to Fred."

Fred tried to explain, his voice low and intense, "Yes, listen! The Torish military must plan to invade Bardia disguised as Bardian soldiers! It's totally against the rules of war—at least the ones I remember from Earth, but—"

Hermann winced. "Don't speak of the forbidden—"

Fred finished, "Although where they'll strike first, I don't know. I imagine Nutman because that's where the College of the Magi is."

Everyone looked at Fred, aghast.

"Eplaithon Baradyah ta Lipplaitha," Hermann breathed. He stroked his wiry moustache, but then he jumped up. "Sir Thomas, I'm taking you back to your father. Tonight! You must be protected from the invasion!" His beady eyes barely touched Fred, as if he were a cigarette butt on the road.

"No!" Tom shouted.

Hermann seized Tom's arm, but Tom knocked his hand aside.

"You must go back home, Tom!" J. T. said tenderly. "For now the rulers of Torpatath are pretending that there is still peace between them and Bardia, but you are the Bard, the very icon of—"

"Tom," said Fred, "it sounds bad. Maybe we'd better go back while we can."

"No." Tom stated, his eyebrows level, jaw set, and his voice firm. "I'm going to Torgard, and from there to Moorway. That's the plan I had in the beginning, and that is what I shall accomplish. And …" he turned to Hermann, "Fred is going with me."

CHAPTER 50

LEWIS JOINS THE ENEMY

In the morning when Lewis awoke, Barth was (*thank God!*) gone. A servant came in and helped Lewis wash his swollen face and dress with new clothes. *Oh great, I get to be medieval.* He was given a midnight blue linen shirt with white lace at the cuffs, a dark brown jacket with gold inner lining, dark brown pants which were too loose on him—a belt with a showy gold buckle held those up—and clean hose with tall brown boots.

Once more in the court chamber, Baron Layhew glared at Lewis, and Lewis, standing, made himself look down as humbly as possible. The huge baron growled. "Tell me about Earth. What did you there before you were sent for?"

With a huge effort, Lewis mastered his response. He answered, keeping his voice calm and polite, "On Earth, before I crossed to Lanthra, I was a physicist. I had a job with Dr. Zhartha, a leading scientist in charge of a project to produce limitless electric power for Earth's needs. Lanthra's prohibition of electronic technology doesn't apply on Earth. Why do you ask?"

The hairy baron, today wearing a black muscle shirt and leather pants, loomed forward and growled, "I'll be asking the questions, *zitta* tongue."

At that moment, Barth showed up, his face puffy and red but otherwise sober. He had dressed formally in a fawn suit with a shiny gold shirt. Sitting near Nark, he crossed his long legs and smiled nastily, enjoying the show. "Louie, that means 'pustule tongue.' You're getting sassy, friend. Just keep on and see what you get for it."

Baron Layhew stared at Lewis like a cat eyeing a little bird. "So, you were a fizz-a-sisst. You were … making e-led-tri-zi-tie. Tell me what that means."

Lewis tried to imagine an explanation that would make sense in Nark's low-tech world of hills and horses and swords and goats. He couldn't, so he didn't even try. He spoke, no tone in his voice at all, "We conceptualized a way to create a tiny singularity—that's a tiny but enormously dense entity called a 'black hole.' One the size of a pinprick would do. Once created, the singularity will sink to Earth's center of gravity. Although the singularity absorbs energy and nothing ever comes out, the turbulence around its event horizon could generate electricity for thousands, even millions of years. All you have to do is tap into it."

Baron Layhew looked blank.

Barth's eyes, however, gleamed with understanding. He patronized, "Our ancient magi achieved that before we helped your Egyptians build the pyramids. Later, of course, Louie, your Bardian buddies outlawed all electronic technology except at a few private clubs such as the College of the Magi in Nutman. I graduated from the University of Nutman with highest honors! And there I learned the secrets of the ancient locating technology."

Until you got fired by Dr. Zadok, Lewis thought, but thought it very wise to say nothing.

Barth jerked his chin toward his brother and said, "Yes, I won a place with my Lord Charon's technology staff, but when dear Nargoleh tried to get into the university, he couldn't pass the tests. Poor, poor brother!"

Nark glowered, eyebrows bristling,

Lewis's jaw dropped. In his head he put two and two together … *Barth is a skilled Lanthran engineer as well as a giant pain.*

Saoma-worshipping Lanthrans have united with Earth's Shields to conquer Lanthra and Earth with overpowering technology from both worlds! Barth is a Lanthran geek! No wonder he's a big player in the Horned Edge plots.

Meanwhile, the air, even eight feet away from the baron and Barth, vibrated with a dissonance that set Lewis's teeth on edge. The clash in the brothers' invisible realm made him feel like he was hearing an augmented fourth interval.

"So," Nark addressed Lewis again. "You found a noretha that guides the way to Earth. Tell me more." The baron crossed his arms and leaned forward to listen.

With no more emotion than a lecturer describing dates and names in ancient history, Lewis related how Patrick and Gracie had found the hot marble, the noretha that Charon's head magus had thrown into the nexus and had lost. He mentioned that he had experienced an attack from the Shields company who wanted him to become a mole in his own company. He told how Fred and he had run tests on the marble, had decided it was a neural network, and had correctly reasoned that they had stumbled across a tool to link to another world.

At that point, Baron Layhew interrupted, "You know about the bizeor of Earth. Tell me about them!" His eyes gleamed.

Lewis narrowed his own eyes. Something about Nark's posture, an extra-intense crackling in his aura, told him that he was close to the man's core issue. *What does Nark want?*

He began, "I don't know that I have ever encountered a demon. *Except for you, Nark!* But I realize that there is evil in the world. Correct that to 'worlds,' both Earth and Lanthra. There must be a logical explanation for evil. Perhaps there are spiritual beings, but science cannot find evidence of those."

Lewis paused, disturbed out of his emotionless state. Unwelcome memories of experiencing true hatred made shivers crawl up and down his back. The home invasion with the nasty Shields threatening his family. The kidnapping and the murdered magi in the College's laboratory. That stinking Kut holding a knife to Patrick's throat! *What? Does this evil brute want to know more about Satan?*

Baron Layhew frowned darkly. He glanced at Barth then looked back at Lewis and growled, "Is that all?"

"That's all" Lewis said. He felt exhausted. A cough spasmed in his lungs, and he bent over, his chest racking.

The baron hit the magistrate's bench with his fist so loudly that Lewis jumped back to a stiff stand. "Tell me more! About Earth's bizeor—and the foroya and Radyah!" His movements were angry, but Lewis, amazed, thought that his eyes pleaded like a small child trying to express a complicated need.

Barth interrupted "Brother dear, don't you mean Saoma? Are you or are you not a member of the Horned Edge? It appears that you fantasize a world of angels, Jesus, and so on, those creations of Earth mythology. You should know that the only real god is Saoma." He added ironically. "Nargoleh, shall I mention to *our* High Magus that you want to be one of *those* people?"

Lewis blinked. *Huh?*

The Baron roared, "To hell with you, little brother!" His face swung back toward Lewis. "Subua from Earth, tell me more! I want to know what is the—" He stopped, stymied by his lack of English vocabulary, and began to sputter, "*Gahalla-tha nethe lag* …"

"Supernatural beings?" Lewis asked, guessing at the unfamiliar words. "Cherubim and seraphim and all the company of heaven?" He now remembered Ezekiel's images of the whirling wheels, the winged creatures full of eyes, the Son of Man on the sapphire throne. "You've got to be kidding!"

His stomach was painfully hungry. He wanted a good drink, and his throat felt hoarse from all the talking, but at least his nose had quit running. Instead, a heavy, clotted pressure had settled in his head and chest. He coughed. It hurt. *Where the hell is this inquisition going? Not to Bible stories—no, I'm not going there!*

Inside, he felt his dragon wriggle, but Lewis set his jaw and stubbornly clamped it down. *I don't believe in angels and demons, or in the Christian God, either—any kind of god.* He answered, his voice flat and firm, "I don't know much about supernatural stuff. Ask me about something real, such as the special theory of relativity."

Baron Nargoleh Layhew demanded, in his poor English, "Tell me about Radyah! The Earth Radyah!" His hand bunched into a fist, and he got up, walking over to stand close to Lewis.

Cooperate, cooperate, Lewis reminded himself. However, he felt too angry to catechize a bloody sadist. Baron Layhew loomed over Lewis who had to tilt his head back to see the man's face. The baron's burning eyes and his greasy flowing black hair intimidated Lewis to the point of making his stomach queasy. Deliberately looking away, Lewis leaned back and crossed his arms.

Barth sneered, evidently enjoying his brother's frustration. Yet, oddly, Lewis noticed a hint of fear on Barth's face, a telltale paling around his eyes. "Wait, brother," Barth interrupted. "Louie boy knows all you want to hear; he's just too stubborn to tell you."

Barth is scared. He brought me here to get points with his big brother, but it's not working. The tension between Lewis's desire to be docile and his stubborn refusal to admit the existence of God clashed. *I don't believe in that religion stuff, and I won't compromise my integrity.*

Thoughts in his mind chorused, *What integrity? You think you still have any left after you helped those devils raid the laboratory? You have a share in the murder, by your compliance!*

But I had to save Patrick! he mentally shouted.

Barth continued. "Don't you understand, Nargoleh? This interview is going nowhere. If you want to know more about Earth gods, you'll have to ask different questions." He stared at Lewis as if to say, *Give him what he wants!* Barth's urgent eyes and pressured voice reminded Lewis of someone losing a giant sale.

Baron Nark growled, "That's right, brother Barth, preserve your lousy present. Maybe you think I'll learn to love you like your dear Lord Charon does, you worthless piece of trash."

Barth's face flushed scarlet.

Baron Layhew ordered, "Go get some wine. I'm thirsty."

Barth sprang out of his chair with a scowl and stomped out from the courtroom.

Menacing, the baron addressed Lewis in his poor English, "Tell me about the bizeor! Tell me about the foroya! Tell me about Radyah! Will you be stubborn with me? Will you murder your young brother?"

Lewis swayed as if he'd been hit by a rock. His whole body trembled so hard that he almost crumpled. With all his small strength, he gripped the wooden railing that kept distance between him and the baron. Lewis whispered hoarsely, "You would hurt Patrick just to hear me talk about a religion that I don't believe in? You're crazy! You're absolutely insane!"

Baron Layhew smiled like a shark about to eat a small tuna. "You will talk with me or, I swear, your brother will ..."

"What? Die?" Barth's high-pitched voice cut through the growing congestion in Lewis' ears. He held a tray that supported a large sweaty pewter pitcher, three polished silver goblets, and three yeast-risen rolls. "Honestly, Nargoleh, is murdering a kid worth that? Just work on Louie's pride a little longer; break him down. I *know* that he knows this Radyah stuff. The bizeor on Earth reported to my Horned Edge brothers that they saw him going to church with his family. Also, in Nutman, I myself saw him attending the chapel with the pious Gregory family and fat little Deirdre." Barth shot Lewis a scathing look. He continued, "Louie boy, talk to my brother, whether you believe or not."

"I ... can ... *not* ... tell you what you want to know!" Lewis whispered intensely.

Baron Layhew drew in a sharp breath; his face went purple. Then it cleared. The man's dark eyes calculated, and his head turned from Barth to Lewis and back again.

Barth's face looked absolutely desperate. However, his eyes gleamed with a sudden idea. "Louie, don't you have a little sister as well as a brother? Hmm, I imagine you'd spill every scrap of religion you've ever heard if she were here."

Lewis felt his breath spill out, the last reluctant exhalation before drowning. "You piece of turd! Would you hurt a little girl as well as my young brother?" His stomach dropped; his chest squeezed hard. *Is this what a heart attack feels like?*

Barth stared longingly at his brother. "Just tell him something, Lewis. Let me give him a gift!"

Cooperate, cooperate, the inner voice chanted, but Lewis stood frozen in fear.

At that moment, Baron Layhew closed his eyes and sighed dramatically, making a decision. He poured wine into the silver goblets, delicately took a yeasty roll, but when Barth reached for a goblet and a roll, Nark slapped Barth's hand away. Red wine splashed all over Barth's fine clothes.

Lips curling with deliberate insult, Baron Layhew handed the second goblet to Lewis. Next, he carefully gave Lewis the second yeasty roll.

Careful not to spill or drop anything, Lewis accepted the food and drink, knowing well the symbolism behind sharing bread with an enemy. *I hate you, Barth. Don't you dare threaten my sister again, or I will find a way to destroy you.*

Dripping with wine, Barth stepped close to Lewis. "Maybe you remember Fred Jontz?" he said, spraying Lewis's face with spit.

Lewis almost dropped the goblet. A little wine splashed onto the floor. It looked like blood. "Have you done anything to Fred?" he asked in a fierce whisper. "Did you murder my friend?"

"Him?" Barth roared incredulously. Laughing, dancing a step, he repeated, "Him? Fred Jontz was your *friend*?

Dumb with rage, Lewis nodded.

Barth held up his arms in mock wonder and crowed, "Your friend was so jealous of you, the teacher's pet, the boy wonder, that he sold you for a pint of beer! Who told us you were the new Bardian expert at the College of the Magi's lab? Who suggested that we use *you* to open the security door so that I could take the essential parts of the thoyo-on? Your friend, Fred Jontz!"

Enjoying the stricken expression on Lewis's face, Barth cried out, "Fred told us how to get into the laboratory—and *you* helped us steal the computer core so we can connect to Earth again! Ha! You're a betrayer, too. Remember how you froze, when we killed Zadok's lab rats, those kindergarten magi? You didn't do a thing to help them." Barth dug into a pocket of his shirt and triumphantly held up a marble that gleamed golden in morning light. "This is your 'hot marble!' Thank you, Louie; thank you, Fred; you gave Charon and me the door to Earth! Thanks for your help!"

All resistance was knocked out of Lewis. He thought about the people he loved: Patrick and Gracie, Deirdre, the Gregory family, even renegade Fred—they would all be crushed by the Torish steamroller. And he was of no use to help anyone ... Unless ...

Switch sides. Join these Saoma-worshipping creeps to rescue Patrick and Gracie. He felt deathly tired, and a fog or film blurred his vision. He was down to his last straw.

You don't need to do this, a breath of a voice said in his mind. *Someone greater than you is taking care of your loved ones.*

Lewis shook his head. Then, looking into Nark's eyes, understanding their unspoken covenant, Lewis drank the wine and ate the roll. A current of mutuality flowed between them. All the nastiness, abuse, and fear had altered him; now he and Baron Nargoleh Layhew shared a same purpose. Out of hate and frustration, he had chosen to triangulate against Barth.

"Stupid brother," Baron Layhew patronized to Barth, "you thought you could buy my favor with this little *risi*?" He looked amused. He threw his emptied goblet, which bounced on the stone floor and rang like a bell, and he crossed his huge bare arms. "Darling brother, your gift is useless to me. However, he's more valuable than gold or diamonds or even *you* to Lord Charon."

Barth glared and hissed, "He will *never* take my place with my Lord Charon!"

Lewis knew what was going to happen and what he should do. *I'll go to Moorway. I'll join the Horned Edge. I'll excel and earn Charon's favor and take Barth's place at Lord Charon's right hand. And then—I'll rescue Patrick and Gracie and send them back to Earth.* A great sadness filled him. *Goodbye, Deirdre.*

CHAPTER 51

RUMORS OF WAR

The sun set over the city of Nutman in Bardia in a big pink splash. Summer moons, little azure Bibo and big copper Wega, appeared against a net of diamond stars. Daniel, the High Magus, watched, but he was not happy. His two daughters and Lewis's sister Gracie had left for Smythe and should be safe, but – he yanked on his white-blond hair – he was still not happy. In Daniel's small, fine hands were several intelligence reports. Each bore bad news.

Somewhere out there is Earth, Daniel thought. *The Planet of the Curse is sending us its best presents, invited by my enemy, Lord Tahei Charon.* Feeling nauseated, he stood in his darkening office, staring out his bay window, his back against the closed door.

He re-read the first report. It was a nasty surprise: Cholera had struck his province. Dozens had died already, and Daniel knew there would be many more deaths. Charon's ally from Earth, the Shields weapons company that included a Saoma-worshipping sect, had dumped feces in the area's reservoirs. "Germ warfare, terrorist style!" Daniel shouted. He crunched up the intelligence report and hurled it across the room.

A second intelligence report noted a massive buildup at his

border of Baron Layhew's Wolf Riders and Lord Charon's Eagle forces. It was not certain when they would invade. If Lord Charon succeeded in connecting to Earth again, not only would he open the door to Saoma's demons, but he would cement his alliance with the Shields. They would bring over their weapons: missiles, guns, tanks, bombs … Daniel closed his eyes as if that would make the problem go away and crushed that report also; the wad rolled over the carpet. *You* will *be overrun,* he remembered the Master telling him.

And last, he held the very worst news, a letter from his friend Sir Edwin Forschwynn, viceroy of the neighboring province. In strong, bold cursive, Edwin had written:

> Here is a copy of the message that Baron Arthur Trager sent me. He has kidnapped my son Thomas and his servant Fred. The ransom note is written in Thomas's handwriting; it is no fake. The baron's messenger brought it to me with my son's lute and his companion's ring. Trager has demanded a huge ransom; I cannot possibly pay it without selling my entire province and all I have.

> It may be that Trager will kill Thomas, the direct descendant of the Bard of Bardia with that bard's talents. Destroying the bard could set Bardia – and indeed our world Lanthra – back for centuries.

> Our nation's 500th Celebration has already begun its gathering in my province. However, any news of Thomas's kidnapping would destroy the morale of all Bardia. I have not made my son's situation public, and I exhort you to keep it quiet as well.

> As I said, Baron Trager sent Thomas's lute and his servant's ring to confirm his message. If you are able to rescue my son – that is, if he still lives – please send the lute to him. You of all people, my canny friend, have the skills and contacts to get it done. However, the servant's ring must be hidden because of a certain inscription from

that world; I'm sure you understand. Do come to the Celebration soon. I fear for you there, and your presence will encourage all of us.

*　　*　　*

Daniel dropped the letter onto his desk. "Oh, my friend Edwin, I am so sorry!" At Daniel's feet lay a lumpy bag with the neck of a lute – *the* Lute – sticking out. The famous instrument looked sad, even dead without its bard.

He stood looking outward but not seeing as mists gathered in the Loudmouth riverbed below. Suddenly his self-control snapped. Daniel yelled and punched the wall. "Why should Lord Charon set himself against me! Why must he worship evil Saoma and want to rule both worlds? Why must we lose the Bard of Bardia? Why, why, why? Why, God, my Master?"

His office door opened behind him, and Daniel stumbled. "What is it?" he snapped.

"Your Excellency," his secretary said in his characteristic mild tone. "Your agent Hermann has returned from Tor with a report. "Will you see him now?"

"In a moment, in a moment." Daniel closed the door in his secretary's face. *I must compose myself!* To the Master, he growled, "All right, you warned me. My plans to protect the province aren't working. In fact, everything I've set in place is falling apart!"

The Master replied, *Are you willing to trust me?*

"Yes – but not very well," Daniel seethed. "You said that my province will be overrun. You told me that I will be captured and taken to Moorway."

Trust me, e bibat. *A little faith is enough.*

Sighing, feeling calmer, Daniel said to God, "Well, at least my daughters Deirdre and Myra and Lewis's young sister Gracie are safe in Smythe." He reopened the door and apologized. "I'm sorry, James, that I lost my temper."

"I understand. You are anxious, Your Excellency," his James

said, bowing. Daniel felt the air clear between them. "Admit my agent Hermann here. Also, James – will you be in for a while tomorrow morning to close out the office?"

His secretary shook his head. "I would prefer not, Your Excellency. My family and I are leaving for the Celebration before dawn." He hesitated.

Daniel answered the unspoken question. "Yes, you may go with my blessing. May your journey be safe and short. I will take care of myself. I must arrange help for the cholera epidemic, and then I will depart to join the Celebration. Now, James, usher in my spy."

Hermann came in. The man, with buckteeth, prominent nose and ears, and beady eyes under a flamboyant hat, bowed low. "Your Excellency, I'm sorry to disturb you so late, but I have news. Aye, indeed," Hermann went on, and his voice was cheerful, "you can ignore the ransom note."

"What?"

"Sir Thomas and his slave are safe. They were indeed kidnapped and held for ransom, but they escaped and are safe."

Daniel felt his entire body blaze with a fierce relief. "Good!"

Hermann's voice lowered. His face darkened. "Your Excellency, I tried to persuade young Sir Thomas to come back to Bardia, but the boy insisted on continuing his concert in Tor to rouse the Patriots. His worthless slave Fred, from that horrible planet, did nothing to stop him!"

Daniel began to respond, but Hermann held up a hand to still Daniel's next words. "Sir Thomas learned that weavers sold a great load of brown cloth to the Saoma-worshipping Torish military. Their troops may intend to masquerade as Bardian soldiers and try to invade your city by trickery."

Daniel considered. "Our city is well guarded. It is surrounded by a camp of soldiers, walled, and entered only by one gate. Nutman is not easy to invade."

Hermann was silent, but the thought came to Daniel, *Do not assume your physical safety, only the safety of your soul.* His optimism cracked and he fought to regain it. Daniel reviewed his plans:

One: Most of my people are already evacuated to the well-defended Forschwynn province. There, the people should be safe. I will be there too, in a few days.

Two: Lord Charon's hunger to invade my province and destroy me has diverted his attention from his own oppressed people. Their revolt is scheduled, and it may succeed.

Three: My daughters and Gracie are in neutral Smythe at Deirdre's estate. Lord Charon's forces cannot reach them there. Even if the Torish succeed in invading Nutman, they will be safe.

Daniel asked Hermann, "How are preparations going for the Patriots' revolt in Tor, especially in Charon's capitol, Moorway?"

With a toothy grin, Hermann slapped his hat on his thigh. "The Patriots have everything organized. The date of their revolt is set. They have yet some time to prepare, and plenty of morale." The spy paused, and he flapped his cloak. "I only wish Sir Thomas was not going to endanger himself in Moorway! I would like to rid him of that bungling *subua* Fred who travels with him! He could yet betray – "

Daniel cut off further discussion. "Stop! I don't want to hear anything from your antagonism toward Fred. True, the demons of Earth infected him. True, he betrayed Lewis and caused him and Patrick to be kidnapped. However, Fred's spirit has changed. Little Gracie has forgiven him, and Sir Thomas gave up his entire inheritance to save Fred from hanging. Now, have you heard anything else?"

Hermann said, "Yes, I have reports from my sources concerning Patrick in Tor. The boy broke his ankle trying to escape after he and *Fean* Lewis were kidnapped. He was very sick indeed. Howe'er, the Patriots found a way to get him out of the hospital and into the care of one of their contacts."

"Thank *Radyah!* And how is Lewis, his brother? Have you

learned anything?"

Hermann let out a deep breath and rubbed the floor with a booted foot. "'Tis said he willingly joined Lord Charon and the worshippers of Saoma. With his help, Charon may well repair his locating system and bring over the weapons from … from the forbidden planet."

"Ah." Daniel felt as if he had been socked in the stomach. *Lewis … a servant of Saoma. Lewis … an open atheist until he and Deirdre fell in love, when he had softened to becoming an agnostic. Now, however, Lewis is working with the enemy. Why?* But he had no answer.

Hermann stated, "Your Excellency, I am ready to return to your mission in Tor. Do you have any additional orders for me?"

"Oh, yes! Go to Moorway immediately! See that Sir Thomas receives the lute. Help the Patriots coordinate the revolt. Do everything you can! You will have to improvise a great deal, but you are my best agent."

"Thank you, Your Excellency, for your trust in me!" Hermann bowed, sweeping the floor with his hat, and swung the lute over his shoulder. He glided out of the door, leaving a faint musty smell behind, like the odor of caves.

CHAPTER 52

LEWIS AND THE HORNED EDGE RING

A few weeks after arriving at Moorway, Lewis Brahmindura swallowed his medicine. Lord Charon, the ruler of Tor, had sent his own personal physician to prescribe it. Dressing for a day of work in Lord Charon's laboratory, Lewis sang aloud and danced, but he still coughed.

Lewis knew that his manic mood was irrational. However, it felt so good that he didn't want to figure out *why*. Dimly, he remembered his transference to the world named Lanthra with his younger brother and sister, Patrick and Gracie, and his best friend, Fred. At first, they had settled in a country called Bardia, where he and Fred had worked under the High Magus, Daniel. He and they had been shocked to know that they could not return home, but the pain had eased when he had fallen in love with beautiful Deirdre, the High Magus's daughter. A sharp, bright thought stabbed his heart and interrupted his dancing spree. *Deirdre! My love! How can I forget you?*

It's too late for you and her, a strange voice said, and stomped on his thoughts and memories.

Now … a complete turn-around … Lewis was working for Daniel's bitter enemy, Lord Charon of Tor. He realized his new position and grinned. "I am so happy now! I'm doing exactly what

I've wanted to do all my life!"

However, a tiny voice inside reminded him: *Fred betrayed you; Patrick and you were kidnapped, and, just several weeks ago, Barth and his horrible brother Nark threatened to harm your brother and sister if you didn't cooperate. But look! Here you are, a magus for Lord Charon, a Saoma worshipper!*

Lewis squashed the rebuke. He congratulated himself, thinking, *Switching sides has paid off. I am now a respected scientist in Lord Charon's hierarchy. And today –* Lewis's smile could have lit an entire planet – *for the first time, I will enter the chamber that houses the portal to the stars.* He began singing again.

Static tickled in his brain, but he brushed it away while he combed his dark hair. It was getting long and wavy … and maybe a little coarse because he kept forgetting to eat. Yet, he saw, his skin and eyes were a warm brown. *I look a lot like Lord Charon. How wonderful!*

His apartment had been designed and decorated for royalty, and it was near Lord Charon's own palace residence. There were no windows – *How long has it been since you even stepped outside to look at the sunshine?* interjected the annoying inner voice.

My apartment is fantastic, he countered. There was plenty of light from tall lamps. His room had a high ceiling curved like a canopy, with a beautiful carved marble lotus at each corner, and white marble walls. An ebony black lattice hid his bed, which was neatly made and covered with slate-gray silk brocade.

Lewis sat at his desk. Humming, he held up his right hand and admired the new ring on his third finger. It was gold with a black diamond – a high status symbol.

Yo, Lewis, didn't you notice what finger that Horned Edge ring is on?

Quickly, Lewis covered his hand. After a moment, feeling stubborn, he opened it to display his ring again. In fact, he was proud of it. *I like it here. I like this room, this desk, and this ring.*

A question came that he didn't expect. *Lewis, didn't you sit at such a desk at your Earth home for journaling, when you wrote that God is nonexistent and irrelevant? Who has protected you to this day? And are you on the side of the people who love you, or the people who mistreat you?*

"No one is mistreating me! I am now a great magus!" he exclaimed aloud. "I am about to become the lead scientist here! I am on Lord Charon's side because, not only will he protect my little brother and sister, he and I will help save the worlds!"

Yes, he was pleased with Lord Charon. His master, the ruler of all Tor, was on the path to become the next High Magus of all Lanthra – and Earth. The man was brilliant and powerful … *I'm like him and he is like me.*

His soul flying with joy, Lewis chanted in his thoughts: *I am brilliant. I am powerful. I have indomitable perseverance. Today, after I talk with Lord Charon. I know exactly what to do. With me in charge, the locating system will work.*

You cannot sustain this mood! the voice in his heart insisted. *And quit taking that mind-altering medicine!*

Lewis paused. His head drooped; he heaved a deep breath. However, rebellious resolve gathering, he raised his head. He declared, "With my talents, I can prevent war on Lanthra, and even on Earth! And I will rescue Patrick and Gracie and get them back home!"

The voice in his head queried, *What exactly is in that medicine?*

"I've never felt better in my life!" Lewis insisted. "Just think – I can bring everything back to the way it was before …" He refused to think about the "before." Humming as he inspected himself again in the mirror, he repeated, "I have everything under control. Soon, I'll rescue my little brother Patrick and little sister Gracie. We'll be together again, and …"

Look around you, a powerful entity inside of him commanded. The voice roared; Lewis felt it as a huge golden dragon coiled in his soul. Lewis sensed that this dragon was not evil, that it was the self that moved toward his true purpose. *You've gotten proud,* the dragon said. *That won't do. I want to give you the desire of your heart, but you will not find that here. And especially not with that Horned Edge ring!*

"Yes, I will!" Lewis told it. The imprisoned beast roiled in his soul. "I don't believe in you," he told it.

Lewis beat his head against the wall to rid it of the conflict. To further distract himself, Lewis circled his head in appreciative awe of the austere, almost holy whiteness of his palace quarters. The dragon interfered again. *Don't you really prefer richer, warmer colors – like the carpets of your Indian heritage? Who is controlling you that you cannot be yourself?*

Impelled by a sudden rage, Lewis smashed his hand onto his desk. The Horned Edge ring cut into his finger, which left drops of red blood on the fine, polished wood. "My room is just the way I like it! My *life* is just the way I like it!"

The voice inside him whispered once more before he clamped it down and threw it out of his head, *No it isn't. The spirit here is strange. And so are you!*

CHAPTER 53

INVASION

Daniel slept through breakfast, which was unusual. He awoke with a tension headache but that slowed him down as he packed for his journey to the Celebration. All the house servants had been evacuated, so he made his own lunch. The afternoon brought paperwork. Finally, in the mild evening, with dew collecting on the tea-rose garden and cooling the air, Daniel walked about the yard, followed discretely by his remaining guards. *I miss my daughters Deirdre and Myra, and Lewis's sweet little sister Gracie. I miss you so much, my dear wife Ielen! I know I will not see you again until the Master comes with the angels to heal the universe.*

He felt that Ielen was close. Tonight, she was feisty. She argued, in his thoughts, *You stayed in Nutman too long. You should have left weeks ago!*

"I needed to stay, and that's that," Daniel replied in his imaginary conversation. "My plans are made, my traps are set, and now I must wait for the Charon's forces to bite the bait. While they are busy here, *my* forces will invade his stronghold."

Go to Smythe! Now! This minute! The heck with the Celebration appearance. Join Deirdre, Myra, and Gracie in their safe haven! Ielen ordered with all the stubbornness of a woman used to command.

"No, dear." Daniel could be stubborn, too. "Trust me! I must keep the enemy focused on my province and this city of Nutman – and not on the Patriots – for as long as possible! My army has troops about these walls to defend the city. All they have to do is hold it for another week, and then …"

Can't you see the error in your plans? They're not the Master's plans; they're your plans!

With a little pepper in his speech, Daniel answered, "Ielen, you're dead. After the Glad-Day – and no sooner, I'm going to the Celebration to encourage my people."

No, go to Smythe! You can't accomplish much at the Celebration. Everybody knows that the king believes the liars who say that you intend to supplant him! King Norhe will try to sabotage you.

"He might," Daniel admitted. "Old Norhe may indeed believe the lies."

I think your plan stinks! Ielen retorted.

The inner conversation faded. Daniel walked a while more, trying to enjoy the well-kept garden. However, the roses' sweet colors turned to gray as evening descended. Feeling gray and tired himself, he left the garden and went back into the house.

*   *   *

He had the bedroom lamp on and a book in his hand when someone pounded on the door. *Who could that be?* Adrenaline surged, and Daniel reached for his sword – *Myra hasn't made off with it this time* – but then he relaxed. *That's what I have guards for. It's probably just another last-minute report.*

Daniel looked down at himself, tousled in striped cotton pajamas. "Too bad," he said to himself, "Forget the protocol. They can see me just the way I am." He wrapped himself in an old terry dressing gown.

When Daniel opened his front door, his heart jumped. His breath caught, and he held onto the doorjamb for support. "Myra!

Deirdre! Gracie!" he cried, flinging the book aside. "What are you doing here? You are supposed to be safe in Smythe!"

He ran out barefoot and in his dressing gown.

Behind the girls on his doorstep stood an entire *harbath* of soldiers with Bardian uniforms, and he took them for part of the city garrison. "Why are you all here? What has happened?"

His younger daughter Myra began crying. Her sobs tore his heart, and he folded her into his arms. "Dear little one, what …?

Lamplight light fell on the company surrounding him. In addition to his daughters and Gracie, he saw his protégé and magus Mark Gregory, his carpenter brother Allen, and their mother Sadie. Daniel noticed others as well, people who had not yet evacuated. "What are you doing here?" Daniel cried. "Has something terrible happened?"

Mark said, looking grim. "These are Wolf Riders wearing Bardian uniforms."

Daniel reeled and would have fallen, except that he was holding Myra. *Master!* he inwardly called. The Master did not reply.

A man in a Bardian lieutenant's uniform growled, "Bind him. Take him with the others to the chapel." He warned Daniel, "If you give no trouble, you'll get none."

Stunned, Daniel let the men secure his hands with a length of cord. They marched him down Garden Lane in his bare feet and dressing gown.

CHAPTER 54

HOSTAGES

Hostages!" Mark Gregory exclaimed in disgust.

He plopped down on the floor of the Nutman chapel, put Gracie in his lap as if she were a very small child, and leaned against a pew. "They caught me coming home after my night shift." He was wearing the black gown of a magus, but it was badly torn, and he had bruises on his face.

Gracie could hear all the conversation, all the murmurs and cries in the church's sanctuary. Yet her soul felt numb.

"They rounded up Mom and me at her house, before supper," Allen snapped. He wore his work clothes, including a woodworker's apron, but no shoes. "We were packing to leave tomorrow for the Celebration." He turned to Deirdre. "O Wise Noblewoman of Smythe, why did you step back in harm's way and let yourself get captured?"

Deirdre swung her thick golden braid. "Allen, shut up! We were kidnapped yesterday, right from my own property! If the queen finds out that Torish soldiers illegally crossed her border, she'll forget that Smythe is supposed to be neutral –

"Shhh," Sadie warned. "They're going around and searching everybody."

In a few minutes, Torish soldiers came to them, removed

several potentially useful objects from Mark and Allen, and then went on. All around them was a low buzz of unhappy conversation, and a few people weeping. "This is dismal," Allen said.

"Where is Daniel?" Sadie asked Deirdre.

"The soldiers took him to the Torish commander. They deliberately humiliated him. They treated him like a criminal." Deirdre's eyes flashed and her right hand made a deadly sword stab gesture.

"What are they going to do with us?" her little sister Myra asked in a small voice.

"They won't kill us. We're hostages. They'll take us to Tor, I think," Mark answered.

An idea came to Gracie. She stirred with excitement, and Mark asked, "What is it, Gracie?"

She said, "Maybe, if we go to Tor, we can find Lewis and Patrick."

The group fell silent.

"Well, I hope so," Mark said. His voice had a forced heartiness to it.

The idea that she might see her brothers again was very comforting. The sticky fear eased away. Gracie snuggled against Mark's chest; he felt warm, like a Teddy Bear. He stroked her curls, the same way Dad back on Earth did.

Tears running down her cheeks, Myra said, "I hope they bring Dad back soon."

Allen hugged her. "Your Dad's a genius, Myra. He may be able to talk his way out of trouble."

"Maybe so," Deirdre said. "Maybe he can negotiate to get us all a nice place to sleep tonight."

"With a hot bath in the morning," said Mark.

"And hotcakes and sausage for breakfast," Allen added.

Everybody laughed.

All at once, the tension drained out of Gracie's body. She felt very sleepy. "I've never slept in a church before."

The others giggled. "Never slept in church? How unusual!" Mark said.

Gracie didn't get the joke and didn't want to take the trouble to figure it out. She relaxed and closed her eyes. Soon she was asleep.

*   *   *

Several hours later, Gracie awoke. Inside the chapel, the light was dim. Most of the people slept or at least rested, although there was a line of people waiting their turn to use the small and now very stinky bathrooms.

Away down the aisle, she saw the front door open. Someone familiar was ushered in. *Daniel!* Both her eyes opened, and she sat up.

He made his way toward them through the crowd of people sitting or sleeping in the pews and on the floor. Gracie saw that he still wore his pajamas and bathrobe, and his curly blond hair was tousled, but he was no longer tied up. She sprang up from Mark's lap. Running down the aisle, skipping and jumping over legs and blankets, Gracie threw herself at him and hugged him tightly around the waist.

Daniel's face was a troubled gray, but he smiled at her and hugged her in return.

Many people left their pews or floor territories to bow low or shake his hand. "Here, Your Excellency. Take my place. Have my water. I can give you a little food."

Daniel greeted everyone that he could and made his way toward his family. He collapsed onto the pew.

"What's happening?" asked Mark.

"Dad, you look so tired!" Deirdre put her hand on her father's arm, and he patted it.

Daniel rubbed his eyes. "Well, the Torish now control the whole city. Someone has betrayed us; the gate was open, and the Wolf Riders rode right into Nutman. Everyone, including the

inner-city garrison, thought they were Bardian reinforcements –
until it was too late. Someone had made a list of names and
addresses so the Torish could round up hostages, who, fortunately,
surrendered. No lives were lost. Of course, Captain Gregory's
troops are in the mountains, but they have retreated into hiding."

His growing audience digested this information. "Thank
God, my husband is still safe," Sadie said softly.

"Maybe Captain Gregory can come and rescue the city," a
youthful magus nearby said hopefully. Like Mark, he looked well
roughed-up.

"Maybe he can, but what about us?" asked one of the women.

Mark told them calmly, because Daniel looked as if he had
talked enough for the day, "We are in no immediate danger. Their
main goal was to seize the College and this city, and that they have
done."

After many more questions, the people in the chapel
dispersed and went back to their places.

Mark stretched and groaned. "These others will be left alone,
I think. The occupying forces will intern them inside the city. But
you, *Hegofean,* will be carted off to Moorway. Hostages!"

Unexpectedly, Daniel chuckled, startling them all. "We're
very fortunate, dear family. Yes, they do intend to take me to Tor
– Radyah has told me this. However, Lord Charon chose a very
good man for the seizure of the city. General Pithesson is a good
man, an honorable man. We won't be abused." He tried to curl up
in the pew, failed, and rolled again to his back, grunting, "… and
to think I voted against cushions for these pews!"

CHAPTER 55

IN CHARGE

When he reached Lord Tahei Charon's office area, Lewis rang a small bronze gong. Charon's personal servant, a tall, gaunt man in a white robe and also wearing a Horned Edge ring, appeared, and bowed the required twenty degrees to acknowledge Lewis's status.

The man led Lewis to a large, circular pillared vestibule. At that point, the servant bowed again, and Lewis stood outside Lord Charon's door, waiting for permission to enter. While he waited, he glanced around. The cold, dry, stony odor reminded him of a monastery.

Or a tomb, the dragon whispered.

"My Lord," Lewis called to announce his presence.

"You may enter."

When he entered, he felt pierced by the room's white marble that was relieved by no tapestries or ornaments, only a long narrow slit of a window high to Lewis's right. A blood-red shaft of sunlight poured through the window, and Lewis thought with surprise, *How can it be sunset already? I just got up!*

Quickly, as evening approached, the room darkened. Dim light from a crystal lamp graced his lord's solemn face, his silky black hair, and long-fingered hands.

Lord Charon sat at a desk on a straight-backed chair. Lewis saw no clutter of paperwork, no dust or ink or pens. He saw the crystal lamp, an alabaster vase of fresh coral red lilies, and a slim upright blade of smoky quartz. He knew that the blade was Charon's personal computer.

Lewis knelt before him, but Charon gestured for him to rise. "Sit down," the ruler said and gestured him onto the plush, zebra-skin settee that faced the desk. "You're looking well," he added, examining Lewis with eyes that were as black as his glossy hair, deep as a depthless pool, with a warmth of genuine liking.

"I feel wonderful, with almost a new identity," Lewis said, only partly joking.

"Yes. You were very sick when you came here," Charon reminded in a gentle deep voice. "You've made quite an improvement since you left Bardia."

"Yes, my lord, thank you."

The voice inside whispered, *You were kidnapped and manipulated into coming here. You were mistreated; that's why you were ill.*

Lewis did not want to remember anything about being a prisoner. He shut down the memory and repeated, "I'm fine now, thank you, Master. Whatever your doctor prescribes gives me a lot of energy."

Charon smiled. "Good," he said.

Lewis waited for his lord to speak again.

With another smile, Lord Charon declared, "I have good news for you. Your brother Patrick will soon join you here. Not only that, but your sister Gracie, also."

Lewis felt all his insides explode into joyful confetti. "When shall I see them?"

"In two weeks. They should arrive during the Council of the Magi."

Feeling hot, grateful tears gathering, wetting his cheeks, Lewis could say nothing.

Charon leaned forward, his eyes bright. "Will you finish your work in time for the Council? You have become familiar with the laboratory with the sonic computer. And today you will be admitted into the locating chamber. I trust you will thoroughly examine it and find the weakness that keeps us from making the connection to Earth."

"Let me think," Lewis said, to give himself time to control his emotions. *I'm about to get my life back. I'll get my family back … It'll be so good to see my brother and sister – and, after I repair Lord Charon's system – my parents! My love Deirdre! Such a sweet thought!*

Finally, he had enough self-control to answer, "Before the Council, I think everything may be ready, but –"

Lord Charon spat, "Do not hedge with me, *Fean* Brahmindura!"

Intimidated, confused, Lewis felt his skin quiver and his stomach do flip-flops, but he made himself speak with calm authority, explaining, "I've become very familiar with your sonic computer system. It draws power from your singularity to enable the nexus between Earth and your … our … world Lanthra. At last I have a good idea why the total connection is not working. The problem is in the tuner, that is, the interface between –"

"Spare me the details." Charon snapped.

Lewis ducked his head, ashamed.

Then Lord Charon's approach changed. The ruler smiled and spoke with a warm voice full of approval, "*Fean* Lewis, you came to me for a reason. What do you want to say to me?"

Lewis raised his head, and he was amazed at his bold courage. "Master, please give me your seal of authority. Let me have me authority over everyone in your laboratory, both your scientists and your staff. Today I will gain my first admittance to the location chamber. I need unlimited and unsupervised access to every part and every place of this project so that it will be done on time, or even ahead of time."

Lord Charon's eyes sparkled with liquid light. *Is he pleased?* the little sarcastic voice in Lewis's head said. *Or is he high – like you are?*

Quelling the conflict inside, Lewis pressed, "I need to do whatever I want, whenever I want, and without questions in the laboratory. Yes, I will get you a fully working system – one that flawlessly connects to Earth – before the Council meets."

A strange nudge inside added, *And you will also copy all the system's records, acquire all the technology, and tell no one.*

Charon searched him for a long time with deep, black eyes. His lips moved, as if he were consulting with someone that Lewis could not see. "Aye," he replied at last. "You may have unlimited and unsupervised access."

He fingered the blade of smoky quartz and made several small motions with his fingers. "Create a personal password. All you need to do is think it. The system will analogue your entire persona into a secure key."

Lewis smiled and thought, *Hot marble.* He remembered the marble only too well: It was the navigation device that connected gravitational entities in the universe. Patrick and Gracie had found it in a field on Earth, after one of Lord Charon's disgruntled magi had hurled it through the nexus. The nexus, before it burned out, had opened the way for Patrick, Gracie, him, and Fred to come to Lanthra. Now it was locked away in Lord Charon's location chamber, and Lewis yearned to get his skillful hands on it.

The ruler returned the blade to its position on the desk. "Remember, *Fean* Lewis, you have two weeks." He sat back with an air of finality.

Lewis knelt, received a blessing and the seal of his authority, and withdrew from Lord Charon's office.

*   *   *

From there, Lewis glided to a certain door that led to the laboratory. "*Golanoya*," he said, "Open," and the laboratory door dissolved. The giant room was domed, containing the sonic-based system that gathered and amplified the horizon energy from Lanthra's singularity. There were also more than a dozen obelisk-like computers projecting 3-D holograms, and the scientists to use them. Lewis cleared his throat. He held up his hand with Lord Charon's seal, a black rod with a blood-red ruby tip. In a loud voice, he minced no words. "I have Lord Charon's seal of authority. Beginning now, I will direct all of you in the repair of the *thoyo-on*."

Everyone in the laboratory stopped working. They stared at Lewis and the seal as if he had usurped the Torish throne. A gasp susurrated through the air. After the shockwave passed, Lewis strode from workstation to workstation, asking different variations of the same question: "Are different methods of testing the system yielding similar results?"

The scientists and staff bowed low as he approached. Time after time, the answer was, "*Alor*. There is no evidence of corruption, yet it will not connect."

Last of all, Lewis went to the two laboratory managers, whose authority he now covered. "Jeffrey, Mildred," Lewis ordered, "Bring the resonance sensors and come with me down to the locating chamber."

Slowly, a pale man with a patchy beard and a tall, intimidating, stocky woman broke off from their stations. They frowned, bowed quite short of the requisite twenty degrees, and Lewis got a strong slam of hostility while they selected tools that looked like silver wands.

"Back up your data now," Lewis said to the others. "After that, repeat the tests to get a baseline, while Jeffrey, Mildred, and I examine a new part of the system."

He swept into a special room off the laboratory, followed by Jeffrey and Mildred. The small room had black polished floor and walls. Ornate gold inlaid patterns depicted scenes from history that Lewis knew dated before the Great Rebellion. To his right, in a freestanding case of spotlessly clear glass, Lewis saw hundreds of jeweled *noretha* – marbles – labelled with Lanthran mathematical script, ready to direct connections locations in the universe.

Lewis methodically examined the noretha and read their labels. While Jeffrey and Mildred shuffled their feet impatiently, Lewis took his time. Finally, he found it: An amber noretha in the middle of the third row – the very "hot marble" that had forced the connection that caught him, Gracie and Patrick, and their friend Fred to Lanthra from Earth. He reached his hand toward the glass case, but then he withdrew it. *Later,* he told himself. *When I can come here alone, I'll get you, hot marble.*

Near the case of noretha stood an ancient door, made of dull metal like platinum, carved with subtle patterns. It had no knob or handle.

"How will *you* get in?" Jeffrey whined, but with a touch of malice. "Did Lord Charon give you our special password?"

"Your special password will no longer work for you," Lewis stated. "You have to have my permission to enter. He drew a deep breath and merely thought, *Hot marble.*

The metal door disappeared. Unlike the location entrance in Bardia where Lewis had worked, before he had been kidnapped, this one was smaller and darker. Golden light glanced onto a bronze stairway that curved downward. Jeffrey sniffed and blinked, his eyes as pale as a goblet full of spit. Mildred snapped, "What do you want us to do that we haven't done already?"

Lewis had no time for power games with subordinates. "Follow me," he ordered and descended the stairs ahead of them. He was about to enter the most important room in the universe.

CHAPTER 56

CHAINS IN THE CHAMBER

Beautiful!" Lewis exclaimed when the last golden spiral of stairs ended in the cave chamber. Amethyst crystals encrusted the ceiling and walls and glittered softly in ambient white light from lamps set into the ceiling like pearls. "This room is a huge geode!"

The chamber smelled cool and mineral, like a glass of ice water in a crystal goblet – except for a faint odor of decay under the chains on the walls. Lewis could not help staring at the chains. "What are these doing here?" he demanded.

"Lord Charon ordered them to be installed," came Jeffrey's weak reply. "He granted the request of the Horned Edge magi." With a smug smile, he flashed his special ring.

Lewis flashed his own ring. "Why? Get those out of this chamber!"

"No." Mildred shook her head and puffed out her chest. "Lord Charon's grandfather ordered sacrifices to Saoma to be done here. The practice will not be changed. We have that right so that we will keep our Horned Edge magi free from traitors' control.

Huh? Lewis thought. *Those horrible sacrifices make no sense.*

"Besides, we only sacrifice non-sentient aliens," Mildred

emphasized, but her eyes slid sideways. "Those Blue People are not human. They are not *homo azure,* as the Daniel's magi sentimentally call them. The Blue People are subhuman, unable to speak or think. The sacrifices serve to control the population and are sweet to god."

Disgusted, Lewis turned away from the chains. His stomach churned, but he knew he could not win that battle by himself. Another time, when he could persuade Lord Charon …

Surveying the rest of the chamber, Lewis stated, "The polished, black stone table in the center is not an altar, but the window to view the stars. It can also be a door, and that is our task, to make the window into a door so that people can pass through from this world to others."

Jeffrey shrugged. Mildred was sour. "Yes, we know that," she snapped. "I used to be in charge of the whole system."

"After Remi died, that is," Jeffrey whispered softly but cruelly, as if to put Mildred in her place. Then he added, with a sidelong glance at Lewis, "Bad things can happen to lead scientists who let the systems break down." He jerked his chin towards the chains bolted into the walls.

"What are you trying to tell me?" Lewis stabbed with his voice.

Jeffrey's face looked pained, even a little afraid. He shrugged.

Lewis felt his face go stony. "We will have no sacrifices, to Saoma or anybody else while I am in authority." He circled the large obsidian-black, oval table, which was the centerpiece of the chamber. Breathing deeply to calm himself, he examined the floor. It was covered with a gorgeous carpet woven in sapphire blue and garnet red. *The floor is covered* … A good guess came to mind, the reason why the locating system could no longer connect. "Pull up the carpet," he ordered.

"What are you talking about?" Mildred put her hands on her large hips. "Do you think we are carpet layers?"

Lewis did not deign to reply.

*   *   *

Under the carpet, the chamber floor was made of polished black quartz. Inlaid on its surface Lewis saw shining metal concentric rings with patterns like Arabic script. He let out a deep sigh of satisfaction. His theory was correct. "These rings and patterns are resonance tuning and amplification structures. When the hot marble, that is, the *noretha,* was thrown though the nexus, the entire locating system strained hard to maintain the connection to Earth. The weakest parts, those rings, burned out when the system overloaded."

Jeffrey and Mildred sniffed and worked slowly, but they finished clearing the floor. Lewis copied the patterns onto a sensitive silver-plated tablet like an old photographic plate. When they were done, he ordered, "Record the tablet's pattern into the sonic computer. Back it up and do it again. After that, activate the system to find and map the dead spots – and then we'll have to repair them."

*   *   *

For the next several days, Jeffrey, Mildred, and Lewis descended into the cave chamber and worked long, hard hours. Carefully, they held their wands to the intricate rings, saying such things as, "This *linath* has resonance, but the next three bilinath do not." Working with very little sleep, they found the sections that had burned out and replaced those sections with new material.

Lewis threw himself into the technical work. His mind jumped and crackled, like the welding arcs used to repair the rings. His senses felt white hot, amplified. And he was delighted to be in control here, Number One, over these magi.

What you are feeling is not normal! the inner voice insisted.

Lewis tried to ignore it. However, there came an inner command. It was so strong and urgent that it cut through all the noise in his head. *Hurry! Copy all the resonance map data along with the rest of the system!*

And he did.

*   *   *

At last Lewis was satisfied that they had repaired the locating system. He ordered a staff party with loads of hors d'oervres and unlimited drinks, and he said to his team, "You've done well. Go and rest." Cheering, Lord Charon's scientists emptied the laboratory. So did Lewis – but he came back.

Speeding to the special room that stored the noretha, and checking to see that he was alone, he thought his password plus the symbols of the mathematical scripts in front of the marbles he wanted. As he thought, the glass pane in front of each choice vanished. Lewis took out three marbles. One was useless, burned out like an old bowling ball with a chunk missing; the second marble, he knew, connected to the coppery moon Wega; and the third was his ticket to Earth. Then he played "musical marbles." Wega's noretha went into Earth's place; the useless marble he laid in Wega's place; and the third place he left empty. He could explain, if anyone asked, that he had thrown out a defective noretha.

As he hid it in his robe, he fingered the marble that had led him and his brother and sister to Lanthra, and he whispered, "We meet again, friend."

CHAPTER 57

SEIZURE

After some time, multicolored sunlight filtered through the chapel windows. However, although people were stirring, a gloomy silence lay thick inside the church. Gracie felt stretched tight like a rubber band about to snap. She had been unable to go back to sleep after Daniel had arrived. *Was it my fault that we all got captured? Is it because I'm from Earth? Suppose I'm tortured? What's going to happen to us?*

Daniel awoke. He got in the long line for the restroom. The people in line waved him on and tried to give him the first place, but Gracie was proud to see that he refused. When he came back, he began to counsel the Gregorys, his family, and Gracie. "General Patterson said he would allow us to go to my house for an hour or two. We can refresh ourselves and gather some clothes for our journey. Especially me," he joked, looking down at his pajamas.

Despite her fear and guilt, Gracie giggled.

Some of the merriment was back in the Daniel's eyes as he whispered, "But that isn't all. Because the commander is so kind, I will have a good opportunity to arrange your escape."

Their gloom changed to amazement. "Excuse my doubt," murmured Allen. "But even your cunning mind has limits."

Sadie picked up on one obvious detail, and said softly, "What about *your* escape?"

Daniel was not listening. His eyes danced, glowing in the morning light coming through the chapel's stained-glass windows. He whispered, "Part of my cellar connects into the ancient foundations of the city. There are tunnels under the entire university circle, and at least one of them leads to the playing field near the outside wall."

Myra's eyes were wide. "Daddy, I never knew that!"

Deirdre admitted, "I did. When I was ten, I found the entrance and explored the tunnels. Mom was furious, not just because I was filthy, but because she was so afraid that I would get hurt or lost. She put a lock on the door, and I never went down again."

"We'll only have a short time, but we can fit a lot into it," Daniel said. "We can take turns bathing, and I will get some clothes, of course. Also, we can eat some breakfast."

*　*　*

About noon, when Gracie was so hungry that she could hardly think about anything else, a dozen Torish regulars came to take them to Daniel's mansion. The lieutenant was not nice. He rudely made them march in a little parade from the chapel and up the hill and through the university gate. Instead of student magi at the gatehouse, there were now Torish soldiers. When they arrived, the lieutenant looked at a gold watch. *That's Lewis' Rolex! Dad gave that to him!* Gracie thought. Anger flooded her chest. *The Torish took after they killed the man who helped us when we crossed over from Earth!*

The lieutenant stated, "You have fifty-five minutes to prepare yourselves. Guards, follow them from room to room, even the bathroom.

"Are we to have no privacy?" Daniel exclaimed.

"I've orders," the lieutenant told him in a cold, intimidating voice.

"My daughter and I will prepare some lunch here. However, your men will not accompany of us into the bathroom," Daniel stated with all his authority. "General Patterson has given no such orders. And you will not watch the ladies dress!"

The lieutenant's eyes flicked sideways, and Gracie noticed. *What a creep!*

"Women get the larger bathroom; men the smaller," Daniel ordered.

Mrs. Gregory stayed with Gracie and Myra as they bathed and dressed, which helped Gracie feel safer. Gracie had just stepped into the tub for her turn when someone rapped on the door. Sadie opened it a crack. "What is it?" she snapped.

"I believe you'll need this." Daniel held out a towel.

"We already have – never mind. Thank you." Sadie accepted the towel. When she had closed the bathroom door, she unfolded the towel. Out dropped an old key. This she tucked into an inner pocket of her sari, and she continued to assist Gracie with her bath.

When Sadie handed Gracie some of Myra's nice clothes, Gracie was surprised. "Here you go," Sadie said. "Now you look like your 'sister' Myra. You both have auburn hair and the eyes to match."

What does that mean? Gracie wondered.

Gracie draped Myra's travelling cloak around her shoulders, brushed her curly hair, which was getting long, and reviewed herself in a mirror. Her freckled face was pale, her red hair was still damp, making her look like a damp kitten. Myra leaned in next to Gracie and the two girls made faces. "We're like twins," Myra observed, and even in such an anxious moment, she and Gracie laughed.

When Gracie and Myra were done, they ran to the kitchen. Deirdre had set out bread and ham from the pantry. "Eat fast," Deirdre ordered.

Gorgeous as ever in her beautiful sari, her long hair braided smoothly, Sadie smiled at them, her face serene as the moon on a clear night. She ate her bread – but no ham – as delicately as a queen. Deirdre wore her blue riding suit and looked regal, too. Myra picked at her food. She wore a maroon riding outfit similar to Gracie's.

Gracie devoured all her food and felt her growling stomach grow warmer and fuller. She was amazed how the meal picked up her spirits.

Daniel, who sat at the table, announced, "I'm so hungry!"

"What, didn't you eat anything?" asked the lieutenant coldly. "You've sat here long enough!"

"Not yet. I wanted to make sure everyone got enough to eat. Maybe there's more food here." Daniel rose and rooted through the pantry. "Ah! There's some headcheese in a jar. Would anyone like a slice of headcheese for your bread?"

All of them shook their heads emphatically. Myra wrinkled her nose. "Dad has some weird tastes," she whispered to Gracie.

Daniel ate a sandwich. After he finished, he sniffed at the last remnant of headcheese and exclaimed, "I thought this tasted a bit off! He tossed the gelatinous meat into the slop pail.

The lieutenant examined his watch, looking cross. "Seventeen minutes," he said.

Gracie did not like the way the lieutenant followed Deirdre with his eyes. He looked at her, well, with bad thoughts.

Allen and Mark came in. The atmosphere seemed to Gracie tense as a high wire. Mark ate a little bread, but Allen sat up straight with his arms crossed.

"What will they do to us if we're late?" Myra asked her father.

"It's all right, *bibath*; we'll be fine."

I hope so! Gracie thought. She began to get scared, and her hands felt sweaty.

"Nine minutes," the lieutenant intoned.

It was finally Daniel's turn to wash up. "If he's still in there when the time's up, fetch him out of the bathroom," sneered the lieutenant. "Clothes or no clothes."

"I won't be long," Daniel told the Torish lieutenant brightly, and went down the hall accompanied by guards.

Allen started to pace. Sadie lost her patience at last. "Allen, sit down! You are driving me crazy!"

Allen lowered his eyebrows. "I don't want –"

She hissed, "I said, Allen, sit down! Have lunch! Everybody's eaten but you!"

Obediently but glaring, Allen sat and began to stuff food into his mouth. "Three minutes," said the lieutenant.

The three minutes passed. Deirdre looked gorgeous, her golden hair brushed glossy and plaited into a thick braid, and the lieutenant alternated between staring at her and looking at his/Lewis's watch. The distracted man let a few extra minutes pass.

The High Magus Daniel, however, did not come out of the bathroom.

Vexed, the lieutenant muttered something and left the kitchen. Gracie heard him beating on the bathroom door, shouting, "'Tis time! Come out!"

There was no answer, and Gracie heard a sharp bang as the lieutenant shouldered the door open. There was a pause; then the man shouted, "Willis! Gabriel! Quickly! The man's having a fit!"

The Torish soldiers and Gracie, Allen, Mark, Sadie, Myra, and Deirdre all ran toward the bathroom.

Gracie had one peek through the door. The bathroom was a mess. Daniel, only half clothed, writhed on the floor holding his stomach. There was vomit on the floor. The room stank ferociously. The lieutenant and the guards shouted at each other. Myra screamed.

"Food poisoning!" Deirdre exclaimed. "It must have been the headcheese!"

"Hold him while I stuff his mouth, lest he puke some more," the lieutenant demanded, totally disgusted.

"Don't! He might choke!" Sadie shouted.

Gracie felt like her world was coming to pieces. *Am I going to lose him? He's not related to me the way my brothers and Mom and Dad are, but to me he's like a dad.* She whispered to Sadie, her voice all weak and trembly, "Is he going to die?"

To her surprise, there was a triumphant glow in Sadie's eyes. She gave Gracie's arm a reassuring squeeze.

The guards tried to control Daniel's spasms while the lieutenant pried his fingers into his mouth, trying to insert a rag. However, Daniel chomped hard with his teeth. "Ow!" the lieutenant shrieked.

From the front of the house, five more guards ran to help. The hallway in front of the bathroom was packed with frantic people, so two guards forced Gracie and the others to retreat to the kitchen. From the bathroom, the lieutenant was still yelling, "Pry his jaws! He will'na release my fingers! Blast you, Willis, hold him down!"

Now Gracie and her companions bunched in the kitchen, including the two guards. Without warning, Sadie grabbed a frying pan from the wall and slugged one of the guards with it. He dropped. Allen leaped on the other guard. "Deirdre!" Sadie cried, "Where's that cellar door?"

Deirdre ran toward the back of the kitchen. Her fingers played the wall in scherzo time. "It looks like part of the wall, except for a small keyhole. I used it such a long time ago … Here it is! But … does anyone have a key?"

Sadie pulled out the key from her inner pocket. She stuck it into the keyhole, but it would not turn.

"Hurry up!" Allen yelled.

"Here, Mom, let me …" Mark grabbed the key and turned it with all his strength. The key bent, but the lock did not turn. Mark tried to pick the lock by inserting a table knife, but the blade broke, cutting his hand. Blood spattered everywhere.

Allen cried, wrestling the guard, "Get going! I can't hold this guy much longer!"

Gracie and Myra huddled together. Still bleeding, Mark pointed to the fireplace and ordered, "Deirdre, get me that thing!" He stuck the kitchen poker into the keyhole, splintering wood, until the entire lock mechanism burst out of the door and left a hole. With the claw of the poker, he pulled, straining, until, with a hideous squeal and flakes of old paint, the door began to open outward.

Gracie cringed. The dark opening into the cellar resembled the maw of a hungry animal. There was a cloud of spider webs across the opening.

Sadie grabbed Myra and ducked into the cellar without hesitation, leaving behind shreds of waving, dusty spider webs. Next, Deirdre put her arm around Gracie, "Let's go, girl!" But Gracie panicked, her stomach squirming and her chest exploding. That black opening – it looked so spooky … There were spiders, and maybe mice or even monsters …

Just then, the soldier that Allen was fighting wriggled free. The Torish man bent his foot around Allen's leg, slipped an arm under his shoulder, and jerked. Allen was forced over, with the guard's foot on top of him. "Help me, Mark!" Allen cried. Mark took the guard down with a fluid toss, kicked his weapons away, and broke a chair over the man's shoulders.

Holding Gracie's hands softly, Deirdre drew her up to the cellar door. "Come on, sweetie; we'll be okay."

However, the other guard that Sadie had hit with the frying pan shook and rolled to his feet. Quickly, he snatched Gracie and pulled her to his chest.

Gracie screamed, a sharp yelp like a car-struck puppy. All her adrenaline rushed to her hands and feet, but she couldn't move because both the man's arms wrapped so tightly around her that she could hardly breathe.

"Surrender, or I'll break her neck," the guard ordered in Lanthran. Deirdre put up her hands. Allen and Mark stopped short.

The man called loudly for reinforcements, *"Marador, marador!"*

Panting, Mark stepped next to Deirdre. His hand dripped blood where the knife blade had slit the skin, and unaware of the bleeding, he wiped his forehead, leaving a long trail of red, then he, too raised his hands.

Allen, however, grabbed the poker and menaced the guard who held Gracie. "Imagine what I can do with this, man! Let the girl go!" The guard shook his head and gripped her throat tightly, and they heard the pounding of many feet. Allen bawled to Mark and Deirdre, "He won't kill her; it's a bluff. Make sure you get out safely!"

Deirdre cried, "I can't leave her!"

"You can't help her!" Allen yelled. He punch-kicked Deirdre through the cellar door, shoved Myra after her, slammed Mark through it with a fist, overturned a cabinet to block the opening, and crouched in front of it.

CHAPTER 58

SUDDEN ANGER

L ewis was eager to see his lord's face when he told him that, probably within one more day, they could positively and certainly connect to Earth. *Lord Charon will reward me! He'll let me go to Earth, he'll reunite me with my family!*

When Lewis approached Lord Charon's throne room in Whitehall, he heard the servant announce, "My Lord, your servant Barth Layhew from Torgard has arrived."

What?

Very quickly, Lewis rounded a nearby pillar to keep from being seen. A hated clear tenor voice resonated through the vestibule, "Greetings, Master." Footsteps and shuffling told Lewis that Barth had entered and kneeled.

Behind the pillar, his heart pounding, Lewis closed his eyes and let out a deep breath. He had hoped that he would never again see or hear the man who had kidnapped him. Forever without Barth was not long enough. Also, *What is my lord doing, seeing that brute?*

Charon's office door closed, but apparently Barth had shut it carelessly because the door eased partially open again. Sounds of the conversation carried well across the marble floor and Lewis's ears were very good.

A heavy thud told Lewis that Barth had plopped onto Charon's zebra-skin covered settee. "Ugh," Barth complained. "It's hot and steamy as a smithy in your city, as usual. Give me my home Torgard any day. The mountains are never as humid as here on the plain."

Lord Charon's pleasant deep voice said, "Have you been given refreshment? I'll call for some ice water."

"Ice water?" Barth snorted. "No thanks. I'll get a real drink later."

He got to his point. "So, Tahei, you got Louie Brahmindura to repair your locating system? How did you manage that? A little session downstairs with the thumbscrews?" He snickered.

Anger drenched Lewis with a hot hose. He wanted to run into Charon's office and punch Barth's teeth out. However, although he clenched his fists, he stayed behind the pillar, listening.

Charon's reply sounded light and smiling. "Nay, nothing like that is necessary. The man is more than willing, as well as very able."

"My Lord Charon, be careful. He cannot be trusted. Put me in authority on this project."

"No," Charon said. "He's brilliant, more than you, Barth. Besides, a daily dose of a powerful solanaceous alkaloid and constant gentle allosuggestion keep him pliable."

Lewis stiffened all over. If he had not heard the words from Charon's own mouth, he could not have believed it. His stomach began to feel very sick. *Is that all I am to the Master? A tool, a dupe?*

Lord Charon said, "*Fean* Lewis manages the project. However, you are loyal, and I want you by my side."

"Well," Barth drawled. "I'm relieved you won Louie over so easily. It's just as well that he decided to collaborate with you, since we lost the one real lever we had on him."

"You mean his brother? Or his sister? Or both?"

Lewis stiffened. His hands trembled and he clasped them

tightly.

Charon's voice sounded dark and angry. "What are you telling me –"

"Patriots," Barth spat disgustedly. "Torgard Patriots. Patrick had been injured – it was Lewis's fault! The blasted Patriots grabbed the boy from the hospital before he even woke up from his surgery. My dear brother Nark rounded up most of the traitors from his city. That was sweet – I got to be there when he gave them to Saoma. One of the nurses at the hospital died by Nark's favorite torture – it was most entertaining. However, no amount of questioning could reveal who took the boy."

Lewis felt a sudden surge of nausea. He put his hand to his mouth to keep from vomiting.

"I need the brother," Charon said stiffly. "Lewis is waiting for him and his sister to join him here in Moorway. You promised –"

Barth replied, his voice defensive, "I searched every brick in Torgard. The boy's description was sent to every garrison in Tor, but the results have been zilch. The Patriots are too well organized in this."

A silence fell. Lewis leaned his head back against the pillar. *Patrick has escaped!* However, he had no room for joy. He imagined what Nark and Barth must have done to the poor nurse. The euphoria, all the pleasant lift in his soul, hardened into hate. He thought, *Barth, I swear I will get revenge for what you did to me and those other people.*

Barth began mouthing excuses over losing his main leverage over Lewis. As he hid behind the pillar, Lewis thought, *He's screwed up badly, and Charon will tan his hide. Perhaps literally.* He could always hope.

However, Barth ended his long defense with a line that froze Lewis to the marrow: "If you need to hook Lewis, besides the drugs and the mind control, there's always his sister. I can make a special trip to fetch her."

No! Lewis silently screamed. *Not Gracie! I wanted her and Patrick to join me here, but not, not, not as prisoners!*

Charon stated, "I have sent for her along with the other hostages from Nutman. However, Barth Layhew, you have stumbled badly."

Another silence settled over the vestibule. Barth began babbling, "Master, forgive me, please forgive me. I will bring the girl and … Patrick."

Charon's voice was sharp, as if puzzled by a new thought. "You came to like the lad, didn't you?" he asked.

Barth made a sudden odd noise, as if he had been drinking beer and had backwashed. He coughed and choked and finally said, "No! I love you with all my heart, with all my life! You alone are my brother and my father!"

Lewis clamped a hand to his own mouth to stifle an exclamation of disgust. *Barth likes Patrick? After tying up my brother and threatening to slit his throat?*

Lord Charon replied softly but cruelly, "Aye, I believe you. By the way, speaking of brothers, you've brought me one in *Fean* Lewis. I've come to love the lad."

Lewis fled. He'd heard enough. Now he needed to think. He needed to plan. He needed to protect his family.

The sequel to *The Hot Marble,* Book 2
THE CAVE CHAMBER
A Soul's Warfare series continues in *The Cave Chamber* where Lord Charon begins his move to join the Shields in their plan to conquer Lanthra and Earth.

All Lewis Brahmindura's drastic efforts seem to fail as the brilliant young physicist struggles to stop the enemies that threaten his brother Patrick and sister Gracie. Lewis faces the deadliest struggle of his entire life, and the greatest threat is inside his own soul.

313

ACKNOWLEDGMENTS

First, thanks to my parents, friends, and generations of people who have believed in Jesus Christ, acted like it, and prayed for me to return to light from darkness. Healing has helped me to analyze my soul from its turbulent depths toward recovery. This journey continues every day, and it has inspired the theme of all my stories.

Thank you for family and friends, believing and unbelieving, who can smell the difference between a sinner and a Pharisee, to help keep me from becoming the latter. You all kept me sane when my mind lived in the abyss.

Because two college friends prayed for me and with me, I crossed that awful abyss. Through them, I came to a *very* interesting place called Christ Center, which is worthy of its own novel. During that time, I also began to learn koiné Greek and systematic Christian doctrine via a mentor, Dr. Louis Brighton. Through him and his family, I met my dear husband, Skip Althoff.

While I was working on my B.A. in English at the University of Kentucky, poet and author Wendell Berry hammered my creative writing. He guided me to write not merely stories, but my heart. However, I needed to learn science to delve into Christian science fiction. My father and sister both worked in the space industry, so I have always been fascinated with stars and other worlds. At Cleveland State University in Ohio, Drs. Rick Perloff, Leo Jeffres, Gary Petty, and other professors taught me to be a Communication research scientist.

With a master's degree in hand, I was able to teach English writing and interpersonal communication at Lakeland Community College. The science of interpersonal communication helped me learn how to understand many of the battles in my soul. Thank you, Ileen Linden, for becoming my friend while I was there.

Published author Dianne Haynes Miley (www.diannemiley.com) helped me with words and beyond words. Linda, my prayer-partner, has been with me all the long, long way. She has published a book of devotions: *Little Letters from Linda at the Lake House*.

Throughout the writing of *A Soul's Warfare: The Hot Marble*, with all my groaning, floundering, and despair, my husband Skip has remained level-headed and encouraging. Our three amazing offspring, Peter, Amy, and Mary, cheer me on always.

There are many other beloved Folks who have helped me. *Thank you!*

ABOUT THE AUTHOR

Rosemary Althoff had already begun writing novels before she majored in English at the University of Kentucky. After missionary work in the Philippines, she obtained a master's degree in Communication Theory and Research Methodology at Cleveland State University. During her career, Rosemary worked for professional textbook publishers, published short stories and devotions, presented public opinion research papers, and taught research and creative writing at various universities. She loves to paint landscapes, play piano, and take hikes

You may contact Rosemary at rosemaryalthoff@gmail.com.